A VOW SO BOLD AND DEADLY

Also by Brigid Kemmerer

Letters to the Lost
More Than We Can Tell
Call It What You Want

A Curse So Dark and Lonely
A Heart So Fierce and Broken

Storm
Spark
Spirit
Secret
Sacrifice

Thicker Than Water

A VOW SO BOLD AND DEADLY

BRIGID KEMMERER

BLOOMSBURY

NEW YORK   LONDON   OXFORD   NEW DELHI   SYDNEY

BLOOMSBURY YA
Bloomsbury Publishing Inc., part of Bloomsbury Publishing Plc
1385 Broadway, New York, NY 10018

BLOOMSBURY and the Diana logo are trademarks of Bloomsbury Publishing Plc

First published in the United States of America in January 2021
by Bloomsbury YA

Bloomsbury books may be purchased for business or promotional use. For information
on bulk purchases please contact Macmillan Corporate and Premium Sales Department at
specialmarkets@macmillan.com

Library of Congress Cataloging-in-Publication Data
Names: Kemmerer, Brigid, author.
Title: A vow so bold and deadly / by Brigid Kemmerer.
Description: New York : Bloomsbury Children's Books, 2021. |
Sequel to: A heart so fierce and broken. |
Summary: Emberfall is torn between supporters of Rhen and Grey, who agreed not to attack for
two months, while Lia Mara struggles to rule Syhl Shallow well and is beginning to question her
alliance with Grey.
Identifiers: LCCN 2020034566
ISBN 978-1-5476-0258-2 (hardcover) • ISBN 978-1-5476-0259-9 (e-book)
Subjects: CYAC: Fairy tales. | Princes—Fiction. | Magic—Fiction.
Classification: LCC PZ8.K374 Vow 2021 | DDC [Fic]—dc23
LC record available at https://lccn.loc.gov/2020034566

ISBN 978-1-5476-0815-7 (special edition)

Book design by Jeanette Levy
Typeset by Westchester Publishing Services
Printed and bound in the U.S.A. by Berryville Graphics Inc., Berryville, Virginia
2 4 6 8 10 9 7 5 3 1

All papers used by Bloomsbury Publishing Plc are natural, recyclable products
made from wood grown in well-managed forests. The manufacturing processes
conform to the environmental regulations of the country of origin.

To find out more about our authors and books visit
www.bloomsbury.com and sign up for our newsletters.

صداقتك لا تقدر
بثمن...بدونك لما
كنت احيا ٢٠٢٠

EMBERFALL

NORTH
LOC HILLS

VALKINS VALLEY

HUTCHINS
FORGE

CASTELLAN
BAY

IRONROSE
CASTLE

CROOKED
BOAR INN

SILVERMOON
HARBOR

RUSHING BAY

COBALT
POINT

OCEAN

CHAPTER ONE

GREY

The weather has begun to turn, allowing cold wind to swoop down from the mountains and sneak under the leather and fur of my jacket. It's colder in Syhl Shallow than it would be in Emberfall, but it's been so long since I experienced the gradual slide from autumn into winter that I've been reveling in it.

The others are clustered around the central hearth that burns in the main room of the Crystal Palace, drinking the cook's first batch of winter wine, but Iisak loathes the warmth, so I'm braving the cold and the dark on the veranda to play dice with the scraver. The only flame burning out here is the lone candle in a glass jar on the table between us.

Iisak shakes the silver cubes in his hands, then lets them rattle out onto the table.

"Silver hell," I mutter as I tally his roll. I'm good at cards, but dice seem to hate me. With cards, there's an element of strategy, of choice, but the dice are moved by nothing more than fate. I toss a coin onto the table to acknowledge his win.

Iisak smiles, and while the darkness paints his black eyes and gray skin in even darker shadows, the moonlight glints off his fangs.

He pockets the coin, but he'll probably give it to Tycho later. He dotes on the boy like an old grandmother. Or maybe like a father missing the son he once lost. "Where is our young queen tonight?" he asks.

"Lia Mara is dining with one of her Royal Houses."

"Without you?"

"They requested a private audience, and she has an obligation to keep them happy." The Royal Houses were putting pressure on the former queen before she was killed, but Karis Luran ruled with an iron fist and she was able to keep them in check. Now that Lia Mara is in power and Syhl Shallow is desperate for resources, the pressure to find trade routes through Emberfall seems to have doubled—especially since Lia Mara has no desire to rule like her mother.

I shrug and gather the dice. "Not everyone is comfortable with magic here, Iisak."

"I assumed as much from the crowd, Your Highness." He glances around the darkened veranda, which is deserted aside from the guards who linger by the door.

"Well," I say noncommittally. "It's cold tonight."

But he's right. It's probably the magic.

I get along with most of the guards and soldiers in Syhl Shallow, but there's a distance here that I can't quite define. A wariness. At first I thought it was because they see me as loyal to Emberfall, and I stood at Lia Mara's side as she killed her mother to claim the throne.

But as time has gone on, that wariness has made itself more apparent every time I heal an injury or drive away an opponent on the training field. It's become more apparent when I go to the armory to put my weapons away, and conversations draw short or small groups disperse.

A strong wind blasts across the veranda, making the candle gutter and then go out.

I shiver. "As I said."

"We should make use of our privacy," Iisak says, and his voice is lower, quieter, nothing that will reach the ears of my guards.

I put a finger over the candlewick and make a circular motion, letting the stars in my blood dance along my fingertips. What once felt like such a challenge is now effortless. A flame crawls to life. "I thought we were."

"I don't need any more of your coins."

I smile. "Well, that's good, because I only have a few left."

He doesn't smile in return, so my expression sobers. Iisak is a king in his own right, though he's living out a year sworn to my service. He was trapped in a cage in Emberfall, and Karis Luran kept him on a chain. I've offered to release him a dozen times, but each time he refuses. It's a type of loyalty I'm not sure I deserve, especially since I know what he's lost: first, a son who went missing, and then, his throne in Iishellasa. When he asks for my attention, I do my best to give it.

"What do you need?" I say.

"It is not just people in Syhl Shallow who fear magic."

I frown. He's talking about Rhen.

My brother.

Every time I think of it, something inside me clenches tight.

"You once said you did not want to be at war with him," says Iisak.

I look at the dice in my palm, turning them over between my fingers. "I still don't."

"You have begun preparing armies on Lia Mara's behalf."

I close my fingers around the silver cubes. "Yes."

"Syhl Shallow's coffers have begun to run dry. You will likely have one chance to stand against him. The losses in the final battle with Emberfall were already great, due to Prince Rhen's creature. A second assault will not be possible." He pauses. "And you granted him sixty days to ready for battle."

"I know."

"As much as you long to preserve lives, these battles will not occur without loss."

"I know that, too."

Another gust of wind sweeps across the veranda, dashing out the flame again. This time, the wind was drawn by Iisak. I've learned the feel of his magic, how it lives in the air the way mine lives in my blood.

I give him a look and coax the flame back to life.

Another gust, and I narrow my eyes. Iisak always pushes. When I first began learning to control my magic, I found it frustrating, but I've come to enjoy the challenge. I keep my finger there, and the flame struggles to stay lit. Stars fill my vision as I try to keep the magic in place. The wind has grown strong enough that it stings my eyes and grabs at my cloak. Iisak's wings flare, but the flame doesn't die.

"Do you remember me saying I was cold?" I say.

He smiles and lets the wind swirl out to nothing.

In the sudden absence of his magic, my flame surges high for a moment, sending wax coursing down the sides of the candle, and I let go.

"Maybe it would be good to show Lia Mara's people how magic can be useful," he says.

I think of the people who've been healed by my magic. The way I've been able to keep enemies away from me, and, more slowly, away from anyone fighting alongside me. "I already have," I say.

"I don't mean you should simply strengthen your military force."

I study him. "You mean I should use magic against Rhen." I pause. "It's exactly what he fears."

"You told him you're sending an army. He'll be prepared to retaliate. He'll be prepared to fight from a distance, the way kings do."

But he'll be powerless against magic.

I know he will. He already was.

"Rhen knows you," says Iisak. "He expects violence. He expects an armed assault. He expects an efficiently brutal attack not unlike the one Karis Luran herself sent. You've assembled an army, and you may as well have made a vow."

"Don't underestimate him." I think of the whip scars on my back. On Tycho's back. "When he's cornered, Rhen can be efficiently brutal himself."

"Yes, Your Highness." Iisak makes the flame flicker again, and it glints off his black eyes. "So can you."

CHAPTER TWO

RHEN

Once again, it is autumn at Ironrose Castle. The first cool wind of the season drifts through my windows and I shiver. I haven't needed a fire in the morning in months, but today there's a bite to the air that has me wanting to call for a servant to light the hearth.

I don't.

For a near eternity, I used to dread the beginning of the season because it signaled that the curse had begun again. I would be newly eighteen, trapped in a never-ending repetition of autumn. I would be alone with Grey, my former guard commander, trying to find a girl to help me break the curse that tormented me and all of Emberfall.

This autumn, Grey is gone.

This autumn, I have a girl to stand at my side.

This autumn, I suppose, I am nineteen for the first time.

The curse is broken.

It doesn't feel like it.

Lilith, the enchantress who once trapped me in the curse, now traps me in another way.

Harper, the first girl to break the curse, the "Princess of Disi" who swore to help my people, is in the courtyard below my window, swinging swords with Zo, her closest friend. Zo was once her guard, too, until she helped lead Grey to escape. I won't take away Harper's best friend, but I can't have a sworn guard displaying divided loyalties.

Tensions are already too high.

Harper and Zo break apart, breathing heavily, but Harper almost immediately reclaims her stance.

It makes me smile. Cerebral palsy makes swordplay challenging—some would say *impossible*—but Harper is more determined than anyone I know.

A light voice speaks from behind me. "Ah, Your Highness. It is so *adorable* how Princess Harper believes she can excel at this."

I lose the smile, but I don't move from the window. "Lady Lilith."

"Forgive me for interrupting your ponderings," she says.

I say nothing. I don't forgive her for anything.

"I wonder how she will fare back in the streets of her Disi, if you fail to win against these invaders from Syhl Shallow."

I freeze. She issues this threat often, that she will take Harper back to Washington, DC, where I would have no hope of reaching her. Where Harper would have nothing and no one to rely on, and no way to get back to Emberfall.

Lilith ignores my silence. "Should you not be preparing for war?"

Yes. I very likely should. Grey gave me sixty days to surrender control of Emberfall before he will help Lia Mara take it by force. He is in Syhl Shallow now, preparing to lead an army against me. I'm never sure whether his motivation is for resources—because I know the country is desperate for access to trade—or whether his motivation is to claim a throne he once said he did not want.

8 Brigid Kemmerer

Either way, he will attack Emberfall. He will attack me.

"I am prepared," I say.

"I see no armies assembling. No generals plotting in your war rooms. No—"

"Are you a military strategist now, Lilith?"

"I know what a war looks like."

I want to beg her to leave, but it will only make her linger. When Grey was trapped here with me, I took solace in the fact that I never suffered alone.

Now I do, and it's . . . agonizing.

In the courtyard below, Harper and Zo are matching blades again.

"Do not chase her blade, my lady," I call.

They break apart, and Harper turns to look up at me in surprise. Her brown curls are twisted into an unruly braid that hangs over one shoulder, and she's wearing leather bracers and a gilded breastplate like she was born to royalty and weaponry. A far cry from the tired, dusty girl whom Grey dragged from the streets of Washington, DC, so many months ago. Now she's a warrior princess, complete with a long scar across one cheek and another across her waist, both courtesy of the horrible enchantress behind me.

When she looks at me, her eyes always search my features, as if she suspects I am hiding something. As if she is *angry* with me, even though she doesn't voice it.

Lilith waits in the shadows at my back. There once was a time when Harper invited me to her chambers to protect me from the enchantress. I wish she could do that again.

I haven't been in her chambers in months. There is too much unspoken between us.

"I didn't know you were watching," Harper says, and she sheathes her sword as if she's displeased.

"Only for a moment." I hesitate. "Forgive me."

As soon as I say it, I wish I could take it back. It sounds like I'm apologizing for something else. I suppose I am.

She must hear the weight in my tone, because she frowns. "Did I wake you?"

As if I ever sleep anymore. "No."

She stares up at me, and I stare down at her, and I wish I could unravel all the emotion that hangs between us. I wish I could tell her about Lilith. I wish I could earn her forgiveness—and win back her trust.

I wish I could undo so many things.

"I don't know what you mean," she finally says. "About chasing the blade."

"I could come show you," I offer.

Her expression freezes, but just for a moment. My heart stutters in my chest. I expect her to refuse. She's refused before.

But then she says, "All right. Come down."

My heart leaps—until Lilith speaks from behind me.

"Yes," she says. "Go, Your Highness. Show her the *power* of your *weapon*."

I whirl, glaring. "Leave here, Lady Lilith," I whisper furiously. "If you are so concerned about my preparations for war, I suggest you find some way to make yourself useful, instead of tormenting me whenever you need a childish diversion."

She laughs. "As you say, Prince Rhen."

She reaches out a hand as if to touch my cheek, and I jerk back, stumbling into the wall. Her touch can be like fire—or worse.

Lilith's smile widens. My hands curl into fists, but she vanishes.

From the courtyard below, I hear Harper call, "Rhen?"

I draw a tense breath and return to the window. The sun has begun to lighten the sky, painting her dark hair with sparks of gold and red.

I'm supposed to be preparing for war, but I feel like I'm already in the middle of one.

"Allow me to dress," I say. "I'll be down in a moment."

CHAPTER THREE

HARPER

I'm surprised Rhen is coming down. I'm surprised he was watching at all, honestly. Since Grey gave him an ultimatum, Rhen has been tucked away in meetings with Grand Marshals from far-off cities, with military advisors, or with his Royal Guard.

Which is fine. When *I'm* with him, a tiny ball of anger burns in my gut, and nothing ever seems to douse it.

The anger makes me feel guilty. Everything he does, he does for his kingdom. For his people. Being a prince—being a *king*—requires sacrifice and tough choices.

No matter how many times I remind myself of that, I can't forget what he did to Grey and Tycho.

I can't forget that I came back here instead of going with my brother.

Instead of going with Grey.

I turn back to Zo, but she's sheathed her sword. Her eyes are tense. "I should return to my quarters."

She doesn't want to be here with Rhen. I hesitate, then frown.

Zo came to the castle months ago, when Rhen was trying to rally his people to defend Emberfall against the invasion from Syhl Shallow. She'd been an apprentice to the Master of Song in Silvermoon Harbor, but she had skills in archery and swordplay, so she applied for the Royal Guard—and Grey chose her, then assigned her to be my personal guard.

We became fast friends—a first for me, after the chaotic life I left behind in Washington, DC. She's clever and strong, with a dry sense of humor, and sometimes I'd stay up well into the night when she was stationed outside my door. We'd wonder what happened to Grey after the curse was broken, or we'd whisper about the rumors over a missing heir, or we'd muse over what would happen to Emberfall if Syhl Shallow attacked again.

But then Grey was found hiding in another city, and he apparently knew the identity of the missing heir—but he refused to tell Rhen. Rhen tortured him to get the information, and he got it—but not in the way he expected. Grey knew the identity of the missing heir, because *he* was Rhen's older brother. He was a magesmith, with magic in his blood. He was the heir to the throne.

He'd never known it. Neither had Rhen.

I helped Grey escape after Rhen tortured him.

Zo helped *me*.

It cost her a position in the Royal Guard. Grey once told me that his guards forswear family and relationships for exactly this reason. She was sworn to Rhen—but she acted for me. Rhen is never cold to her; he's too political for that. But there's an edge between them now. Like the ball of anger in my gut that won't go away, I'm not sure it will ever soften.

I want to beg Zo to stay, because every moment I spend with Rhen feels prickly. But asking Zo to stay feels selfish.

Asking her to help Grey was probably selfish, too. Zo and I are friends, but she was my guard. Did she help me out of friendship, or out of obligation? I'm not even sure if it matters. She helped me, and now she's out of a job—a job she loved.

Rhen isn't heartless. He gave her a year's worth of pay and wrote her a letter of recommendation, both of which she keeps in her quarters—but she hasn't left, and he hasn't forced her out.

She wanted to be a guard. She gave up her apprenticeship. She says she doesn't want to leave me alone while everything is so precarious, but a part of me wonders if she doesn't want to go home carrying the weight of the choices she made. Of the choices *I* made.

I've hesitated too long. Rhen comes through the doorway to the courtyard, trailed by two of his guards. He's tall and striking, with blond hair and brown eyes, and his clothes are always finely detailed, right down to the ornate hilt of the sword at his hip or the silver hand-tooled buttons of his jacket. He moves with purpose and athletic grace, never a hesitation in his step. He moves like a prince. Like a king. A man born to rule.

But I can see the subtle changes. The shadows under his eyes have grown slightly darker. The edge of his jaw seems sharper, his cheekbones more pronounced. Unease has taken root in his eyes over the last few weeks.

His guards take a place by the wall while he strides across the courtyard toward us. Zo sighs.

"I'm sorry," I whisper to her.

"Nonsense." She curtsies to Rhen, even though she's in breeches and armor. "Your Highness."

"Zo," he says coolly. His eyes shift to me. "My lady."

I inhale to try to say something to ease the tension between them, but Zo says, "If you'll forgive me, I was just about to return to my quarters."

"Of course," says Rhen.

I bite my lip as she moves away.

"She is running from me," Rhen says, and there's no question in his gaze.

I bristle immediately. "She's not *running*."

"It certainly seems like a retreat."

Wow. Someone certainly seems like a jerk. "Zo is allowed to be mad, Rhen."

"So am I."

That stops my mouth from forming whatever words I was going to say. I didn't know that he was still angry at Zo. I wonder if he's still mad at me, if I'm not the only one with this burning core of anger in my belly.

Before I can ask him, he draws his sword. "Show me what you've learned."

I put my hand on the hilt, but I don't draw it. I'm not entirely sure why—especially since I told him to come show me. Maybe it's because he said it like an order. Maybe it's because his mood feels belligerent. Either way, I don't want to face him with a weapon.

I glance away. "I don't want to do this anymore." I turn toward the door he just came through. "I should go get dressed for breakfast."

I hear him sheathe his sword, and then his hand catches my arm gently. "Please."

It's a broken word. A desperate word that cuts the tiniest hole in my anger.

"Please," he says again, and his voice is so very soft. "Please, Harper."

He has a magical way of saying my name, his accent softening the edges of each *r* to turn a couple syllables into a growl and a caress all at once, but that's not what gets my attention. It's the *please*. Rhen is the crown prince. The future king. He doesn't plead.

"Please what?" I say softly.

"Please stay."

He means right now, but it feels bigger. Broader.

A memory flickers into my thoughts, from a year ago. Mom was already sick, cancer invading her lungs, and Dad had blown through our family savings trying to cover what insurance wouldn't. He made bad choices to get money, choices that put our family in danger. When Mom found out about it, she told me and Jake to pack our things. Dad was crying at the kitchen table, begging her to stay. I remember my big brother shoving things into a duffel bag while I sat on his bed and stared with wide eyes.

"It'll be okay, Harp," Jake kept saying. "Just get your stuff."

It wasn't okay. None of it was okay. At the time, the thought of leaving was terrifying. I remember being relieved that Mom relented, that we stayed. That *she* stayed.

Later, as things got really bad, I remember wishing she hadn't.

I stare up into Rhen's eyes and wonder if I'm making the same choices. Jake left with Grey. My brother will be on the other side of this war.

I take a breath and blow it out. "I don't want to fight."

I'm not talking about swords, and I think he knows it. Rhen nods. "Shall we walk instead?"

I hesitate. "Okay."

He offers his arm, and I take it.

CHAPTER FOUR

RHEN

My guards trail us as we walk. Harper's hand on my arm is light, as if she might pull away at any time. Grey used to say I would plan my moves twenty steps ahead, and he's right—but all of my moves now seem to be directed by another. I can't plan out twenty moves when the enchantress might change course after the second or third or fifteenth.

I want to tell Harper about the enchantress so badly—but there are so many ways that could go wrong.

I kept this secret for more than three hundred seasons. I can keep it again.

"You are angry with me," I say quietly.

Harper doesn't answer, but then it really wasn't a question. She's been angry for weeks. For months.

The cobblestone path begins to thin as we approach the wooded path that leads into the forest. I expect her to turn when we reach the tree line, to keep our walk short, but she doesn't. We step into the early morning dimness of the woods, letting the silence swallow us up. The trees haven't fully changed, but red and gold leaves are plentiful, drifting through the air to litter our path.

"On my first night here," says Harper, "when I rode through these woods and I went from sweating in the heat to shivering in a snowstorm, it was the first moment I really believed you about the curse."

I glance at her. "Not the music that played on its own?"

"Well, that was . . . something. But going from early autumn to late winter was literally a smack in the face." She pauses. "And then finding Freya and the kids . . ." She shakes her head.

"Ah. You saw how far my kingdom had fallen. The true depth of the curse."

"No! I didn't mean it like that."

"I know. But the truth remains." I remember this too, when Grey and I rode out after Harper's attempt to escape, when I was worried about what she would find. I'd spent so many seasons confining myself to Ironrose Castle that even I was unaware how difficult life had become for my subjects. I'd known they were hungry and poor, but I hadn't realized how much. I hadn't thought I could do anything for them unless I broke the curse.

Harper showed me I was wrong, that the curse wasn't preventing me from providing for my people—and then she broke the curse anyway.

Yet Lilith is still here. Still making my life hell, just in another way.

I put my hand over Harper's, where it rests on my arm, and she glances up at me in surprise. For an instant, I expect her to jerk her hand away, but she doesn't. It's the tiniest allowance, but it holds so much meaning.

This is why Lilith holds so much power over me. Too much emotion is churning in my chest. I have to draw a breath.

"What's wrong?" she says.

Everything. But I can't say that. "We only have six weeks before Syhl Shallow will attack, and no matter how many times I try to plan a path to victory, I feel I am destined to fail."

She's quiet for a moment, and she looks back at the path. "You think Grey will win?"

I hope he doesn't. I have no idea what Lilith will do if he does.

I have no idea what will happen to Emberfall if he does.

"Lia Mara once came to me hoping for peace," I say. "And Grey has aligned himself with her. He has already begun to endear himself to my people. You've heard what happened in the town of Blind Hollow." My guardsmen tried to take Grey—and ended up in a battle with the townspeople. Grey apparently used magic to heal anyone injured in the fray. "They know Emberfall is still weak. Grey did not have to give us a warning of their intentions."

"I hear a 'but' coming."

"But . . . it is one thing to be a ruler wishing for peace, and entirely another to be a subject wishing for vengeance. They may have allies here, but I am unsure of what support they have in Syhl Shallow. Lia Mara is one woman. Grey is one man." I glance at her. "Much like you and me, my lady."

"You think they'll have a hard time staying in power?"

"I think they will face a lot of challenges, regardless of whether they win or lose this war. I think it will not be easy to have power shift from a woman like Karis Luran, who held her throne by violence and fear, to a woman like Lia Mara, who seems to value compassion and empathy."

Harper keeps her eyes forward. "Well, I value those things, too."

"I know."

My words fall into the space between us. She is hoping for me to say that I value those qualities as well, and I *do*, but not in the way that she means. Not in a way that would matter to her.

The gulf between us feels so vast.

Harper frowns when I say nothing more. "I guess compassion and empathy isn't winning *us* any followers either."

I hesitate. "Despite the harm Syhl Shallow has caused to Emberfall, it may not be easy for my people to rally around me, when my entire claim to the throne relies on the line of succession—putting Grey ahead of me. When his magic seems beneficial, not a threat. When my promises of military support have worn thin and proved to be inaccurate."

"Because of Disi," Harper says.

"Yes."

"And that's my fault."

She sounds both bitter and repentant. I draw her to a stop and look down at her. "My lady. You cannot possibly feel responsible for failing to produce an army."

She sighs and starts walking again. "Well. I do." She glances behind us at the guards, then drops her voice. "It was a lie, Rhen. And now everyone looks at me like I've let them down—or that I'm working with the enemy."

"Your brother, the 'crown prince of Disi,' fled to Syhl Shallow with Grey," I say. I cannot keep the tightness out of my voice. "How could they not?"

She says nothing. Her hand is tense against my arm.

"This sucks," she finally says.

"Indeed."

"So what can we do?"

We. Such a small word, but it tightens my chest and makes it hard to swallow. It's more than I deserve, surely. I want to pull her against me, to bury my face in her neck and remind myself that she's alive, that she's *here*, that she's safe.

But she's angry with me, with the choices I've made.

I force myself to be content with her hand on my arm. With the word *we.*

She's asked me for action. When Lilith asked, I balked.

When Harper asks, I want to leap.

"Many of my Grand Marshals have closed their borders," I say. "They seem unwilling to acknowledge my right to rule. We were able to stop the rebellion in Silvermoon Harbor, but not without cost. I would be a fool to assume my people are content." I pause. "Perhaps we should follow Grey's lead."

"You want to declare war?"

"No. I want to ask for unity."

She shudders. "You want to go back to Silvermoon *now*? It was scary enough when we went before." She's quiet for a moment, and I know she is remembering our first visit to Silvermoon Harbor, when we were ambushed—and would have been killed, if not for Grey. "What if we ride up to the gates and they shoot you?"

"They won't," I say.

"How do you know?"

"Because I don't intend to go to them." A plan has begun to form in my mind. "I intend to invite them here."

CHAPTER FIVE

HARPER

Freya, my lady-in-waiting, is lacing me into a corseted gown. The bodice is white silk, with red stitching and golden grommets edged by rubies, laced over the top of a layer of shimmering red voile spilling over crimson underskirts. The laces of the bodice are gold satin. The neckline is low and daring, and if I try to bend over, I'll have a wardrobe malfunction. I generally gravitate toward the breeches and sweaters—the *wool blousons*, as Freya calls them—in my wardrobe, and I have dozens of stunning dresses for when I need to dress up, but this is by far the most gorgeous thing I've ever worn. Even my boots are red leather with gold trim along the heel.

Rhen sent word to all of his Grand Marshals a week ago, and I've been dreading this "party" since the instant he mentioned it, but it's nice to feel pretty for five minutes. As much as I try not to think about it, the scar on my cheek and the limp in my step are a constant reminder that I'll never be classically beautiful or effortlessly graceful. I'm confident in my strengths, but that doesn't mean I don't think about my weaknesses.

Lately, I've been wondering if the choice to stay here is a weakness.

But where would I go? I can't go back to Washington, DC—and even if I could, what would I do? We disappeared in the middle of the night, facing a man with a gun. Our family's apartment has probably been emptied out and rented to someone else now. I have no identification, no documents, nothing.

Without warning, I think of my mother, and the memory of her death almost smothers me. We lost her because of cancer. We lost everything else because of my father.

My chest grows tight, and I can't breathe.

"Here, my lady," says Freya. "Look." She turns me to face the mirror.

It's a huge testament to this dress that it jerks my thoughts away from a downward spiral. In the mirror, it's even better than it looked laid across the bed. "Freya," I breathe. "Where did you *find* this?"

"Ordered by His Highness." Her blue eyes flick up to meet mine in the mirror, and her voice drops. "In the colors of Emberfall."

"Oh." I lose the smile. It's not just a pretty dress. It's a political statement.

"From what I understand," she adds as she smooths my skirts, "he ordered a dress for Zo as well."

"Really?"

She nods.

Freya is ten years older than I am, and since I helped rescue her and her children from an attack by Syhl Shallow's soldiers, she's been my lady-in-waiting in the palace. In a way, she's also been like a surrogate mother. She knows about Zo and what we did for Grey. She knows how it's driven a wedge between me and Rhen—and maybe driven a sliver between me and Zo.

It might have caused tension between me and Freya too, because I know how she feels about Syhl Shallow. Their soldiers destroyed her home, leaving her and the children shivering in the snow. Leaving them with *nothing* until Rhen offered her a position here in the castle. But the night Rhen had Grey and Tycho beaten, she was as horrified as I was. She'd never speak a word against Rhen, but I remember the hard set of her jaw, the way her breath had trembled.

I need to stop thinking about this. It was months ago. I made a choice. I stayed.

And it's not like Grey isn't planning to strike back.

"Why did he order a dress for Zo?" I say. Zo wasn't planning to come to the party. She doesn't like being in a position that reminds her of being a guardsman, and she definitely doesn't like being in the same room as Rhen.

If he sent her a dress, I wonder how she took it. Worse, I wonder how he *meant* it. When it comes to strategic planning, Rhen can be downright brilliant—but he can also be an epic ass.

Freya arranges my hair across my shoulder, adjusting a pin here and there. "Well, I presume he hoped she would attend with you." She pauses. "Perhaps His Highness wants a guard-who-is-not-a-guard at your side. Jamison said the soldiers are antsy because it is rumored that an attack from Syhl Shallow could occur at any moment."

I glance at Freya in the mirror. "When did you talk to Jamison?" The soldier was one of the first to lend support to Rhen and Grey when I convinced them to leave the grounds of Ironrose and help their people. He's another person who hates Syhl Shallow, after one of their soldiers took his arm and destroyed most of his regiment when he was stationed in Willminton. Now he's a lieutenant in the regiment stationed nearby, but he's rarely inside the castle.

"When I took the children to visit Evalyn last week," she says. "We saw him on the road back." She pauses. "He was very kind. He accompanied us to the castle."

"Oh." I'm not sure what to make of that. I used to spend so much time with the guards and soldiers. I would train alongside them. I'd be included in their banter and gossip. For the first time in my life, no one treated me like a liability. Like I was incapable. I felt like I belonged.

Now every interaction I have feels weighted with suspicion. I didn't realize how important that feeling of belonging had grown until it was gone.

Now the only person I train with is Zo.

I have to clear my throat. I wish I'd known Freya was going to see Evalyn, because I would have joined her, just for an excuse to talk to *someone*. But maybe I wasn't welcome.

I hate this.

A knock sounds at my door, and my breath catches. It's probably Rhen, so I call, "Enter."

It's not Rhen. It's Zo. The door swings open and she strides in, wearing a dress in a darker crimson than my own, her bodice so dark it's almost black, with cherry-red lacings. Her muscled arms are bare, her braids twisting down her back to her waist.

"Wow," I say.

Zo smiles and offers me a curtsy. "You too."

"You didn't tell me you were coming."

She shrugs a little. "I . . . wasn't sure I was." She strokes her hands along the skirts and sighs. "But it would be foolish to offend the crown prince again."

I frown.

"Don't look like that," she says. "I thought maybe you'd want a friend anyway."

Against my will, tears fill my eyes, and I step forward to hug her.

Her arms are tight against my back, but she says, "You'll undo all of Freya's hard work."

"You're such a good friend," I say. "I don't deserve you."

She draws back to look at me, her eyes searching mine. "Yes, you do."

Freya steps forward and begins pinning tiny white flowers into my hair. She has red ones in her hands, and I expect her to add them, but she turns to Zo. "Here," she says. "A finishing touch."

Zo holds still, her hands gentle on mine.

In another life, we'd be getting ready for prom, not getting ready for a party that's really an excuse to build alliances in anticipation of war.

I draw a shaky breath.

Zo's eyes are steady on mine. "You rallied them once before," she says quietly.

"I have no armies this time," I whisper. "I have nothing to offer."

She regards me soberly, then leans in to kiss me on the cheek. "You had none then, Princess."

That's true. Somehow I'd forgotten. My breathing steadies.

When I first came here, I knew what was right. I risked my life for this country. So did Grey, a thousand times over. I would never have allowed anyone to make me feel guilty for helping the people of Emberfall. I would never have let anyone make me feel like I'd made a poor choice by helping Grey.

I shouldn't be allowing it now.

As we turn for the door, I catch a glimpse of us in the mirror. The dresses are truly stunning together, a clear signal that we stand for Emberfall.

Rhen once asked me to be his ally, to present a united front to his people. To stand at his side. This . . . this is different. I'm not a billboard.

Anger, familiar and not entirely unwelcome, builds in my belly, chasing away everything else.

"Wait," I say, pulling Zo to a stop. "Freya?" I tug the bow of my bodice loose. "We're both going to need another dress."

* * *

Rhen has spared no expense, and considering that he only issued a summons for this "party" a week ago, I'm sure it wasn't cheap. The call for loyalty to Emberfall is evident in every red tablecloth, in every gold candlestick, in the massive crest hung over the fireplace in the Great Hall. Musicians have been stationed in the corner, their playing lively and vibrant, a melody chosen to project confidence. The castle doors stand open, allowing the night air to flow into the space. Guards stand at assigned intervals, their weapons and armor gleaming, while servants carry loaded trays to the tables. I can smell the food from the top of the staircase.

The hour is still early, so only a few dozen people fill the room. These will be the true loyalists, the Grand Marshals and their Seneschals from towns who've already sworn fealty to Rhen. These will be the people who want to be seen arriving first, as if they're among the prince's inner circle, even though Rhen himself hasn't deigned to join them yet. They've brought their own guards, too, which isn't unusual, but a bunch of armed men and women lining the walls doesn't make for a very welcoming party.

A page at the top of the staircase steps forward as if he's planning to announce us, but I wave him away. My heart thrums in my chest, and I smooth my hands along the navy blue of my skirts. The last thing I need is for Rhen to hear us being announced without him. He'd be pissed, and I'd probably knock him down the stairs.

I hate feeling this way.

Zo studies me, and as usual, she can practically read my thoughts. "We have not yet been announced," she murmurs. "We can return to your chambers. There is still time to wear the dresses he selected."

"No." I glance at her and wish I could read *her* thoughts. "I mean—we can. If you want."

Her eyes stare into mine. "I didn't want to before."

That makes me smile. I squeeze her hand and head down the stairs.

Without being announced, we don't draw much attention. I'm sure Rhen knows every single person here by name, but I don't know them all, especially the people who are from more distant cities. I spot Micah Rennells, a trade advisor who meets with Rhen once a week. He's one of the least genuine people I've ever met, and the false flattery he lavishes on Rhen makes me want to stick a finger down my throat. Zo and I head in the opposite direction, toward a table that has been laid out with glasses filled in an alternating pattern of red wine and glistening gold champagne.

Wow.

"You think anyone will even notice we're not wearing gold and red?" I whisper to Zo, and she grins. I take a glass for each of us, and it's tempting to drain mine in one swallow.

Then I turn around and find myself face-to-face with a short-ish man with weathered, tan skin, gray hair, and troubled blue eyes. If I met him in Washington, DC, I'd say he looked like retired military, because he has that kind of stature: fit and trim and very upright. His clothes are elegant but also simple: a dark jacket buckled over a red shirt, calfskin breeches, and tall, polished boots with worn laces.

"My lady," he says in surprise, and his voice is rough and raspy but not unkind. He offers me a bow and glances past me before returning his eyes to mine. "Forgive me. I did not realize you had joined the party."

When he extends a hand, I take it and curtsy. "I haven't been here long." I search my memory banks for his name and come up with nothing. I bite the edge of my lip before reminding myself to knock it off. "I'm so sorry. I don't recall if we've met before."

He offers a small smile. "We have, but it was a different time, and I have not traveled to Ironrose since Karis Luran was driven out of Emberfall. I am Conrad Macon, the Grand Marshal of Rillisk."

Rillisk. I freeze. Rillisk is where Grey went into hiding after he ran from his birthright. When we spent months thinking he was dead.

Conrad's expression goes still as well, and that troubled look returns to his eyes. "I was a bit relieved to receive His Highness's invitation to attend tonight. We have heard rumors that Rillisk may have fallen out of favor after . . . after the false heir was found hiding in our city." He pauses, and the tiniest note of desperation crawls into his voice. "We have always been loyal to the Crown, my lady, I assure you we had no idea—"

"Of course," I say quickly. "Rhen has no doubt." I think. I hope.

Relief blooms in his eyes. "Oh. Well. Perhaps the rumors will quiet. Since the heir—" He stumbles over his words. "Forgive me, since the *false* heir was captured in Rillisk, we have struggled a bit for trade, and we are not a seaport town—"

"Silvermoon *is* a seaport town," says another man, "and we are also struggling." I turn and recognize this one. Grand Marshal Anscom Perry, from Silvermoon Harbor. He's got thick hair, thick pale skin, and a thick midsection that's asking a lot from his jacket. I liked Marshal Perry's amical demeanor when we met him in Silvermoon, but then he attempted to close his gates on Rhen.

I'm surprised he's here, honestly.

"Marshal Perry," I say evenly. "It's a pleasure to see you again."

"It's not a pleasure to be here," he says, blustering. "The invitation implied I'd be brought by force if I didn't show up willingly. I only have so many soldiers left."

I falter and glance at Zo, but she meets my eyes and gives a minute shake of her head. She's no longer a part of the Royal Guard. She doesn't know what messages Rhen sent.

"I am certain you misunderstood," I begin.

"You are certain?" says a woman's voice, cutting me off. Marshal Earla Vail of . . . oof, I can't remember. She's from somewhere north of here, a town near the mountains that lead into Syhl Shallow. She's in her seventies, with thick graying hair and dark brown skin. Despite her age, she wears a sword on one hip and a dagger on another. "Much like you were certain that your father would send an army to help protect Emberfall?"

"My father's army was not needed," I say tightly. My heart is slamming along inside my rib cage.

"Emberfall was victorious thanks to Princess Harper alone," says Zo, and there's heat in her voice.

"Not without loss. Perhaps your father's army stands ready to assist Syhl Shallow," says another man, and enough people have begun to swarm around me that I can't even see who's speaking.

"Yes," says Conrad. "Have Disi's alliances shifted? Your crown prince has joined with those monsters over the mountain."

"Perhaps their princess has," says Marshal Vail, staring at me pointedly. "Karis Luran may be dead, but those soldiers from Syhl Shallow slaughtered people by the *thousands*—"

I suck in a breath. "I am *not*—"

"What kind of game is Disi playing?" says another woman. "Are you here to distract the prince while your father's armies lend support to Syhl Shallow?"

"That's not what's happening," says Zo, her voice low and tight.

"Or perhaps Princess Harper has been kept out of the negotiations," says Marshal Perry.

"I have *not* been kept out of negotiations," I snap, but I hear someone make a scoffing sound near my shoulder, and two of the Grand Marshals exchange a glance. They all begin to press closer, and I wish I could call for guards. But since I helped Grey, Rhen's guards have made it very clear that they are sworn to him—not to me.

"Why are you not accompanied by the prince?" Marshal Perry continues.

"I . . . well, he . . . ah—"

"My lady," Prince Rhen says smoothly from behind me, and I jump.

The people surrounding me back away so quickly that it's like they're being dragged.

"Your Highness," they say. The men bow. Ladies curtsy.

Rhen ignores them, his eyes finding mine. He steps forward to take my hand and kiss my knuckles, but I can't read anything in his expression. "Forgive me," he says, using my hand to draw me close.

His voice is warm and low in a way I haven't heard in . . . a while. "I did not realize I would be so delayed."

I swallow. "Forgiven."

He turns to face the people, keeping my hand wrapped in his. "The night is young. Perhaps we can spend an hour enjoying each other's company before we begin arguing over politics?" He nods to the servants laying food along the tables. "Or at least wait until after the food is served. It would be a pity to waste this fine meal. Anscom, the valet in the corner is pouring sugared spirits. I remember how much you enjoyed a glass with my father."

Marshal Perry of Silvermoon clears his throat. "Ah . . . yes. Of course, Your Highness."

Rhen offers them a nod, then looks at me. "Shall we, my lady?"

Shall we what? But he rescued me, and he's not being a jerk, so I nod. "Yes, certainly."

He turns to walk, keeping me close, his pace slow and languorous.

I look up at him. "Where are we going?"

He draws me closer and leans down a bit, his lips brushing against my temple in a way that makes me blush and shiver because it's so unexpected. I'd forgotten he could be like this. He hasn't said a word about the dress, either.

Then he says, "To dance."

I almost trip over my feet. "Wait. Rhen—"

"Shh." He leads me onto the marble floor, and his hand closes on my waist.

We're surrounded by dozens of people, many of whom just accused me of being a traitor. I hadn't expected them to be like . . . *that*, and I definitely don't want to dance in front of them like none of it bothered me. But I also don't want to cause more of a scene than I already have.

"I hate to dance," I whisper.

"I know." Rhen turns to face me, and his hand finds mine. "I hate to be thrust into political maneuvering without preparation. Yet here we are."

My mouth forms a line, but the song is slower now and I'm not as hopeless at this as I once was. I let him lead. "You're mad."

"Do I seem so?" he says affably.

"Uh-huh."

"I thought I was hiding it rather admirably." He pauses, and his eyes search mine. "Is your intent for us to be at odds here, my lady?"

I study him, trying to figure him out. There's a part of me that's happy he's angry, that I'm not the only one battling resentment here. There's a part of me that's immeasurably sad, too. Like I could punch him in the face and then run off sobbing.

"If it is," Rhen continues, "I wish you had come to me, instead of demonstrating it to all of Emberfall."

I frown and look away. He might be able to look happy while all of this is going on, but I can't do it. Music swirls through the room, and I remember that first night he taught me to dance on a cliff at Silvermoon. When I said to him, "I want to make sure it's real." He wanted it to be real, too—and for the longest time, I felt like it was.

But then I started to doubt myself. To doubt him.

When I say nothing, Rhen's voice turns careful. "Were you displeased with the gown I had sent for you?" He pauses, his voice gaining the barest hint of an edge. "Or was the displeasure Zo's?"

"It was *mine*," I say. "If you're pissed at me, don't take it out on her."

He looks a bit incredulous. "You believe I would?"

"I believe you'll do whatever you want to do."

His hand tightens on mine, and he turns me a little more sharply than necessary. "I have been more than fair to Zo."

That's probably true, and I glance away. "Fine."

He's quiet, but I can feel the tension in his body now. No one else has dared to enter the dance floor, so maybe they can sense it.

"I don't want to be a pawn," I say tightly. "That dress made me look like one."

"I rather doubt it."

He probably means it like a compliment, but it feels dismissive. "It made me *feel* like one." I swallow, and my throat is tight. "So I asked Freya to find me another one." He inhales, and I add, "Don't take it out on her either."

He doesn't flinch from my gaze. "I have done nothing to your friends, my lady. And I would never hold them accountable for *your* actions."

"Is that a threat?" I demand.

He blinks, startled. "What? No. I do not—"

"Because Grey spent his life doing everything you asked, and the first time he didn't, you strung him up on that wall."

He jerks back like I've slapped him. We're not dancing anymore. There's suddenly an icy distance between us. Music pours across the dance floor, but we're motionless in the center of it. The crowd has gone silent, and there's a weighted tension in the air.

I'm breathless, too.

I can't believe I said that.

Until the words fell out of my mouth, I never admitted to myself that I *felt* that.

Rhen's gaze could cut steel. So could mine, I'm sure.

Zo appears at my side. "My lady," she says smoothly. "A matter requires your attention."

My body feels like it's turned to stone. Rhen hasn't moved, and I can't breathe. I probably could have slapped him and generated less interest.

Maybe he's right—I should have talked to him privately. But I can't undo what's been done. I can't unsay what's been said.

I grab hold of my skirt and give him a curtsy. "Your Highness."

Without waiting for a response, without even a backward glance, I stride out of the hall.

CHAPTER SIX

RHEN

I'd forgotten she could be like this.

Right now, I'm so angry that I want to tell Lilith to go to hell, that she can take Harper back to Washington, DC, and I'd be glad of it. I'm alone in the middle of the dance floor, and while our words weren't loud enough to carry very far, there's no disguising our argument as anything other than what it was. As piqued as I am with Zo, I am glad she took Harper away before we said anything else.

Dustan strides across the dance floor to stop in front of me. "My lord."

He's been my guard commander since Grey left. He's strong and competent, and generally well liked. He was part of a private army in the west before I put out the call for more guardsmen, and he was one of the first to swear to me. Where Grey could be stoic and aloof, Dustan is more jovial, and he has a good rapport with the guards. He was an easy choice when I was desperate.

But while he's good at doing what I say, sometimes I wish he were better at doing what I *don't*.

Grey would have stopped Harper from entering the party without me.

Grey would have interceded before Zo did.

Grey would have—

I need to stop thinking about Grey. He's gone. He's my enemy.

You strung him up on the wall.

The words are like a dagger she plunged into my chest, and it's hard to breathe around it. I wish Dustan had brought me a glass of sugared spirits. Grey probably wouldn't have done that either—but he would've thought to tell a servant to do it.

"Go after her," I say to him.

He frowns. "My lord—"

"Go after her," I say again. The castle is full of people whose motivations—and whose loyalties—would scatter across a map. Harper just made me a target, but she made one of herself as well. "Keep her safe. Make sure she doesn't leave the grounds."

"You believe she would?"

I remember the numerous times Grey and I had to race after her in the beginning. "Right now, I'd be more surprised if she stayed here." I turn away.

He hesitates. "But—"

I turn back, and there must be enough ice in my eyes, because he gives me a nod and says, "Yes, my lord. Right away."

Grey wouldn't have hesitated.

Finally, a servant approaches with a tray, and I seize a glass of wine. It takes every ounce of my self-control to keep from downing the entire thing in one swallow. As it is, I drain half.

One of the Grand Marshals approaches. Conrad Macon, from Rillisk. Because of his city's distance from Ironrose, I don't know him well, but that's not a bad thing. The only Grand Marshals I know *well* are those who live nearby—or those who were at odds with my father.

Conrad has been quick to respond to any request since Grey was captured within his borders. And he showed up here tonight.

"Forgive me," he says, and his voice is conciliatory. "I did not intend to cause tension for the princess."

"There is more than enough tension to go around," I say. "You are not the cause of it."

He looks relieved to hear that. "Ah . . . yes, my lord. I agree." He hesitates. "I understand you are preparing the army for another attack by Syhl Shallow."

Now I do drain the glass. "Yes."

"Rillisk has a small private army, as you know," he says. "I know you have faced . . . conflict with Silvermoon. But I was speaking with the Grand Marshal of Wildthorne Valley, and we believe that by aligning our soldiers, we could present quite a large force in the west, which may be large enough to prevent any other cities from attempting to defect to the false heir's rule."

My thoughts were still tangled up in what Harper said to me, but this gets my attention. "You believe your armed forces would be enough to stand against Syhl Shallow?"

"Well, Marshal Baldrick has a woman in his employ who's been able to discern information from Syhl Shallow's soldiers."

"A spy," I say.

He winces. "More of a mercenary," he says, his voice low. "From what I understand, she's not cheap. But she was able to infiltrate their forces before, and she kept Wildthorne Valley from suffering many losses."

If there's anything I have, it's plenty of silver. In Emberfall, five years passed without much activity from the royal family, because I had no need to spend a single copper. It's part of why Syhl Shallow is so desperate to take over. "Have Marshal Baldrick plan a visit with this mercenary," I say. "If money is a concern, I'll make it worth her while. I would like to hear more from her directly."

"No need," Conrad says. "He brought her with him."

———

Chesleigh Darington is younger than I expect, somewhere in her mid-twenties, with waist-length dark hair, olive skin, and calculating gray eyes. She has a scar on her cheek similar to Harper's, though Chesleigh's stretches into her hairline over her ear, where the hair has grown back in a narrow white streak. Unlike the rest of the women at the party, she's wearing trousers—black calfskin, laced boots, and a slender tunic in deep purple. She's more armed than most of my guards, and I notice that several of my guardsmen hover close when she joins us at a table in the corner.

Marshal Baldrick and Marshal Macon sit at the table, sipping from glasses of wine, looking proud that they've brought something to offer. In another lifetime, I might be dismissive about their gloating, but tonight, I want people to envy them. I want people to seek my favor. I need Emberfall to be whole to stand against Grey. He's already endeared himself to many of the northern towns, and I am on rocky ground with Silvermoon Harbor. It's likely a miracle that Marshal Perry even showed up tonight.

I wish Harper had not stormed out of here.

I trace my finger around the stem of my wineglass and pay attention to the matter at hand.

"You believe you have information on Syhl Shallow's military?" I say to Chesleigh.

"Not just on their military," she says. "I can cross the border at will."

I frown. "How?"

"I speak Syssalah. I'm familiar with their customs, and they've come to see me as a citizen."

I lean in against the table. "How?"

"I was born there."

The Grand Marshals at the table exchange a glance, but Baldrick clears his throat. "Chesleigh is loyal to Emberfall."

My eyes don't leave hers. "Why?"

"Because their queen slaughtered my family." Her words are even and unaffected, her eyes cool. But I was a monster created by the enchantress, and I slaughtered my own family, so my tone is just the same when I speak of it. I know how much anger and fury and loss can be hidden by a pair of cool eyes.

"When their army first came through the mountain pass," she continues, "I was surprised how easy it was to lose myself among their ranks. Few people in Emberfall speak Syssalah—and even fewer would walk right up to a Syhl Shallow soldier without fear after what they've done. Bold women are rarer here, but they're common in Syhl Shallow."

"And they let you cross the border?" I say. "Just like that?"

She gives me a darkly conspiratorial smile. "They believe I am a spy."

I don't smile back. "How do I know you're not?"

"How do you know anyone is not?" She glances at the Grand Marshals at the table, then back at me. "I understand your . . . *princess* from Disi did not bring about the military forces that were promised. That the royal family perished while under the king of Disi's protection. Perhaps *she* is the spy."

"I thought we were here to talk about what *you* could offer," I say.

"We are." She pauses. "I can assure you that my word is good."

"Prove it."

She draws back in her chair and takes a sip from her glass. "I don't work for free, Your Highness. A girl has to eat."

She's very forward. I can see why she wouldn't have an issue assimilating in Syhl Shallow. I'm used to polished doublespeak from the men at this table, so a forthright request is almost . . . refreshing. "Fifty silvers," I say easily.

She smiles. "Two hundred."

Marshal Macon snorts with laughter and someone else mutters a curse, but I don't smile. "You must be very hungry."

Her eyes flash. "You have no idea."

"Fifty," I say again.

"You won't negotiate?"

"Not yet."

She studies me for the longest time. "There is a narrow passage through the mountains, three or four days' ride northwest of here. It's not wide enough to support the movement of troops, but it's unguarded from this side."

I straighten. "And?"

"It's wide enough to allow small contingents of soldiers at a time, and after their forces razed many of your smaller cities, they could begin setting up camp inside Emberfall." She pauses. "Without notice."

I go still. "Has this already begun?"

She shrugs and takes a sip of her wine.

I narrow my eyes. "I could find out for myself by sending scouts."

"Yes, and it would take you a week and possibly the loss of those scouts." She drains her glass, then smiles. This one looks genuine, and it turns her expression from calculating to something more intriguing. "Is that *truly* worth another hundred and fifty silvers, Your Highness?"

No. It's not. "One hundred now," I say to her. "One hundred when I've verified what you told me."

"You'll risk men anyway?"

"I'd rather risk a few now than risk my entire army on your word." I pause. "Now. Tell me."

"Forces have already made camp on the western side of Blackrock Plains, just at the base of the mountains."

The Grand Marshals gasp.

I don't. "How many?"

"At least a thousand."

Silver hell. A thousand enemy soldiers are stationed in my country and I had no idea.

A part of me goes cold at the thought. Grey gave me warning. Even *Lilith* gave me warning.

I didn't want to believe it.

I have to bite back a shiver. I glance at one of my guards. "Find General Landon." He gives me a quick nod and rushes off. I look back at Chesleigh. "I will pay you your silver and verify your story. If you're giving me the truth, return to Ironrose in a week and I'll pay you the rest."

She doesn't move. "I can tell you about more than just the soldiers, Your Highness."

"What else?"

Her eyebrows go up.

"There is a difference between hunger and greed," I say.

"Is there?" she says innocently.

"One hundred fifty now."

She hesitates, and I can tell that she's weighing whether to play me for more. I've never bartered with mercenaries, but I've seen my father do it, and I know from experience that once you set a level, they'll only ask for more the next time. She won't get more than that out of me today, and maybe my expression gives that away.

"A faction has formed in Syhl Shallow," she says. "There are many who fear magic. Many others who want no part of it among their people. There are records and ledgers of the magesmiths, of the things they could do, of the ways they were vulnerable." She pauses. "There are those who oppose the queen, and her alliance with this magesmith."

I go still. "Are you a part of this faction?"

"I could be."

"How are they vulnerable?"

"I have heard that magic can be bound into a certain kind of steel forged in the ice forests of Iishellasa. This steel can be fashioned to bear magic itself—or it can cause wounds that are impervious to magic. Many of these artifacts have been lost to time, but some can still be found in the Syhl Shallow villages where the magesmiths once lived."

"Preposterous," blusters one of the Grand Marshals.

But it's not preposterous. Grey once wore a silver bracelet that the enchantress bound to his wrist. It allowed him to cross the veil into Washington, DC.

I have no idea where it ended up. But I know such a thing exists.

My breathing goes thin, and my thoughts race. Is there a weapon that could harm Lilith? Has the solution been in Syhl Shallow all this time?

"I have heard rumor of one such weapon," says Chesleigh. She shrugs. "Doubtless there are others."

"Such a weapon could be used against the false heir," I hear one of the Grand Marshals murmur.

No, I think. *Such a weapon could be used against Lilith.*

This feels like a risk. There is no proof. No surety. It's not as if I could ask Lilith herself. Even now, I want to cast a glance around, as if she could be listening to this very conversation.

I say, "Could you retrieve this weapon?"

Her eyes flash. "It will cost you."

"For this, you can name your price."

CHAPTER SEVEN

HARPER

The sun set hours ago, and the stable hands have long since gone to bed. The silence is heavy around me, but I don't mind. Silence means I'm alone. I'm not entirely sure where I'm going, but I'm not dragging Zo down with me this time. I sent her back to her quarters with the assurance that I'd head for my own.

Instead, I'm in the stables, and this dress is cut for riding. I have Ironwill saddled in three minutes, and I'm on his back in one. I don't really know where I'm going, but I don't want to be *here*. I cluck softly to the horse, and we trot through the stable doorway.

A hand appears from nowhere, grabbing the rein. "Whoa!" yells a male voice.

Ironwill spooks, then spins, then rears.

I gasp and tilt sideways. The horse skitters, his iron shoes striking the cobblestones frantically. I scramble for purchase, but I'm going to hit the cobblestones. It's going to *hurt*.

Instead, I'm caught, arms closing around me, stopping the fall.

It's dark, and half the people in Emberfall hate Rhen right now, so I shriek and struggle, my hand finding the dagger at my waist.

"My lady. *My lady.*" Dustan's voice. My feet are set roughly against the ground.

I fight to right my cloak, shoving unruly hair out of my face. I'm gasping, my breath making quick clouds in the air. Another guard has hold of Ironwill's reins, and the horse prances, tossing his head.

I glare at Dustan. I've been ignoring him for months, since he was a part of what Rhen did to Grey. Since he was the one to tell Zo she was relieved of her duties. Since he turned from someone I thought might be a friend—into someone I've grown to resent.

My heart is still in my throat. "What is *wrong* with you?"

He doesn't look any happier to be here than I am. "His Highness ordered me to keep you on the castle grounds."

OH, DID HE.

I'm breathing hard, my thoughts full of venom. He's blocking my path now, standing like he's ready for me to take a swing at him—or bolt.

Both sound like a good idea. "Give me back my horse," I bite out.

He looks aggrieved. "My orders were to keep you on the grounds and keep you safe."

"I'm right here. I'm fine." I take a step forward and reach for the reins, but Dustan steps in front of me.

"If you force my hand, I will accomplish that by locking you in your quarters."

I feign a gasp. "You will? Such *chivalry.*"

He ignores my tone. "Would Grey not have done the same?"

I freeze. I remember a time when Rhen and I were arguing, and I pulled a dagger. Grey pulled a blade to stop me, and Rhen said, "He'll take your arm off if I order it."

I asked Grey about it later. *I follow orders, my lady. I bear you no ill will.*

He definitely would have done the same.

It takes some of the wind out of my sails.

I frown and start forward. Dustan steps to block me.

I grit my teeth. "I'm going to take the saddle off," I say darkly. "If that's all right with you."

He studies me for the longest moment, then steps back. I jerk the reins out of the other guard's hands, then stroke a hand down Ironwill's cheek. He chews at the bit and swishes his tail, looking aggrieved himself.

I wish I were nimble and limber, that I had the kind of skills that would let me leap onto Ironwill's back and gallop out of here, trampling Dustan in the process. But I'm not and I can't, and if I tried, Dustan probably *would* drag me back to my room to lock me there.

Back in the stall, I loosen the girth, then slip the saddle off the buckskin's back. I'm not trapped, but I feel like a prisoner anyway. I trade the saddle for a brush and ease the soft bristles against Will's coat. At some point, Dustan gives the other guards an order to stand outside the stables, but he stations himself across the aisle to stand against the opposite wall.

I ignore him, leaning into the brush, and the silence settles in around us. My anger is flailing, wanting a target, leaving me tense and fidgety. A chill has crept into the stall, and I bite back a shiver, pressing closer to the horse. It doesn't help, and I shiver harder, sucking a shuddering breath through my teeth.

"My lady." Dustan speaks from behind me, but I don't turn.

"Go away."

"You should return to the castle if you are cold."

"No."

He says nothing, and I wonder if he's still standing there or if he's returned to his spot across the aisle.

I can't decide if I'm being rude or if he's being a jerk, and honestly, I don't care. I stop brushing and press my forehead into Ironwill's neck, breathing in the scent of hay and horseflesh. He's warm and familiar and was a constant source of solace for me in the beginning.

I have learned that when you go missing, I should check the stables first.

Grey said that to me, on my second day in Emberfall.

Against my will, my eyes fill, and my throat tightens. I lost my mother to cancer, and then I lost my friend when Grey fled, and then I lost my brother when he went to help.

And I'm the idiot who stayed here. Because I believed in Rhen. Because I believed in Emberfall.

I sniff the tears back, but I do it quietly, because I don't want Dustan to know. I shiver again, clutching my forearms to my abdomen.

Dustan sighs. A moment later, a cloak drops over my shoulders.

I turn, and I'm sure there's fire in my eyes, because Dustan holds his hands up. "You don't need to be cold to spite me."

The cloak is warm from his body, and I want to throw it back at him, but that feels petty—and I really am cold. I swallow the tears that sat ready, then put the brush against the buckskin's coat again, using a little more force than necessary. "You don't need to pretend to be kind."

Dustan is quiet for a moment. "I heard what you said to His Highness. In the Great Hall."

"Good for you." I'm sure everyone heard it.

"Do you truly believe that is why he gave the order for what he did to Grey and Tycho? As some sort of . . . retaliation?"

"I don't want to talk to you, Dustan."

"And do you believe that if I'd refused to obey, that the prince would have simply chosen another path?" He pauses. "Or do you think he would have relieved *me* of my duties, then given the order to another?"

The brush goes still along Ironwill's shoulder.

"Do you think," Dustan continues, "that *Grey* would have refused such an order, if given?"

No. He wouldn't. I have to swallow hard.

"Grey's *final words*," Dustan says to my back, "were swearing an oath to an enchantress who nearly destroyed Emberfall. You can fault His Highness for the choice he made, and you can blame me for following the order he gave, but Grey could have simply admitted the truth—"

"Enough. Please." A stupid tear slips down my cheek.

I don't want Dustan to be right—but he is. Grey let me see glimpses of who he could be—gentle and kind—but there was a reason I called him Scary Grey. There was a reason I found him terrifying in the beginning.

And as much as I don't want to admit it, there was a reason Rhen had to go as hard as he did to get an answer.

Grey would never have yielded. I begged him to tell Rhen what he knew. I *begged* him, and he refused. I don't know if it's pride or if it's something that was drilled into him when he was in the Royal Guard, but Grey would never have given up that information.

Rhen couldn't stop until he had it. Not with all of Emberfall at risk.

I take a long breath and blow it out. I finally turn and look at Dustan. He's standing in the stall doorway, leaning against the frame.

"I still hate you," I say.

"Yes, my lady." His expression is inscrutable. I wonder if he hates me, too.

But some of the tension between us evaporates. Not all of it, not by a mile, but enough that I can feel it. No pretense, no hidden motives. We might not *like* each other right now, but we understand each other.

I wish it could be that easy with Rhen, but there's too much between us. It's one thing to understand why Dustan followed the order and why Rhen gave it. It's entirely different to have seen the aftermath. To know it wasn't done to some criminal plotting against the country, that it was done to *Grey*.

As if my tumultuous thoughts summoned him, the main stable doors are drawn open, and Rhen himself steps through. Dustan immediately snaps to attention.

I turn back to the horse. "Party over so soon?"

He says nothing for a moment, then, "Commander. Leave us."

I hear Dustan's quiet deferral, and then we're alone. I smooth the brush along the horse's coat, but Rhen must step up to the stall door, because Ironwill shifts his weight and turns, forcing me to step back. The buckskin pricks his ears and stretches out his neck to blow puffs of air at Rhen's hands.

Traitor.

Rhen strokes a hand down the horse's face. "I'm surprised I didn't find you ten miles away."

"You ordered Dustan to trap me here."

"Half of Emberfall seems ready to take action against me. Syhl Shallow stands ready to attack." He pauses, and his voice is low. "Surely you know I ordered him to keep you here for your safety, not as my prisoner." Another pause. "Especially once you demonstrated to my Grand Marshals that we are not in accord."

I say nothing. Every muscle in my body is tense, waiting for him to fully pick a fight, to finish what we started on the dance floor.

But . . . he doesn't.

Rhen's patience always takes me by surprise. He expects everything to be done on his command, but somehow it's more powerful when he doesn't command anything, and instead simply . . . waits. I resume my brushing, following each stroke with my palm, finding comfort in the warmth of the horse and the repetitive motion. Eventually, my shoulders loosen. My chest doesn't feel like it's going to cave in.

"I'm sorry," I say quietly, and as I say the words, I discover I really mean them. "I shouldn't have done that . . . there."

"I do not deserve an apology," he says, and his voice is equally quiet. "Indeed, I feel as though I owe you one."

When I say nothing, he adds, "You are so angry with me." He hesitates. "I believe there has been too much unsaid between us for too long."

I peek over at him, but his eyes are on Ironwill, and the horse has pressed his head against Rhen's chest. Rhen's hand is against the animal's cheek, his long fingers stroking the sleek fur in the hollow of his jaw.

It reminds me of the day Rhen was a monster, a creature summoned by Lilith's magic, bent on destroying everything in his path. He'd never been docile for anyone in his monster form, he'd never even *known* anyone—not even Grey. But he quieted for me. He was massive, at least ten feet tall, part dragon and part horse, with fangs and talons, his scales and feathers glittering in luminescent colors. I thought he was going to kill us all, but he'd put his head against my chest and blown warmth against my knees.

The memory is so powerful that my breath catches. I look back at Ironwill.

"My lady?" says Rhen.

I shake my head slightly. "What's . . ." I have to clear my throat. "What's unsaid on your side?"

"I should have spoken to you about Grey before I made a choice of what to do."

I hold my breath.

"I thought . . . ," he begins, then hesitates. "I thought you understood my reasons, but perhaps—"

"I do." I peek over at him again. My voice is rough. "I do understand your reasons." I have to look back at the horse. "When you did that," I whisper, "you were so much more frightening than you ever were as a monster."

He inhales sharply, but I don't look at him. I can't look at him.

"Because you made a *choice*," I say, and my voice breaks. "Because it was *you*. Because it was someone I cared about. Because it was horrible."

Tears fall, and I press my forehead into the horse's neck. My fingers tangle in Ironwill's mane. "Because you needed to do it. Because I didn't want to know *you* could have done it."

"Harper." He's at my side suddenly, his voice soft and broken. His finger brushes against my cheek, his touch feather-light, as if he worries I'll turn away from him.

I don't. In a way, I wonder if I've been turning away from him for too long.

His eyes burn into mine. "Please, Harper, please know this. I begged him to tell me. After what Lilith did, I could not—I could not risk my people." Those tortured shadows shift in his eyes. "Forgive me. Please. Do you think it cost me *nothing*?"

The emotion in his voice makes my throat tighten and sends fresh tears to my eyes. It's not the apology—it's the acknowledgment that he felt hurt and loss the same way I did. I wait for his apology to bounce off that coiled pit of anger in my stomach, but it doesn't. For the first time, I realize that the bulk of anger isn't at the people around me. It's not about Rhen.

It's about myself.

He made choices here, but so did I. His choices were about Emberfall. Mine were about Grey.

We were both wrong and both right at the same time, and the realization of *that* is what finally makes the anger ease and shift and become a bit more bearable.

I sigh and press my face against his chest, and his arms come around me, tight against my back under the cloak, pulling me against him. I feel his breath in my hair, his heart thrumming alongside mine.

It feels good to be in the circle of his arms. I'd somehow forgotten.

"I don't want to be in this weird holding pattern anymore," I say against him.

He's quiet for a moment, and then he says, "I do not know what this means."

I blink, then a startled laugh escapes my throat. He's met enough girls from Washington, DC, that I don't often trip him up with an expression, so when it happens, it takes me by surprise.

I draw back and peer up at him. "It's like . . ." I have no idea how to explain what an airplane holding pattern is to him, and it doesn't even matter. "I mean I don't want to keep doing the same thing over and over again, waiting for something to happen to knock us out of it." He's frowning, so I add, "I don't want to keep fighting with you."

"Nor do I." He strokes a tear off my cheek. "I should have told you."

And I should have asked. I should have *known*. I sniff. "You— you needed to do it. And I would have stopped you."

"No. You would have helped me find a better way." His eyes don't leave mine. "You always help me find a better way."

That's part of the problem. I don't know if there *was* a better way. He did what he did to protect Emberfall. Rhen's first obligation is his people—he's never hidden that from anyone. But his feelings for me are high up there, too. Standing here now, feeling his breath in my hair and his heart beating against mine, I don't think I made the wrong choice in staying.

We stand for the longest time, his hand idly stroking my back, mine tracing the buttons on his chest, until the moment changes, growing heavier. Sweeter. Warmer. I inhale, or maybe he does, because my name is a whispered purr on his lips, and then his mouth finds mine.

He's hesitant at first, as if he's still worried I'll pull away, but I don't, and he's immediately more sure. His hands land on my waist, trapping me against him. His tongue brushes mine, and my fingers tangle in his hair. It's been so long since he kissed me like this, and it takes my breath away. Warmth swells in my body, a tiny flicker of flame at first, but quickly racing through my veins to send heat everywhere. He makes a low sound in his throat, and before I'm ready, my back hits the stall door.

"Ouch." I giggle.

"Forgive me," Rhen says again, and he actually looks repentant.

"I'll survive."

A light sparks in his eyes, and Rhen tugs me into the aisle, letting the stall door fall closed. I take advantage of the narrow distance he's suddenly granted us, and I yank at the buttons of his jacket and the buckle of his sword belt all at once.

Then his mouth claims mine again, and my fingers stop working.

His don't. I distantly hear his weapon strike the floor, and then his jacket is gone. I can feel the warmth of his skin through his shirt now, the long sloping muscle of his back. He strokes a hand up the front of my corset, lighting a fire when his fingertips brush along the barely exposed skin of my breast, and I curse the fact that Freya tied the knots so tightly.

Maybe I *should* have worn that other dress.

The thought makes me flush and cling to him, because it's unlike him to be quite this forward. We've slept *beside* each other dozens of times, but we've never actually *slept together* for a hundred different reasons—one being that the last woman he had sex with cursed him for an eternity.

He's never specifically said as much, but if we had to rank reasons, I'd bet good money that it would find a spot among his top five.

The fact that we always seem to be at odds would probably be up there, too.

It feels good to be kissed by him again. To be *held* by him. Some-times Rhen is so hard, so decisive and challenging, that I forget he can be gentle. Tender. I forget that he can strike a match with his kiss and turn my insides into a bonfire.

"I've missed you," I say softly, because it's true, so true that it almost pulls tears into my eyes again.

He goes still, which I don't expect, and then exhales against my neck. His breath shudders. His hands slow, holding me tight, hold-ing me still. There's a different tension in his body now, a whisper of sorrow in the air.

I lean against him. "Rhen?"

It takes him forever to look up and meet my gaze. The aisle is dim, his eyes pools of darkness. He touches my cheek, his fingers light at first, until his palm is against my jaw and his thumb traces over my lips. "This is the dress you first wore to Silvermoon."

I frown. "You remember?"

"You looked like a queen." His eyes find mine again. "You *look* like a queen."

"It's a great dress."

He inhales and blows it out slowly. "I did not tell you about Grey because sometimes I think your will is stronger than mine."

"Sometimes?" I tease, but gently, because he seems so fragile.

"Just as before," he says, "I did not tell you because I feared it would put you in harm's way."

Before. It takes me a moment to figure out what he's talking about, but then I do. Before the curse was broken, when Lilith was torturing him night after night because he'd come close to finding love with *me*. I basically had to force him into my room because he wouldn't willingly put me at risk—but he's never denied me anything.

I would have asked him not to harm Grey, and he wouldn't have done it.

My heart gives a jump in my chest. I was wrong before. It's not that he puts Emberfall first.

He puts *me* first.

"Rhen." I stare at him. "Did something happen at the party?"

"The party was a success," he says. "I met a mercenary from Wildthorne Valley who offered insight into troop movements. She spoke of weapons in Syhl Shallow that could stand against magic."

"Wait—what?" I blink at him. "You're not telling me something." I study the sharp lines of his jaw, the shadows under his eyes, more pronounced now in the dark.

I should have asked.

I consider how he's been these last few weeks. The way he's tense and jumpy, how he never seems to sleep anymore. The way we're supposed to be preparing for war—but he doesn't seem to be *preparing* anything at all.

If Rhen is anything, it's prepared.

I square my shoulders and look at him. "You don't want to go to war," I guess.

"If I do not, Grey will take Emberfall," he says. "He will ally with Syhl Shallow, and their people have slaughtered ours by the *thousands*. He is not a king, Harper. He has no experience in ruling a country."

"Is that it?" I say, narrowing my eyes. "Or is it his magic that you're afraid of?"

He flinches at the word *magic*.

"I don't believe Grey means you harm," I say quietly.

"In truth, my fears do not concern Grey."

I go still. There's a note in his voice I can't parse out.

"Rhen." I step into him again, until we breathe the same air. "Tell me what you're afraid of."

Finally, his eyes meet mine. "Lilith."

CHAPTER EIGHT

RHEN

Harper is frowning up at me. I long to draw the words back into my mouth, to erase the enchantress's name from this moment.

Harper is so lovely in the dimness of the stable aisle, her curls coming a bit loose from their pins, her lips flushed and swollen from kissing me. Her eyes are full of concern, and I wish I could reverse time by the span of one minute, so I could steal that worry from her expression.

But I can't do this again. I can't keep this from her any longer.

"Lilith?" she says.

The name still has the power to make my heart skip with fear, and I flick my eyes to the shadowed corners of the stable, as if Lilith might appear right here, right now.

She doesn't.

Harper's frown deepens. "But Lilith is dead."

"No. She is not." I take a breath, and my voice drops. "She has been here, to Ironrose. She has returned with magic, and threats, and a clear desire to make me miserable."

Harper takes a step back, and it hurts to let her go. I expect to see betrayal in her expression, but there's none.

There's resolve.

When she speaks, her voice is level. "When? Where is she? What has she done?" Without waiting for an answer, she looks at the door and raises her voice. "Dustan! Guards!"

"My lady—"

The doors are thrown wide, and four guards sweep into the aisle, weapons drawn, eyes seeking a threat.

I give her a withering glance, then stoop to grab my jacket and sword belt. At least *she* is fully dressed. "Stand down," I say to the guards. "There is no cause for alarm."

"Yes, there is." Harper's voice is like steel. "If she's back, you shouldn't be alone."

Dustan has sheathed his weapon, but he glances between us. He's definitely picked up on the tension in her voice. "My lord?"

I sigh and shove my arms through the sleeves of my jacket. "Commander. I will retire to my chambers."

Harper inhales to make more demands, I'm sure, but I give her a level glare and hold out my hand. "Join me, my lady?"

She scowls, but she places her hand in mine. We stride out of the stable, but I hesitate as we cross over the threshold, my eyes searching the darkness for the enchantress.

Harper notices, because her step falters, too, and she glances up at me. I force myself to keep walking.

"Talk to me," she hisses. "How can you say something like that and not tell me anything more?"

"I planned to, but you called for guards." She is so *impulsive*. A cold breeze whispers against the bare skin of my neck and I shiver.

I want to be inside. I want to be in my chambers. I want to be locked behind a door so thick that no one could penetrate it.

None of that would matter. Nothing stops Lilith.

We reach the rear doors of the castle, and a footman leaps to hold it open. Once we're out of the chilly night air, I feel better. Less exposed. Dustan sticks close to us, and I want to send him away. I already saw what Lilith did to Grey, season after season. I have no desire to see it inflicted on more of my guardsmen.

But Harper has clearly spooked him. Once we reach my chambers, Dustan stations himself outside, along with three other guardsmen. He inhales like he's going to say something, but I close the door in his face.

My eyes flick to the corners before I look at Harper. "I suppose I should be glad you did not alert the *entire* castle."

"Don't you dare get mad at me."

"I am not mad. I am . . ." My voice trails off, and I sigh. I set my sword against the wall, then run my hands down my face. I have no idea how to finish that statement. *I am . . .*

Regretful.

Resigned.

Exhausted.

And the worst: *ashamed.*

Speaking those words would seem to give weight to my faults, and I've done that enough already.

"I do not know what I am," I say.

"Did she show up at the party?" Harper draws an angry breath. "You should have kept Dustan with you. You shouldn't have sent him after *me*, of all people—"

Silver hell. "Harper. *Stop.*"

She stops.

"Lilith has been here for *weeks*." I pause. "Months."

I watch as she absorbs this information, as her face shifts from worry and fear to confusion and bewilderment. I expect her to yell, for this to fuel her tirade, but instead, she turns thoughtful. "Months." Her voice grows softer. "Rhen. *Rhen.* Why wouldn't you *tell* me?"

I hesitate, and she sucks in a breath, pressing a hand to her abdomen. "It's me. She threatened me."

"Yes."

Harper presses her palms together in front of her face, then blows out a breath. She drops into a chair in front of the hearth. "Okay. Start at the beginning. I thought Grey took her to the other side and killed her."

I ease into the chair beside her. "He certainly tried. She bears a scar on her neck—and for all the other injuries he attempted on *this* side, she's never had a scar. He may not be aware she lives."

"And what does she want?"

"She wants me to win this war."

"Why? Why does she care?"

"Because she wants to rule Emberfall. She blames my father—my *country*—for the destruction of her people. She wants the throne."

"Then why doesn't she just kill you?"

"You see that my dispute with Grey has already put us at risk of civil war. She wholeheartedly admits that she cannot claim the throne and expect my entire kingdom to bend a knee to her. She is powerful, but not *that* powerful."

Harper considers that for a while. I wait, listening to the fire snap in the hearth. I have been terrified of this moment for . . . for *ages*. I did not want Harper to know. I did not want her to be at risk. But

I did not realize how desperate I was for a confidante until she demanded this truth.

The thought tightens my chest, and I have to swallow the emotion. I still remember the night I met the enchantress, how she tried to charm my father first, and he had the good sense to turn her away.

I didn't, and I've been paying the price ever since.

Harper's hand falls over mine. "Don't hide," she says. "Talk to me."

She's kinder than I deserve. "When Grey and I were trapped in the curse, he was the only person who knew how terrible she was. It is . . . difficult to share that with you. Even now."

"What does she want to do to me? Leave my body parts all over Emberfall?"

"Worse. She has threatened to return you to Disi."

Her hand goes still over mine, and her expression freezes. "Oh."

I hold my breath, worried that Lilith will show herself and make good on her threats, but the room remains quiet. The enchantress does not appear. The fire continues to snap.

Harper continues to exist at my side.

"So she wants you to win this war. She wants you to be king." Harper hesitates, and her eyes search mine. "And she wants to be at your side once you are."

I nod.

She's quiet for a moment. "Do you really want to go to war with Grey?"

"I see no other way for Emberfall—"

"Stop." She puts up a hand. "Do *you*, Rhen, really want to go to war with your *brother*?"

I sigh and rise from the chair, moving to the side table, where I uncork a bottle of wine. "He may be my brother in blood, Harper, but he is not my brother." I pause to pour. "He ran instead of telling me the truth. He stood in front of me and kept this secret. *He* declared war on *me*."

"No, he gave you sixty days—"

"To prepare for war." I drain the glass and pour another. "His letter was quite clear."

"He said, *do not make me do this*."

"I've made him do nothing. He can stay there and I can stay here and we can all be at peace." I drain this glass, too, especially because I know this is not true. Syhl Shallow was struggling, desperate for resources and trade, before the curse was ever broken. My father had been paying a tithe to keep Grey's birthright a secret, but once I was cursed and my father was dead, the tithe stopped being paid. Five years of silver stayed in my coffers—and Syhl Shallow went lacking.

It's why Karis Luran sent soldiers into my lands, and it's why Grey is promising to do the same thing if I do not ally with Lia Mara.

Harper appears at my side and takes the glass away. "If Lilith is around, the last thing you need to be is drunk."

That's debatable, but I push the cork back in. I haven't been drunk in months. Not since the night Grey returned Harper to Washington, DC. Before we knew anything about his birthright. Before the curse was broken.

You are incorrigible. I have no idea how I put up with you for so long.

Grey's words. The only time I've ever seen him drunk. Probably the truest words he ever said to me.

He stood with me on the castle parapets before I turned into a monster the final time. I sought to sacrifice myself. I was going to jump. I was terrified.

He stepped up and took my hand.

My throat tightens. I yank the cork free and drink right from the bottle.

"Wow," says Harper.

"Indeed." My voice is husky.

She takes the bottle this time. I drop into the chair in front of the fire and run my hands across my face.

"Why didn't you tell me?" she says quietly.

"Because I cannot lose you again," I say. "I couldn't put you at risk."

She's quiet for a while, and I don't have the courage to look at her. Weeks of anger were bad enough. I have no desire to see disappointment or censure in her expression.

Her fingers drift along my shoulder then, and she curls into the chair with me, her skirts falling across my lap, her head tucking into the hollow beneath my chin. She is warm and solid and sure against me.

She doesn't hate me, and I nearly shudder from the relief of it.

"That's why you were putting on such a show for the Grand Marshals," she says. "Because you need to put on a good show for Lilith."

"It needs to be more than a show if we're going to stand a chance against Syhl Shallow." I pause. "But yes."

"I wish I'd worn the dress now."

"I have never seen you as a pawn," I say, and mean it. "Wear what you like."

She falls quiet for a while, breathing along my neck for so long that my thoughts begin to scatter and drift, either from exhaustion or the wine. Or both.

"You used to take Lilith's torments so she wouldn't hurt Grey," Harper whispers.

I remember the endless misery the enchantress would visit upon us both. Some days it was boredom, while others it seemed to be vindictive, or a punishment for crimes only she could fathom. Nothing she did would kill us, not when the curse was in effect, but the pain was very real.

I would draw her attention off Grey when I could. He did not earn the curse, I did. He should have fled during the first season, when I first changed.

Sometimes I wish he had.

"It was all I could do," I say to Harper. "Only his loyalty kept him by my side. No one deserves an eternity of torture for *that*."

"Grey once told me it was his duty to bleed so you would not."

I know. I heard him say the words.

I thought of them when I watched a whip split open the skin of his back.

I long for that wine bottle again.

"You didn't have to take it all on yourself," Harper says. "And you don't have to now."

"I do not know how to defeat her—"

"Together," she says. "The way we did before."

She sounds so sure.

"Yes, my lady," I whisper, and I drop a kiss along her temple.

I wish I felt the same.

"Your Highness."

My eyelids flicker. The room is cold and dark, and my left arm has gone numb. Harper's weight is heavy with sleep, her breath slow and light against my skin. The fire has burned down to embers.

"Shh," the voice says. "Do not wake your princess."

I blink slowly, my eyes seeking a face in the shadows. It's unusual for a servant to enter my chambers after I've retired for the night.

Then Lilith's fine features snap into clarity, and I jerk in alarm.

"Shh," Lilith says again. "I'd hate for her to wake and force me to take her back to Disi."

My heart has leapt into a panicked race, pounding so hard that I'm sure it'll wake Harper. "Leave me," I whisper. "Please, Lilith."

"You told her the truth," she says.

She makes it sound like a weakness, and I clench my jaw. "I will not hide your crimes any longer."

"I commit no crimes." She leans closer, until her lips are a breath away from mine. Her eyes glitter in the darkness.

I hold very still. I would give every scrap of silver in Emberfall to my new spy if she could appear with a weapon that would stop Lilith right this moment. My fingers long to grip tight to the girl in my arms, as if I could keep her safe by sheer strength of will. "I have made preparations to go to war. I will stand against Grey. I have done as you asked."

"Good boy," she breathes. Her lips brush against mine, and I snap back. Harper shifts in my arms.

Lilith smiles. "No matter what you tell her, she cannot cross the veil without my assistance. If I take her away, you will have no way to reach her."

"I will do as you ask," I say. "You have my word."

"Good." She traces a finger along the scar on Harper's cheek before I can jerk her away.

Harper startles awake, slapping a palm to her cheek. Her breathing is quick and rapid. "Rhen. What—who—*you*." She goes very still in my arms.

"Yes. Me." Lilith's eyes flash with danger in the darkness, and she hisses the words like a snake. "You weak, broken, worthless little—"

Harper launches herself out of my arms, and I realize a moment too late that she's seized the dagger from my belt.

"No!" I cry. I remember the last time she threw a weapon at the enchantress.

But Harper doesn't throw it. She drives the blade right into Lilith's midsection, throwing her weight into the movement and bringing the enchantress to the floor. Harper kneels on her arm, then wraps the fist of her free hand in Lilith's hair.

She leans down close. "Go ahead," she whispers. "Take me home. Let's see how long you live on my side."

Wind swirls through the room, making the candles go out and the flames in the hearth flicker. Lilith is gasping, either from shock or pain. "I will make you *pay*—"

"He's doing what you want him to do. Did Grey give you that scar? I bet I can make a bigger one."

"Harper." I can't breathe. "Harper, please."

Lilith is practically drooling with rage. "I will *end* you—"

"Then do it. Lose the only leverage you have." Harper leans down closer. "You're the weak one," she whispers. Lilith screams in rage, then slashes her free hand against Harper's arm.

Harper cries out and snaps back. Blood has appeared in three long stripes across her bicep.

My door swings open. Guardsmen charge in, drawn by their screams.

Lilith disappears, leaving nothing but the dagger and a stain of blood on the floor.

Harper slaps a hand over her arm. She's all but wheezing. "Is it bad?" she says. "I can't look at it."

I'm staring at her, and it takes a moment for my eyes to leave her face. I pull at her fingers gingerly. The sleeve of her dress is shredded, the slashes bleeding freely.

Dustan appears at my side, and he drops to a knee.

"Brandyn," he says to one of the guards. "Fetch a physician. The princess will need stitches."

Harper sighs. "More scars. Great."

I can't stop staring at her in wonder.

"What?" she says.

I have no words. "How—how did you—" I break off. "*How?*"

"I hate her," she says simply. "It wasn't hard. Or do you mean, how did I know how to pin her like that?"

"Who?" says Dustan.

"Yes," I say.

"Easy." Harper picks up the blade, wipes it on the skirts of her ruined dress, and holds it out to me, hilt first. Her eyes are fierce and determined. "Zo taught me."

CHAPTER NINE

LIA MARA

When I used to imagine being queen, my dreams involved my people finding peace at last. I would rule with gentle firmness instead of my mother's vicious brutality, and my subjects would thrive. No one would fear me. I never *wanted* to be feared. I thought my people would rejoice.

I never thought someone would be begging me to sever limbs right in the middle of my throne room.

"Your Majesty," whispers Clanna Sun, the woman who used to be Mother's chief advisor—who is now *my* chief advisor. "You will need to take some action."

"You should cut his hands off," growls the woman in front of me. Her name is Kallara, and she owns a small farm far to the north, right along the Frozen River. Her hands are gnarled and her skin is weathered from a lifetime of hard labor. "Even if an apple falls from the tree, it doesn't make it free."

"I didn't steal an apple!" snaps the man, another landowner named Bayard. "I planted on *my* land."

"It's *my* land," shouts Kallara.

"Mine!" he roars. His cheeks are red, his eyes bulging out with fury.

"Not surprising that a man lacks the intelligence to measure distance," says Kallara. "Perhaps our wise queen will grant your lands to me, and I can put you to work in the fields where you belong."

"I *was* in the fields where I belong!"

"Cut all their hands off," Nolla Verin, my sister, mutters from her throne on my opposite side. Ellia Maya, another advisor who's always been close to my sister, laughs under her breath. Nolla Verin flashes her a smile.

I sigh and glance at the window. Prince Grey is outside on the fields, Jake and Tycho by his side, overseeing the training of our soldiers. In the beginning, Grey would sit with me while I heard complaints from my subjects, but not everyone speaks the language of Emberfall, and he's still learning Syssalah. It's not a failing, but I've heard whispers about arrogance and ignorance, and I'm not sure which is worse. My people already question whether I am ruthless enough to rule following my mother's death.

All of this is so much more complicated than I ever imagined.

At my side, Nolla Verin clears her throat emphatically.

I jerk my eyes away from the window and glance at Clanna Sun. "Whose land is it truly?"

"They both bear deeds showing ownership of the acreage, Your Majesty."

Of course they do. I hold back another sigh.

"Forged, I'm sure," sniffs Kallara.

"Enough." They would never bicker like this in front of my mother. I glance across the room where the scribes take down every word we say. "Scribes," I say. "Review the deeds for accuracy. Verify my mother's seal." I look at Kallara and Bayard. "We will meet again in a week's time—"

"A *week*!" says Kallara. "Preposterous."

"Her hands," whispers Nolla Verin. "Take them off, sister."

Ellia Maya steps forward. She has long dark hair that she keeps bound up in braids, and she carries herself like a soldier. She was an officer in the army before proving herself during the last battle in Emberfall, after which my mother granted her a position as an advisor. "A minor punishment would make others hesitate to contradict you."

"Yes!" Nolla Verin smiles sweetly. "Perhaps just one hand, then?"

She sounds like she's teasing, but I can hear an undercurrent of frustration. She would have cut their hands off already.

In all truth, Nolla Verin wouldn't be allowing subjects to air their grievances at all.

A steward steps forward to take the deeds from the farmers. Bayard passes his over without hesitation, and he offers me a bow. "I appreciate your wisdom, Your Majesty."

Kallara tightens her grip on the paper instead. "Your mother would *never* have questioned me."

My mother would never have *tolerated* her. I actually doubt either of these people would have had the courage to bring this complaint to the Crystal Palace at all. Both Nolla Verin and Clanna Sun have mentioned that the number of people requesting mediation has increased tenfold.

In a way, it's what I wanted. Less violence, less blood. Less death. Less fear.

In a way, it's not.

"Release the deed," I say to her tightly.

Kallara takes a step back. "This is ludicrous." She rolls the paper into a tube. "Fine. Side with a *man*, then. I shouldn't be surprised." She spits at Bayard. "*Fell siralla.*"

"I did not side with a man," I say. "I asked you to release your deed so I could fairly—"

She spits at me, then turns her back, striding for the door.

Beside me, Nolla Verin, Ellia Maya, and Clanna Sun all suck in a breath. The other subjects waiting their turn uncomfortably exchange glances.

My mother would have had Kallara executed right here. Or maybe not an execution at first. She would have had the guards disable her in some painful manner, then would have left the body bleeding on the stone floor, a warning to any others who would dare such insolence.

I can't do that. I can't.

Nolla Verin glances at me, and when I say nothing, she stands. "Guards!" she snaps. "Stop her."

I whip my head around to glare at my sister. She shouldn't be issuing orders for me. Two guards have peeled away from the wall anyway, and they've taken hold of Kallara by the arms. She's spitting profanity at me now. Bayard is staring wide-eyed.

"Don't look at me like that," whispers Nolla Verin. "You must take action. You know you must."

I look back at the guards. "Take the deed. We will determine the truth of whose land it is."

"And cut out her tongue," says Nolla Verin. "For spitting at the queen."

"Wait. What? No!" I say, but the guard has already pulled a blade, and my words are lost in the sound of Kallara's sudden screams

of protest. Blood is spilling from the woman's mouth down the front
of her dress. Her screams devolve into keening, a garbled, wet sound.
Her knees give way, but the guards keep her upright.

I'm frozen in place, my own breathing very shallow. At the base
of the dais, Bayard has gone pale. I see several of the others shift and
glance at the door, as if their complaints should possibly wait for
another day.

I'm no stranger to this kind of violence, but it's still upsetting.
I don't want it in my throne room. I don't want it done on my sister's
order.

You must take action. You know you must.

I wish I'd had another minute. Another second.

But Kallara was leaving. She'd spit at me. She'd sworn at me.
She'd refused an order.

And I didn't do anything. My hands are trembling for so many
reasons.

"Take her out of here," I say, my voice low and tight, and the
guards begin to drag her. I glance down at Bayard. "The lands are
yours unless the deeds prove otherwise. Return in a week's time for
my judgment."

"Yes." His voice breaks a little. "Yes, Your Majesty." He gives a
hasty bow and shuffles backward.

I turn to look at Nolla Verin. "Don't do that again."

"Did you hear what she was saying? Someone had to do it."

"I would have addressed it. You do not need to undermine me."

"She was leaving. Were you going to send her a letter?"

The worst part of all of this is that my sister is right. I glance at
the window again. On the training field, the soldiers have broken
apart into sparring groups. I've lost sight of Grey and the others,
which must mean they've joined the fighting.

I consider what Kallara just said before the guards took her ability to speak. *Side with a man, then. I shouldn't be surprised.*

Mother never ruled with a man at her side, and I was raised with the belief that no queen needed a king in order to rule effectively. But Grey is the true heir to the throne of Emberfall, and ruling together could bring peace to both our kingdoms.

I never thought any of my subjects would see a man at my side as another brand of weakness.

I think of all the meetings where Grey hasn't been invited. The dinners, the parties. The whispers about whether he will truly side with Syhl Shallow against his home country of Emberfall. The queries about whether I am strong enough to rule if I want a man on a throne next to me.

I don't know if that means I should have Grey here for all of this—or if it's better for him to be on the fields.

I know what Mother would think.

Some of the people waiting for an audience have filtered out.

It's not because of me. It's because of my sister.

I sigh and look at my remaining guards. "You will wait for *my* order before taking action. Am I understood?"

"Yes, Your Majesty."

Their words sound hollow. I don't know how to fix that. Nolla Verin is murmuring with Ellia Maya now. I think they must be talking about me, but then the advisor nods and rises to leave the room. When my sister looks back at me, her expression isn't repentant at all. She looks smug.

I have to fight to keep from scowling. Clanna Sun claps her hands. "Who is next? Bring forward the next issue."

A girl in a long, dark cloak shuffles forward. She's short, with broad shoulders, with a spill of lank auburn hair that hangs across half her face. She seems very young to be approaching the queen with an issue I am expected to solve, but maybe that's the hesitancy of her steps. She seems to be trembling.

My heart softens. These are the subjects I want to help. The ones who would have been afraid to approach Mother.

"Come forward," I say gently.

"Yes, Your Majesty," she whispers. She peeks up at me and eases all the way up to the dais. Her voice is so quiet, wavering a bit on the syllables. "I am truly grateful for an audience with you. I . . . I have brought you a gift." Something made of glass glistens in the shadow of her cloak.

I hold out a hand. "Come," I say again. "Have no fear."

She takes hold of my hand and steps up onto the dais. Her fingers are tiny and trembling, her palm damp. Stone rings adorn her fingers. Her eyes flick to Nolla Verin and Clanna Sun, and she wets her lips.

"What can I do for you?" I say.

She withdraws her gift. It's a crystal bottle, the neck wrapped in gold and red silk. She snaps her fingers, and the stones of her rings spark, catching the silk. A small flame erupts.

I suck in a breath and jerk back. A guard starts forward and I hold up a hand.

The girl smiles. The crystal sparkles under the flame, the silk disintegrating into sparks that fall at her feet. "Your gift, Your Majesty."

I hesitate. It's lovely, like a lamp with a wick on the outside.

"Magic," she whispers, "will destroy you."

Then she throws the bottle against the stones at my feet, and fire erupts around us.

CHAPTER TEN

GREY

The best thing about swordplay is that it needs no translation.

Most of the soldiers speak Emberish well, but many don't—and many *choose* not to. I've discovered that many lapse into Syssalah when they don't want me to know what they're saying.

I'm not fluent yet, but I've learned enough of their language to know when they're talking about me. I know they don't trust me—or my magic. Many of them think I'm too young, too loyal to Emberfall, too much of an outsider. Too . . . male. *Fell siralla* was once a bit of an endearment between me and Lia Mara, but I've learned that here in Syhl Shallow, it's a real insult. *Stupid man.* No one has the courage to say it to my face—yet—but I can see it in their eyes. I can hear it muttered under their breath when I give an order they're not in favor of.

In Syhl Shallow, men are appreciated for strength and fighting, which seems fine on the surface, until I discovered that it means men are mostly valued for their ability to carry heavy loads and die in battle.

I'm definitely not valued for any skill with magic.

Despite the challenges I face, I'm happier on the training field with a sword in my hand. Language and politics don't matter once a blade is flying. All that matters here is skill.

I face six opponents. Four are soldiers in Syhl Shallow's army, two women and two men. One is my guard Talfor, and the other is Jake, my best friend and closest ally. Iisak soars high overhead, feeding his power into the air. It took me a long time to recognize the feel of his magic, because it's not stars and sparks the way my own is. It's a feather-light touch from the wind on a calm day, a bite of cold rain on my cheek when the sun hangs high overhead, a needle of ice to slip under my armor and make me shiver. He can slow the air, making my opponents' movements a fraction more sluggish. It would slow me, too, but I can use my magic to accelerate my swordplay. I feel the magic of his resistance and slice through it, holding off all six blades with lightning speed.

One of the men, a captain named Solt, ducks my sword and tackles me around the midsection, using brute strength to do the same thing.

Iisak's magic makes the fall slower, but somehow it hurts more. The soldier draws a dagger, aiming for my throat, but I'm quick, and I use my bracer to block before he gets close.

"You can't slice through everything," he says, and there's an edge in his voice.

Captain Solt doesn't like me. He's not the only one.

I duck out of his hold, trying to reclaim my weapon, but he kicks it out of reach and tries to pin me. He's a second too slow, but he has the strength to make up for it, and we end up rolling, grappling, fighting for purchase. He's got my arm wrenched back, and I wouldn't put it past him to pull it right out of its socket. Solt would likely kill me if he thought he could get away with it. I taste dirt and blood on my tongue, but my sword is only an inch—maybe—

An icy blast of wind rockets across the field. "*Magic*," Iisak calls.

Ah. Yes. *Magic*. Sparks and stars flare in my vision, and I cast my power into the ground. Fire blazes up from the dried grass around us.

Solt swears and lets me go, scrambling back, smacking at his arm where the fire caught. His eyes are dark with irritation. The sparring matches around us have drawn to a close, and now we're the center of attention. The other soldiers shift away from the charred ground and speak under their breath in Syssalah.

I let the flames die as another blast of cold wind sweeps across the field. Jake steps over to me and puts out a hand to pull me to my feet. I take it, then claim my sword and drive it into its sheath.

My eyes are on Solt, though. "That wasn't the point of the exercise."

"We fought," he says darkly. "You used magic. Your plan, yes?"

He says *magic* in the same voice he'd use to accuse me of cheating. Not quite mockery, but definitely contempt.

This feels dangerously close to insubordination—if we're not there already. But he's got the respect of most of the soldiers on this field, and he's good with a sword. I need him as an ally, not an enemy. Still, the tension between us thickens the air.

There's only one other soldier here who isn't wary—or disparaging—of my magic. Tycho stands a short distance off, sheathing his own sword. He's only fifteen, and small for his age, but he begged for a chance to train with the recruits. At first, the younger soldiers all but refused to spar with "the boy," but Tycho put one of them on the ground in less than twenty seconds, so now they grudgingly allow it.

He's watching the standoff between me and Solt.

Jake steps closer. "Let's do it again," he says equably. Jake's very good at playing the peacemaker, at pulling the tension out of a moment without making anyone yield ground.

"Fine," I say. I cast a glance up at the sky and whistle to Iisak.

The soldiers mutter again, shifting back into their formations. This time I don't need any translation. They've reluctantly allowed the scraver to help us train, but they do not see him as an ally. He was enslaved by Karis Luran, and is now oath-bound to me, but they do not trust him.

In truth, most of them do not trust *me.*

Iisak eases to the ground beside me, his wings folding neatly. "Your Highness," he says, his voice rasping on the words. He doesn't need to call me that, and I've told him not to, but he says it reminds others of my role here.

"Five minutes," I say to him. "We'll go again."

A horn blares from the palace, and I startle. So do most of the others around me. The horn sounds again before I can speak. Then a third time, followed by a pause. It's louder than their battle horns, almost deafening.

A gasp goes up around me.

I look at Talfor, my guard. "What does it mean?"

He's gone pale. "An attack."

"Rhen?" says Jake. His voice has gone tight. "Is he attacking?"

"No," says Talfor. "An attack on the queen."

Lia Mara is in her chambers, prone on the bed, but it's hard to see past the press of guards and advisors surrounding her. Her eyes are barely open, her skin ashen. As I get closer, I notice tears glistening on her cheeks, and my chest tightens as my heart gives a kick. Nolla Verin is on her knees beside her sister, clutching Lia Mara's hand, kissing her knuckles. On her other side is Noah, a doctor formerly of Washington, DC, but now known as a healer from Disi. He's pressing a dripping roll of fabric against her legs.

Then I see the blistered, reddened flesh. The blood. The charred fabric. The soot on Nolla Verin's robes and cheeks.

"He's coming," Nolla Verin is murmuring. When she sees me in the doorway, her eyes flare wide. "Grey. There was an attack." Her voice breaks. "There was—she was—you have to heal her."

I'm already beside the bed, pulling at the soaking fabric, looking for the source of damage.

"Slow," says Noah, grabbing my wrist. "Slow. There's a lot of glass."

Then I see the small pile beside him, each piece bright with fresh blood.

I hesitate, my eyes finding his. "What happened?"

"Some kind of bottle bomb." I must be looking at him blankly, because he says, "A Molotov cocktail. I don't know what you'd call it here. An incendiary—"

"Magic," someone hisses.

"*Not* magic," Noah says emphatically. "This was done on purpose, but it wasn't magic."

"How do you know?" demands Nolla Verin.

"The prince was using fire on the training fields," says one of the advisors. "Perhaps his magic went awry—"

"It wasn't magic!" Noah snaps. "If you bring me a bottle and some lantern oil, I can make another one right here."

They gasp. "The healer has made a threat—"

"It's not a threat," I snap. I look over my shoulder at Jake, but he's already beginning to move the crowd of people out of the room.

More carefully this time, I pull at the soaking linens. The skin underneath is badly burned, the smell sickly sweet. Smaller bits of glass cling to the skin.

Lia Mara winces, then tries to shift. Her eyes flutter open. A sob escapes her throat.

"Easy," I say softly. "Easy." I take a breath and press my hands against the worst of the damage, closing my eyes, summoning the stars of my magic. Her breathing shudders, and I wish for my magic to be faster, but I know from experience that if I try to force it, the stars will scatter away into nothing.

There's so much damage, though. I can feel her anguish. I can hear it in every breath.

"What happened?" I say, and my voice is rough and low.

"A girl," says Nolla Verin, and her voice is fierce, but tears sit on her cheeks, too. "She came up to the dais, under the guise of making a plea. She said she had a gift, and it looked like a lantern. But then she threw it at her feet, and it—it burst. Lia Mara's robes caught—the draperies caught—fire was everywhere—"

"Where is the girl?" I say.

"She's dead, Your Highness," says one of the guards who's remained in the room. Her voice is nonplussed, as if there would be any other fate for someone who'd dare attack their queen.

I understand the impulse, but when I was in the Royal Guard, we'd try to leave someone alive to question. Now we'll have no way of knowing who sent her or whether she was truly working alone.

Lia Mara takes a slower, steadier breath. The skin of her calves is no longer red and raw. The remaining bits of glass have slipped free to land among the bed linens. I glance up and find her eyes. "Where else are you hurt?"

She shakes her head quickly. "I'm not. I'm—I'm fine."

"You're not fine," says Nolla Verin. "You were *attacked*."

Noah draws the wet cloths away. He looks at the guards. "Send for fresh linens."

The guards hesitate. Exchange glances.

I don't know if it's about me or if it's about Noah, but it's definitely a hesitation born of mistrust, and I'm glad when Nolla Verin snaps, "*Now.*"

Attendants bring fresh linens and new robes. Nolla Verin pulls into the corridor to speak with Ellia Maya. Jake tells me he will inquire as to what happened, then he slips out of the room as well. I stand with folded arms and watch as the sheets and blankets are replaced. Noah waits by my side.

"You are certain this was not magic?" I say to him quietly.

"I think it was made to *look* like magic." He pauses. "When people are afraid of something, it's easy to bolster their fear."

I think of the soldiers on the field, shifting uncertainly when we worked through the drills. I think of the voices of Lia Mara's advisors when Noah mentioned the weapon.

Now that the immediate danger has passed, the fear in my chest has dissipated, allowing room for anger to crowd in.

No one should have been able to cause so much damage.

It's probably better that Jake is going to make inquiries about what happened. As Prince Grey, I am expected to be political and controlled.

Right now, I want no part of either.

Once the attendants leave, Lia Mara looks at Noah. "You have my thanks, as always."

He smiles, then claps me on the shoulder before turning to leave. "It was all Grey this time."

She looks up at me, and I'm sure my mood is no secret. "Forgive me for interrupting your training sessions," she says. She pauses. "You may return to the fields if you like."

I can't tell if she's teasing me or if she is trying to put on a brave face, but it doesn't matter. I won't be dismissed as easily as Noah and her advisors. "You were attacked. I will not leave this room."

"You will have to leave *eventually*," she says.

We're alone now, but her guards wait just outside the open door. It's rare that we have complete privacy, and even so, there is much gossip about my relationship with their queen. "If you wish to rest, I will remain in the hall."

She puts out a hand. "No." Her eyes find mine, and in that moment, I see her fear, her uncertainty. "Stay."

I step forward to take her hand, easing onto the side of the bed, sitting beside her in the silence of her chambers. She should have moved into the queen's rooms months ago, but she still resides in the same space she occupied when we first met, when she was not a princess, when Nolla Verin was destined to be queen.

Her wounds have fully closed, and her linens have been changed, but blood stains her robes and marks of soot linger on her skin. I should call for an attendant, but her fingers wind tightly through my own, so I do not move.

"*Fell vale*," says Lia Mara, and I look down.

Gentle man. Far from it. I want to fight something into the ground. There's a part of me that regrets that they already killed her attacker—for reasons that have nothing to do with interrogation. "I don't feel very gentle right now," I say.

She uses my grip on her hand to pull herself to sitting. I should protest, but before I can, she tucks herself into the circle of my arm, her back against my chest, her head nestled under my chin. She draws my arm into her lap, and I hold her tight and sigh.

"See?" she says softly. "*Gentle.*"

"I should be at your side when you allow an audience with your people," I say.

She says nothing, and I add, "I would have seen her intent. I would have stopped her before she caused so much damage."

Lia Mara begins unbuckling my bracer, and I want to resist, but her fingers are light and deft—and I'm generally powerless when there is something she wants. "You cannot know that," she says.

"I *do* know that."

She inhales to protest, and I turn her in my arms so I can face her. My hands are on her waist, and though I'm not rough at all, she winces.

I freeze. "Forgive me. Are you still hurt?"

"Just a bit sore."

I feed magic into my hands again, then lean in to press my forehead to hers. "Your guards should not have allowed her to draw so close. I do not know if that was through fault or deliberation, but either way, I should be at your side."

She says nothing, but I feel her hesitation.

"What?" I say.

"There was another woman bickering with a man over land rights. My guards obeyed Nolla Verin's order before I could say otherwise."

"This was before you were attacked?"

"Yes."

"They are not loyal," I say immediately. "You should choose others."

"She is my sister. She was to be queen. They *are* loyal."

"They should not have followed her order." I pause. "And she should not have given one."

Lia Mara says nothing. She loathes discord. I know she wants peace for her people—and for mine in Emberfall. She wants to rule without violence and fear.

I am not sure her people want to be ruled that way.

She leans into me again. Her breath is warm and sweet against the bare skin of my neck.

"What would you have done?" she says quietly.

"I don't think you want to hear what I would have done."

My voice is dark, and she cranes her head around to look up at me. "You would not have hacked your way out of it with a sword."

"No. I would have dismissed the guards. At the very least, I would have demanded they swear an oath right then and there. And I would have dismissed your sister."

"What? No!"

"Nolla Verin *was* to be queen—but she is *not*. There is enough doubt in Syhl Shallow, and for her to undermine you—and for your guards to obey her—I worry this attack will embolden others."

"She is supporting me."

"She is weakening you."

Lia Mara goes very still against me, and for a moment, I'm worried my anger has gotten the best of me. I don't want *us* to be at odds.

But then I realize her heart is pounding in her chest. Her

fingers are gripped tight to the arm I have wrapped around her. She's not angry.

She's *afraid*.

That steals some of my anger, replacing it with a fierce protectiveness. I brush my lips against her temple. "Fear not," I say softly, the same words I once spoke to her in Blind Hollow, after a soldier from Emberfall had put a knife to her neck. "No one will touch you again."

CHAPTER ELEVEN

LIA MARA

By morning, the wall hangings and velvet carpeting have been replaced, leaving my throne room looking exactly the same as it did yesterday, but there is still an acrid scent of old smoke or burned fabric that seems to cling to the air. I don't want to feel reassured by Grey's presence at my side today, but I am. Mother never wore a weapon in front of her people, because she said it implied she did not trust them. But Grey is fully armed, and he's made no secret of it. His expression is locked down and closed off, as distant and cold as I've ever seen him. Princess Harper once called him Scary Grey, and she's right. When he looks like this, he truly is frightening.

Jake is here, too, along the wall with the guards. He should be out on the training fields, or spending time with Noah, or practicing swordplay with Tycho, but instead he's here, his cool eyes assessing everyone who comes through the doors. He's far less stoic than Grey, a bit more flippant and irreverent, but he's grown every bit as dangerous as the sword-wielding prince at my side.

And while I trust them both, it's clear that my guards don't. I've heard enough whispers in the halls this morning to know that everyone suspects magic as the source of my attack. I suppose it's easier to think the worst of Grey and his companions than to imagine someone from Syhl Shallow would take action against the throne. The thought makes *me* shudder. I don't want to think about my people wanting me dead. I don't want to think about failing as queen.

Grey said Nolla Verin might be weakening my position, but it's not her. It's me.

My sister isn't here today anyway. She told me she would be working with Ellia Maya, trying to determine where the woman who attacked me came from. Iisak says she was no magesmith, but she must have known people would suspect magic, that her actions would deepen the distrust of Grey and his ties to Emberfall. By law, if she killed me, she could have claimed the throne herself—but Nolla Verin could have buried a sword in her belly and taken it right back.

Was that the goal? To put my sister in power?

Do people think that would be better?

I wish I could feel like I did yesterday, optimistic about how I can rule differently from my mother, but all morning I've been rigid in my chair, now wondering who might be a threat. It's making me tense and distracted, and more than once Clanna Sun has had to lean in and whisper, "Your Majesty, they are waiting for an answer."

Every time someone moves toward me, I think of the girl. Of the explosion. Of the searing pain, the way the glass barreled into my skin.

"Lia Mara."

Grey's voice, low and intense and just for me. I blink and look over at him.

His eyes meet mine, then flick down. I realize I've wrapped both arms across my abdomen. My breathing is trembling.

I swallow and straighten, then look back at the elderly woman standing before the dais. She's peering up at me in confusion. I can't even remember her complaint. Something about chickens or roosters or maybe something entirely different. Maybe she hasn't even made one yet. Her hands are twisting around the handle of a basket.

"Your Majesty?" she says.

Yes, I should say. *What is your complaint?* But I keep staring at the way she's working her hands around the handle. I'm wondering if she has a hidden weapon. A bloom of sweat breaks out on my forehead.

This is ridiculous. She's probably eighty-five years old.

But I can't speak.

"The queen has been taking callers all morning," says Grey to Clanna Sun, though his eyes are on me, and his next words are a request, not a demand. "Perhaps we could retire for a time?"

I should refuse. I *want* to refuse.

I don't.

I expect Grey to return me to my chambers, or perhaps to the library, which has been my source of refuge since I was a child. Instead, he leads me to the large doors along the front side of the palace, which open to splashing fountains and a long marble staircase that descends into the city proper.

Guards will follow us wherever we go, but I hesitate on the threshold.

I'm such a fool. I've never been *afraid* of my people. I refuse to start now.

Grey says nothing, but I'm sure he noticed. He notices everything.

The streets in this part of the city are busy with both foot traffic as well as horses and carriages. It's not common for the queen to quite literally walk right into the street, so we generate more than a few stares, before people scurry to bow and curtsy. My guards fan out so we have a good distance from the people, though Jake follows more closely.

I glance up at Grey. "Where are we going?"

"There's a tavern not too far from here that serves sliced beef that's been fried into twists of pastry. *Hushna Bora*. Do you know it?"

Hushna Bora. The Wild Horse. I don't know it—but I love that he thinks of a tavern. Nolla Verin would have found it scandalous. *The queen*, I imagine her hissing, *should not eat with commoners*. My mother would never have deigned to eat at a tavern either—which makes it tempting all by itself, even if he hadn't mentioned the food.

But a tavern will be full of people. Full of strangers.

"You hardly ate at breakfast," Grey says. "And I thought you might like a walk." His voice is easy, revealing no tension or concern, but then his hand rests over mine and he gives my fingers a gentle squeeze.

This is one of my favorite things about him. He could easily take control. He could have taken over in the throne room, and I wouldn't have stopped him. He could be questioning my guards and making demands.

But he's not. He's not yielding, either. He's . . . he's *supporting*.

His voice drops. "Rumor of the attack will spread. It is important that you do not seem afraid."

I have to swallow again. My fingers tighten on Grey's arm. "I am afraid." I speak the words so softly that I don't want to hear them.

"I know." He pauses. "But I also know you are stronger than your fear." He nods ahead and inhales deeply, as if he's unaware that his words have lit me with a warmth I didn't realize was missing. "Can you smell the food? Let's surprise them with their queen."

———————————

The food is as good as Grey promised. The patrons cleared a space for us in a dim corner, but we're near the hearth, so it's warm, and the guards have formed a wall between us and the rest of the customers, so we're safe. Jake and one of Grey's guards are playing dice at a table near the bar, where they'll be able to keep an ear out for trouble. For the first time all morning, I've been able to take a deep breath.

Honestly, it feels like the first time in *weeks*.

"Better?" says Grey.

I meet his eyes and nod. "Better." I pause. "I almost wish we could stay right here for the rest of the day." I glance away, ashamed that I've admitted that. "But that would be hiding."

"Do not think of it as hiding. Think of it as . . . strategic positioning."

I make a very unqueenly sound. "Said by someone who never hides from anything."

"I hid with you in the woods for days on end."

"That was different."

"How?" He pauses, his voice changing, becoming wry. "And I strategically positioned myself in Rillisk for months."

I've heard his stories of Rillisk, how he fled Ironrose and took a job as a stable hand. How he worked in the shadows with Tycho, until the day he volunteered to fight in the stead of a man who was injured, and ended up revealing himself to Dustan, the commander of Rhen's Royal Guard.

"Iisak once asked me why I took a job near the lowest rungs of Emberfall's society," Grey says.

I pick at a twist of dough left on my plate. "Why did you?"

He shrugs a little. "I'm not sure, really. I like horses. I knew how to do the job." His voice has grown heavy, and he hesitates, fiddling with the handle of his knife. "My life had been so entwined with loss and fear and anguish for so long. I think I longed for . . . simplicity."

Because of the curse. "If only Rhen longed for the same."

Grey frowns. "In truth . . . I think he does." He pauses. "I sometimes wonder if his actions were not solely due to fear of magic, but resentment that the curse was broken, yet he was still trapped. Envy that I was able to find freedom while he was not."

I suck in a breath, because Rhen's actions toward Grey and Tycho were truly terrible, and this seems to make them more so. "You can't excuse what he did, Grey."

"I surely can." He looks at me steadily. "I fled my birthright—but it allowed me to escape, for a time. It allowed me to find myself in a way I never could during the curse. Rhen never had that opportunity."

I lean in against the table. "He had you *whipped*—"

"The enchantress *tortured* him. Many times, and far worse than a flogging." Grey's shoulders are tense now, his hand still against the knife, his eyes cold and dark. "There were days when . . . when . . . when she—"

He breaks off suddenly, and takes a long breath, which is very unlike him. "Well. Your mother would likely admire her methods. But Rhen wouldn't allow Lilith to torture me." His eyes shy away from mine. "So she did it to him. Season after season."

Grey rarely talks about the time during the curse, when he was trapped alone with Rhen in that castle. When he does, his tone grows heavy. He blames himself for so much, I know, but this is the first time I've learned this about Rhen.

It's the first time, the *only* time, I've been able to garner a kernel of sympathy for the man.

"You never told me that," I say softly.

He looks away. "What's done is done."

I reach out a hand and rest it over his. There are scars along his wrist, marring the smoothness of his skin, from before he knew how to use magic to heal himself. They're nothing compared to the scars on his back from what Rhen did.

Grey tenses for a moment when I touch him. I've learned that he's always startled by a gentle touch, because he went so long without it. He grew so used to being alone that touch and kindness became foreign.

He eases quickly, then turns his hand to capture mine. "None of these things matter if we are going to march on Emberfall to claim his kingdom."

"Do you think there's any chance he'll yield?" I ask. "We gave him sixty days."

"When I was dragged in front of him in chains, Rhen released me and said we should have been friends." Grey hesitates. "I thought, in that moment, that he might yield. That he might allow me my freedom." Another pause. "That he might trust me when I said I was trying to protect him."

Instead, the very next night, Rhen chained Grey and Tycho to a wall and ordered his guards to find a pair of whips.

"He won't yield," I say.

"No." Grey's expression is cool again, the emotion of a few moments ago locked away. "I won't either."

"How go *your* efforts with the army?"

Grey grunts and draws himself up. "Many of your soldiers don't seem to want magic on the training fields with them." He pauses. "Many don't seem to want *me* at all."

"But you are our *ally*," I say fiercely.

"It was not long ago that I was your enemy," he says. "There are soldiers I faced in battle who I am now commanding. That would not be easy for me, so I can understand why it is not easy for them."

I set my jaw. I know he's right. Maybe I'm naive to think it could be any other way.

"So we're about to lead a fractured army into Emberfall, to face a fractured country."

"Yes." He sighs heavily. "Our mission of *peace*."

I sigh too. It feels wrong to bring peace with an army—but I cannot sacrifice my people to a cursed prince's pride.

A serving girl steps between the guards to come remove our platters.

As she moves near me, light glints on a bit of glass. I have a flash of memory of the woman who attacked me, and I gasp and flinch away.

Aria, my guard, is at my side in less than a second. She has a blade drawn. So does Grey.

The girl shrieks and drops a plate. Bits of food scatter across the floor. She blanches, dropping to her knees, stammering an apology.

Grey and Aria exchange a glance, and then his eyes shift to me.

"It is fine," I say in Syssalah. "*I'm* fine. It was—a misunderstanding."

The girl is gasping, almost crying. "Forgive me, Your Majesty—forgive me—"

"It's all right." I'm gasping a bit myself. "Rise. Please."

The tavern owner rushes over, an older woman with a mass of curly gray hair pulled into a tight knot at the back of her head. She grabs hold of the trembling girl's arm, dragging her upright. "Forgive us, Your Majesty. I will see that she is punished." Then, without hesitation, she draws back a hand as if she's going to slap the girl across the face right there in front of me.

"No!" Furniture scrapes as I find my feet. I catch the woman's wrist. It was a strong swing, and I only dull the blow.

But the woman stumbles back. "I—Your Majesty—forgive me. I thought—I thought . . ." She looks appalled. The girl's breath is hitching in her chest as she looks from me to the tavern owner, her expression stunned.

They likely thought I would have appreciated the abuse—or that I would have taken any disappointment out on *her*.

My mother surely would have.

"I know what you thought," I say. "But I do not revel in punishment. The girl did nothing wrong." I straighten and look at Aria and Grey. "Put up your weapons. No one meant any harm here."

They do. The girl curtsies and ducks to pick up the fallen platter. She's whispering apologies again, and her hands are trembling. The tavern owner is wringing her hands, uncertain.

I look at her. "Prince Grey spoke highly of your tavern, and I am pleased to discover that the food has been excellent. Your girl has been dutiful. We are grateful to you both. I will be sure to tell my Royal Houses to dine here as well."

The woman gasps. "Your Majesty."

My heart is beating at a rapid clip in my chest. "We would like to finish our meal, if you please."

"Yes." She curtsies. "Yes, of course. I will send another bottle of our finest wine."

She retreats. We sit. My cheeks feel hot, and I'm not sure I can meet Grey's eyes. I'm embarrassed that I caused a scene.

But then he leans in. "As I said," he murmurs, and there's pride in his voice. "You are stronger than your fear."

That makes me look up. I just flinched at . . . at *nothing*. I almost caused a girl to get slapped across the face—and maybe worse. "I don't feel very strong."

He looks pointedly at the serving girl, who is now on the opposite side of the tavern, speaking with two others. They glance in our direction a few times.

"They seem to think you are," says Grey.

I blush. "I am glad you brought me here."

"As am I." He reaches out a hand to brush his fingertips along my jaw, and I go still. Much like the moments when I'm gentle with him, his softness takes me by surprise, especially since he was just on his feet with a weapon in his hand. It's a side of himself he so rarely shows, especially in public.

He draws back and sighs. "Though I cannot be off the training fields *all* day." He hesitates, his eyes holding mine. "Perhaps your soldiers should see their queen."

"I'm glad you're my ally now," I say. His eyebrows lift, and I blush, because it sounds so sterile out loud. "I wouldn't want to face you on a battlefield."

"I wouldn't want to face you on a battlefield either."

"Liar," I say, and I'm teasing, yet also serious. "I could never defeat you in battle."

"On the contrary." He takes my hand and kisses my fingertips. "You know all the ways to make me yield."

CHAPTER TWELVE

GREY

I've spent what feels like a hundred lifetimes being a guardsman, but I've never truly been a soldier. Even still, I know how to fight, how to train as part of a unit. I know what it looks like when soldiers are committed to a cause, unified in their desire to support their leaders.

I know what it looks like when they're not.

Under Karis Luran, the soldiers and guards were fiercely united. There was a sense of honor to serve their queen—but also swift and brutal punishment for those who failed to perform. I remember standing on this same field with Karis Luran at my side, watching a commanding officer put a dagger through the hand of a man who was repeatedly too slow during an exercise. She'd nodded her approval.

Lia Mara would never have stood for such a punishment.

These soldiers expected Nolla Verin to take the throne, a girl who, at sixteen, was every bit as vicious and calculating as her mother. But by law, Lia Mara is queen, and soldiers who've been trained to be as merciless as possible seem to be faltering when confronted by a leader who eschews brutality.

I'm not sure if I expected the soldiers to be better or worse in Lia Mara's presence, but they're the same—which says enough. They're never truly insubordinate, but they're a second slower to follow orders than they should be. They hold my eyes a moment longer than necessary. They mutter and shift and exchange glances when they think I'm not paying attention.

For weeks, I've thought it stemmed from a lack of trust in me.

Today, seeing it in front of Lia Mara, I wonder if it's a lack of trust in *her*. She may have inspired gratitude in that serving girl with gentle kindness, but that won't work here.

My eyes flick across the groups sparring on the grounds, the more experienced officers leading the newest recruits in drills. I'm not surprised to see Nolla Verin among them, her hair in twin braids she's twisted across the back of her head. The soldiers fighting with *her* aren't defiant and shifty at all—but she'd probably pin them to the turf if they were. I expect to see Tycho in the group, but when I cast my gaze across the younger recruits, I discover that he's not on the battlefield.

"Jake," I call. "Where's Tycho?"

He steps out of his sparring group and shoves sweat-damp hair back from his forehead, looking over at the recruits. "I have . . . no idea."

Solt, the captain who gives me the most trouble, is leading the sparring group in front of me, and he snorts without missing a parry with his sword. "Probably fawning over that demon," he says in Syssalah, and his opponent, a younger recruit named Hazen, snorts with laughter.

They mean Iisak. Solt might think I can't understand him, but I do.

Lia Mara definitely does.

"The scraver is a friend and ally," she says coolly. "As is Tycho."

Solt disarms Hazen easily, but neither of them are taking it seriously now. "Yes, Your Majesty." He salutes her with his sword, touching the flat side of the blade to his forehead, but there's no deference in his tone. Instead, there's a hint of mockery.

Lia Mara sucks in a breath to retort, but her eyes are locked on his sword, and she seems to freeze.

It's like the moment in the tavern, but this time, he really does have a weapon.

If I can feel her fear, likely everyone else on this field can feel it, too. I see the moment it registers in Solt's eyes, because there's a flicker of surprise, quickly followed by disdain. Even Hazen's expression is shadowed with impudence when he mutters under his breath to one of the other soldiers.

Solt exhales dismissively, then sheathes his sword and turns away to allow another two to spar.

"Captain," I snap.

Lia Mara catches my hand. "Grey." Her fingers are tense against my palm, her voice barely a whisper. She expects me to do what Nolla Verin did, or possibly what her guards did. She expects me to undermine her, to rule over her. Maybe she even thinks I'll draw my own sword and spill his blood right here in the grass. I can see Nolla Verin watching, and she definitely would.

I don't. "Run the drill again," I say.

Solt hesitates, and his eyes narrow, but he turns back. Hazen frowns and steps back out of line, casting a dark look my way.

No one here likes me.

But they fight. Swords clash and spark in the sunlight.

The battle ends exactly the same way. Going through the motions, making little effort. Following the order to the letter, but nothing more. Hazen mutters something to Solt.

I don't know the word he used, but the tone is enough.

"Again," I say.

They fight again.

"Again."

Again. Again. Again.

They're both breathing heavily by the time they break apart the tenth time, but the insolence is gone from Hazen's eyes. When I order them to do it again, he nods and ducks his head to shove sweat out of his eyes.

But Solt doesn't lift his sword. His chest is rising and falling rapidly. "We've run it enough," he grinds out.

I stare at him and wait.

He stares back, until the moment shifts, thickening with animosity. We've drawn some attention from the closer sparring groups, because many of them have broken apart, watching, sensing the tension between us just like yesterday. Jake has sheathed his weapon, but he's edged closer like he sees trouble brewing.

I didn't get along with Jake at first, but it was nothing like this. That was me and him. This is me against an army. An army expected to fight on my behalf. An army full of men and women who might *die* on my behalf. In their eyes, I'm young and untested, a man from an enemy kingdom allying myself with a girl who took the throne from her sister.

A girl who's clinging to my hand instead of ordering Solt to be dragged over broken glass or whatever Karis Luran would have thought of.

Solt hasn't looked away, and the anger in his dark eyes makes me think he might draw his sword on me instead of Hazen. For real instead of a drill.

Solt takes a step forward, and my hand twitches near the hilt of my weapon.

But Hazen taps the flat of his blade against the other man's greaves. "Captain." His tone is resigned. Subdued. *"Rukt."*

Fight.

Solt mutters under his breath and draws his sword. He's tired now, so he's a little slower, his movement more labored. He's a man who relies on strength instead of speed. For the first time, Hazen puts his heart into the drill. He pushes hard against Solt's defense, and he's rewarded with an opening. He disarms the other man, and Solt swears.

"Hazen," I say. "You've earned a rest."

Hazen is panting, jerking at the buckles of his breastplate. "Thank you." He hesitates, then gives me a nod. "Your Highness."

I freeze. Since Karis Luran died, it might be the first time someone has offered me any kind of deference on this field.

I keep my eyes on Solt. "Again." My eyes flick to another soldier, someone who snickered when Solt made a comment about Tycho. "Baz."

Baz isn't snickering now. He's quick to obey. Solt gives me a glare, but he fights when Baz draws a blade.

At my side, Lia Mara speaks, her voice is low and quiet, just for me. "How long are you going to make him do this?"

"Until he takes it seriously." It sounds petty, petulant even. In a way, it is—but it's also not. I need them to respect me. I need them to respect *her*. We're on opposite sides of the same coin: I'm every bit as frustrated as Solt. At least he can burn off his anger on the field.

But with every day that passes, we draw closer to the time when *everyone* will have to take this seriously, or Rhen's soldiers will run us through. My magic can't protect the entire army.

"He could refuse to fight," she says.

"His pride won't let him do that."

And it doesn't. Solt spars with Baz for six rounds.

He learned his lesson with Hazen and wins all six—then glares at me derisively when I say, "Again."

We've gained the attention of most of the soldiers on the field by now, and I don't care. Solt is breathing hard. Blood is in stripes on his sleeves where he's gotten sloppy on defense, pink where it's been diluted with sweat. His arms are shaking.

Pride or not, he won't win many more. I can tell.

Then again, desperation always makes for a good ally.

"Again," I repeat. Baz coughs, but he lifts his blade. I glance at the other soldiers. No one looks defiant now.

I was right. In this match, Baz is able to knock the blade right out of Solt's hand. The soldier goes down. Baz has a weapon against the other man's throat in less than a minute.

"Baz," I say. "You've earned a rest."

Baz steps back and nods. He glances at Hazen, then back at me. "Thank you. Your Highness."

Solt reclaims his sword and shoves himself to his feet. His breathing is ragged now. He looks like he wants to vomit on the field. No, in all truth, he looks like he wants to run me through and then vomit on my corpse.

Good. I inhale to tell him to do it again.

"Enough," says Lia Mara. "If you please, Prince Grey."

I glance at her. Her voice is strong and clear.

"Of course," I say.

Solt is still panting, sweat dripping off his jaw, but he looks at her in surprise.

"My mother would have made an example of you," she says to him. "Burned off your fingers or forced you to swallow boiling oil. You know this, I am sure." When he says nothing, her eyebrows go up. "Answer me, please."

Please. They see her courtesies as weakness. Rhen did too. They're wrong. She's not weak at all.

His breathing has slowed a bit, and he nods. "Yes, Your Majesty."

"You believe I will not be so cruel," she says. "Is that correct?"

He hesitates. If Karis Luran asked that question, it would be a trap. It would be a trap from Rhen, too. But Lia Mara is forthright with her kindness, and I think that is what's most unexpected here. I watch as a flicker of uncertainty crosses his expression. He wonders if he's pushed her too far.

"I do not believe you will rule as your mother did." Solt's eyes flick to me briefly, but she notices.

"Prince Grey can be as vicious as my mother," she says. "You may not have seen it, but I have. You are lucky that he respects my hope to rule without violence. I believe he would have ordered you to fight until your hand was too weak to hold that sword. I am tempted to let him." She pauses. "But you're a good soldier. I can see your strength and talent. I would not like to see it wasted. Do not force my hand."

It's a good speech, but her fingers have a death grip on mine. I'm the only one who can feel her uncertainty. This isn't like the moment in the tavern. It's not even like the moment she was attacked by a clear enemy. This is one of her soldiers—and she's worried he *will* force her hand.

But I wish she could see herself as I do. As *they* do, right now in this moment. Because this is when she's most impressive, when her strength shines through her words. Rhen was such a fool to turn her down when she came seeking peace. Even today, I made them fight, but she made them stop.

Solt nods, then drops to a knee. There's no repentance in his gaze, but there's a shred of respect, which is better. "Yes, Your Majesty."

Lia Mara looks up at me. "I should return to the palace. I have duties to attend to. Will I see you at the evening meal?"

"Yes, of course." I pause. "Should I return with you now?"

Her eyes meet mine, and I know she hears what I am not saying.

Do you want me to remain at your side?

Lia Mara lifts her chin. "I can manage."

"I have no doubt." I lift her hand to kiss her knuckles, and she blushes.

"Well," she says coyly. "Perhaps you should not take too long."

That makes me want to follow her immediately. But I have a field full of soldiers, and I've gained ground. I can't lose it now.

When she turns away, I look back at Solt, then offer him a hand to pull him to his feet. He eyes it derisively for a fraction of a second but must think better of it, because he clasps mine.

I'm no fool. There's no love lost between me and this man.

He begins to turn away, but I hold fast. "She was wrong."

He hesitates, glancing from my hand to my face. "Wrong?"

"She said I would have ordered you to fight until you couldn't hold a sword." I lean in, keeping my voice low. "She was wrong. I would have tied it to your hand."

CHAPTER THIRTEEN

GREY

By the time I call for a break on the training fields, Tycho has not yet appeared. Solt made a comment about the scraver, but Iisak is as driven by duty as I am. He wouldn't call Tycho away without telling me—and Tycho himself wouldn't skip drills. He loves sword-play more than breathing.

The soldiers have begun heading back to their quarters, and I stare after them. I should return to the castle to check on Lia Mara, but concern set up camp in my chest when I first noticed Tycho was missing, and it hasn't gone away yet.

Jake has sheathed his weapons, and he comes to my side. "I wish Lia Mara hadn't made you stop," he says, his voice low even though most of the soldiers have already moved off the field. "I wanted to see that guy puke on his boots."

"Me too," I say, and he grins.

When I don't smile back, he says, "What's wrong?"

"Tycho missed drills."

"His unit leader said he was off his game this morning, and he asked for leave to skip the midday meal. Want to check the barracks?"

The youngest recruits sleep in the farthest building from the fields, near the stables and the edge of the forest that leads up into the mountains. Tycho has a room in the palace, but as the weeks have worn on, he's spent more nights here to build a rapport with the soldiers.

We check the barracks and the stables, but he's not there. When we walk past the armory, Solt is splashing water on his face from a bucket, speaking in low tones to another senior officer. She must call his attention to the fact that we're nearby, because he glances over, and he swipes the water out of his eyes. His gaze could cut steel.

"Your Highness," he says in Syssalah, his tone so cold that he might as well be telling me to dig myself a grave.

My steps slow, but Jake grabs hold of my bracer and drags me along. "Kill him later. Come on. If Tycho wasn't feeling well, maybe he went to the infirmary."

The palace has two infirmaries. One houses a healer named Drathea, an older woman with a pinched mouth and surly demeanor who says the healing arts are better left to the feminine mind. She wanted nothing to do with Noah, who proved himself better at curing fevers and stitching wounds and treating ailments in his first week in Syhl Shallow. Regardless of his talents, he still leaves many in the palace feeling wary and uncertain. I don't know if it's his supposed allegiance to me or to Emberfall, or if they believe he has some magic of his own, but Lia Mara doesn't want to make her people uncomfortable. She gave Noah a space at the northern end of the palace, which leaves him closer to the training fields and the barracks.

I once asked Noah how many people come to him after Drathea fails to cure their ills, and he graciously said he doesn't keep track—and then Jake leaned in and whispered, "I've seen his notes. He's up to seventy-six."

I know which one Tycho would visit.

By the time we stride through the palace, my worry has grown into a tension around my gut that I can't shake loose. Tycho isn't naive, but he's young. Not overly trusting, but innocent.

I was so preoccupied with Lia Mara's safety that I didn't take a moment to wonder about the fate of the rest of my friends. No one would dare to hassle Iisak unless they wanted to see their skin in ribbons while taking their last breath, and Jake is more than capable of fending for himself. Noah is savvy and cynical, and he's endeared himself to enough people here that he doesn't face the same kind of grudging acceptance that I endure every day.

But Tycho . . . My breathing has gone tight and shallow by the time I stride into the infirmary. "Noah. Have you seen—"

I stop short. Noah is sitting on a bench by a low table strewn with an assortment of instruments. Tycho is right beside him. A small orange kitten is on his lap, chewing on one of his fingers.

"Grey." Tycho leaps to his feet when he sees me, scooping the kitten onto the table. The animal hisses at me, then scrabbles at the wood, leaps to the floor, and dashes out of sight.

Tycho looks from me to Jake, then at the fading light in the window. "Silver hell." He grimaces. "I missed second drills."

"I knew they'd come looking eventually." Noah glances at us. "Hey, Jake."

"'Sup," says Jake. A platter of nuts, cheese, and fruit sits forgotten at the corner of the table by Noah. Jake shoves it to the side to cock a hip against the wood, then grabs two apples.

He tosses one to me, and I snatch it out of the air, but I don't look away from Tycho. He's in an army uniform, trimmed in green and black, the colors of Syhl Shallow. His leather-lined breastplate and greaves are still buckled in place, though his sword and bracers are on the ground beside the table. His blond hair is shorter than it was when we were stable hands at Worwick's Tourney, and his frame is a little leaner, a little more muscled from all the time he spends with a sword in his hands. But there's a youthfulness to him that hasn't been stolen away yet, an edge still waiting to be chiseled.

There's also a shadow in his eyes, something I haven't seen in months.

My eyes narrow. "Are you unwell?"

"Oh! I—no. I'm fine. I had—I had—" He falters.

I frown. I don't want to be irritated, because this is unlike Tycho—but my role here is so precarious. I can't chastise Solt for failing to take drills seriously if my own friends are going to skip out. I can't expect a unified front from the Syhl Shallow soldiers if I can't demonstrate it from within my own circle.

"What happened?" I say.

"Nothing." He swallows. "I didn't—I didn't realize the hours passed so quickly."

Before I was trapped in the curse with Rhen, I watched the royal family of Emberfall dance around truth with ease, so I can tell a lie when I hear one. "You've never lied to me before," I say. "Do not start now."

Tycho flushes.

"Grey," says Noah. The easy tone is gone from his voice. "Leave it."

I go very still. The day has been too long, too full of threats from both inside and outside the palace. I don't want to have to worry about half-truths and indecision here.

Tycho must read the darkening thoughts behind my eyes, because he ducks to grab his bracers and weapons. "Forgive me," he says quickly, and his voice is low and repentant.

Maybe Jake can sense my mood too, because he says, "Tycho. Find your unit leader and see if you can run the drills now."

Tycho was moving toward the doorway, but at that, he hesitates.

Noah looks at Jake, and some unspoken message must pass between them, because Jake straightens, pushing away from the table. "You know what? Never mind. I'll do it." He takes another bite of his apple. "Come on, T."

Once they're gone, the infirmary falls very quiet. I don't like feeling at odds with Noah. He has an easy sensibility: never aggressive, never overbearing. His bravery is simple, uncomplicated. Like the day he left Rhen and Ironrose behind, when Noah feels strongly about something, he's calm and collected about it, but his will is iron strong.

So is mine.

He's regarding me evenly. "He's only fifteen, Grey."

"I was seventeen when I joined the Royal Guard."

He snorts. "Maybe you've been twenty for too long, because there's a lot of ground between fifteen and seventeen."

He's probably right on both counts, but I don't like it. "When I was fifteen, I was trying to run my family's farm."

"And how did that turn out?"

His voice is quiet, not cruel, but the words hit me like a dart anyway. He knows how that turned out. My family nearly starved. It's the very reason I joined the Royal Guard: I could forswear my family, and they would be rewarded richly for losing me to the castle. I don't need the reminder of my failures or my sacrifices, especially not right now. "Do you seek a fight with me, Noah?"

"No." His tone doesn't change.

"*I* did not force Tycho into the army," I say fiercely. I take a step forward. "It was his choice to join the recruits. I did not demand—"

"Hey." He lifts a hand, and his voice is placating. "I know you're under a lot of pressure. I'm just asking you to take it easy on him, okay?"

I hesitate, then run a hand across the back of my neck. My frustration is not with Noah. It's not even with Tycho, really.

If I'm being strictly honest with myself, my frustration isn't with the soldiers here, either.

It's with Rhen. It's with myself.

I sigh and lean against the table.

Something bats at my ankle, strong taps that I can feel through the leather of my greaves. I look down and see the kitten has emerged from under the table, and it's smacking at my boot laces with its paws. I lean down to scoop the creature into my hands.

It immediately digs in with claws that seem to rival Iisak's. I let go with a swear, and it bolts under the table again. Blood appears in stripes across my fingers.

Noah is laughing. "That kitten only lets Tycho and Iisak touch him." He reaches for a square of cloth. "Cat scratches get infected easily. Let me get you—" He stops short and sobers as the wounds on my fingers magically close. "Well. Never mind. I forgot."

The air between us goes quiet again. The tension has lessened a bit. Maybe it was all on my side to begin with. "What happened?" I say. "Why did Tycho come here?"

Noah hesitates. "I don't want to betray his trust."

"If the other recruits are bothering him, I should know."

He shakes his head slightly. "I don't think they're doing anything wrong. I think they're . . . just being soldiers." He pauses. "When the guardsmen first took Tycho from Rillisk, he hid in the infirmary with me then, too."

In Ironrose. When Rhen captured me. The guards took Tycho prisoner to use as leverage against me. He clung to the shadows and refused to speak to them.

When we worked at Worwick's in Rillisk, Tycho was afraid of soldiers there, too. He'd make himself scarce when they came to the tourney, or he'd stick by my side in the stables. I spent an eternity as a swordsman, but Tycho was never afraid of *me* in Rillisk. He was the first person I trusted. I might've been the first person *he* trusted.

I'd keep your secret too, Hawk.

Hawk.

He was never afraid of me because I wasn't a swordsman. I was a stable hand, and then an outlaw, and then a reluctant prince.

He's grown into himself so much here that I'd forgotten that.

"Does he want out of the army?" I say to Noah quietly.

"If you asked him that, I think you'd break his heart."

I look at him in surprise, and Noah adds, "He's worried he'll disappoint you."

I glance at the window. Across the field, Jake and Tycho have taken up sparring positions, their shadows long in the fading light. Men like Solt will rely on strength instead of speed, and sometimes it makes them lazy and overconfident. Tycho never takes anything for granted, and I watch it play out in his skills whenever he's on the field. It's part of why he earned respect from the other recruits. He's willing to risk his life in this war, and he demonstrates it every day. And not because he believes in Syhl Shallow or my right to rule. Because he believes in me.

"Tycho has never disappointed me," I say.

"Maybe he needs to know that."

I think on that for a moment, unsure what to say. I feel like I am failing in so many ways here.

A hand raps on the doorjamb, and an older woman with deep brown skin hesitates in the doorway. I recognize her as one of the shop owners in the city who does metal work. Her eyes flick from Noah to me. "Healer," she says in Syssalah. She extends her hand, which is wrapped in wet cloth. She says something else, but I only recognize the words for *burn* and *forge*.

Noah can fix a lot of ailments, but a bad burn will ache for weeks and likely scar. "I can help you," I say, but she draws her arm back against her body warily.

"*Nah*," she says, shaking her head. "*Nah runiah.*"

No magic. I frown.

Noah speaks to her, and his tone is comforting, reassuring. He glances at me. "I'm not useless yet," he says.

His tone is wry, but there's an undercurrent to his words that I can't quite parcel out.

I inhale to ask what he means, but he's frowning at the woman, trying to ask her questions and understand her answers in broken Syssalah. I quietly move toward the door, and the woman looks relieved that I'm leaving.

"Hey, Grey," Noah calls after me, and I hesitate in the hallway.

"For the record," he says, "you've never disappointed us, either."

"Do not judge too soon," I call back, but he's already lost to his patient, and my words drift on unheard, while his words lodge in my heart, both a reassurance and a reminder.

I have an hour until dinner, so I tighten the buckles on my breastplate and head out to join Jake and Tycho.

CHAPTER FOURTEEN

LIA MARA

My afternoon drones on, and I find myself looking at the windows more often than not. It's difficult to be still, sitting attentively while advisors and representatives from my Royal Houses talk about our preparations for war. It's impossible to focus on grain stores and the late harvest when my brain wants to fix on every glimmer in someone's hand. The palace feels claustrophobic, as if I could be trapped in a hallway with assassins hiding behind every door, while the training fields left me feeling vulnerable and exposed. I don't like either option. I'm relieved when I can retire to my quarters to dress before dinner.

My room has always been a sanctuary, and it's no different now. I send for a tray of hot tea and lock myself inside, curling onto the chaise longue by the window. I used to hide here and read when I grew bored of court politics and my mother's machinations.

Or rather, I used to *strategically position* myself here. The thought makes me smile. I can see Grey from my window. He seems to have found Tycho, because they're sparring with Jake in the fading light.

But as I watch, the smile slides off my face. I was unprepared for the tension between him and the soldiers, especially the officers. A year of military service is mandatory in Syhl Shallow, but many of the men and women on the field have made a career of it. It was once considered an *honor*.

Few of the people I saw today seemed to consider it an honor anymore.

I don't know if that's because of me, or because of Grey. Or because of us both.

A knock sounds at my door, and I jump, my heart pounding hard against my ribs. I have to remind myself that an assassin wouldn't knock, and my guards wouldn't let many people get that far anyway. It's probably the tea I just requested.

Either way, it takes me a moment to call, "Enter."

My sister breezes through the door almost before I say the word, letting the heavy wood panel close behind her. She's still wearing her armor and weapons from the training fields, but somehow she wears them more elegantly than the gauzy belted robes we wear at court. Her hair gleams in its braids, her cheeks still pink from the chill in the air outside.

"I've been waiting to talk to you all afternoon," she says. "You should have let Grey make that man fight until he was coughing blood on his boots. Mother would have."

As if I don't compare my failings to my mother's victories every second of every day. "Hello, my dear sister," I say tersely. "Please, do not hesitate to speak freely."

She puts her hands on her hips. "What are you doing in here?

I thought you were meeting with the advisors about the food stores for the winter."

"I was." I glance back at the window. "What are *you* doing here? I'm surprised you're not still on the field, making some poor soldier beg for mercy."

"Ellia Maya was able to discover the identity of the woman who attacked you," she says. "She lived in the city, not far from the palace. We do not believe she was working alone."

I go still, thinking of how Grey and I strode through the city streets this very morning. I bite back a shiver.

Nolla Verin isn't done. "Ellia Maya said her home was filled with documents on the history of magesmiths. There are records of weapons that are impervious to magic—weapons that were used against them in the past."

"Weapons?"

"None were found." She hesitates. "But that does not mean they don't exist. The girl had drafted letters to the Royal Houses asking them to stand against our alliance with magic. She was not the only one who had signed them."

This time I do shiver. I knew the distrust for magic was strong in Syhl Shallow, but I was unprepared for an organized objection.

"How many?" I say quietly.

"Not many. The guards are tracking them down." Nolla Verin pauses. "Many seem to have fled. Their homes have been ransacked."

I say nothing, and my sister moves close. "Lia Mara." She puts a hand over mine. "After what happened yesterday . . . are you all right?"

I look back at her in surprise. Nolla Verin can be so callous, so brutally practical, that I forget she can also be caring and dutiful.

When I don't say anything, she sits beside me on the chaise. She smells like sweat and leather and sunshine, and I'm reminded of how Mother originally chose her to be heir. Sometimes I wonder if she wouldn't be better at this. Solt would not have been defiant on the training fields. That assassin wouldn't have dared to draw close. I can hardly imagine Nolla Verin listening to petty complaints at all.

I'm still irritated that she issued orders in the throne room yesterday—but I'm also envious that she had the strength to take harsh action, when I did not.

"Lia Mara." Her voice is soft, and she reaches out to touch my hand, and I realize I've drawn my arms across my midsection again.

"I feel like such a fool," I whisper, and then, against my will, my eyes fill with tears.

Nolla Verin *tsks*, and she pulls me against her. She's younger than I am, but just now, I feel like a child. I lean against her shoulder, the edges of her weapons pressing into my curves, while she strokes my hair down my back.

"There, there," she says after a moment. "Tell me who I can stab for you."

I giggle and straighten, swiping at my tears. "You're terrible."

"I'm committed." She's only teasing a little bit. Her eyes search mine. "When Mother named me heir, when she announced her intent for me to marry Prince Grey, she did so without yielding her ability to rule. The people of Syhl Shallow had nothing to fear."

I snort. "But now they fear *my* rule."

"Yes," she says simply. "They fear magic. They fear your alliance with a prince of an enemy land." Her voice hardens. "Instead they should fear *you*."

"I don't want anyone to *fear* me."

"Ah. So you hope to coddle them into loyalty." She rolls her eyes, then clutches her hands to her chest mockingly. "Please don't hurt me, assassins! Would anyone like a sweet pastry?"

"Stop it." I shove her hands away and stand. "I want my people to know I *care* for them. I want them to feel confident in my abilities to protect them without making them cough *blood* on their *boots*."

She frowns. "Then you must show them you will not stand for insurrection. That you will not stand for disloyalty."

"I don't need to be *cruel*—"

"No." She points out at the field. "But you're asking them to fight for you. You're asking *me* to fight for you."

"You don't have to do anything you don't—"

"Ah, *sister*." Nolla Verin swears. "How can you ask them to fight for *you* when you won't fight for *yourself*?"

The words draw me up short, and I stare at her. Is that what I've been doing? I don't know. I can't tell.

"I might be able to fight for myself if you didn't feel the need to issue orders on my behalf," I say tightly.

She snaps back, "I wouldn't feel the need if you weren't so determined to allow peasants to spit in your face."

"I don't need to cut out someone's tongue to prove a point."

"Maybe you should! No one can tell you have a point to *prove*."

I glare at her. She glares back.

I wish I hadn't cried on her shoulder now. It makes me feel immeasurably weak, especially since she's standing in front of me adorned in leather and steel, fresh off the training fields, when I was hiding in my room.

I straighten. "Thank you for sharing your thoughts," I say through my teeth. "I have to prepare for dinner now."

A knock sounds at my door, but neither of us moves.

"Enter," I finally call.

It's a serving girl with the platter of tea I ordered. She's young, with flushed cheeks and red hair pinned into a knot at the back of her head. Her eyes are fixed on the tray, which is almost as wide as she is tall. She eases into the room and bobs a curtsy that makes the dishes rattle. She has to clear her throat. "Your Majesty." Her eyes flick to Nolla Verin and her voice trembles as she sets the tray on a side table. "Your H-Highness. Shall I pour a cup for you both?"

Nolla Verin folds her arms and says, "Certainly," just as I say, "My sister was just leaving."

"Fine," we both say simultaneously.

I fold my arms as well. The girl hesitates, then she must decide that this means my sister is staying, because she sets two rattling cups in their saucers. The sound of the sloshing liquid is loud in the tense space between us.

The girl lifts the saucer in one hand and moves toward me. Her eyes are downcast, and the way the dish vibrates makes me wonder if she's been chastised by my mother in the past. She reminds me of the flinching barmaid in the tavern.

"Thank you," I say gently, but I keep my eyes on my sister. I reach for the saucer.

The girl releases the dish and bobs another curtsy.

Then, without warning, her hand swings.

I'm so focused on Nolla Verin that I almost don't see it coming, but my nerves are on edge today, and my body ducks to the side without my willing participation.

It doesn't matter, anyway. Nolla Verin is a better fighter than I'll ever be, and she already has a blade free. My sister's dagger is in the girl's chest and my cup of tea is shattered on the floor before I even realized what happened.

"Guards!" Nolla Verin is shouting, but my gaze is fixed on the girl on the floor. She's gasping, choking on blood. Her hands flail limply at the blade embedded in her chest.

"You—you—" she's gasping.

Nolla Verin kicks her in the ribs, and the girl's eyes flare wide. She makes a loud choking sound as her lungs beg for air.

My sister spits at her. "You're lucky you'll be dead before I can give you what you truly deserve."

I grab my sister's arm. "Stop." I stare down at the girl as guards swirl into my chambers, weapons drawn. "*Me*. Me what?"

Her eyelids flicker. Her hands grasp at the blade. "You ally us with monsters."

Then her eyes stop moving and her hands stop struggling, and she just lies there, dead.

The attack causes so much uproar that I wonder if I'll ever find a still moment again, but in a way, I don't mind the chaos, the questions, the intense scrutiny from Grey and my sister when they interrogate the guards. Clanna Sun begs me to move into the queen's chambers, but I don't want to leave my room. I feel like it's my last source of refuge. Servants took away the body and the velvet floor coverings, replacing them efficiently while I clung to the corner and tried not to watch for hidden weapons.

It takes hours before the last of my guards and advisors clear out, leaving only Nolla Verin and Grey to have a heated discussion just outside the door. Nolla Verin's voice is low, but my sister already made her position clear. She probably wants to execute all my guards and start fresh. Maybe she's already given an order to do so. Maybe people would obey.

The thought makes me angry. I don't want to know.

That thought makes me frown. I *should* want to know.

Nolla Verin was right. I should be fighting for myself. The proof was quite literally left gasping for breath on my floor.

I shudder and move to the window, which has long since gone dark. The room is warm from the fire in the hearth, but a chill sneaks around the window joints anyway. I should pull the draperies to block the draft, but I already feel trapped. Frost glistens at the corners of the glass, and I know Iisak must be on the roof above.

You ally us with monsters.

Maybe I have, but right now it's reassuring. I wouldn't expect anyone to come in through a third-story window, but Grey once climbed a rope to get into these chambers, so I know it's not impossible.

The door clicks softly, and I don't know if I'm more panicked at the thought of being alone or being attacked, but I whirl before I can stop myself.

Nolla Verin is gone, and Grey stands alone beside the door. His dark eyes search my face, and I have no doubt he can read every worry in my expression.

"I have sent for a meal." He pauses. "Your sister has selected the guards stationed in the hallway. I will join them once the food arrives. Jake will relieve me at midnight—"

"Please don't." The words come out as a whisper, and he stops, regarding me.

"Lia Mara. You have been attacked twice now." He hesitates. "I would not feel comfortable returning to my chambers—"

"No. I meant—" My voice catches. "I meant I don't want you to leave."

His eyes narrow just the tiniest bit, and I wish he weren't so good at concealing any emotion. A bloom of heat finds my cheeks, and I have to glance away. We're so rarely alone together. Even when we are, it's for moments at a time, with an open door and a guard stationed nearby. My people are so sensitive to the idea of me needing a man at my side that I've made every attempt to put them at ease, to demonstrate that my alliance with Grey will be about my people *first*.

But now he's here, the door closed, the night pressing against the windowpanes.

He hasn't said anything, and I have to turn to look out the window again. "Forgive me," I say quickly. "I am being improper." I pause. "I am being foolish as well."

"You are being neither." He speaks from beside me, and I nearly jump. He crossed the room so silently. He's bound up in leather and blades as usual, but the spark of light on silver makes me think of what Nolla Verin said about weapons that could stand against his magic.

"Nolla Verin said there are rumors of weapons that could be used against a magesmith." I look up and find his eyes. "Against *you*."

"She told me the same." He gives me a level gaze. "If someone bears such a weapon, they are welcome to try."

I shiver. Maybe that's why I'm the target. I know how to defend myself—but not like Grey does. Not even like my sister does.

Now that he's standing close, I sense a flicker of fatigue in his frame. I hadn't noticed. I should have.

"You deserve to rest," I say.

"So do you." He sighs. "Fate always seems to conspire against us both."

"Fate." He believes in it, but I don't. I reach out and catch his hand, winding our fingers together, tracing my thumb along the edge of his bracer where it sits against his wrist. "I don't like the idea that these attacks might be predestined. That our entire attack on Emberfall might be predestined."

He's quiet for a moment. "I often find comfort in the thought that fate has already drawn a path beyond what seems impossible."

"This war seems impossible?" I don't find that thought reassuring at *all*.

"Yes." He pauses. "But so did the curse. Our journey here to Syhl Shallow. My escape from Ironrose." Another pause. "My childhood." He glances at me. "Your mother."

I cling to his hand and look out the window again. He's so warm beside me, and I'm suddenly very aware of his presence. I don't think we've been alone in my chambers with the door closed since the night he crept past the guards to sneak in. Then as now, he was such a gentleman, bound by duty and honor. We shared sugared plums beneath the window, trading secrets and stealing kisses until my mother came bursting through the door.

The instant I think of kissing him, my cheeks burn, and I have to keep my gaze fixed on the window. His palm against mine feels too warm now, too intimate, but it would be more awkward to let go. He's here to keep me safe, that's all. I'm glad he's trussed up in buckled leather while I'm draped in yards of belted fabric. Allies first. Anything more is a mere hope that we have to deny until we achieve peace.

But as I listen to the softness of his breathing beside me, the last thing I'm thinking about is peace, or war, or even the threats against my life. I cast my glance slightly sideways, until I catch a glimpse of his profile in the shadows, the curve of his lip, the angle of his jaw, the bare start of a beard that always seems to rob him of a bit of his severity.

Without warning, he turns to look at me, and my breath catches. I'm trapped in his gaze.

A knock sounds at the door, and I jump a *mile*.

"Be at ease." Grey lifts my hand to kiss my fingertips, and sparks light all the way up my arm—but then he lets go. "This will be our dinner."

He heads for the door, leaving me to melt into a puddle by the window.

Did fate have to send dinner right this moment? I want to ask.

But I don't. I straighten my robes, steel my spine against the new burst of anxiety about servants entering my quarters, and remind myself of how to be a queen.

CHAPTER FIFTEEN

LIA MARA

I don't expect to have an appetite, but once the platters are uncovered, I find that I'm ravenous. I was tense and fidgety at the thought of another servant entering my room, but Grey didn't allow the young man to even cross the threshold. Instead, he ordered a guard to bring the tray in, and he stood between me and the guard while the food was placed on a side table.

Now we're alone again, and the food is steaming between us. I'm afraid to touch anything.

Grey is studying me, and he says, "I can have a guard taste it."

I'm being ridiculous. I have tasters in the kitchens, anyway.

But still.

"No, no," I say after a moment. But I don't touch the food.

Grey gives me an ironic glance, then swiftly slices a small piece of everything on his plate and tries it all.

I stare at him with wide eyes. He has magic that would keep him safe, surely, but—

"It's fine." He lifts his plate and gestures for us to switch. "Take mine."

I feel sheepish, but I swap with him anyway. I imagine sitting here alone, staring at a platter, watching it get cold while I deliberate over whether someone would poison me. I'm so relieved that he stayed, that he's *here*, that I nearly burst into tears over my food. I have to swipe dampness away from my eyes.

"Indeed," says Grey. "Your chef's roasted chicken often brings me to tears, too."

His voice is so dry that it makes me giggle through my tears. "In a good way?"

He grimaces. "No. She may as well light it on fire."

I laugh outright. "It's far better than all that shellfish in Emberfall." I make a face.

"Blasphemy." He isn't smiling, but his eyes are dancing, so I know he's teasing. "Tycho and I used to race each other across Rillisk for the best steamed crabs in the city."

"I wasn't sure there was anything worse than shellfish until you mentioned *running* to get it."

That startles a laugh out of him, and the sound lodges itself in my heart. He's so reserved that smiles are earned, and true laughter is hard won. Every time it happens, I feel like I need to lock the sound away in a box to treasure for later.

Then he says, "The barmaid, Jodi, was a friend."

Maybe it's the way he says *friend*, or the way he mentions a girl's name, or the fact that she was a barmaid, but something inside me sits up and pays attention. "A friend?" I say, trying to sound casual but likely failing miserably.

"Yes. A friend. Nothing more." He shakes his head a little.

"I was too . . . too wrapped up in fear of discovery for anyone to be anything more."

"All your strategic positioning?"

"Mmm," he says noncommittally, and I smile. I wait, but that's all he says. For a moment, I wonder if that's meaningful, if there was more between them that he doesn't want to admit. But I should know better. For someone who reveals so little about himself, he's incredibly forthright. There's never a hint of artifice or deceit.

The silence that builds between us has no strain to it, and my earlier emotion has softened into something warmer. Better. Gentler. It makes me wish we never had to leave this space, that my world was confined to these quarters. Just me and him and this roaring fire, nothing outside the window but the night sky.

The thought feels immeasurably selfish.

I have to clear my throat before tears can form again. "I saw you on the fields with Tycho. I haven't seen him in days. Is he well?"

"I'm . . . not certain."

It's not an answer I expected, so I snap my gaze up. "Why?"

"I suspect he may be struggling with his chosen role."

"Well." I uncork a bottle of wine and somehow restrain myself from pouring thrice as much as I usually would. "He is not alone in that."

"No." Grey sighs. "He's not." He pushes his glass toward me.

He almost never drinks. I raise my eyebrows.

He shrugs.

I pour.

I've drained half of mine before he reaches for his glass, but he takes the smallest sip before setting it back on the table. His eyes follow my motion, though, watching the tilt of my glass, or maybe the curve of my fingers around the stem, or my lips or my throat or—

I need to put this glass down. My cheeks are on fire, my thoughts a million miles away from where they should be.

He's tracing a finger around the base of his glass, and I blush. "I thought we were both going to be reckless," I say.

But of course, he's never reckless. Never careless.

Grey confirms it when he says, "I should be with your guards, Lia Mara."

He's probably right, but the words pierce my heart. Then I realize he hasn't moved. Those dark eyes are still fixed on me, his long fingers still tracing endless circles around the glass.

Fight for yourself, Nolla Verin said.

I swallow. "I want you to stay with me," I whisper.

He closes his eyes and draws a breath, and then *he* drains half his glass.

Abruptly, he sets it down and shoves the wine away. "Silver hell. That will lead nowhere good."

I don't know if he means the staying or the wine, but I want to challenge him to drink it. For once, I want to see him lose control.

The very thought makes me flush. At least one of us is being responsible. The whole reason he's here is to keep me safe. To keep assassins out. He can't very well do that if he's drunk.

I push away from the table and return to stare out the window, resting my fingertips against the icy chill of the frame. The cold is startling and stabilizing, and I take a deep breath. "Go if you must," I say. "My guards will likely welcome the—"

Hands close on my waist, and I gasp.

"Shh," he murmurs, holding me still. His breath touches my

hair, the skin of my neck. His hands are always so gentle, but I can feel his strength. My heart gallops along in my chest, but I want to lean into him, to let his arms close around me and capture my thundering pulse.

"There will be talk," he says, his voice low and intent. "Even if I do nothing more than stand guard inside your door while you sleep, your guards and servants will talk. There will be no quelling the rumors."

I think of him on the field, facing Solt, doing what he can to control my soldiers without defying my wish to rule without violence, trying to maintain control without giving the impression that he's countermanding me. I consider everything Nolla Verin said and wonder if I've been crippling everyone around me with my own self-doubt. I've spent so much time worrying about what everyone else wants, worrying about how they see *me*, that I haven't given a moment's thought to what *I* want.

"Then let there be talk," I finally say.

"Lia Mara—"

"I don't care." I turn in his arms and look up at him. "Wait. Do . . . you?"

"It would be difficult for your people to think any less of me." Grey frowns. "But I do not wish for them to think less of *you*." He lifts a hand to trace a lock of hair that's fallen against my cheek.

"I think rather highly of you," I say softly. His thumb brushes along my jaw, and I shiver.

"I'm relieved someone does." His finger strokes down the length of my neck, so lightly, like he's not sure if he should dare. His touch is almost weightless as his hand drifts across the slope of my shoulder—before he draws back.

I catch his wrist, digging my fingers into the leather there. His eyes spark with light from somewhere, and we stand there breathing at each other.

My blush deepens, and I glance at his hand sheepishly. "As if you couldn't break my hold."

"As if I'd want to."

"As if—"

He leans in to press his lips to mine, and I suck in a breath. My fingers are still wrapped around his wrist, but it feels like he has caught *me*. His mouth is warm against my own, slow and intense, drawing a small sound from my throat when his tongue brushes mine. I don't know if I let him go or if he breaks free, but his hands are suddenly on my waist, lighting a fire inside me. My back hits the cold frame of the window, making the panes rattle.

I gasp in surprise, but he captures the sound with his mouth, his weight against me now, heavy and addictive. We've kissed before, but he seems closer than he's ever been. His kisses have grown more insistent, more sure. More of a challenge than a question.

My hands drift along the muscles of his arms to his shoulders, his chest, seeking skin but only finding so much leather, so many weapons. His fingers play at the edge of my belt, where I'm a little ticklish, and it makes me giggle and squirm—until his other hand slips lower, finding my hip through the robes, making me flush and gasp in an entirely new way.

I break the kiss, tucking my face into his neck, breathing hard against the sweet warmth of his skin. I can't think. I can't speak. I want to laugh. I want to cry. "Grey," I whisper. "Grey."

"*Faer bellama*," he says against my hair. "*Faer gallant*."

Beautiful girl. Brave girl.

My eyes fill, and I draw back to look at him.

He lifts a hand to brush the tears away, then leans in to brush his lips against my damp cheek.

"*Faer vale,*" he says.

Gentle girl.

My hands find his neck, my fingers stroking the hair at his nape as I inhale the heady scent of him.

He begins to pull away, but I hook my fingers in the straps along his chest and hold fast.

He stops, his eyes searching mine, but I dodge his gaze and fix my eyes on the buckles. I take a deep breath and begin to unfasten one.

He goes very still.

My cheeks are on *fire*. Once again, our breathing is very loud between us.

"There are a lot of buckles, you know," I say, but my cheeks are burning. I can't look at him.

He smiles. "As you say."

His hands are quick and deft, easily three times faster than mine, born of a time when he was trained to adorn himself in armor to face an immediate threat. But the leather and weapons are in a pile on the floor in *seconds*, leaving him in a linen shirt and calfskin trousers. At least, I think so. I barely have time to register that he's still dressed before he's kissing me again.

Oh, I was so wrong before. Now he's closer than ever, the thin fabric of his shirt doing nothing to hide the warmth of his skin. There's nothing hesitant about his kisses now, and I drink in the taste of him until I feel like I'm drowning. He can surely feel my heart pounding against his own, especially when his hand sweeps down the length of my body, tugging at my robes, hiking the silk higher, baring my calf, my knee. His hand finds the bare skin of my outer thigh just as his hips meet mine.

I suck in a breath and cling to him. I forget how to breathe. I forget how to think. I want to feel all of him at once. I tug at his shirt, and my knuckles are rewarded with the smooth slope of his waist, the gentle curve of muscle leading toward his rib cage.

Then my fingers settle over the harsh edges of his scars. I can't tell if he freezes or if I do. Either way, my hands slow. Stop. Slip away.

Grey has drawn back a few inches. His eyes are dark and inscrutable now.

I've only seen his scars once, when we were on the run from Emberfall. We'd taken shelter in a cave in the mountains, and he didn't realize I was looking. Even then, it was only a brief glance, a tiny glimpse of something terrible. Noah has seen the worst of it, from before Grey was healed, but otherwise, he's kept the marks hidden. Even when Princess Harper first brought him clothes, he refused to let her see what had been done to him.

Maybe the scars make him feel vulnerable, or maybe they're a reminder that someone he once trusted could cause such torment, but the air between us has shifted. There's a shadow where a moment ago there was light.

I don't know if it's pity for his anguish or awe at his strength or rage for what was done to him—or some emotion I can't even identify. Whatever it is, I reach for him again, sliding my hands under his shirt. He's tense now, but he doesn't move. When my fingers drift across the marks, he shivers, his breath catching the tiniest bit, but he doesn't pull away.

I push off the wall and step into him, pressing my lips to the skin at the base of his neck, letting my hands travel up his back, holding him against me. I can feel his heart beat against mine, quick and fluttering like a trapped bird, but as I hold him, as my fingers trace the lines and my breath warms his neck, his tension eases. Calms. Settles. His head dips and he presses kisses to my temple, to my cheek, his fingers tangling in my hair.

"As I said," he whispers, his voice a low rasp, "you know all the ways to make me yield."

This is different from the wildfire attraction of a moment ago. More powerful. More precious. This is trust. Faith. Hope.

Love.

He kisses the shell of my ear, adding a little nip with his teeth before withdrawing. He reaches up to pull the shirt over his head, and all the breath leaves my lungs in a rush. The firelight paints his skin with gold and shadow, and I'm flushed and dizzy with desire and fear igniting in my belly. Suddenly I'm shy, my hands fluttering against my abdomen as he bends to yank the ties on his boots. But he must notice, because he pauses for the briefest moment, peering up at me.

"Should I re-dress?" he says, and there's no censure in his voice, no judgment.

"No. No!" I shake my head quickly. I have to make my voice work. "Grey—Grey, you should know—"

I can't say it. Flames are eating up my ability to think. He's too lovely, too fierce, too male, too . . . oh, too *much*.

He kicks his boots free. Without warning, he steps forward and scoops me into his arms. I yip and grab hold of his neck, but it puts our faces very close. My free hand is against his bare chest, and I have to force my eyes to meet his.

"I should know what?" he says, and his voice is low and gentle, just for me.

"I've never," I whisper.

"Ah." He carries me to the bed, and now it's my heart's turn to want to escape its cage. But he eases me onto the coverlet, then climbs up to lie beside me. Mere inches of space exist between us, and I want to close every inch.

Then he says, "I haven't either."

It's so unexpected that I nearly fall off the bed. "But—you were a guardsman! How is that possible?"

He shrugs a bit. "I was seventeen when I was sworn to the Royal Guard, and we forswear family, so courtship was not allowed. Some of the others would visit the pleasure houses in the cities, but that wasn't for me." He traces a finger along the line of my robes, along my shoulder, across my neck, and then down the front of my chest.

I shiver and my breath catches, but he leans in to press another kiss to my lips. "You'll have to forgive my inexperience."

"You'll have to forgive mine—" I begin, but his gentle hand slips under my robe, and my back arches into his touch, and I find I can't think at all.

"I've heard many stories," he says against my cheek, his voice teasing as he drags his teeth along my jaw. "You read so very many books." His thumb strokes against a sensitive bit of skin, and I gasp again.

He draws back enough to find my eyes, and he smiles. "Surely, we can figure it out."

CHAPTER SIXTEEN

GREY

I'm rarely asleep long enough to be woken by the sun, but the room is dim with early morning light when my eyes finally open. The fire has fallen to embers, and I can taste a chill in the air, but Lia Mara's blankets are enough to keep me warm, especially with the queen herself curled up beside me.

She hasn't woken yet, but her forehead is pressed to my shoulder, her red hair spilling into the space between us, shining in the pale sunlight. Her knees are drawn up to press against my outer thigh. I am torn between wanting to wake her so I have the pleasure of seeing her eyes, and wanting to let her sleep so I can continue to watch the sunlight drift along the bare curve of her shoulder. I am torn between wanting to stay by her side until the end of time, and wanting to find every single person who would dare wish her harm so I can put a blade through them myself. I have felt protective of her for ages, of all my friends, but this . . . this is different suddenly. Not an obligation. An imperative. A fierce urgency.

I am supposed to be meeting with the army officers and Lia Mara's generals this morning, likely right this very moment, but I find I cannot leave her side.

Lia Mara inhales deeply, and then her lips press to my arm before her eyes even open. I reach over to stroke the hair back from her face, and her eyes open the tiniest bit.

"I was worried," she says softly, "that I would wake and you'd be gone."

"Still here." I trace a finger over her mouth, and she touches a kiss to my fingertips. "Though I am to meet with your generals about the reports from Emberfall—"

"They can wait a bit longer." She shifts closer until her legs tangle with mine, and I forget everything but the feel of her skin and the taste of her mouth.

Minutes or hours or decades later, sunlight floods the room. I'm buckling my bracers into place while Lia Mara is blushing at me from under her blankets.

"If you don't stop looking at me like that," I say, "I will be forced to spend the day here."

"Do you mean that to be a warning? Because it sounds like a promise."

That makes me smile, and I lean down to kiss her. "Don't tempt me, you lovely girl." She attempts to hook her fingers in the neckline of my shirt, but I grin and bat her hand away. "Later."

She flops back against her pillows and feigns a pout. "I suppose I do need to be a queen, at least for a short while."

"I will ask Iisak to stay with you when I cannot," I say, and she sobers. Her mock pout turns into a true frown.

"I really do wish we could stay here," she says softly.

I pick up my sword belt and loop it around my waist. "I once heard Rhen's father—my father, I suppose—say that if you cannot make your people love you, you should make them fear you." I pause. "Respect is rarely born out of anything else."

"My sister said the same thing." She studies me as I buckle my weapons into place. "I don't want people to fear me, Grey." Her voice is very soft. "Do you think that makes me a weak queen?"

"No." I step over to the bed and press a hand to her cheek. "You can be a strong queen without being your mother, Lia Mara."

The instant I say the words, I realize I don't know if they're true. The soldiers on her training fields would disagree with me. In Emberfall, King Broderick was certainly never known for being *kind*. And while Rhen is devoted to his people, he's not opposed to being brutal when he sees the need for it. The scars on my back—on Tycho's back—are proof enough of that.

Maybe Lia Mara can read the hesitation in my eyes, because she presses her hand over mine. "Nolla Verin thinks I am too lax."

"Your sister is vicious because your mother expected her to be." I pause. "She expected the throne, and she knows no other way to rule."

She stares at me. "You . . . don't trust her," she says carefully.

"I trust her to behave exactly as Karis Luran would."

She frowns. "Nolla Verin says I need to learn to fight for myself if I expect others to fight on my behalf. Mother would have agreed."

"Nolla Verin is wrong."

"She is?"

"You are *queen*, Lia Mara, and you took that throne by force.

You already know how to fight for yourself. I've seen your strength and bravery countless times." I lean down to kiss her. "Now it's time to show your people."

⁘

Jake is waiting in the hallway when I finally emerge. He's leaning against the opposite wall, his arms folded across his chest. If I didn't know any better, I'd say he was dozing, but I've learned that Jake is very good at looking bored and inattentive when he's actually quite the opposite. His eyes widen, and he straightens when he sees me. I'm not sure what about my appearance is telling, but he hooks a thumb in his sword belt and smiles. "Well, hi, Grey," he says, too casually. "Nice night?"

I was a guardsman long enough to recognize *this* type of taunting, so I ignore him and look at Lia Mara's guards, two women this morning. I only know one of them, a stony-faced guard named Tika who was loyal to Karis Luran.

"No one is to enter the queen's chambers without an escort," I say to them both. "I will speak to the scraver Iisak about remaining at her side throughout the day."

They exchange a glance, then Tika nods. Her expression does not change. "Yes, Your Highness."

I turn to stride down the hallway, but I'm not surprised at all when Jake falls into step beside me.

"Don't start," I say.

"You do realize you're blushing."

I'm not. At least I hope I'm not.

He grins. Silver hell.

"You must be exhausted," he continues, "after . . . ah, *standing guard*."

I give him a look and wonder how much of this I'm going to have to endure.

"What?" he says innocently.

I mimic his always-irreverent tone. "Don't be a dick, Jake."

He lowers his voice and mimics my severe one. "As you say, Your Highness."

I smack him on the back of the head, and he laughs—but he quickly sobers. He's quieter as he says, "I've been waiting till we were out of earshot to tell you this, but . . . her guards were going to storm in there."

"What?" I look at him in surprise. "When?"

"Around midnight." He pauses. "Apparently there's worry that you would cause her harm."

I stop short in the hallway and round on him. "That *I* would cause—"

"Shh." He doesn't stop. "Keep walking."

I keep walking. "She has had two attempts on her life while I was nowhere near."

"There are a lot of rumors." He pauses. "Their law says whoever kills the queen gets to rule Syhl Shallow, right? One of the strongest rumors is that you intend to kill Lia Mara and claim the throne for yourself."

"Why would I need to? We are already *allies*." We pass a servant in the hallway, and my expression must be fierce, because he quickly bows and scurries out of the way.

"They don't trust magic, Grey. They don't trust *you*." He takes a deep breath. "There are factions in the city who think Syhl Shallow needs to take a stand against your magic. They're worried you're manipulating her to gain control of her army, and once they've marched on Emberfall, you'll take control of everything. Then their queen will be dead, and no one will be able to touch you because of your magic—"

"Enough." I sigh and run a hand down my face.

They think I am manipulating her because they *do* see her as weak. She wants to be a peaceful queen, but that means we will battle uphill at every turn. If I take control of her army by force, we will seem to be at odds. If I don't . . . we will struggle to hold them together at all.

Not for the first time, I wish for Rhen's counsel.

I want to shove the thought out of my head, but as usual, it lodges there. He was not without his faults . . . but he would not be in this predicament. He was raised to do this, raised to *rule a kingdom*. He has the skill to outwit his opponents when they make themselves known. It's why he was able to run Syhl Shallow out of Emberfall the first time—and likely why he was able to keep Lilith at bay for so very long.

It's why I need this army to respect their queen and to follow me. Rhen will sense the slightest weakness and exploit it. My magic is worthless if we can't move our forces into Emberfall. My claim to the throne is worthless if his people will not support me.

I once told Rhen not to get mired in self-doubt, and now I'm facing the same thing.

We've reached the final turn before the hallway that will lead to her strategy room, and I stop. I can hear the cacophony of voices echoing from here. Nolla Verin stands near the doorway with an advisor, Ellia Maya, and they seem deep in conversation. We're too far to hear their words, but Nolla Verin casts a disapproving glance my way. I want to cast a disapproving one right back, but I'm sure they've all been waiting awhile, and that will do nothing to improve my position.

I look at Jake, who has stopped with me. "So I am to meet with generals and officers who already hate me and now think I am merely using them as a means to an end." It's no wonder Solt and the others glare at me with disdain on the training fields.

Jake stares back at me steadily. "Don't take this the wrong way, but . . . aren't you?"

I frown.

"Isn't that the point of an army? *Any* army?" Jake continues. "When Harper first dragged me and Noah into Ironrose, I was hoping you'd get trampled by a horse, but I still fell in with that 'good of Emberfall' crap. I still risked my life. A lot of that was for Harper—but then a lot of it was for . . ." He pauses, then rolls his eyes, looking abashed. "Well, *you*, you idiot." He glances meaningfully at the hallway. "They're still here. They must believe in *something* you're doing."

I was not raised to be a prince. I am not a general. I was not even a soldier.

I don't know how to make them believe in what I'm doing when I'm not entirely certain *I* do.

"Go." Jake punches me in the shoulder. "Do you need a pregame pep talk?"

"What?"

"No guts, no glory. Get your head in the game. Go big or—"

"Jake."

"*Grey*." He hits me in the center of my chest, where the emblem of Emberfall is embedded in the leather: a gold lion and a red rose entwined, encircled in green and black, the colors of Syhl Shallow. The armor was once a gift from Karis Luran, in honor of our future alliance.

"Syhl Shallow needs to ally with Emberfall to survive," Jake says fiercely. "You know that. They know that. Karis Luran herself knew that."

"As I know that." Lia Mara speaks from the hallway, and I turn to face her as she strides across the marble floor, her guards trailing behind. She has changed into fresh robes in layers of green, with a thick black belt laced into place at her waist. Her red hair hangs over her shoulder in a silken curtain. Her eyes are bright, but her mouth is solemn, and my heart skips at her beauty.

Jake bows to her, and at first I think it's mockery and I'm going to have to punch him. But then he says, "Your Majesty," in Syssalah, and I realize it's not. Perhaps I *should* get my head in the game.

She smiles. "Jake. Good morning."

"We were discussing strategy before meeting with the army officers," he says.

"I heard a bit of your *strategy*," she says, not fooled. "I'd like to join you. If I may."

As if they were not *her* generals and officers. As if I would not grant her everything she asked.

I nod. "Always."

She reaches for my arm and draws close enough that I can catch her scent, like oranges and vanilla. "I thought that showing a distance between myself and my armed forces would make my people realize that I will not quickly resort to violence." She hesitates. "I believe it has done quite the opposite. I do not want my soldiers to think I do not need them. I do not want my people to think we are weak."

They would never, I want to say, but it would be a lie. Her people are worried and uncertain, and it's clear.

It's impressive that she sees that. It's more impressive that she *admits* that.

"Besides," she says. "I disagree with what you said. I don't need to show them *my* strength."

These words are said more clearly, and Nolla Verin straightens at the end of the hallway when she hears them.

I glance down at Lia Mara in surprise. "You do not?"

"No." She keeps her eyes ahead, fixed on the challenging gaze of her sister, but her fingers tighten on the bend of my arm. "This is not about Syhl Shallow alone. This is about forging an alliance between our countries. This is about learning the ways magic can be an asset, not a threat. This is about more than violence and power. This is about education, and knowledge, and communication." She looks up at me, and her eyes are intense. "If my people must see strength, then we need to show them *ours*."

CHAPTER SEVENTEEN

RHEN

It's been two weeks since Lilith showed herself.

Two weeks—leaving Emberfall with less than a month until Grey brings his forces here.

I'm not sure which causes more dread to fill my chest. I'm not even sure it matters.

This morning, Harper is just outside my window again, sparring with Zo. We are to ride for Silvermoon later, because their Grand Marshal has grudgingly sworn his private army to defend Emberfall, and I want to see the state of his forces myself. My spy, Chesleigh Darington, is expected to return from Syhl Shallow by this evening with reports on their army, on whether she bears a weapon she thinks I will use against Grey—a weapon I hope to use against Lilith.

There are too many hopes. Too many fears. Too many unknowns.

The air has turned colder, bringing icy winds to cross the farmlands surrounding Ironrose, promising a bitter winter to come. The guardsmen now wear wool beneath their armor, and steel fire barrels have been placed at each of the sentry stands surrounding the castle. Heavy cloaks have been dragged out of chests, and the servants have added a feather down blanket to my bed. I remember once wishing for winter to find the castle, despairing at the end of every season that autumn would begin again. I forgot how quickly the days would turn shorter, how a chill could find every corner of my chambers.

Once we pass the solstice, snow will begin to blanket the mountains between here and Syhl Shallow, making travel difficult. It's hard enough to feed an army when there's a healthy harvest, and a lot more difficult to keep people motivated to fight when they're cold and hungry. That will affect Grey's army as well as my own.

Or maybe it won't. Maybe he can magic food right into the mouths of his soldiers. Maybe he can drive away the snow and ice and trap Emberfall in a perpetual autumn again. Maybe he can wrap himself in magic so he's untouchable the way Lilith was.

The thought makes something inside me clench tight, and I shiver. I don't want to think of Grey as being like Lilith. I don't want to think of him using magic against me.

I don't want to think of him having magic at all.

I remember a time early in the curse when Lilith sought to punish me for refusing to love her. We stood in the courtyard where the roses and honeysuckle were in bloom, the air full of their perfume. This was only the third or fourth season, after Lilith had seen my monster destroy my family due to her enchantments, but she still held some delusional hope that I would find a place for her in my heart.

She ran a finger across my cheek, drawing blood with her touch, sending fire through my veins so quickly that I fell to my knees. Grey grabbed her wrist and tried to stop her, but she turned on him instead. The bones in his fingers snapped, one by one. When he tried to jerk back, she grabbed hold of his wrist, and the bones cracked there, too. Then something in his leg, because he collapsed. I remember bone jutting from the fabric of his trousers. The sound of bones breaking still haunts me.

"Stop!" I yelled at her, coughing on my own blood. "Stop!"

But she didn't stop. She drew his sword and drove the weapon into his abdomen. When he hit the ground, she yanked it free, then drove it straight through his shoulder, pinning him to the turf in front of me.

His free hand was trying to draw another weapon, but she caught that wrist too and proceeded to break the rest of his fingers. I remember the sound of his breathing, fractured and panicked as he tried to free himself with hands that wouldn't work. He was swearing at her, cursing fate, cursing magic.

But never cursing me.

I was able to drag myself to her side, and I grabbed hold of her arm. "Please," I begged.

"Oh, now you want to beg?" she'd crooned, her voice light and sweet despite the blood on the grass around her. She reached out to cup my jaw, and I flinched, expecting pain, but her fingers were cool against my skin.

"I like it when you beg," she whispered, leaning closer. "Do it some more."

Then she broke my jaw, and when I cried out, she knocked me onto my back. She knelt on my chest as my ribs cracked from her magic. She proceeded to pull every tooth from my mouth with her bare fingers, letting them drop into my throat until I was choking on bone and blood and begging for death. Her skirts pooled around me in piles of silk, and a honeybee droned somewhere nearby—or maybe that was me, keening from the pain and desperation of it all.

I don't know if she answered my prayers or if fate did, but I woke in my sitting room as if her torture had never happened, Grey at my side, the curse beginning once more. The memories weren't gone, though. For so long, they felt like a nightmare I'd just awoken from. I'd close my eyes and hear bones breaking. I'd swallow and taste blood.

That evening, I ordered Grey not to defend me from Lilith.

"I am sworn to defend you," he said.

"You are the only remaining guardsman," I snapped, as if that were somehow a failing, because I somehow didn't realize how very meaningful that was. But the curse was torment enough. I couldn't endure the prospect of watching her destroy someone else, season after season, for her own entertainment—because of a choice *I* made. "If you will not obey my orders, you will *leave*."

He stayed—until he didn't.

And here we are.

Grey will bring magic back to Ironrose, and he will take something I do not want to give. And there is a tiny part of me that worries I deserve all of it.

Outside my window, swords clash, and Harper cries out. A blade rattles along the cobblestones.

I stride to the window. "Harper!"

"I'm all right. I'm all right." She takes Zo's outstretched hand and pulls herself to her feet. My eyes search her form, but there's no blood, no obvious source of damage.

Harper looks up at me, and I am relieved that the ready anger that used to cloud her eyes has dissipated. Our moments together now remind me of the last weeks of the curse, when she knew the enchantress was tormenting me, night after night, so Harper would hardly leave my side, day or night.

I should be protecting her. Instead it feels as though she is always protecting me.

She dusts herself off. "I suck at this."

"You are chasing her blade again, my lady."

She fetches her weapon from where it landed. "Come show me."

I stare down at her, at the way curls have pulled free of her braids and the wind has painted pink along her cheekbones. Weeks ago we stood just like this, and I was worried she hated me. Now I'm worried she pities me.

"Of course," I say.

By the time I make it to the courtyard, Zo has vanished. A week ago, I saw her frequent retreats as a weakness. Something worthy of disdain.

Since the moment Harper struck Lilith with a dagger, I have regretted those thoughts.

Dustan and three other guardsmen have trailed me to the court-yard, but they take up positions along the wall. I bite back a shiver and wish I'd thought to grab a cloak.

Harper lifts her sword, so I draw mine, but I'm struck by the realization that we haven't faced each other like this in months— not since before Grey was dragged back to the castle in chains. Her stance is better than I remember, more balanced, which I know is a constant struggle for her. Something else to be grateful to Zo for, I suppose, because Harper does not spar with anyone else.

I begin with a simple attack from above, and she blocks it easily to counterattack. Her movements are precise but practiced, though I'm impressed at her speed. But when she blocks again and I withdraw to regroup, she follows the motion.

It puts her off balance, and I snap the blade right out of her hand.

"Ugh," she says as she reclaims the weapon.

"You do not need to chase your opponent," I say. "If someone is truly your enemy, they will come back to you."

She stops and stares at me, and I realize what I've said. I wonder if she's thinking of Grey—who didn't try to come after me.

I'm thinking of Lilith, whom I can't shake loose.

Harper's eyes flash with challenge as she steels herself. "I'm not very patient."

"As if you need to tell me." Her conviction is one of the very first things I ever admired about her. I lift my blade.

We do it again. And again. By the eighth time, a bloom of sweat glints on her brow, but her expression is fiercely determined. She worries about her balance, about her left side weakness, but her footwork is almost flawless. It must be the result of careful practice and repetition, because it's not something that would come naturally to her. It's impressive, but it also tugs at chords of sadness in my chest.

I taught her how to hold a bow, how to dance, how to station an army. But when it came to swordplay, she first learned from Grey.

I don't know if I'm distracted or if she finally convinces herself to wait, but she doesn't come after me when I disengage. I'm not ready for it, so when I attack, she's prepared, and she hooks my blade with her guard. Metal scrapes against metal, then locks into place, all but pinning us together. Our breath makes quick clouds between us in the chilled air.

Her eyes are wide and surprised, so I smile. "Well done."

Her cheeks turn pink. "Did you let me do that?"

"My lady." I feign hurt. "You wound me."

That pink on her cheeks turns into a true blush. We're so close together, blades crossed between us, but there's no strain, no tension.

I wish I had something I could give her. Something that would steal away the sting of all my wrongs. I know I can't undo what I've done or erase the mistakes I've made. Forgiveness can't be bought, but I'm not entirely sure how I could earn it either.

She wets her lips, then unlocks her sword from mine. "Thank you for the lesson."

I lift a hand to brush a tendril of hair from her cheek, and when she leans into my touch, I let my hand linger, my thumb stroking the very edge of her lip. I want very badly to lean in and kiss her, but even this feels precarious. With Harper, everything must be earned. Patience is rewarded.

I kiss her on the forehead instead. "You should dress for our journey to Silvermoon," I say, and my voice is rough.

"Freya already laid out a gown." Her gaze searches mine again. "I won't take long."

Dustan holds the door for her when she approaches, but none of my guards follow her into the castle. They won't unless I order it. They're sworn to protect me, not her. There are so many rumors about Disi's failures, about the true heir to the throne, not to mention the very real threats from Lilith, that even if I ordered them to keep her safe, I'm not entirely sure anyone would risk their life on her behalf. The only one of my guards who ever did is now preparing to wage war against me.

As I turn to head into the castle myself, I realize that's not true.

The Royal Guard quarters sit along the lowest level of the castle, lining the rear hallway to the training arena, on the opposite side from the kitchens and the servant quarters, and the closest to the stables. I have little occasion to be down here, and in fact I cannot remember the last time I was. When Grey and I were trapped by the curse, he selected chambers near my own, because there was little sense in my sole guardsman being out of earshot.

When I turn down the shadowed hallway, a long-buried memory rises to the surface. I must have been six or seven, old enough that I'd learned how to escape the watchful eyes of my nurse or my tutors. Young enough that I was curious about spaces in the castle that I was not allowed to frequent. In my memory, I was seeking the dungeons, because my sister Arabella insisted they were haunted, but I found myself in this hallway, wide-eyed when I realized that the loud, angry voices I'd heard from the stairwell were not from ghosts or prisoners, but instead guardsmen having a heated argument.

Until that day, I'd never seen a guardsman put a foot wrong. I'd never heard one speak in anything more than a measured, deliberate tone, always with deference to the royal family.

But that morning, I watched as one guardsman shoved another into the stone wall, and two more tried to pry them apart. Their words turned into a fiery string of profanity that would've made my mother blush, but I was *fascinated*.

Then one of them saw me, because he swore and hissed, "The prince. The *prince*."

They jerked apart and snapped to attention. I was so startled by their reaction that I did, too. I know now that they were probably afraid of earning a reprimand, but I was worried about being found here and angering my father. I wasn't so young that I hadn't learned the ramifications of his temper.

One of them must have finally found the courage to peel him-self off the wall—or maybe he could read my own fear—because he approached and said, "Your Highness. Have you lost your way?"

I don't remember what he looked like, or even what his name was. I don't have any idea why they were arguing, or whether it con-tinued once I was out of earshot. I just remember that his voice was kind, and I knew I would not be in trouble. I remember that he was startled when I took his hand, the way I would do when I went for a walk with my nurse.

I remember it being the first time I realized my father's guards—*my* guards—had thoughts and feelings and actions that had nothing to do with the royal family, that they all would speak an oath, but it would mean something different to each man or woman who gave it.

This memory brings another. This one is less welcome.

Do you regret your oath?

I do not.

This is our final season, Commander. You must know you can speak freely.

I do speak freely, my lord.

My chest tightens, and I have to breathe through it. I don't want to think of Grey, but as usual, my thoughts give no heed to what I *want*.

I stop in front of a door near the end of the hallway. Dustan and Copper, another of my guards, have trailed me here, and I can all but feel their curiosity in the air around us, but they won't ques-tion me.

Usually my presence is announced, but I am already at odds with Zo, and I do not want to stand on ceremony, so I knock at her door.

"Ugh!" she yells, her voice muffled from the other side of the solid wood. "Go off, you fools."

I raise my eyebrows and turn to look at Dustan. He meets my gaze steadily. "Some of the guardsmen may harbor a bit of resentment that she has remained in her quarters."

"Do you?"

"No, my lord."

I wonder if that's true. He must harbor a *bit* if he's allowing it to continue unchecked.

He clears his throat. "She does not endear herself. Her violin can be heard through the hallways hours before sunrise."

I almost smile. It's no wonder Zo and Harper are friends.

"I can *hear* you out there plotting," Zo says from the other side of the door, her tone sharp. "Don't you have better things to do with your time?" The lock rattles, and the door swings open. Zo has one hand wrapped around a dagger, and the other balled into a fist.

She takes one look at me and her eyes flare wide. "Oh!" She lowers the dagger. "Your Highness. I—forgive me—" She drops into a curtsy. "I should not—my words were not—"

"Not for me. I know. May I come in?"

The surprise vanishes from her eyes, replaced with a hint of suspicion. For a moment, I expect her to refuse, and I'm not sure what I'll do. There's probably a part of her that wants to use that dagger on *me*.

But she doesn't. She takes a step back, drawing the door open wide. "Of course."

I step into her quarters. The room is small but well appointed, like all of the guards' lodgings. No windows, because the Royal Guard could not be vulnerable to attack, but there are a few narrow slats between the bricks to allow fresh air into the space. A wide lantern hangs in one corner, casting shadows along the whitewashed walls. A small wood stove sits in the other corner, thickening the air with warmth. At the foot of the bed is a wide chest, and a slim closet lines the front wall. The table is covered with books and parchment and a writing set. A rack is built into the rear wall to hold weapons and armor, but Zo doesn't have much of that anymore, and one of the racks holds her violin.

Dustan and Copper have followed me inside, and there's hardly room for all of us to stand. Zo watches as I take in the state of her quarters, and her gaze flicks to the guardsmen at my back. When my eyes return to hers, she swallows.

"I would have left without resistance, Your Highness," she says quietly.

I frown. "What?"

"The guards are unnecessary. I would have left at your order. I know . . ." She hesitates and seems to brace herself. "I know you believe I would act in defiance to the Crown, but I would not—"

"Zo. You think I am here to order your dismissal?"

She glances at Dustan and Copper again. "I . . . yes?"

"No," I say. "I believe I acted too hastily when I stripped you of your role with the Royal Guard."

That cynical look is back in Zo's eye. "You do?"

"My lord," says Dustan, his voice tight.

I ignore him. "Yes," I say. "You acted to protect Harper. You followed her order. Did you not?"

"Yes, Your Highness," she says slowly. "I did." She glances at Dustan again. "If you are here to offer me back my position among the Royal Guard, I do not think it will work."

"That is not my intent."

"Oh." She frowns. "Then . . . why are you here?"

"I worry for Harper. The enchantress has made her threats known. An attack from Syhl Shallow is imminent. We may have spies in our midst. Many of my cities have refused to acknowledge my rule. All of Emberfall is at risk."

The cynicism slides off her face. "I know." She pauses. "I worry for Harper as well."

"Because she is your friend."

"Yes."

I glance at Dustan. "I understand that the Royal Guard has expressed . . . ah, *displeasure* at the fact that you continue to reside among their ranks?"

She frowns as if trying to figure out the path of this conversation. "Harper does not want me to leave."

I offer a shrewd smile. "And I hear you enjoy entertaining the other guards in the early dawn hours."

"They love it," she says flatly.

"I would offer you another set of chambers," I say. "Opposite Harper's." I pause. "And I would like for you to accompany us when we leave Ironrose later today."

She studies me. "Why?"

"I feel she would be more assured at having you close. As would I."

Her eyes turn a bit flinty, and she inhales to respond, but then must think better of it, because she says nothing.

"I would ask you to speak true," I say. Her eyes flick to the guardsmen at my back, so I add, "Dustan. Copper. Wait in the hall."

They do, but they leave the door open. I don't fear Zo any more than I fear Harper herself, so I reach out and close it in my guard commander's face.

"You and I have been at odds," I say. "I no longer wish it to be so."

She curtsies again. "Well of *course*, Your Highness." The sarcasm in her tone isn't strong, but it's there.

"I asked you to speak true," I say levelly. "Do you not believe me?"

"I believe you care for Harper. I believe you want something from me, and it is *inconvenient* if we are in a state of conflict." I watch her steel herself again. "I do not believe you understand why we are at odds to begin with."

Her voice is cold and frank, so I let mine match. "You acted in defiance of my orders and you lost your position in the Royal Guard. What is to misunderstand?"

"I did not defy an order. I did not betray you. I did not betray my oath." Her shoulders are tense now, her eyes flashing with anger. "I protected Harper. She would have gone after Grey by herself, and you well know it. You put all of us in an impossible situation."

"*I* was in an impossible situation," I say tightly.

"I know!" she says fiercely. "We all know!"

"You do *not* know—" I begin, but I catch myself. As always, my anger, my frustration, is not with the person in front of me. I break off and sigh. The wood stove snaps in the corner. When I can speak again, my voice is more measured. "If you understand the circumstances, then why are we at odds?"

"You ask *why*?" She looks incredulous. "Because Harper is my *friend*."

It's such a simple reason. Or it should be. But it's not.

"Harper and I have resolved our differences," I say.

"Until the next time, when you do *not*."

I almost flinch. I am beginning to regret coming here, and I'm unsure if that's because she is challenging me, or if it's because she is right to do so. "So you are to hate me for . . . ever? Is that your position, Zo?"

She inhales like she intends to breathe fire, but she stops and lets it out on a sigh. "No. I do not hate you." She pauses. "But you have an entire kingdom to rally behind you—and an entire kingdom to protect. Harper has no one—yet still she stays. For you."

Those words hit me like a blow. My chest is suddenly tight, and I have to breathe through it.

"Her brother asked her to leave," Zo continues more quietly. "To go with them. To go to Syhl Shallow."

"I know."

"Grey did not."

I stare at her as the impact of those words sinks in. Grey didn't ask, and Harper didn't leave.

But she might have, if he had.

I don't like the doubts that this conversation has sown. Harper stayed. She *stays.* For me. Just as Zo stays for her.

"I believe I owe you a debt of gratitude," I say. Her eyebrows go up, but I'm not done. "And an apology." My voice lowers. "Harper did not mention that the guards were harassing you."

Zo shakes her head. "She doesn't know. And I understand their frustration."

We fall quiet for a moment. I wonder how much longer Dustan will give me privacy before opening the door to make sure Zo isn't feeding my body parts to the wood stove.

"Did you truly think I was coming here to dismiss you from the castle?" I say.

"Of course."

Of course. It reminds me of the way Harper faced me on the dance floor, when she told me not to take out my frustrations on her friends. It makes me wonder if everyone expects the worst of me.

I'm not unused to this feeling, but it's different now, when I am not trapped by the curse, when decisions are mine alone and have far-reaching effects.

I do not like it.

"In truth," I say, "I was coming to offer you a new position."

"As . . . what?"

"A guard."

She looks exasperated. "The Royal Guard will not—"

"Not a guard for me," I say. "A guard for Harper."

Her mouth snaps shut.

"There is too much uncertainty in my kingdom right now," I say. "No matter what orders I give, I know the Royal Guard will value my life over hers. You, I think, will not."

She says nothing. Her eyes have closed off now, and I cannot tell if she is in favor of this idea, or if she resents me for asking.

"You have trained with the Royal Guard," I continue. "You are well suited to stand at her side when we are in public."

She still hasn't said anything, so I hold her gaze. "Or you can refuse. We can continue as we have."

"Have you asked Harper if she wants this?"

That question throws me. "No. I have not."

She sighs. Says nothing.

"Well," I say. "You have my thanks for your consideration." I begin to turn for the door. Disappointment isn't an unfamiliar emotion *at all*.

But then I turn before I reach for the handle. "Zo. Please." I pause. "You were right. Harper will risk herself without hesitation."

"I know. I'm trying to decide if I should say yes before Harper has a chance to say no."

That makes me smile. "So you are not refusing?"

"Of course not." She doesn't smile back. "How much are you willing to pay?"

"What salary would suit you, Zo?"

Her eyes narrow, and she names a figure that's more than twice what the guardsmen make.

I don't know if this is an effort to challenge me on Harper's behalf or on her own, but either way, it doesn't matter. "Done," I say easily, and her eyes nearly bug out of her head. "I will send servants to help move your belongings. We would like to leave for Silvermoon within an hour. I trust you can be ready?"

"But—yes? Yes." She has to clear her throat. "Your Highness."

"Good." I reach for the door.

"You know," she calls behind me, "for Harper, I would have done it for free." She pauses. "I was curious how much it was worth to you."

"I would have given you ten times as much." I think of the moment Harper plunged a dagger into Lilith's chest. I have to put a hand against my midsection to shake off the sudden emotion. "For Harper, I would have given you everything."

CHAPTER EIGHTEEN

HARPER

I'm glad it's finally cold outside, because one of the things I miss most about Washington, DC, is the ready access to antiperspirant. Freya has half a dozen jars of lotions and potions and powders to make me smell good, but none of them stop me from sweating. I'm halfway through unbuckling my bracers when I turn the corner to head down the hallway, but I hear low voices from the room beside mine, and I stop short. Freya's voice is familiar, but it takes me a moment to place Jamison's. I've only ever known him as a temporary guard and then a soldier, as a man who lost his arm in battle and watched the army from Syhl Shallow destroy his entire regiment, but was willing to put a uniform on again to serve Rhen.

The slow, gentle murmur of his voice takes me by surprise. Clearly Freya knows him as more than that. I hesitate in my doorway, and a small smile finds my face. She mentioned Jamison on the night of Rhen's party, but their low voices make me wonder if there's more between them than just casual friendship.

I bite my lip and shift to ease into my room silently, not wanting to disturb them. Things here are so precarious, so *uncertain*, and it gives me hope to remember that love can bloom anywhere, even in the darkest times.

But then I hear Freya's breath hitch, and Jamison says, "I must. I *must*."

She's crying? Her door is open, so I grab hold of the doorjamb and rap my knuckles against the frame. They snap apart, but not so quickly that I don't notice that they were pressed up against each other, Jamison's hand stroking the hair down her back.

Freya swipes at her eyes hurriedly. Tendrils of her blond hair have pulled loose from the ribbons holding it back from her face, and her cheeks are mottled red. There's a damp spot on the shoulder of Jamison's uniform, but he stands at attention when he sees me. "My lady," he says.

"Oh, my lady," says Freya. She swipes at her eyes again. "Forgive me."

"Don't apologize." I hesitate in the doorway. "Are you all right?"

"Of course. Of course." But her breath hitches again.

My eyes sweep the room, looking for the children, but they're not here. "Are the kids all right?"

"Oh! Yes. Dahlia and Davin are down in the kitchens. The baby is next door, asleep." She takes a long breath and smooths her hands along her skirts. At her side, Jamison is silent and stoic. I can't read anything from his expression.

"Oh," I say. "Well. Good."

I say nothing. They say nothing.

Suddenly this is all kinds of awkward.

"I heard—well, you were crying. I just—you know what? Never

mind. Not my business." I back away from the doorway. "I'll just—I'll be in my room."

I feel like such an idiot. My face is hot, and I close myself into my chambers. I peel the bracers from my arms and unbuckle the sword belt, then toss my weapons and armor into a pile by the fireplace to let the sweaty leather dry. I sigh and attempt to unlace the boned linen corset that makes a good replacement for a sports bra—but it ties behind my back. I've never understood why so many clothes here require help to get in and out of. Some days, I'd give anything for a T-shirt.

My door whispers open, and I don't turn, because my face is still burning. "I'm so sorry," I say. "I didn't mean to interrupt. You were crying. I wanted to make sure you were okay."

Freya's cool fingers brush mine away, and she takes up the lacings along my spine herself, but she doesn't say anything. I can't tell if she's mad or if she's still emotional and she wants some space.

"I can do this myself," I say quietly. "If you need to be with Jamison right now."

Her fingers jerk the laces hard, pulling the fabric so tight against my rib cage that I can't even draw breath to cry out.

"No, my dear," says a vicious voice that is definitely not Freya's. "I think I need to be with you."

"Lilith." I can barely gasp the name. I struggle against her hold, trying to turn, but she pulls the lacings even tighter. A T-shirt would rip from this pressure, but this corset was made to last. My ribs feel like they're going to snap in a second. I try to inhale, but I can barely squeak in a breath. I scrabble at my neckline, but there's no give.

I just tossed all my weapons in the corner. Like an *idiot*. I have to swallow this panic. I have to think.

Luckily, I've got months of training with Zo to fall back on.

I throw an elbow back, and I'm gratified to hear Lilith grunt, but she doesn't let go.

Instead, it feels like her fingers sink through the corset into the skin of my back, and all I feel is fire. Ice. A million needles through my spine. I can't see. I can't breathe.

"You see?" she says, and her voice is like a roar and a whisper all at once. "I don't need to kill you to control him. I just need to leave reminders of what I can do."

I'm flat on the floor. She's on my back. I think I've vomited from the pain. I can't tell. I can taste blood and bile. Everything hurts, and I'm sobbing against the marble.

"I know," she croons. "I'm truly terrible."

I can't answer. My thoughts won't organize enough for speech. I thought I knew pain. I thought I was so fierce and brave, and now I'm crying on the floor.

"You stand beside him," Lilith hisses, "as if he is worthy of it. As if he has not caused a thousand harms himself."

I grit my teeth against the blinding pain. I know what Rhen did to his people, but I know he did all of it while he was a vicious monster created by Lilith herself. He blames himself for all of it, but he shouldn't. "He—he never—he never—"

"Oh no?"

My vision goes dark, but the pain lingers. Suddenly my thoughts fill with a memory: Grey and Tycho chained to the wall in the courtyard, torches flickering in the darkness, shadows dancing as Rhen gave an order. A line of fire traces across my back like the bite of a lash, and I try to cry out, but my voice is ragged and broken.

"I'm sure you think I caused that, too," she says viciously, and her breath is hot against my ear. I flinch away.

"I had nothing to do with this one," she says, and the image changes, becoming a room here in the castle. Rhen is standing by a table in his chambers, buckling his jacket into place, but he looks . . . different. I can't quite put my finger on why.

"My guards will call for your carriage," he's saying, and his voice is cold, dispassionate. "I've sent for tea."

"But, Your Highness . . ."

I can't see the woman who's speaking, but I know the voice. It's Lilith. I'm seeing him through her eyes. From the angle, she must be looking at him from the bed.

This must be before the curse. I'm terrified and fascinated.

The scene continues. A light knock raps at the door, and a young servant enters carrying a tray of tea and delicacies. Rhen completely ignores him, and the boy looks like he's used to being ignored by royalty. He eases the platter onto the table, but when he tips the pot to fill a cup, it's slightly off center, and the cup falls, shattering on the marble floor. Tea splashes everywhere, including Rhen's boots.

The boy flinches and glances at Rhen. "For-forgive me, Your High—"

"Guards." Rhen doesn't look at him.

A guard appears in the doorway, and I'm startled to realize it's Grey. Again, like Rhen, he looks slightly different. Not younger, just . . . not the same. Maybe it's the expression in their eyes or the weight of their presence—or maybe it's something they haven't lost or earned yet.

Before Grey has a chance to say anything, Rhen says, "Get him out of here. Make him regret that." He gives a nod to Lilith and says, "Farewell, my lady."

Then he turns for the door.

Grey's eyes are cold. He grabs the cringing boy's arm.

Scary Grey.

At my back, present-day Lilith whispers, "They're all beasts, aren't they?"

The vision goes dark, and I'm returned to the pain so swiftly that I cry out.

Lilith's fingers twist, and I feel like my bones are being pried through my skin.

"You think I am the villain," she says, and pain licks through my veins. "You think I am the monster. But who made the choices here, Harper?"

I choke on a sob. I'm still facedown on the marble, and my tears gather on the floor.

"Rhen's family killed my people," she says. "And you blame me for wanting revenge? You see for yourself, he was a monster before I ever arrived."

"No," I gasp. "No—you're the—"

"I expect to see military movement, *Princess*," she hisses. "I expect to see him yielding to *me*, not to you. Am I understood?"

Her fingers jerk. Spots flare in my vision, and the marble beneath me turns black.

For a moment, I think I've passed out, but no, the floor has changed. I'm lying on asphalt. I try to lift my head, and I see the pale gray concrete of a curb, and the rusted slats of a storm drain. A candy bar wrapper is stuck there, the edges fluttering in the wind.

I'm back in Washington, DC.

"No!" I cry. If she leaves me here, I have no way to get back. No way to help Rhen. No way to—

A car horn blares, and I whip my head around. An SUV is headed right for me.

I scream, and it vanishes. I'm back in my chambers, the scream echoing in my throat.

"Remember," Lilith says, her breath hot on my ear. "I can control you just as easily as I can control him."

"No," I shout. I brace myself against her weight, as if I can throw her off. "No."

A hand seizes on my shoulder, turning me over. I surge upright, swinging wildly, screaming in rage, clawing with my hands.

"My lady. *My lady.*" The male voice forces me still, and I realize why my fingers were clutching at leather and buckles instead of skin and silk.

Dustan is kneeling beside me, and my fingers have a death grip on his armor. She didn't break my spine. She didn't break anything at all. My back feels wet, though I can't tell if it's sweat or blood, and my abdomen is achy and sore. I'm trembling so hard that my teeth clack together. My breathing is loud and panicked in the space between us.

Dustan and I aren't friends, but we're not enemies either. I can't make my fingers let go. Instead, I put my face against his armor and cry.

I don't know how long I sit there, but it's not long. Rhen can't find me like this. He's already terrified that Lilith is going to return. I unclench my fingers and push back from Dustan to find that he's not alone. Freya and Jamison stand behind him, and there's another guard in the doorway.

I wipe my eyes. "Am I bleeding?"

Dustan searches my face, then casts a glance down at my body. "No." He pauses. "The enchantress was here?"

"Yes." I wish I could stop shaking. Freya gasps. Her hand clutches at Jamison's.

Dustan begins to straighten, inhaling like he's going to issue an order to the guard who's waiting in the hall, and I know—I just *know*—he's going to call for the prince. Rhen will absorb my panic and fear, the way he always does, and he'll allow it to double his own. Lilith will continue to control him.

I scramble to my feet and ignore the spots flaring in my vision to grab hold of Dustan's arm. "Commander." My voice sounds like I'm speaking through gravel. "You can't tell Rhen."

He looks at my hand, and his voice drops. "My lady. I cannot keep this a secret—"

"You *can*. Dustan, you must."

He stares at me, and his expression says he absolutely cannot.

"Please." I dig my fingers into his bracer. Grey would never have yielded, but Dustan might. "Please, Dustan. She wants—she wants him to put his army in action. She wants to force his hand. We can't let her. Not like this."

His eyes are hard, and I don't think he'll agree, but then Jamison takes a step forward. "If this enchantress wants military action, she will have it. His Highness has ordered forces to the border."

I blink up at him. "He has?"

Freya nods. Her cheeks are still pink from crying, but her tears are dry. "Yes," she says. "Jamison is part of the regiment assigned to the mountain pass."

I glance between them. I want this to be good news, because Lilith will be abated—but it's not. The regiment assigned to the mountain pass will be the first to encounter troops from Syhl Shallow.

And possibly the first to die.

As always, everything is so complicated here.

I can't think. I can't *think*.

I rub my hands over my face and take a breath. "Dustan. Please. Don't you see that she's trying to use me to manipulate him?"

"Yes. I do."

"Then we can't *let* her—"

"I also know that he rules Emberfall." He pauses. "And you do not."

"Look," I say. "We're going to Silvermoon. He's trying to bolster support, right? If we tell him this happened, he might not go at all." My insides still ache, and I try not to think about how much it's going to hurt to ride a horse in an hour. I try not to think about the fact that Rhen might never let me leave my chambers if he hears what Lilith just did.

I try not to think about what Rhen did to Grey and Tycho when he felt betrayed. Lilith just showed me how Rhen acted when a boy spilled tea in his chambers. I've never seen Rhen do anything like that *now*, but I know there's a sliver of that inside him still.

I try not to think of how Rhen will react if Dustan keeps something from him.

"Let *me* tell him," I offer. "Just . . . let me wait until when we get back." Dustan still doesn't look like he's going to concede, so I say, "It's just a few hours! What's the difference?"

He looks at me steadily for a long moment, then sighs. I'm not sure if that's assent or exasperation, but either way, he doesn't tell the other guardsman to fetch Rhen. He takes a step back and turns for the door. "You had best prepare, my lady. His Highness will be ready to leave shortly."

"Yes. Yes, of course." I start yanking at the bodice ribbon that will probably need to be cut free after Lilith pulled it so tight. "Freya, will you—"

"Yes, my lady. Right away." She pulls away from Jamison, giving him a long look.

Wait. I didn't mean to stop whatever was between them. "No. I'm sorry. You can finish . . . whatever."

Jamison shakes his head. "I should return to my regiment, my lady." He holds tight to Freya's hand before she can pull away, and he bows to her, pressing a kiss to her knuckles. "I'll send word when I can."

Then he's gone, and her eyes are welling.

"I'm sorry," I whisper. "You and Jamison . . . I didn't know."

"I hardly know myself," she says. "We've only just been talking." She brushes the tears off her cheeks and squares her shoulders. "Forgive me. We should—"

I step forward and wrap her up in a hug. My insides ache and pull and I have to force Lilith's effects out of my head, and I hold on to my friend.

Freya's not like Rhen. She lets me hold her, and her face presses into my shoulder—but only for a moment. She begins to pull away. "I am being inappropriate—"

"I've cried all over you a dozen times," I say. "I can return the favor."

That makes her breath hitch, and she says, "I've lost so much, and I didn't want to dare hope . . . oh, I can't think about it." She draws back. "Did you hear the commander? You must dress."

I was right about the corset. We have to cut the ribbon to get it free. We're both quiet and contemplative as she helps me into the pieces of a fancier gown, then urges me onto a stool in front of a mirror to try to tame my curls.

In the mirror, her eyes are still red and swollen.

I hate this. All of it. Every time I get a five-minute break from worry, something new pops up to smack me in the face. Or stab me in the back or whatever Lilith did.

"I can ask him to keep Jamison here," I say softly. "To assign him to—"

"No," she says curtly. "And he would not want that anyway. He considers it a great honor to protect Emberfall." She pauses. "As do I."

"I know." I swallow. "Me too."

Her hand settles on my shoulder, and she gives it a squeeze. "I know. Your bravery now is proof. Your bravery every *day* is proof."

I put a hand up to rest over hers, and I squeeze in return. My eyes suddenly feel damp. "You once told me that when the world seems darkest, there exists the greatest opportunity for light."

She nods at me in the mirror, but then her eyes fill again. "Sometimes I worry that the light can be doused too easily."

"Then we just light it again," I say, even though I'm not sure this is true. But I can't look at her tearstained face and say anything else. Again, I'm reminded of my mother, how she stood by my father for so long, even though he kept making the wrong decisions. I think of Rhen, and I wonder if I'm doing the same thing. My voice almost wavers and I have to steady it. "We light it again and again, as many times as we have to."

Her eyes meet mine, and she takes a steadying breath. "Yes, my lady."

A hand raps on the door frame, and I turn, expecting Rhen, but instead, I find Zo there, fully dressed in the leather armor worn by the Royal Guard. I have to do a double take. She looks severe and stoic, and I straighten. "Zo?"

Something in her severe countenance shifts, and she cracks a small smile. "His Highness hired me."

I almost fall off my stool. "You're back in the Royal Guard?"

"Ah . . . no. I'm to be *your* guard. And only yours."

I want to tackle her with hugs, but now that she's in a uniform, it probably wouldn't be seemly. I squeeze Freya's hand again. "See?" I say to her. "Another light."

CHAPTER NINETEEN

RHEN

Before the curse, I had attendants who would help me dress and prepare, valets and manservants who would lay out clothes or shave my face or fasten my buckles. Servants who would have spooned food into my mouth if I'd ordered it.

When the curse took over and the entire castle staff fled—or died—I was left with no one but Grey. For weeks, I felt helpless. I had no idea where my valets stored my underthings. Or socks! I wore boots without them for days, simply because I could not find them. I had never once shaved my own face, and when I tried, I nearly cut my throat.

I remember finding Grey outside my chambers, standing at attention in the deserted, silent hallway.

"Commander," I said sharply. "You will show me how to shave."

He stared at me for the longest moment, and I felt like such a spoiled fool, especially when confronted with the clean-shaven face that he'd clearly accomplished himself, while I was standing there pressing a silk handkerchief to my neck to stop the bleeding.

I waited for his expression to shift into scorn or disdain. For him to inwardly sigh. We were the only two people left in the castle, and there wouldn't have been much I could have done about it. He could have turned the moment into something humiliating.

He didn't. "Yes, my lord," he said equably. "Do you have a kit?"

I expect the memory to sting, but for some reason, this one doesn't.

Since the curse was broken, I've hired servants to fill most of the roles in the castle, but I haven't bothered to replace the attendants in my own chambers. Something that seemed like a necessity now feels like a frivolity.

Today, though, I wish for an advisor to help me decide how to dress. When I visit my cities, I usually wear tailored jackets and polished boots, silk and brocade trimmed in silver or gold. Never as ostentatious as my father would have been, but enough to signify who I am. Not a subject, not a soldier. A prince—their future king.

For this visit to Silvermoon, however, I need to look ready to command an army.

I tie the laces of a thick linen shirt, then buckle rich leather armor into place over top. Red fabric lines the breastplate, matching the crimson rose paired with a golden lion on the insignia in the center of my chest, and a gold crown has been hammered into the leather directly over my heart. I thread my sword belt into place and add a dagger, then add laced bracers to my forearms that reach all the way to my knuckles. The weight feels solid, secure, and it's surprisingly reassuring. Maybe I'm the one who needs the reminder of who I am, not my people.

I catch a glimpse of myself in my long mirror, and my eyes shy away. I haven't worn this armor in months, not since Grey and I were forced to venture off the grounds of Ironrose to chase after Harper, when threats of Syhl Shallow first made themselves known. I have no desire to get lost in those memories right now. I seize a cloak from a hook and buckle it into place along my shoulders.

When I emerge from my chambers, Dustan and Copper are waiting in the hallway.

"Call for horses," I say as I stride into the hallway. "I will see to Princess Harper."

Copper gives me a nod and heads toward the stairs, but Dustan falls into step behind me. "My lord," he says to my back. His voice is low.

"Commander." I don't see Zo in the hallway yet, but Harper's door is open. Light spills across the carpeting in the hallway.

"I must speak with you before you see the princess."

I don't stop. "If you have further concerns about Zo—"

"The enchantress has been in the castle."

There's very little he could stay that would yank me to a halt, but that achieves it. I round on him. "What?"

"The enchantress visited Princess Harper. She—"

"When?" I demand. "Why did you not tell me at once?" Panic wraps around my heart, and I stride down the hallway. "Was she harmed? Was she—"

"My lord. Stop." He all but grabs my arm. "Please!" he says. "Allow me to finish."

I stop. My breathing feels too quick. I cast a glance at her doorway again.

"It was not long ago," he says quickly, his voice a quiet rush. "The princess was unharmed. The enchantress only issued threats." He pauses. "But Princess Harper asked that I keep this information from you."

My pulse is still thundering in my ears. Lilith went to Harper? She issued threats? I know how the enchantress gets her point across, and I have to suppress a shudder.

But then my thoughts seize on Dustan's final words.

Princess Harper asked that I keep this information from you.

I can't move. For days, I've been terrified of the enchantress returning.

Now it has happened, and Harper sought to keep this from me.

This feels like betrayal. It shouldn't, but it does. It's no different from the many times I kept information from *her*, but fury and fear still spin through my gut to wind together.

Then I have another thought. My eyes snap to Dustan's. "Has this happened at other times?"

"Not to my knowledge."

A moment ago, the weight of this armor felt reassuring, but now it feels like a fabrication. Like I am only feigning competence. I kept the truth from Harper because I wanted to keep her safe. I did not want her to recklessly risk her life on my behalf.

She keeps the truth from me because she does not think I can handle it.

I have to draw a steadying breath. I want to confront her. I want to hide. I'm resentful. Humiliated. Afraid.

Angry.

Harper must think that Dustan was going to keep her confidence, because otherwise she'd be out in the hallway right now, pleading with me.

"Who else knows?" I say to him, and my voice is rough.

"Copper. Freya. The soldier Jamison."

So she not only asked my guard commander to keep a secret,

she did it in front of others. I thought we had found a path to honesty and mutual respect, but perhaps I was wrong. My jaw is tight.

"Fine," I say. I turn to storm down the remaining distance to Harper's chambers.

I remember the second day she was here, she packed up foods from the kitchens to take to people who were lacking. Grey and I had to chase after her—*again*—and I asked why she did not ask for assistance.

Because I didn't think you would do it, she said.

Shame curled in my belly at the time.

This moment does not feel unlike that one.

I stop in her doorway. A part of me was worried I would find her trembling and anxious, somewhat broken after facing Lilith. But she's not. She's resplendent in a violet gown meant for riding, a black leather corset laced along her waist, with a dagger belt drooping over one hip. Her hair is braided into twin plaits that are pinned to her head, with a few curls escaping, and her eyes have been lined in dark kohl. She doesn't look afraid. She looks like a warrior princess.

She had been speaking in low tones to Freya and Zo, but she stops short when she sees me. Her eyes flare wide. "Rhen."

Do you have so little faith in me? I want to say.

I think I know the answer, and some of my waiting anger withers like my confidence. I feel as though we stare at each other across a distance of miles. I hate this.

So many words wait for a chance to escape my lips, but all I say is "I have called for horses, my lady."

When I turn away, Dustan is taking a slip of paper from a servant who bobs a quick curtsy to me. Dustan reads it quickly and says, "Chesleigh Darington has returned from Syhl Shallow with information."

My spy. I have a war to wage. There are more important things at risk than my pride.

Harper appears in the doorway. "Rhen," she says. "What's wrong?"

I lock away any emotion and say, "Nothing at all." I look at Dustan. "Tell Chesleigh we are about to depart for Silvermoon Harbor."

"I will have the servants prepare a room for her to wait—"

"No. Give her a fresh horse. I want her to come along."

CHAPTER TWENTY

HARPER

I was so relieved to know Rhen hired Zo to ride at my side today, to think we're finally on the same page and working toward a common goal that will satisfy Lilith. But now we're riding to Silvermoon and he's as cold and aloof as ever, choosing to ride alongside his spy instead of with me. I should be happy—he's talking about military strategy and taking action. But my insides still ache from Lilith's treatment, making me uncomfortable and short-tempered as we ride for miles, and I can't help but think something has happened between *us*.

Maybe it's Chesleigh. I've heard her name spoken a dozen times, sometimes with reverence and sometimes with scorn, about how she's demanding piles of silver in exchange for valuable information about Syhl Shallow, how she has information about a faction that is standing against magic. She's ingratiated herself with Rhen's generals, and clearly with the prince himself. For some reason I envisioned a grisly, weathered soldier, someone older and jaded by war and politics. I didn't expect someone less than ten years older than me, someone with brutal confidence and clear skill, someone who's captured Rhen's attention not with flirtation or flattery, but with sheer competence.

I don't want to resent her. Especially not for those things. It's *good* that we have someone competent working alongside us. But I keep thinking about how I've spent months learning how to find my balance during swordplay so I can protect myself, while this woman has been to Syhl Shallow and back with something to offer the kingdom. Lilith is using me to manipulate Rhen in this war, and I can't even stop her. It makes me feel more like a hindrance than a help.

I don't like these thoughts.

I can't shake them loose.

I remember when I first arrived in Emberfall, how I thought it would be so easy to help Rhen's people. I would throw a few pastries and meat pies into a satchel and deliver them to the inn.

It would not be enough to feed all of my subjects, Rhen said.

Yes, but it would feed some of them, Rhen, I replied.

Some, but not all.

I remember thinking that should be enough. And it was, for a while. But the *all* comprised so many people.

I keep thinking of Freya's tears over Jamison. She *has* lost so much.

Zo rides close. "You have said very little since we left Ironrose." She peers at me. "Are you unwell?"

"Oh. No, I'm fine." I can't very well say that I'm feeling insecure. I straighten my back and tell myself to get it together. "I was listening."

Chesleigh is talking about soldiers stationed just inside Emberfall's border. "They've met no opposition, so the forces have been doubled," she's saying. "They've made camp some fifty miles northwest of Blind Hollow, at the base of the mountains. But they have orders to hold their position."

They've met no opposition because we don't have enough people to fight this war long term. I wonder if this is why Rhen is sending Jamison's regiment to the border—to prevent Grey from gaining more of a foothold than he's already got.

"At least Grey is still honoring the sixty days," I say.

Rhen glances at me over his shoulder. "I would not consider stationing forces in my lands to be *honoring* anything at all."

His tone is bitter. Before I can comment on it, Chesleigh says, "Nor would I." She glances at me. "Do *you* have any experience with military strategy, my lady?"

Okay, now I want to resent her.

No, that's not true. It's a simple question. An honest one.

"Very little," I say.

"It was your *brother* who was leader of your king's army, is that correct?" She glances at Rhen. "And then he fled with that traitor."

"Jake isn't a traitor," I snap.

Chesleigh glances at Rhen, and then back at me. "Prince Jacob has stationed himself as Grey's second. He trains with their military and answers to no one but Grey or the queen herself. If he is not a traitor, then he was never loyal to Emberfall at all—and perhaps never to Disi either."

Wait. *Wait.* Her sentences hit me like bullets from a machine gun, like I can't react before more slam into me. I haven't seen Jake since the day he and Grey returned to the castle, since the moment they declared war, since my brother had dinner with me and said, "Yes, Harp, I'm going back." The way he paused and said, "You could come, too."

And I didn't.

I knew he and Grey had moved past their early hatred of each other. I knew my brother was on the other side of this war.

I never thought about him being at Grey's right hand. I never really considered him plotting against Rhen. Against *us*. When he was here, in Emberfall, he and Noah kept to themselves. He certainly never made any effort to endear himself to Rhen—and honestly, Rhen wasn't quick to remedy that himself.

But my brother has never hesitated to do what he believes needs to be done—even if that means getting his hands dirty. For the first time, I wonder what he thinks of this war. Is he taking a stand *against* Rhen? Or is he taking a stand *for* Grey?

Or is it *neither*? Is he taking a stand for himself, something he believes in?

Am I on the wrong side here?

I wonder if this is what happened to my mother—if she was buried by self-doubt when it came to my father and his choices. I don't know. That scene Lilith showed me keeps playing in my brain, when Rhen ordered Grey to drag the serving boy out of his chambers for spilling a little tea.

They're all monsters, aren't they?

Rhen has turned back to Chesleigh without acknowledging her comments about Jake. I can't tell if that's out of kindness to me or if he genuinely doesn't care. Either way, that old familiar knot of anger has re-formed in my belly, fighting for space against the uncertainty.

"Before you left," he says tightly, "you mentioned there were certain . . . artifacts in Syhl Shallow."

Artifacts. What kind of artifacts? I hate that there are clearly secrets he's still keeping from me.

Or maybe they aren't secrets at all. Maybe it's just military stuff that he wouldn't bother to share.

I need to turn my brain off.

"You mentioned I could name my price," she says.

Something in my chest clenches tight. "I can't see Rhen saying that."

He looks at me, and if his eyes could shoot laser beams, they would. "About this, I did."

What is his *problem*? I set my jaw. He once told me to never offer all I have, because someone would ask for it. What if Chesleigh asks for the whole kingdom? What is he willing to sacrifice for an advantage in this war?

She doesn't. "A thousand silvers," Chesleigh says.

My heart gives a jolt. It's a *lot* of money. He offered five hundred silvers to find the heir, and people were ready to kill each other to claim it. At my back, Zo gives a low gasp.

"Tell me what you have," says Rhen.

Chesleigh draws a dagger from her belt and holds it out. "Made of steel from the Iishellasa ice forests," she says. "Impervious to magic."

Rhen takes the blade from her, and he weighs it in his hand. The weapon looks aged, with braided leather around the hilt that seems to have thinned in spots from wear. But the blade itself is polished silver, and it looks sharp enough to cut through stone.

He looks back at her. "It could be just a dagger."

She shrugs. "Indeed. It could be. The blade will cut through flesh regardless." She pauses. "I have no magesmith handy. Do you?"

Impervious to magic.

I have no magesmith handy.

I stare at Rhen, but he's looking at Chesleigh. "A thousand silvers." He slips the dagger into his belt. "Done."

Does he mean to use this weapon against Grey? Or Lilith? Or both?

I'm scared of the answer—because I think I already know. This is like the moment he chose to string Grey up on the wall. He didn't tell me, because I didn't want to know. I don't want to know now. I don't want to think of him plotting to kill Grey.

But of course, this is war.

In a move that surprises no one, Rhen has decided to inquire about strategy. "How big of a force does Syhl Shallow have remaining?" he says.

"At least a thousand soldiers," she says. "They've been training hard. Twice a day."

"His soldiers will be fit and prepared for battle," says Rhen. "As will mine. I've given orders to send a regiment to the border this morning."

At least I know about *this*. I'm spurred into offering, "Jamison mentioned that."

"Yes," Rhen says, and his tone is almost clipped. "I heard you spoke with the lieutenant."

I inhale to snap at him, but Chesleigh's head is turned just a bit, and I'm aware that we have the attention of everyone in our traveling party. At my side, Zo murmurs, "My lady."

I clamp my mouth shut. I let my horse drift back a bit, putting distance between me and him. I'm so . . . something. I can't even pick apart my own emotions, but I want to give Rhen the finger, and at least that's better than sobbing.

I wish I hadn't come along. I'm not even sure why I'm needed right now, especially when riding feels like torture, each step jolting through my body and reminding me of what Lilith did.

When we reach Silvermoon and leave the horses in the livery, Rhen says, "My lady, you will surely be bored with my negotiations with the Grand Marshal. Chesleigh will be able to accompany me to discuss our plans." His tone is a bit cold. "Perhaps you would like to walk the market with Zo?" He holds out a pouch of coins.

I might have been able to keep my mouth shut while we were walking, but there's only so much I can take. I shove the coins back at him. "I've got my own money. Thanks." I offer him a belligerent curtsy and turn away.

At my back, I hear Chesleigh chuckle and say something under her breath.

My hands form fists. The only thing keeping me from swinging one is that Chesleigh looks like she could knock me flat without breaking a nail.

Zo quickly says, "Come, my lady. Which stall would you like to visit first?"

"Let's hit the bowyer," I say, making no effort to keep my voice down. "I have a feeling I'm going to want a weapon later."

* * *

What's really sad is that I never travel anywhere without Rhen, so I *don't* have my own money.

Despite my tumultuous emotions, I'm glad to be walking the

stalls in the late autumn air instead of listening to Rhen and the Grand Marshal. I really don't know much more than basic military strategy, despite the number of times I've watched Rhen pore over his maps and discuss troop placements with his advisors. When they're little steel figurines on a map, it's easy to forget that the whole point is to chart out the locations of real live soldiers who will be expected to kill or defend. I care about people. I don't like thinking of ways to kill them more efficiently. For months, I had nightmares about Syhl Shallow's first invasion, when Rhen was a monster who tore the soldiers apart. Night after night, I'd hear the cries of men and women whose limbs had been severed, or the screams from people whose intestines were spilling out of their bodies, or I'd see the blind eyes of people who'd never draw another breath.

And we're just going to do it again. I should have let Lilith take me back.

"Harper," says Zo, and I swallow and blink at her.

"Sorry," I say. "It's been a long day." I pause. "Thanks for getting me away from Rhen. I don't know why he's being so . . . whatever." I blink away tears. "It's really good to see you in armor again."

Zo smiles. "It is good to wear it again." She gives a self-deprecating shrug. "I was worried you would be upset that His Highness did not ask you first."

"No." I shake my head quickly. "No, I've felt guilty for . . . forever. It was my fault that you lost your job."

She looks at me like I'm crazy. "No. It wasn't."

"I shouldn't have made you go after Grey—"

"You didn't make me." She takes a breath and blows it out through her teeth. "You wouldn't have had to make me."

I think back to that moment when we stood in the small yard

behind the inn, when Grey and Tycho were so injured from the flogging that they could barely stand. Back then, even though Lia Mara
was not destined to be queen, she offered to grant them safe passage
to Syhl Shallow. She offered them an escape from Rhen.

"I've wondered a thousand times if I should have gone with
them," I say quietly, as if the words need courage to be spoken fully.

Zo nods, her expression musing, which makes me think she
wonders the same thing.

"Would you have gone?" I ask, and my voice is very soft because
I'm not sure I want the answer.

It's probably not even the right question anyway.

Should I have gone?

As usual, I don't know if I'm more angry at Rhen or more angry
at myself.

"Yes," says Zo, and I flinch. She looks at me. "I would have gone,
if you had wanted to go. But you did not just stay for the prince.
You stayed for Emberfall." She swears and looks away. "The guards
should know that. His Highness should know that."

Tears flood my eyes again, and there are too many to blink
away. I'm sure I look super regal right now. I glance around at the
merchant stalls to find that many people are peering at me with
dark curiosity, but there are a few glimpses of outright hostility.
Rhen is not popular here in Silvermoon. Neither am I, I guess. Or
maybe they don't know who I am. This is the first time I've ever
visited a city without Rhen by my side.

Either way, it makes the tears dry up real quick.

I wish I'd taken the pouch of silver. Rhen always says that a little bit of honest coin in someone's palm can shift loyalties. It would
sound callous and manipulative from anyone else, but I've seen his

generosity toward his people, the way he's bolstered business and trade across Emberfall. Grey has supporters here, people who would rather see him on the throne because so many people blame Rhen for the kingdom's downfall during the time of the curse. But they forget that Rhen was the one to bring this country back from the brink of ruin.

I can see it here in Silvermoon, the changes since I first visited: No one is thin anymore. Clothes, while simple, are not worn threadbare. Shoes and boots seem well-tooled and free of holes. At the food stalls, plates are piled high with roasted meats and spiced vegetables, and goblets are filled to the top with wine, not halfway as they were the first time we visited.

But they believe someone else is heir, so none of that matters.

They believe my inability to produce Disi's "army" left them vulnerable, so none of that matters.

I'm guilty of it, too, I realize. Rhen did so much good—*so much good* that I used to be in awe at his never-ending work ethic—but as soon as he took action against Grey, it seemed to overshadow everything else.

I sigh. We wander. The marketplace doesn't seem crowded, which takes me by surprise. There's a weird feeling in the air. It's not hostile, and I can't quite figure it out, but it's leaving me unsettled. I thread my fingers through silken fabrics and examine blown glass figurines. Everyone is cordial—at least to my face—but I can't help remembering the first time we were in Silvermoon, when Rhen and I were attacked, and we barely escaped alive.

I have to swallow my nerves. It's not like that now, but I'm keenly aware that I only have Zo at my side.

By late afternoon, no one has tried to kill me and I'm starving.

The ache from whatever Lilith did has gone away, and my pride won't let me seek out Rhen. He's probably busy anyway. Zo and I have made it to the back part of the market, where the vendor stalls are twice as wide, selling more expensive goods: finely tooled weapons, beaded gowns, leather and furs, and polished jewels. Silvermoon's guards and enforcers are more plentiful back here, and I relax a little bit.

When we draw near to the musician's stall, Zo's eyes light up, and a short, round woman in a dress of dyed homespun wool dashes out from behind the counter. She looks to be near fifty, with weathered tan skin and gray hair that's been cropped short. Her smile is brighter than the sun.

"Zo!" she cries, rushing toward us. "Oh, Zo, you are a *sight*." Then she stops short and grabs hold of her skirts, bobbing a quick curtsy to me. "I beg your pardon, my lady."

I can't help but smile back. "No need."

"I know better than to run at a member of the Royal Guard," she says, with a bit of feigned awe in her voice. "Even if I knew the guard when she was still tripping over her braids in her rush to beat my boys at whatever nonsense they were getting up to."

"Someone had to," says Zo. She's smiling. "My lady, this is Grace. Her husband is the Master of Song for Silvermoon. Grace, this is Princess Harper of Disi."

Grace's face freezes for just the briefest moment, making her smile seem a bit forced, but then she curtsies again. "I am honored."

"So am I," I say. "Zo speaks fondly of her time as his apprentice." This is true, but I also know Zo hated that her parents forced her into music when she longed to be a soldier or a guard. She spent every free moment she had learning swordplay and archery.

As someone who was once forced into taking ballet with bribes of horseback riding lessons, I think it's the first thing Zo and I ever bonded over.

"Where is Master Edmund?" says Zo. "Will he be playing later?"

Grace hesitates again, but then she waves a hand. She probably intends for it to look casual, but it seems a bit forced. "Oh, he's with the crowd that went to meet the prince."

I frown. "The crowd?" There wasn't supposed to be a crowd. Rhen was supposed to meet with the Grand Marshal about his soldiers or his army or some kind of military planning. We didn't bring a contingent of guards to meet a crowd.

Especially in a town like Silvermoon, where Rhen's popularity is questionable at best.

A spike of fear drives right through my spine. I might be pissed off, but I don't want something to happen to him.

I don't want him to be forced to take an action he'd later regret.

Zo is already two steps ahead of me. Her eyes are on the people around us suddenly, as if she senses a threat. "Harper," she says urgently, her voice low. "We should—"

"I know. Let's find him."

CHAPTER TWENTY-ONE

RHEN

No one has tried to kill me, but this feels like an ambush all the same.

Hundreds of merchants and laborers pack the courtyard in front of the Grand Marshal's home. They're angry, all shouting questions at once. They want to know why they should pay taxes to the Crown if I'm determined to remain allied with a country that failed to produce an army. They want to know why soldiers forced their way into Silvermoon when the Grand Marshal attempted to block access a few months ago. They want to know how we're going to stop another invasion from Syhl Shallow.

They want to know why I think I have any right to be here.

I can't answer any of their questions like this—and it wouldn't matter anyway. They're too loud, too angry. Dustan and the other guards have formed a barrier between me and the people, but I only brought eight guards for this visit. Our horses are stabled in the livery, so we can't flee.

I do not understand how fate can consistently deliver such conflicting results all at once. I'm at odds with Harper again—but I have a dagger at my waist that could stop Lilith. I finally have insight into Syhl Shallow's movements—but I have an angry crowd at my feet.

Dustan has a hand on his sword, but he hasn't drawn it yet. Neither have the others. Right now, the people are just angry, but a weapon has the potential to turn anger into a death sentence. I've heard Dustan's reports about their attempt to take Grey when he was in Blind Hollow, how the townspeople turned on the guards and soldiers and drove them out of the city.

Rebellion is contagious, my father used to say. All it takes is one unchecked rebel and you'll have a dozen more in a matter of days.

This is more than a dozen. I wore armor as a symbol of strength, but now I'm wondering if it's going to be a necessity. My earlier frustration with Harper has vanished, replaced with a biting panic that she's somewhere in the marketplace, mostly unguarded.

I can't even send a guard to find her, because they'd have to fight their way through this crowd first.

Anscom Perry, the Grand Marshal, is on the steps with me, standing to my left, but he looks a bit smug. His own guards surround the courtyard, but they're taking no action. At this point, I'm not even sure whose side they'd be on if a fight erupted.

Chesleigh is off to my right, and she looks grim. She's got a hand on her own weapon. She brings me stories of unity and progress in Syhl Shallow, of *preparation*, and here I can't even meet with a man about aligning his private army with my own.

I felt like a failure for the entire duration of the curse.

Now I feel like a failure for an entirely different reason.

I look at Marshal Perry and keep my voice low. "You will ask them to disband."

"Why?" he says, unimpressed. "Do you not always ask your people to speak true?"

"Not like this and you know it."

A man shouts from the crowd, "You lied about forces from Disi!"

"You aren't the rightful heir!" shouts a woman.

Another man rushes forward and shoves one of my guardsmen, but he's quickly knocked to the ground. A child nearby screams. The guard begins to pull a sword.

"Hold!" I snap, and the guard hesitates. "I will hear your complaints, but I will not—"

"Liar!" shouts a man. "Liar!"

Quickly, others bring up the same chant. That man shoves my guardsman again, and I can feel the guard's frustration when he's been ordered not to draw a weapon. When the shove is unchecked, the crowd begins shoving at my other guardsmen. Someone spits in Dustan's face. He sets his jaw and holds his stance.

Chesleigh pulls closer to me. "Sometimes making an example of one gets the attention of many."

"If we draw blood first, this will end in a massacre. Possibly of my own men."

"I'm not talking about the crowd." She looks at Marshal Perry. "I'm talking about making an example of him."

"The courtyard is surrounded by my own guards," he says with a laugh. "Go ahead and try."

Months ago, when I traveled to Hutchins Forge with Grey, we were ambushed, but it was nothing like this. The Grand Marshal

and his Seneschal had plotted to manipulate me out of silver, and
when they failed, I was forced to make an example of the Seneschal.
I ordered Grey to kill him—the first time I'd ever given an order to
end someone's life. I'd caused a lot of destruction as a monster, but
it was the first time I'd been responsible as a *man*. It was horrible
then.

It would be horrible now.

My heart is pounding like someone has drawn a weapon on *me*.
This is like the moment Grey refused to reveal the name of the heir.
Emberfall is in danger, and my hand is being forced.

Every time I need to take an action like this, I hate it.

I hate it. But I see no other way out.

"You will tell them to stand down," I say tightly.

"I will do no such thing," he snaps.

"This is treason."

"It's not treason if you're not the rightful heir."

"Commander," I say, and my voice is rough.

He turns to look at me, and my guardsmen are well trained.
Another guard shifts to take his place. Dustan's hand is still on his
sword. Spit is still wet on his cheek.

I don't want to do this. Grey always made it seem as though it
was easy to take action, to accomplish these horrible things. I always
thought it would get easier every time I have to put lives at risk, but
it doesn't. It gets harder.

Marshal Perry must realize that I'm serious, because he takes a
step back. His guards have begun to shift forward. "You think you
can hold your people together this way?" he shouts. He spits at *me*.
"You're no better than Karis Luran."

My pulse is a roar in my ears. I inhale to give an order. His blood will be on the stones, and there will be no way to undo it. I can't undo what I did to Grey, either, but there was no other choice.

There is no other choice now.

I can all but hear the crowd suck in a breath. A pause, a hesitation.

A boy shouts from amid the melee. "Father!" he screams. Others are holding him back, but he jerks free and runs for the steps. "Father!"

"Luthas," snaps Marshal Perry, and his voice is ragged. "Luthas, get back."

"Rhen!" shouts Harper from somewhere distant. Her voice is so faint that I almost don't hear her. "Rhen!"

I turn to find her fighting her way through the crowd, Zo at her back. The people rock and shove against her, but she's fearless and gutsy and elbows her way past them. My heart lights with both relief and panic at the same time. Anyone could have a blade. Anyone could use her against me right here and now.

"Father!" shouts the boy.

"Luthas!"

One of my guards steps forward, his blade drawn.

I remember Grey at my side the last time we came to Silvermoon. I was speaking of the Royal Guard's prowess in battle. *It was once said that approaching the royal family was a good way to lose your head in the street.*

I jerk my eyes away from Harper, and I jolt forward, toward the boy. "Hold!" I snap. "Hold!" But the crowd is too loud, the tension too palpable. The guard's arm begins to fall.

I shove him away, throwing up an arm to deflect his blade. The sword falls against my bracer and skids off. The guard stares at me in shock.

The boy is on the ground, his arm up, his breath high and keening.

I look up, searching the crowd for Harper. As my eyes lift, the shouting around us changes. "It's the princess!" they yell. "The princess full of *promises*."

"Dustan!" I shout. "Find her!" But then I meet her eyes in the crowd—and just as suddenly, Harper disappears from view. My vision narrows with singular focus. I forget the Grand Marshal. I forget the people. I forget the war and the enchantress and the guards at my side.

I'm unaware of leaving the steps. I'm unaware of drawing my weapon. I'm in the thick of the crowd, shoving people away, resorting to my sword when they don't move quickly enough.

"Release her!" I shout. "Do not *touch* her." My rage burns the air around me, hot and thick. When I make it to Harper and Zo, they're on the ground, but the men surrounding them fall back.

Zo seems uninjured, but she's on one knee, her dagger up, blocking Harper. Harper's dress is torn, a long rip from the shoulder into the bodice. A panel of the skirts hangs awkwardly in the dirt. Her dagger is gone. She's got a swath of dirt across her scarred cheek, and she's panting, clutching a hand to her side, but she's trying to get to her feet.

I put out a hand to help her, but I want to bury this sword in the chest of every single man surrounding them. I want to do it *twice*.

Harper's breath hitches, and my eyes lock on hers.

"I'm fine," she says, but her voice wavers, belying her confidence. "I'm fine." But then her weak leg gives way, and she begins to fall.

I catch her, pulling her against me. It's only then that I realize she's trembling.

We've caught the crowd in a moment of indecision. There's still so much violent promise in the air. I can't tell if the people are more alarmed at what I was about to do—or at what *they* were about to do. My guards are at my back, and to my surprise, Chesleigh has followed them down off the steps with weapons in hand.

I look at the men and women surrounding us. "You will let us pass," I say. "Or I will execute every person who stands in our way."

"Rhen," Harper whispers against my armor.

"I mean every word," I snap, and I must look deadly serious, because a few of the men shift and shuffle back a step. These aren't soldiers. These are merchants and dockworkers. Weavers and butchers. Few of them are armed. Children stand among them.

They came with questions and accusations. They might have spit in Dustan's face and shoved my guards, but they didn't come for bloodshed.

I'm the one who almost brought it.

Dustan steps in front of me. His own sword is drawn. "Clear a path," he says sharply.

They do.

"Rhen," whispers Harper. Her fingers dig into my arm, and she tries to take a step, then stumbles. "Wait. I don't—I don't think I can walk. Just—just give me a minute—"

We do not have a minute. I sheathe my sword. "Hold on to me," I say, and I draw her arm across my shoulder, then scoop her up into my arms. She's so fiercely determined that I expect her to protest, but maybe she's as shaken as I am, because her fractured breath trembles against my neck.

As we stride out of the courtyard, the shouted questions and accusations resume. I keep my eyes forward, my arms tight around

Harper, striding all the way to the livery to fetch our horses. I want to be thinking of ways to resolve this, to earn back the respect of the people here. To build my army, to create a larger show of strength against the forces Grey is readying against me.

But instead, all I can think about is how I came here hoping to project a show of strength and purpose, and now this feels like a retreat.

I think of how my people almost died at my hand, when they simply came seeking hope and change.

I look down at Harper, and I think of what she did—what she *stopped*—and what she risked.

This might feel like a retreat, but at this moment, I don't feel as though I've lost anything at all.

Harper and I haven't ridden double since the first day she arrived in Emberfall. Then, she'd tried to escape from Ironrose and ended up saving Freya and her children. We needed extra horses, so Harper rode at my back when we went to the Crooked Boar Inn to secure a room for the others. She hated me then.

She might hate me now, honestly. I have no idea.

Then again, I don't *think* so. Her arms are tight around my waist as Ironwill steadfastly canters along the road. She did not balk when I considered her pained expression and offered to share a horse.

But she hasn't said anything since we left the city.

Nor have I.

My feelings of betrayal from hours ago, when I learned of Lilith's visit, have wilted and shriveled into nothing. That felt petty and impudent, the way I was in the early days of the curse, when I thought

I could stomp my foot and give an order and the world would right itself. She was trying to protect me, as I've tried to protect her. In the castle, in front of my guardsmen, it made me feel weak and powerless. But when I saw Harper overwhelmed by the men in that crowd, I . . . I forgot everything else.

Once we've put a few miles between us and Silvermoon, I let the horse slow to a walk. At my back, Harper remains silent. Dustan rides close, but the other guards have fallen back. Chesleigh is among them, riding beside Zo.

On the steps, Chesleigh said, "Sometimes making an example of one gets the attention of many," and those words keep ringing in my thoughts. It feels like something my father would have said. My father would have killed Marshal Perry without hesitation. My father wouldn't be in this mess.

I keep telling Harper that Grey isn't suited to be a king when I have no idea whether *I* am.

"I'm sorry," she says quietly.

Harper's soft voice at my shoulder takes me by surprise. No, the *apology* takes me by surprise.

I turn my head slightly, seeking her eyes, but she's looking out at the countryside, her cheek pressed to my shoulder.

"I just wanted to warn you," she continues. "I mean . . . I guess you didn't need it. But I'm sorry I . . . I ruined whatever you were going to do."

I spend a moment trying to figure out her tone. It sounds suspiciously similar to the way I feel: Uncertain. Ineffective. Vulnerable.

"You ruined nothing," I say.

"Well, you were about to say something to the crowd, and I came crashing in—"

"I was about to order the death of the Grand Marshal. One of my guards was about to slaughter his son."

That shocks her into silence, and I can't tell if that's a good thing or a bad thing.

"As you see," I continue. "You ruined nothing. You stopped me from taking an action I could not undo." I pause. "I want my people to have faith that I will do right by them. I have spent so much time resorting to violence that it has begun to feel like the only solution."

She's still quiet, but I sense her judgment riding on the cold air. Ironwill tugs at the reins, so I give him another few inches to stretch his neck, then reach out a hand to rub the itchy spot under his mane, just where he likes.

"I thought you were mad," Harper says.

"Mad?" I feel her shift, so I turn my head and catch a glimpse of her blue eyes. "I am furious that Marshal Perry sought to trap me. I don't think his intent was violence, but it could have quickly turned to that. I am angry that I anticipated gaining another few thousand soldiers for the King's Army, and now I am leaving empty-handed."

"No—I mean, I thought you were mad at me."

I hesitate, then rest a hand over hers, where she grips tight against my sword belt. Her fingers are cold from the wind, but they grow warmer under mine. "No. I am grateful that you thought to warn me." Another pause, as I consider the order I was about to give. "I am grateful that you arrived at exactly that moment."

She's quiet again, but this time it's contemplative, so I wait.

Eventually, she says, "But . . . you were pissed off before. You were being such a jerk on the way to Silvermoon."

"Ah." I frown. "I was struggling with thoughts of betrayal."

"Betrayal." Her voice is hollow. "Like . . . with Chesleigh?"

"What?" I turn my head again. A cold breeze rushes across the fields, making her shiver at my back. "Betrayal with Chesleigh? I do not understand."

She ducks her head. "Never mind. What kind of betrayal?"

"Lilith came to you."

She freezes. I can feel the shock reverberate through her body. "Dustan told you."

"He is my guard commander. Of course he told me."

She straightens, her head lifting from my shoulder. "I should have known." She raises her voice. "Hey, Dustan. Maybe you should—"

"Harper." I keep my voice low, placating. "You once asked me not to fault those close to *you* for their loyalty."

She clamps her mouth shut, then sighs. "Ugh. Fine." She pauses. "He didn't have to lie about it."

"Neither did you."

She says nothing to that.

"Did Lilith harm you?" I say.

"Nothing that left a mark." She takes a deep breath. "She's awful, Rhen."

"I know." I pause. "Did you not think I would be able to bear such news?"

"If I don't want to be your pawn, I don't want to be hers, either." She hesitates. "I'm not going to let her use me against you."

"Yet she sowed discord anyway." I sigh bitterly. "It is her *gift*."

Harper says nothing to that. We ride in silence for the longest time, until Ironwill grows antsy and I draw up the reins.

"Thank you," Harper says then, and any ire in her voice is gone. "For pulling me out of the crowd." She shivers. "You looked like you were going to level the courtyard."

I cluck to the horse, and he leaps forward into a gallop, eager. Harper clings tightly to my back. "For you, my lady, I would have leveled the entire city."

CHAPTER TWENTY-TWO

HARPER

Something has shifted between me and Rhen, and I'm not sure what it is. Like something has cracked in him. It doesn't create a new tension between us. Instead, it feels . . . good. Like it was something that needed to break.

You ruined nothing. You stopped me from taking an action I could not undo.

He seems relieved. I think that's the most startling thing of all: his relief. I'd somehow forgotten that he doesn't want to resort to drastic measures, that at his core, he wants the best for his people.

Once we arrive at Ironrose, Rhen leaves Zo and the guardsmen to tend to the horses and find lodgings for Chesleigh, then helps me into the castle, mostly carrying me until we reach the stairs of the Great Hall, where I demand that he set me down.

He doesn't. "You could hardly dismount from the horse," he says. "I will see you all the way to your chambers."

"I can hold the railing."

"Hmm." He strides up the steps like I'm weightless. "I have seen the results of your other attempts to refuse assistance, so you'll forgive me for insisting."

"I never refuse assistance!"

He snorts. "Harper."

Harrrrperrr. The way he says my name makes me blush and shiver. He must notice, because a light sparks in his eyes when he stops in front of my chambers and eases my legs to the ground. I put a hand on the wall to keep my balance, which is a challenge even when I don't have a twisted ankle.

My other hand doesn't let go of his arm. There's a gouge in the leather of his armor, so I look down. There across the buckles is a deep rivet that's gone down into the steel. One of the buckles has been sliced clean through.

I frown. "What happened?"

"I told you: one of the guards was going to kill the Grand Marshal's son. I stopped him."

I open my mouth. Close it. I thought he meant with . . . with an *order.* Not his arm. He's lucky he didn't lose his hand.

"I'll call for your lady-in-waiting," Rhen says softly.

"No!" I think of Freya's tears earlier. "Don't bother her. I'm okay."

His eyes skip across my form, the torn dress that's only holding on to my left shoulder by a few threads and a prayer. "You will need assistance in dressing."

"I just need to unlace the corset. Could you—" I realize how this is coming out, and I flush. "I mean—I don't mean—never mind."

He feigns a gasp. " 'I *never* refuse assistance,' " he teases, his voice light and mocking.

"Fine." I lift my chin. "Unlace it."

The corner of his mouth turns up, his expression becoming slightly wolfish, which is *rare* for him. "Right here in the hallway, my lady?"

I smack him in the middle of the chest, which is ridiculous, because I'm smacking leather-coated armor, but he catches my wrist anyway, his fingers gentle yet secure against my skin. His eyes are intense and piercing in the dim light of the hallway.

I stare up at him until my heartbeat is a roar in my ears. My lips part slightly, and a breath escapes. He feels closer, intimidating yet not, reminding me of the moment in the crowd at Silvermoon when he looked ready to take them all on. For *me*.

I'd forgotten he could look like that. I'd forgotten he could *be* like that.

I swallow, and his thumb strokes over the base of my palm before he lets me go. His voice is lower, softer. "I will call for Freya."

"No." I catch his hand, and he waits. My cheeks feel like they're on fire. In a minute, his guards will be done with the horses and they'll appear in the hallway, or Freya will hear us out here and come to check if I need her. Either way, I'm going to lose all my courage in a second, and my instincts are telling me that Rhen and I have been fighting our way to this moment for ages now, and I can't let him go.

"Come in," I whisper. "Please."

For half a second, my heart stutters, because I expect him to refuse.

Instead, he nods. "Yes, my lady."

My chambers are warm, candles already lit in preparation of my arrival, the fire burning high in the hearth. Rhen helps me to the low sofa near the window, then drops to a knee to unlace the boot on my injured ankle.

"I can do that—" I begin in protest.

He silences me with a look. When he pulls the boot free, it's both agonizing and a miracle. I can see the swelling even through my stockings. Rhen frowns up at me. "I should call for a physician."

"No. It's fine. It's just a sprain. It's okay if I don't stand on it." I make a face. "It's not like I don't already have a limp."

He pulls the laces on the other boot, then drags that one free, too. He's hardly touched me, but I shiver anyway, goose bumps springing up all along my arms.

That gets his attention, but not for the right reason. "You are cold," he says, straightening. "I should fetch a blanket."

"You should remove your armor," I say, and his eyes flash to mine. "I mean." I clear my throat and tuck a loose strand of hair behind my ear. My eyes skip away from his and land on his sword belt, which is not better. I look at the wall instead. My face is on fire. "I'm fine. The armor—it's uncomfortable."

He studies me. I can't look at him now. He saved my life like a fairy-tale prince, and now I'm a blushing puddle in a chair.

A knock at the door saves me.

"My lord," calls a voice.

"Dustan," says Rhen. He touches a gentle finger to my chin. "I will return in a moment."

There is something wrong with me. I press my hands to my cheeks as if that will cool them. I need to think. I need to hear what he's saying, what orders he's giving. I need to know what he's *planning*, so I can act accordingly—

And then Rhen is back and I have no time for any of that. I can taste my heart in my throat.

He's unbuckling the sword belt, slipping the leather across the buckle. I've seen him do it a million times, and it shouldn't make my heart flutter, but it *does*, and I have to look away again.

"I have asked Dustan to send for dinner," he says quietly. He rests the sword in one of my armchairs, and then his nimble fingers turn to the buckles on his bracers. "Zo said you did not have a chance to dine in Silvermoon."

"No," I say, but it's a miracle my brain can focus on what he's saying, because my eyes are transfixed by the movement of his hands. The bracers land on the armchair next. He only unbuckles one half of the breastplate before jerking it over his head and tossing it with the rest of his armor. Somehow that's more alluring than the slow, agonizing removal of everything else.

He's always so buttoned up, so *perfect*, that it feels like a privilege to see him in trousers and shirtsleeves, just that lone dagger left at his waist. His blond hair is in a bit of disarray, and the first shadow of beard growth has appeared on his jaw.

But then he's done, and standing there, studying me so intently that I have to hold my breath.

"I should call for Freya," he says, and his voice is a touch lower. "You will want to dress."

I don't want to call for Freya.

I swallow, then nod at where my lady-in-waiting has hung a sleeping shift and a dressing gown beside the wardrobe. "She already laid out my clothes." I hesitate. "If you could handle the lacing up the back."

His eyes narrow slightly, but his gaze burns into mine. "As you say."

He fetches the clothes, then helps me stand, and I brace a hand against the arm of the sofa when he moves behind me. He's so close that I can feel his warmth and hear his breathing. When his hand brushes my shoulder, moving my hair to the side, I nearly jump.

But then his fingertips slow against my skin, tracing a line lightly. "You're bruised here."

I crane my neck around to see him, and there's a thunderstorm in his eyes. "Am I?"

"Lilith?" His voice has taken on a new weight. "Or the crowd at Silvermoon?"

"Either? Both. I don't know." I pause. "Does it matter?" I say humorlessly.

"It does to me." His breath eases against my skin, and I go still. "You did not need to keep her a secret, Harper."

Harrrrperrr. I close my eyes and inhale. He shouldn't be allowed to say my name like that when I'm . . . I don't know what I am. Like this.

He's quiet for a moment, and then the laces of my corset tug and loosen as his fingers work the ties. "I did not intend to be cruel on the ride to Silvermoon. Forgive me." His hands slow. "It was a blow to my pride. To think that you believed a visit from Lilith would undo me."

"What? No." I whirl to face him, jerking the ribbons free of his hands. It's too much movement on my ankle, and my leg begins to give way.

Rhen catches my waist, holding me upright. There's hardly an inch of space between our bodies.

"No more lies between us," he says, and his voice is gentle but firm.

"I wanted to protect you," I whisper.

"As I want the same for you." He lifts a hand to trace the line of my face. "Perhaps we are both determined to go about that in the wrong way."

I stare up at him until I realize what he's saying. Have we spent so long seeing each other's vulnerabilities that we forgot each other's strengths? Is that why it was such a shock to see him stride through the crowd at Silvermoon?

"Shall I finish?" he says, his voice a gentle rasp.

It takes me a moment to realize he means the dress. His hands are barely holding the loosened corset in place. I have an underdress beneath it, so I'm not in danger of everything falling to the floor, but still. Since coming to Emberfall, I've learned what people mean when they talk about a glimpse of ankle or shoulder being sexy.

I turn in his arms, and his fingers take up the lacings again. The corset finally gives, and I toss it onto the sofa, folding my arms against my chest instinctively. Rhen doesn't move from behind me. His hands have settled on my waist again, and I can feel every finger. A tiny gasp escapes my mouth.

"The skirts as well?" he says, and he's moved closer, because his voice speaks right to my ear, his breath warm on my neck.

I can't breathe. I nod quickly.

He doesn't hesitate. His fingers brush the small of my back as he works the lacings there, and my entire body flushes. "Ah, Harper." His mouth finds my shoulder, and a tiny sound leaves my throat. The lacings give, and the skirts pool on the floor, leaving me in the thin underdress. I don't know if my knees will keep holding me.

They don't need to, because Rhen's arm snakes around the front of my body, pulling me against him, and I hiss in a breath. His mouth finds my neck, his free hand sliding along my hip. I'm dizzy and breathless, but everywhere he touches, it lights a fire inside me. I try to turn, to face him, but he's strong enough to hold me in place, his hands slow and seeking, his teeth grazing the sensitive skin of my neck.

"Rhen," I whisper. My hands fall over his, but I'm not sure if I want him to stop or keep going. "Rhen."

"My lady?" he says, and there's a touch of humor in his tone—but there's a true question there, too. His hands have stilled.

I lean into him, into his warmth, into his strength. This thin fabric leaves nothing to the imagination, and goose bumps spring up along my skin when I realize how *very* closely we're pressed together. I shift slightly against him, and Rhen makes a low sound that's half growl, half plea. The hand at my hip tightens.

A knock sounds at the door. "Your Highness," calls a muffled voice. "Dinner has arrived."

Rhen sighs, then rests his forehead against my shoulder. "Silver hell," he says, his voice both rueful and amused. "Fate must truly hate me."

I laugh under my breath, then draw his hand up from my hip to kiss his knuckles. "Grab my dressing gown," I say. "Maybe fate is giving us both a breather."

CHAPTER TWENTY-THREE

HARPER

I'm glad there's food to keep my hands busy, because I can't look at Rhen without blushing. Every time my eyes flick to his, I'm distracted by his mouth, by his fingers, by the way he lifts a glass to his lips.

I have to think. I have to talk. I have to . . . something. Otherwise I'm going to keep imagining the feel of his hands on my body.

I take a gulp of wine. "Rhen? What are you going to do about Silvermoon?"

He hesitates, like he needs a moment to think of how to answer for the same reason I needed a moment to think of a question. "I'm going to send word to the Grand Marshal that if his merchants and citizens would like to discuss their grievances, I will listen to their complaints if they are willing to present them in an orderly fashion."

That's not at all what I expected him to say, and I stare at him. "But . . . what about the army? Wasn't that the whole reason we went there?"

"Yes." He drains his own glass of wine. "Though in truth, I have no idea whether he had an army that would be willing to fight on my behalf, or if that was merely a means to get me to Silvermoon on his own terms."

"So what are you going to do?"

He rises to top off my glass, then refills his own. "I've been fighting against my people for months, Harper, trying to get them to unite once again. Today I nearly killed a man for daring to allow his people to question me." His voice turns grave. "I have no idea what I am going to do. But spilling blood in front of a crowd is not going to forge any kind of path to *unity*."

My whole body has cooled. I can't stop staring at him. "Wow."

He takes a sip from his glass. "My lady?"

Okay, maybe my entire body hasn't cooled. I blush again, then wince. "I . . . I don't know how to say this."

"No lies between us."

"Right." I smooth my hands against the silk of the dressing gown, feeling it slide along my knees. "I'm realizing that I got so caught up in the poor choices you made I forgot that you knew how to make good ones."

His eyebrows raise, but he thinks before he speaks, which is probably something I should have done.

"As did I," he says. "With you."

That's unexpected. I want to say that I don't know what he means.

But I do. He's talking about me helping Grey.

Just like I'm talking about him hurting Grey.

But I suppose we can add other things to that list. Like when he kept Lilith a secret.

When I did the same thing.

All the times I didn't ask for his help—and all the times he didn't ask for mine.

I swallow and look away. My body has gone cool from the track of this conversation, but like those moments we spent together in the barn, it feels good to have naked truth between us. "I keep thinking about my mother, and whether she made a bad choice in staying with my father. Jake and I spent so much time resenting him for everything he put us through. Like . . . if he'd been knocking her around, that would've been one thing. But he wasn't. He wasn't a bad husband or father. I think he was just . . ."

My voice trails off.

"A bad man," Rhen finishes quietly.

I flinch.

Rhen is quiet for the longest moment. "Do you fault your mother for staying with him?"

"Sometimes," I say, and the word almost causes me physical pain to speak it. "But then I wonder what that means about me."

He thinks about that for a while, and I know he's drawing the parallels I'm afraid to voice. When he speaks, I'm surprised that his voice is contemplative, not defensive. "I think of my father often. I've told you how he was never faithful to my mother. I think of how he had a secret child that he sent away to be raised in poverty. I think of how I could have had a brother, how I could have been second in line for the throne." Emotion tightens his voice, but only for a second. "How I never would have been a target for Lilith at all, how the magesmiths would not have been driven out of Emberfall. I sometimes wonder if the man was ever faithful to anyone who should have earned his devotion—or if he only thought of what *he* wanted in each moment of his life, and simply acted accordingly." He pauses. "I wonder if he would see me as a failure—and I also wonder if I would want a man like that to see me as a success."

I'm staring at him. The "secret child sent away to be raised in poverty" was Grey. This is the first time I've ever heard Rhen mention a brother with something akin to longing in his voice.

"What I have to remind myself," he says, "is that my father was dealt a different hand by fate than I was. Just as your mother's was different from yours." He pauses. "Do you fault yourself for staying with me, Harper?"

If he asked me the question in a challenging way, my hackles would immediately go up. But maybe that's why he doesn't. His voice is level and calm, a true question.

And it's such a *good* question, one that hits right at the core of every emotion I've felt over the past few months. I was angry at Rhen.

I blame myself.

Somehow, though, the way he's presented this has pulled the sting out of it. Maybe it's the realization that we both bring different experiences and different expectations to every challenge we face, those cards that fate deals. He's the tortured prince, and a million choices layered on a million other choices got him here. I'm the broken girl from the streets of DC, and I got here the same way.

Maybe my father thought he was doing the best he could.

Maybe my mother thought the same—and that's why she stayed.

Maybe that's all Rhen is doing.

He doesn't wait for an answer, but maybe he doesn't have to. Rhen's eyes shy from mine, and he picks up his glass. "I was surrounded by guards and weapons in Silvermoon," he says, "so I looked at all those people like a threat. But until the moment they fell away from you, I don't think I realized that all they wanted was . . . was a chance to air their grievances."

I hold very still. There's so much weight in his voice, I can feel it pressing down on the room.

He looks at me. "Much like Lia Mara simply wanted to forge a path to peace." He takes a long swallow from his wineglass. "Much like Grey wanted to spare me the fight to keep my throne."

"Rhen," I whisper.

"On that night in the Crooked Boar, there was a moment when you challenged me, when you commented that I was looking for a path to *victory,* when the curse required me to find a path to *love.* Do you remember that?"

Yes. I nod.

"I think of that moment often. I wonder if fighting against Lilith for so long made me forget that not every interaction is a challenge that I must win." He makes a humorless sound. "I wonder if Grey knew that, too. He often realized things about me before I myself ever did."

That longing note is back in his voice, and I shift closer to him. "You . . . regret what you did."

He nods, then drains the glass. "Very much. For so very many reasons."

He misses him too, I realize. But those shadows are back in his eyes, and his hand must be tight on the glass, because his knuckles are white.

He's afraid of the magic. That's the crux here, the basis of all this conflict. That's been the problem in this kingdom for far too long: the magic and the fear of it. That started before Rhen was even born—and then he met Lilith. Here, magic never stood a chance.

I gingerly put weight on my good foot, then reach to take the wineglass out of his hand. Then, like the night he first told me about Lilith, I curl into the chair with him, tucking my head under his chin, feeling him sigh against me, some of the tension easing out of his body.

I reach between us and grab the hilt of the dagger he bought from Chesleigh for an impossible sum of money, with no proof of whether it works. *Impervious to magic.* A weapon to bring down a magesmith. I pull it free.

Rhen catches my wrist, but his grip is gentle, his eyes on mine.

I rub a thumb against the hilt. "Despite everything, I do not think Grey would use magic against you, Rhen."

"This is war, Harper. He will use everything at his disposal."

"You're going to war because you're afraid of *Lilith*. You're risking your people—*his* people—because of *Lilith*. Grey asked for peace. Lia Mara asked for peace." I pause, thinking of that moment in the stables when he told me I would have helped him find a better way. He teased me about how I don't ask for help, and he's right: I don't. He once promised me anything within his power to give, but I don't like to ask for anything at all.

Maybe I should.

"Rhen," I whisper. "I'm asking you for peace."

He's almost rigid against me. Rhen does not back down from a challenge. Syhl Shallow caused a lot of damage to Emberfall—but so did Rhen himself. And Karis Luran is dead.

And Lilith wants a victory. Not an alliance.

He takes the dagger from my hand and turns it over, pressing a finger against the blade, but not hard enough to draw blood. "I have already sent a regiment to the border," he says. "And so has he."

"So . . . send a message. Ask for a conversation."

"If I send such a message, Lilith will—"

"Lilith is not the crown prince of Emberfall."

For an instant, he goes still. I'm not sure he's even breathing. But then he exhales against my hair, and he says, "Indeed, Harper. Neither am I."

My heart is pounding in my chest, but I shift to look at him. His brown eyes are dark, glinting with gold from the fire.

"You are right, my lady," Rhen says, his voice soft and resigned. He tosses the dagger onto the table. "As before, the only way to defeat Lilith is not to play."

"You're going to yield to Grey?" I almost can't believe I'm saying the words.

"I will try for peace." His eyes flash, a hint of that familiar spark in their depths. He traces a slow finger over my lips. "I am not yielding to Grey. I am yielding to you, Harper. For *you*."

My eyes fill. I wish he could see what he looks like right now. What he *sounds* like. I think somewhere in his brain, this feels like defeat, but it's not. Once again, he's putting his people first. Not just his people, but the subjects of Syhl Shallow, too. He's taking the hit so others can thrive. I've always thought that his greatest strength is when he's patient, when he waits, when he doesn't *demand* and instead waits for others to give.

I press a hand to his cheek. "For the good of Emberfall."

He smiles. "For the good of—"

I silence him with a kiss. It's gentle and soft and a bare press of my mouth against his, but every cooled nerve ending under my skin sparks a new flame. He makes a low sound in his throat, and then his hands land on my waist. I'm suddenly straddling his knees, my shift and dressing gown spilling down his legs. He pulls me closer, until I'm flush against him, my fingers tangling in his hair. I'm gasping, warmth gathering in my body, but the feel of his mouth on mine is so addictive that I don't know if we're slowing down or speeding up.

Then his hand finds my thigh beneath the layers of silk, and I suck in a breath. I'm wearing *nothing* under these gowns, and if his fingers move another inch, that's not going to be a secret. His mouth lands on my neck, though, and the thumb of his free hand strokes over my breast, and I shudder.

But then he stops. His hands venture no farther. He's breathing against me, his forehead against my neck. The air is suddenly full of hesitation. Uncertainty. Fear.

He's so strong and sure that it takes me by surprise. But I remember why we've never gone this far before.

My hands disentangle from his shirt, and I wind my arms around his neck, pressing close. I brush my lips against his jaw. At first he doesn't move, and I realize he's withdrawing the way he always does. Protecting me. Protecting himself. From memories, from fear, from the very real threat of an enchantress who takes every small joy and twists it to torture him in the most effective way possible.

"Don't yield to her," I whisper. "Don't even yield to the memory of her."

He draws back a little, just enough so I can meet his eyes.

"Don't yield to me either," I say, and I have to swallow past the sudden emotion in my throat. "Yield to yourself. Yield to forgiveness. Yield to happiness. Yield to this moment. It's not hers. It's yours. It's mine. It's ours."

"Ah, *Harper*." He closes his eyes, and for a moment, I think he's going to turn away from me. But then I'm lifted from the chair, swung into his arms for the second time today. He kisses me so deeply that I don't realize he's laid me on the bed until I feel his weight against me, and his hands are tugging at the skirts of my dressing gown.

This time, when his hand skates up my thigh, he doesn't stop. I almost cry out when his fingers touch me, but he catches my gasp with a kiss. He's so slow and determined that I can't think past it. My entire world centers on the feel of my body and the touch of his hand, at the heat pooling in my belly. I instinctively reach for him, my hand seeking skin, pulling at the suddenly irritating fabric of his shirt. My fingers find his waist, the smooth muscle of his abdomen, the tied belt of his trousers.

My hand drifts lower, and he hisses, then grabs my wrist.

"It has been a *very* long time," he says.

It startles a giggle out of me. Then he moves his other hand, and my back arches involuntarily. I see stars and clutch at the bedsheets. "Not too long," I say, when I can breathe.

He grins, and possibly for the first time in my life, I see Rhen blush, just a bit. He leans down to kiss me. "Let's see how much I remember."

CHAPTER TWENTY-FOUR

RHEN

Harper is curled against me, her breathing slow and even, but sleep eludes me as usual. The darkness presses against the windows and swells into the room like a silent visitor. The fire in the hearth has dropped to glowing embers, providing little light, but I don't mind. In the dark, it's easy to pretend there are no worries waiting for me outside her chamber doors. I'm warm and content, and Harper is at my side.

I want to touch her, to reassure myself that she is real, that she is *here*, that fate must not hate me as much as I thought.

Yield to yourself. Yield to forgiveness. Yield to happiness.

Happiness—is that what this is? The word doesn't feel strong enough. I forget, so often, that the most powerful moments in my life rarely end up being about my kingdom, or about a war, or about even my subjects. I forget that the world can narrow down to two people, to a moment of vulnerability and trust. To a moment of love that seems to outshine all the rest.

I told Harper that it's been a very long time, but being with her was like the first time. The only time it's ever meant so much. I want to wrap myself around her and never let go. I want to bury a sword in the chest of anyone who'd dare to hurt her.

As if my thoughts wake her, Harper shifts and blinks up at me. "You're not sleeping."

I roll up on one elbow and trace a finger along her cheek, then take a moment to revel in the fact that I *can*. We spent so many weeks treading carefully around each other that it feels like I have finally earned the privilege to touch her. "You sound surprised."

She blushes and nestles under the blankets until only her eyes and her curls are visible. "I thought you'd be tired."

I touch my nose to hers and whisper, "I am."

She doesn't smile. Her hand slips from under the blankets to press against my cheek. I turn my head to place a kiss on her palm.

She's still studying me. "Are you . . . are you still going to try for peace?"

She says it hesitantly, as if she expects me to walk back my vow. Last night, she spoke of her father, of all the ways he disappointed her mother, and I wonder if she worries the same about me. It tugs at my happiness, but I know trust is not something you win once, but is instead something you must earn over and over again. I nod and watch relief bloom in her eyes.

"I will send word to the regiment at the border to hold their position. I will have a delegation send word to Syhl Shallow that I would like . . . I would like to hear his terms." It's harder to say the words than I expect. So much has happened between me and Grey, and I cannot ignore the fact that he now bears magic. That he now stands with a country that caused so much harm to Emberfall.

Negotiating some kind of treaty with him feels akin to negotiating one with Lilith, and my chest tightens.

"It'll be okay," Harper whispers. "It'll be okay. I promise."

She cannot promise. She does not know.

"Anything is better than all-out war," she says, and my eyes lock on hers.

"Anything?" says a female voice in the corner of my room, a glittering shadow near the hearth. Ice slips down my spine at Lilith's voice. "Anything at all? Are you *sure*, Princess?"

"Get out." My eyes snap to the side table, where I tossed the dagger Chesleigh brought me. It's behind Harper, just out of arm's reach.

The enchantress slides out of the shadows. Normally, she's laced up in elegance and finery, the perfect courtly attire of a lady, but tonight she's in a violet dressing gown tied with a stretch of black satin, the fabric shifting across her body as she slips out of the darkness.

"*Such* a turn of events," she says, her voice a dangerous hiss of sound.

"He told you to get out," says Harper.

Lilith doesn't stop approaching the bed. "He does not command me, girl." Her voice is edged, angry, which is unusual. Normally she's playful. Truly *terrible*, but playful while she's wreaking havoc.

"What do you want?"

"It sounds as though you are attempting to change the terms," she says. She reaches the bed, and instead of stopping, she climbs onto the blankets, crawling toward us, her movements slow and languorous. Harper clutches the sheets to her chest and shoves herself backward until her shoulders hit the headboard.

Lilith smiles, but she doesn't go after Harper.

She goes after me. Her hand strokes up the length of my leg under the blanket, and I try to scramble back.

But she freezes. Harper appears beside her, the dagger clutched in her hand. "Care to lose an eye?"

My heart stutters in my chest. I don't know if Harper knows what that dagger could do. I don't know if it works at all. As always, I have so many hopes and so many plans and so many wishes, but the results always depend on fate.

And fate seems to hate me so very much.

"This reminds me of another time," says Lilith, and that dark look hasn't left her eyes. "When the sheets were rumpled and warm and the room was full of privileged satisfaction."

She slashes her nails across my body. They slice through the sheets. They slice through everything. Fire tears across my abdomen.

"Rhen!" shouts Harper. She lurches forward with the dagger, but my vision is full of spots and flares and I can't tell if she makes contact.

"When the room was full of blood," says Lilith.

She does it again. I can taste my own blood, and I don't know if I've bitten my tongue or if there's just so much of it. I can't feel anything but the pain, and her weight is on my body now.

Harper screams.

Lilith screams.

"Run," I shout to Harper. "*Run.*"

Lilith's face appears above mine, and blood is in a long crimson streak on her face. "You were *mine*," she hisses. Her nails claw down the front of my chest. I swear her nails scrape my ribs, and I cry out. "You thought your broken girl could stand against me with *that*?"

Harper is shouting, but my brain can't make sense of the words. I don't know if she's hurt, if she's fighting, if she's running, if she's dying.

Lilith's nails drag across my face. I feel my eyelid pull and tear, and suddenly that eye is blind with a wash of blood—or worse.

More shouts fill the room. My guards, led by Dustan and Zo.

"Harper," I gasp. "Harper, run."

"Stop!" Lilith screeches. "*Stop thinking of her!*" The windows shatter, exploding with glass that rattles across the floor. An icy wind sweeps through the room. I swing a fist to strike at her, but she catches my arm, and I feel the bones grind together. The pain is blinding. I try to breathe through it. I try to *live* through it.

She grips my jaw, and her eyes fill my vision. "You're going to watch her die," she says, her breath hot against my lips.

"I'm going to watch *you* die," I grit out.

She smiles—but then she's ripped away from me. I blink through blood and see Dustan bury a sword in her abdomen. She gasps, clutching at the blade. For an instant, he looks viciously victorious, but I know better.

"Run," I choke out. I can't watch her harm my people. "Get out. That is—an order."

Lilith takes hold of the blade bare-handed, dragging it free, the look on her face almost euphoric. Her silk dressing gown has spilled open, revealing a stretch of naked body, the sword bringing blood and other viscera with it. There's another wound, higher, pouring blood from her shoulder.

Dustan stares at her in horror.

He needs to run. He needs to run. He needs to *run*.

"Run," I gasp. "Dustan—"

Lilith tears out his throat with her bare hands.

His body drops, lifeless.

She turns for the guards who were standing at his back, their swords ready. In her fist, she's clutching the skin and muscle that she tore away from his neck, blood dripping down her wrist.

They blanch. Their swords clatter to the ground. They run.

I've seen it all before, when she first issued the curse.

It's no better the second time.

My eyes finally find Harper. She's got a bloodied dagger in her hand, but Zo is in front of her. I barely register that Zo has found my bow and quiver in the corner before an arrow is flying.

One strikes the enchantress through the neck. Then another through her shoulder. Another through the leg. Lilith staggers to her knees.

Another through her back. The enchantress is hissing, jerking at the weapons. She pulls one free of her neck and blood spills down her shoulder, but the wound closes just like the others in her abdomen.

That one slice in her shoulder remains unhealed, and blood continues to pulse from the wound. I stare at it, but my eyes don't want to focus and all I can think about is Harper.

Zo grabs the last arrow from the quiver. Her eyes are wide and afraid, but she takes aim.

"Rhen." Harper tries to limp past Zo to get to me.

"Go!" I cry. I try to get off the bed, but my knees won't hold me. "Zo—get her out. Get her out."

"No!" Harper screams.

Lilith stops jerking at the arrows. She's braced a hand against the floor, and she's wheezing now. This won't stop her, though, I know.

It'll just make it worse.

She grabs Dustan's lifeless wrist, pulling one of his throwing blades free. I realize what she intends to do, and I leap for her.

I'm too slow to stop the throw, and all I do is affect her aim. The blade doesn't drive into Harper's chest or neck—it buries itself in her upper thigh. She falls.

Lilith scrabbles for another.

"Zo!" I call. "Get her out. Get them all out."

Zo fires her last arrow, and it takes Lilith in the shoulder, throwing her forward. It puts us eye to eye again. But behind her, I see Zo drag Harper into the hallway. Zo is shouting orders at the guards who must be running to assist.

My body is in agony. I can't stand. I can't move. But suddenly it's silent. I'm alone with the enchantress.

For the longest time, I listen to Lilith's wheezing breath. I listen to my own.

The world begins to go spotty. Blood is pooling on the marble floor around me. Maybe she's finally done it. Maybe she's killed me.

But Harper got away. She got out.

Eventually, I hear a sickening pop, and I realize Lilith is pulling the arrows free, one by one.

Pop. Pop. Pop.

I blink at her. Only one eye works. I reach a hand to touch my cheek and find a mass of broken skin and blood. I try not to whimper, and fail. I wish for death to find me.

Lilith leans down and kisses me. There's blood on her lips. "I like you better like this," she whispers.

She got away. I lock my thoughts on that. Only that. Lilith can do what she wants to me. Harper got away. She's safe. Zo will keep her safe.

"Finish it," I breathe.

"Oh, no, Your Highness." She kisses me again, and my body involuntarily shudders. "You know I need you." She traces a tongue across my lips. "Now wait here while I go rip out her heart, the way you ripped out mine."

CHAPTER TWENTY-FIVE

HARPER

There are dead guards littering the castle hallways. Some are pinned to the walls with their swords, while others have terrible slash wounds. Blood coats everything. I remember the first week of the curse, when I discovered a room that represented what Lilith had done to Rhen and Grey. It was horrific.

This is like that, times a hundred.

Lilith must have been doing this for *hours*. Slowly and methodically killing his guards and servants, so we'd have no idea. I was begging him for peace while she was guaranteeing it would never be possible.

Freya and the children would have been in the room right beside us. Sweet, gentle Freya.

The thought of her dying at Lilith's hands almost makes my knees buckle. Zo half drags me past all of it. I can't decide if I should be helping her or fighting her. The throwing blade caught me in the thigh, but it was a glancing blow and it fell free. I know you're not supposed to pull a blade out of a stab wound, but I have no idea if it's okay for one to fall out on its own. Blood already soaked through my sleeping shift, and between the knife and the sprained ankle on top of my CP, I feel like a marionette with a broken string.

The night air is cold and smacks me in the face when we get outside, but Zo doesn't stop. I'm barefoot and panting in the stable aisle by the time she eases me onto a bench beside the stalls. It's the middle of the night and the stables are deserted. Her own breath is fractured and broken, making panicked clouds in the cold night air. Her hands are shaking as she starts unbuckling her breastplate.

"Stop," I say. My hands are flailing, wringing, uncertain where to settle. "Stop—what are you doing—"

"Here." She jerks the breastplate over her head. It sounds like she's wheezing.

"Zo—we have to go back. I have this dagger. We just need— we just need—she'll—she'll—"

She shoves the breastplate into my hands. "Put it on. I'll saddle a horse."

"Zo—"

"Put it on!" she shouts.

She's never yelled at me. I don't think I've ever heard her raise her voice. I'm so startled that my fingers start fumbling with the buckles automatically. The horses must feel our panic, because they're all circling their stalls restlessly. One of them kicks the stable wall.

"We have to go back." I'm babbling. Keening with each breath. Every time I blink I see Lilith's fingers ripping the front right out of Dustan's throat. I see Rhen's abdomen turned to ribbons of flesh. Like it was nothing. I wasn't strong enough. I wasn't fast enough. "She's going to—she's going to—"

"We have to run." She pulls a bridle out of the closet beside Iron-will's stall, followed by a cloak that she tosses at me. "Put that on."

I'm shaking so badly I can barely get it around my shoulders. "Zo—"

"We are *not* going back."

"We—we can't leave him—"

"She killed every guard in the castle," Zo says. It takes her four tries to get the bridle buckled onto the horse's head. "Can you ride?"

A boot scrapes against the cobblestones at the opposite end of the aisle, and Zo whirls, drawing her blade.

A stable boy swears and stumbles back. "I heard the horses—"

"Run," she says to him. "Get off the grounds."

"But—but—"

"Run!" she snaps. He nods quickly and darts through the door.

A cold wind whips through the aisle, making the stall doors rattle, and I shiver. "Zo. We need a plan. We need—"

She rounds on me. Her eyes blaze into mine. "What are we going to do, Harper? She *tore out* the commander's *throat*. With her *bare hands*."

She's right. I know she's right.

We need to get help.

I don't know who can help with this. She slaughtered all the guards. My breath hitches again.

Zo doesn't wait for an answer. She moves to the next stall and jerks the closet door open. Another blast of wind swirls through the aisle, reminding me of my first night in Emberfall, when the weather in the woods changed from autumn warmth into a heavy snowfall. The horses resume their pacing. A few give a nervous whicker. That one down the aisle kicks the wall again.

Every hair on my arms stands up.

I don't know what I can feel, but it's not good.

Zo appears in the doorway of the stall, and I know she can feel it, too.

"Zo," I whisper. "Zo, we need to go."

She leaves the second horse and returns to Ironwill, boosting me onto his back before I'm ready. Her foot slips into the stirrup, and she climbs up behind me. Without hesitation, she clucks to the horse, and we fly out of the stables.

The wind hits us hard and fast and nearly unseats me. Clouds have filled the sky, blocking the moon, plunging the grounds into darkness. I've got the reins, and Zo's got her arms around my waist.

"You should've kept the armor," I say breathlessly.

An earsplitting screech splits the night, the loudest, most terrifying sound I've ever heard. Ironwill's ears flatten and his back bunches underneath us, and he bolts like a . . . well, like a spooked horse.

"What is it?" Zo breathes into my ear. "What is she doing? Can she . . . can she shape-shift?"

"I don't know. I don't know." She made Rhen change shape, but I've never seen her do it. That doesn't mean she can't.

Zo remembers the monster Rhen became. Is that what's behind us? Did she do it again?

I steal a glance over my shoulder. All I see is the black sky, flickers of darkness. Another screech pierces the air. Ironwill flies into the woods, jerking at the reins, his hooves pounding into the ground.

We need to get through the woods. I don't know why, but there's always been something about the edge of Ironrose's territory that seems to limit Lilith's power. We need to get through these woods, and then we can figure out a plan to rescue Rhen.

Without warning, my throat chokes on a sob.

At my back, so does Zo's. Her arms grip tight.

I don't have words. I don't know what to say. My thoughts are in a blind panic. I keep searching for hope, but there's none. Everything is bad.

That screech rings out again. Something shoves into us, and Zo cries out.

"Zo!" I scream.

"Keep going," she says, redoubling her grip on my waist, but she's pulling at me, as if something has a grip on *her*. "Keep going!"

I dig my heels in to the horse's sides, but it's almost like Zo is on the ground, pulling me back. In a moment I'm going to be yanked off this horse.

Then she lets go. She's gone, her scream echoing in my ears, matched only by the screeching behind us.

I haul back on the reins, but Ironwill bucks and bolts and nearly gets me off his back. "Zo!" I cry. "Zo!"

Claws seize my upper arms, and I shriek in surprise. I'm being pulled, yanked, dragged.

"Let go of me!" I cry, and I wrench my arms free. Those claws hook on the armor that I never fully fastened, and suddenly, I'm being choked.

I have an image of Rhen pulling half-fastened armor over his head, ducking free of it. My chest catches with a sob, but I grab the breastplate and flip it up hard, scraping my face in the process.

But it works. She lets go. A screech of rage echoes behind me.

I cross the tree line out of the woods, duck close to Ironwill's neck, and we flatten into a gallop. My tears soak into his mane, and the wind catches my sobs, but nothing pursues us beyond the woods. We run and run until the darkness swallows us up.

CHAPTER TWENTY-SIX

RHEN

I lose track of time. There's a slow, incessant dripping somewhere to my left, but I don't know if it's been going on for hours or minutes or seconds—or years. I don't know if I've lost consciousness or if I've been awake this whole time.

The pain hasn't gone anywhere.

My left eye won't open, and my right eye is crusted with blood that drags at my eyelashes when I blink. Dustan's dead body is inches away. Blood has formed a puddle on the floor between us, but I can't tell where mine ends and his begins.

I remember this. From the first time, when she killed my guardsmen. When she turned me into a monster that killed my family. *I remember.*

I don't want to remember.

I lift a hand to touch my face, but I find torn skin and shredded flesh, and I suddenly can't breathe. I jerk my hand down, but the motion is too quick, and I whimper.

"Problems?" says Lilith, and I clench my good eye shut.

She doesn't wait for an answer. "Look what I've found," she says, and something loud and heavy clatters to the ground in front of me. Bits of blood and worse things splash up to hit me in the face, and I jerk away.

But it forces my eye open. It's an armored breastplate.

Zo, I think. But it could be anyone's. Any of my people. It's just a piece of armor.

Then a pile of red flesh lands on top of it. For the longest moment, my brain can't make sense of it. It's just a pile of bleeding muscle.

But then I realize what it is, and my own heart stops.

"Her heart, Your Highness," Lilith whispers. "As promised."

CHAPTER TWENTY-SEVEN

HARPER

If I were in the mood to think about mystical connections, I'd find it interesting that the Crooked Boar Inn seems to have become a place of solace and comfort when something goes wrong at Ironrose. But tonight, all I can think about is Rhen being torn apart while all his guards and soldiers are dead.

All I can think about is Zo, ripped right off the back of the horse while I galloped away. Or Dustan, his throat torn out right in front of me.

I press my fingers into my eyes and try not to sob while Evalyn, the innkeeper's wife, stitches up the wound on my leg and wraps a poultice around my ankle.

"Here, my lady," says Coale, the innkeeper, his voice a low rasp as he hands me a mug full of warm mead. My fingers are shaking, but I take it.

"The creature has returned?" says Evalyn, her voice hardly more than a whisper.

"I don't—I don't know what it was." I wish Rhen were here. He'd know a way to spin this, to get his people to rally and fight Lilith.

But of course if Rhen were here, if he were fine and well, there'd be no one to fight.

I was right yesterday. I should have just told her to leave me in Washington, DC. I should have told her to take me there originally.

I can't fight her. I can't ask anyone else to fight her either.

And I know if I go back, she'll just kill me. She'll probably do it right in front of him.

Rhen has spent his life hating magic, but right this second, I wish I had a shred of it, because I'd—

My thoughts freeze. The world seems to tilt on its axis, just for a second.

I don't have any supplies. I don't even have any clothes aside from a cloak and my dressing gown. The only weapon I have is this priceless dagger that was worthless in my hands.

But I suddenly have a plan.

"Evalyn," I whisper, and I almost shudder when I speak, because I have already asked so much of everyone in this room. "I don't—I don't have any silver, but I need your help."

She exchanges a glance with Coale, and new tears well in my eyes. I don't know what I can use to bargain. I don't even know *when* I'll get more silver.

But I've been poor before. I've been desperate before. Rhen teased me about asking for help—but I know what it's like when no one is around to give it.

"If you can't," I say, breathing away the tears, "I understand. I know—I know times are hard for everyone—"

"My lady." Evalyn puts her hands over mine and squeezes tight. I look up and meet her eyes. "You've done so much for us," she says. "So has the prince. All we have is yours."

"Tell us what you need," says Coale, his deep voice rumbling. He strokes at his thick beard. "We are well stocked for winter."

I swipe at my eyes. "I need clothes. And a map. And enough food for . . ." I do some quick calculations, trying to remember all the times Rhen talked about distance and travel time. I have no idea whether this will work, but I have no other options. "Four days. I think. Maybe five."

Evalyn's eyes widen. "My lady. Are you returning to Disi?"

"No." My tears dry up as hope flares in my chest for the first time. "I'm going to find Grey."

CHAPTER TWENTY-EIGHT

GREY

"Again," says the scraver, and despite the icy chill in the twilight air, I have to swipe sweat from my eyes. I'm breathing harder than I do after a long bout of swordplay or drills.

Honestly, I'd *rather* be doing swordplay or drills. It's been weeks of this. "I hate magic," I mutter under my breath.

"Yet you expect to coax it to your will with such adoring words? *Again.*"

I give him a narrow glare, but then I crouch and touch a hand to the ground, trying to send my power into an ever-widening circle. Some aspects of magic have come easily, like drawing flame from the wick of a lamp, while others have been more difficult, like knitting skin back together to heal. But sending power away from myself is proving the most challenging of all. It feels like running in an infinite number of directions at once—while tied to a boulder. Like I'm trying to tear myself apart and hold myself together simultaneously.

We're in the woods beyond the training fields, and snow flurries drift through the branches overhead, collecting in the grass between my fingers. My power feels each one strike the ground as I try to let my magic expand. I feel each blade of grass, each fallen branch. The warmth of the lone lamp I set near the base of a tree, which was unnecessary when we began but is now casting thin shadows along the ground. I achieve ten feet. Twelve. A hare leaps into a thicket, and I send my power to follow.

My power snaps back to me. It's like being shot with an arrow. I rock back and sit down hard.

I sigh.

Iisak drifts down from the high branch where he'd taken roost, landing silently in front of me. He's barefoot and bare-chested as usual, his dark gray skin like a shadow in the darkness, but knife-lined bracers are buckled to his forearms. Snow is collecting in the black hair that curls to his shoulders, drifting across the stretches of his wings.

"You run yourself too thin, young prince," he says.

I grunt. Maybe I do. But right now, I'd rather rely on skills I *know* will protect me in a battle than skills I haven't yet mastered.

"This should be effortless," he presses. "You should spend fewer hours on the field with your soldiers and more—"

"More here in the woods with magic?" I give a humorless laugh and spring to my feet. "Reports say that Rhen has sent soldiers to the border, and my magic can't stop them all. Spending less time on the fields isn't the answer."

"If you reached for your magic before reaching for a blade, perhaps you would not need to worry."

"Everyone here in Syhl Shallow thinks magic is a *threat*," I snap. "There are secret factions in the city that plot the queen's death."

"I believe they plot *your* death."

"Ah. That's better." I scowl. Iisak would have me practice magic until dawn if he had his way. I sometimes wonder if he is so focused on our success here because he regrets his failures with his son, the long-lost *aelix* of Iishellasa. I wonder if he dotes on Tycho and lectures me in an attempt to fill a chasm of loss. Right now, I don't care. This lesson in magic reminds me of the way I drove Solt through his drill, and it's not a fond memory. We've been at this for hours, and I was exhausted before we even started.

I nod at the knives Iisak wears. "I'm done with this. It's your turn."

"I hate weapons," he growls, and I can't tell if he's mocking me or if he's serious.

"Come on," I say. "I've already missed dinner." He's pretty lethal on his own, and I've seen him tear soldiers apart with his bare hands. But that all requires close proximity, and he was captured once before. A bow and arrows proved too cumbersome in flight, but the knives and bracers don't slow him down.

Like me with the magic, he's reluctant to practice with something that doesn't feel natural.

He slips a blade free. "One would think your mood would improve from all the time you spend with the young queen, but—"

"Knives, Iisak."

"Perhaps you should spend more time *sleeping*, instead of—"

Silver hell. I draw one of my own blades and throw it at him.

He leaps into the air, quicker than thought, and my knife drives into the ground a few feet beyond where he stood. He laughs, and a bitter wind tears through the small clearing. His wings flare, sending snow flurries spinning, but I catch a flash of light on steel an instant before he throws. I snatch my dagger and knock the knife away before it can embed itself in my shoulder, and I almost miss the second one that aims for my leg. It nicks my thigh and skitters into the underbrush.

I gather the knives from the ground. "You've been practicing."

"Quite a bit," he says. "Tycho is eager to have a student."

Tycho. My irritation is happy to have a new target. Tycho missed drills again this afternoon. It's the fifth time. His unit leader should be dealing with it, but she hasn't, and I'm not sure if that's out of some kind of deference to me or if they're happy to let him fail. Either way, it's one more fracture in the unity of the army here, and it's not as if we need more. I'm glad the boy is spending time with Iisak, because he is quite noticeably dodging me.

"I didn't know you were practicing with Tycho," I say. I wonder if Iisak is doing it for Tycho's benefit—or for his own.

"I am certainly not busy helping you with *magic*." Iisak throws again.

I scowl and knock the blades out of the air. "Put them in a tree," I say. "Not me."

"You look as though you long for distraction, Your Highness."

Maybe. Probably. The shadows are growing longer, the flakes of snow shifting to sleet that stings my cheeks. At breakfast, Lia Mara was rapt as Noah explained the reasons for the changes in the weather, how the *precipitation* would fall as snow thousands of feet up in the sky, and then melt and refreeze to form sleet. One of her advisors leaned toward another and whispered, "How can he know such things? I do not trust these outsiders and their *magic*."

Lia Mara overheard and cut them off with a terse, "Knowledge should not be greeted with scorn. You would do well to listen to Noah."

They silenced immediately, but I saw their exchanged glances.

Iisak's knives drive into the tree at my back with an audible *thock* each time. They were good throws, the blades driven deeply into the wood. When I reach to pull them free, Iisak slams into me from the side, his claws hooking into my armor, sending me to the ground. It knocks the wind out of me, but I roll and catch his ankle so he can't fly. He tries to claw at me, but I'm used to his antics now, and I don't let him get in a hit.

In seconds, he's pinned, one wing trapped under my knee, his throwing knives in my hand, one pointed at his throat. We're both breathing hard.

I usually don't mind sparring with him. Often I *enjoy* the challenge, because Iisak has no hesitation in breaking my bones and drawing my blood—along with the actual talent and skill to accomplish it.

Tonight is different. The sleet is falling harder now, stinging my eyes and creeping under my armor. Iisak probably loves it.

"If you don't need the practice," I say, "I'm hungry." I all but drop the throwing knives on the center of his chest and uncurl from the ground.

He slides them into their sheaths. "As you say, Your Highness." With a parting nod, he launches himself into the air, and in seconds, he's lost in the swirling darkness and branches overhead, probably off to find dinner for himself. I fetch the flickering lantern and walk.

The sleet grows heavier, slicking my hair and soaking under my armor, making a racket on the tin roofs of the soldier barracks just beyond the trees. I ease out of the woods onto the path, startling the soldiers on duty, but they quickly stand at attention and salute me. It's later than I thought if they've changed shifts. These two are adorned in hooded oilcloth cloaks over their armor, but it's still a miserable assignment in this weather.

"Who is your commanding officer?" I say to them. "I'll see that you aren't stationed here overly long."

They exchange a glance, trying not to shiver. "Captain Solt."

I inwardly sigh. Of course.

The paths between the barracks are deserted because of the weather and the late hour, and I wish I had thought to bring an oil-cloth cloak of my own. Lights twinkle along the wall of the palace, and I look for Lia Mara's chambers, because I'm sure she's waiting for me. Sure enough, a shadow darkens half her window, and lightness fills my heart for the first time today. I suddenly wish I *could* send magic tearing across the grounds, because I'd lace it with fierce longing and gentle wistfulness and unfettered hope, emotions I only dare to share with her.

Unbidden, my magic seeps into the ground, spreading farther with each step, almost like a light in the darkness that only I can see. I should have invited her to join me and Iisak, because her presence is always a reminder that my power never responds well to force, and instead needs to be invited to play. I feel each path, each drop of ice that strikes the ground, each stone along the base of each barrack. This has to be more than fifteen feet, but I try to relax into the feel of my magic as I walk, giving it little attention, as if it's a skittish horse that can be spooked by nothing more than eye contact.

Then my magic flickers against . . . something. A person? An emotion? Whatever it is, the sensation isn't positive like my thoughts of Lia Mara. But it's too quick, and I can't grab hold of it, and my sudden focus sends my magic spiraling back to me like the crack of a whip. I stay on my feet this time, but I drop the lantern and stop short. The lantern cracks with a little tinkle of glass and goes dark. I can't hear anything over the sleet.

Immediately, I think of the threats against Lia Mara, and I change course, striding between the darkened buildings, wondering if I should call for the guards by the woods or if that would be over-kill for a *feeling*. Still, there have been attacks on the queen. A faction against magic has formed in the city. As Iisak said, they likely plot my death as well. Just as I'm about to turn back for the guards, I hear a raised voice near the recruit barracks. A man is speaking in Syssalah, his tone thick with anger. I sigh and wonder if I'm going to have to break up a fight.

But I turn the corner and discover it's Solt. He's pinning a cringing recruit to the wall of the barracks with a hand against his shoulder.

Tycho.

I should demand an explanation. I should stride right up and call them to attention.

Before I've thought through everything I *should* be doing, I've shoved Solt away from Tycho with enough force that I nearly get him off his feet. He recovers faster than I'm ready for—I guess he can be quick when he wants to be—and he takes a swing at me. I dodge the first punch but not the second. He catches me right in the jaw, and it sends me to the ground, but I use momentum to roll. I have blades in my hands before I'm fully upright. Solt is a second slower, his hand on his hilt, his sword half-drawn before recognition dawns in his eyes.

He didn't know who I was when he threw that punch, but he knows now.

"Stop!" Tycho is yelling. He's got his hands up between both of us. Sleet slicks down his face. "Stop! *Nah rukt!*"

Don't fight.

Solt hasn't let that sword slide back into its sheath. He's never liked me, and there's a battle in his eyes as he wars with whether we should settle this right here. I'm sure he can see the same battle in my own. Blood is a sour taste in my mouth from where he hit me. He's stronger than I gave him credit for.

But then he straightens, letting the weapon fall back into place. He glowers at me through the weather. "Forgive me, Your Highness."

For half a second, I'm irritated that he withdrew so swiftly. But now Tycho's worried eyes are locked on *me*, not Solt.

I put my weapons away and spit blood at the ground. "Return to your quarters," I snap.

Solt salutes me sharply and turns away. After a brief hesitation, Tycho does the same thing.

I catch his arm. "Not you."

He looks up at me. When we were in Rillisk, he always seemed so much younger than fifteen, but time and experience keep whittling that away. Noah's warnings are loud in my memories, so I say, "Are you all right?"

He seems startled, like he wasn't expecting the question. When he tugs his arm free, I let him go, but his eyes skip away, dodging my gaze. He bites back a shiver. "I'm fine."

"He was pinning you to the wall. What happened?"

"No—he was—it wasn't . . . he wasn't hurting me."

The rain pours down, well and truly soaking through my armor now. I'm ice-cold, and the inviting warmth of Lia Mara's chambers feels like it's hours away. "Talk to me, Tycho."

He stares back at me steadily but says nothing. A new thought curls into my brain, dark and sinister.

"Is he threatening you?" I demand. "Is he harming you in some way? Are the others taking some kind of—"

"No! Grey." His eyes clench closed, but only for a moment, and then he squares his shoulders and looks back at me. "Captain Solt is fine. He was—he was *talking* to me—"

"I could hear him from two barracks away. Try again."

When he still offers nothing, I sharpen my tone to make it an order. "Tycho. *Talk.*"

He does shiver now, and I'm not sure how much is the weather and how much is me, but his eyes seem to shutter a bit. "He caught me sneaking back. It was . . . it was a reprimand."

I freeze. "A reprimand."

"He said I have an obligation to support my unit. He said that my absence will cause the other recruits to think they don't have to follow orders." His cheeks flush. "He said that if I hold a favored position with you, that I should do my best to prove it's earned, not given."

Silver hell.

His eyes shy away again, and he scowls. "He said a lot of other things, but I couldn't keep up with all the Syssalah."

I study him, but I must be quiet a moment too long, because he finally looks back at me, and any hint of immaturity has vanished from his expression. Just contrition and a little bit of belligerence. This is a soldier looking at a commanding officer. "I won't miss drills again." He hesitates, then tacks on, "Your Highness."

I almost correct him. He's never called me that before, and I've certainly never demanded it. The sleet slices through the air between us, and Tycho shivers again.

"Go," I say. "Return to your quarters."

He salutes, then sprints across the muddy grounds until he disappears between barracks.

I glance back up at the palace. Lia Mara has disappeared from her window. I know Jake or Nolla Verin will be stationed outside her room along with her guards, so I'm not worried, simply longing for her presence. That, and dinner and a warm fire. A chance to lose this sodden armor.

Those will have to wait.

I turn away from the palace and head back along the path through the barracks.

Instead of heading toward Lia Mara, I change course to go find Captain Solt.

CHAPTER TWENTY-NINE

GREY

The sleet has changed over to snow, collecting quickly in the grass and on the buildings, silencing the rattle on the tin roofs. In Emberfall, on the other side of the mountains, I doubt that snow has found Ironrose Castle yet. We only have a matter of days until we're due to advance across the border, to make good on my vow to Rhen, and I hope the weather doesn't get ahead of us.

My boots crunch through the frozen grass, and I draw to a stop in front of Solt's door. His curtains are drawn against the night, but smoke curls from his chimney and there's a glow at the edge of his window.

Ah, Tycho. I sigh and lift a hand to knock.

It takes him a moment to answer, and when he does, he looks surprised to see me. He's already removed his armor, and now he's in a simple linen shirt and calfskin trousers. His dark hair is damp and mussed up, his skin still ruddy from the cold.

His eyes turn immediately wary. Considering Karis Luran's

punishments or our last interaction on the training fields, he's probably ready for me to light him on fire.

"Tycho told me why you stopped him," I say.

"The other recruits have noticed his absence," Solt says. His accent is thick, thicker than many of the others', and I wonder if my language is as much of an effort for him as his is for me. "They need to be able to trust him to be ready."

"I agree." I hesitate. "I'm glad you had words. I shouldn't have stopped you."

Now it's his turn to hesitate. That wariness hasn't left his eyes. "His unit leader should have handled it."

"Yes." I pause. "And *I* should have handled it."

He studies me. Wind sweeps across the path, sending snow swirling.

"You have soldiers stationed by the woods," I add. "They should change shift every four hours in this weather."

His eyes turn flinty. "I have ordered them to change every two, but if you insist on four—"

"No." I feel as though my evening has been full of missteps on my side. "Two is fine." I take a step back and give him a nod. "Forgive me for the interruption." I pause. "Then . . . and now."

"Of course, Your Highness." This is said with a bit of bitterness, but a bit of genuine surprise, too. He steps back to hold the door open. "Would you like to come in?" he says. "I have *meleata* on the fire."

Meleata is seasoned rice that's been boiled with milk and dried beef, and it's a common dish among the soldiers here because it's easy to make and store. At first I thought it was awful, but I've learned that everyone makes it differently, affecting the taste with their own favored seasonings. Solt's quarters are filled with the aromas of oranges and cinnamon, which is inviting, especially considering my empty stomach.

But . . . it's Solt.

His gaze turns challenging, and I realize he expects me to refuse. That might be the only reason he offered at all.

I step forward through the snow. "I will. Thank you."

The door closes behind me, and despite the company, I'm grateful for the warmth. Solt keeps his quarters orderly, which is somewhat unexpected. He's always struck me as someone who skirts the line of what's acceptable in a soldier—but his talk with Tycho and now the state of his quarters make me wonder if I judged too quickly. His bedding is tucked in neatly, his armor hung near the fire. "You are welcome to disarm," he says.

"Am I?" I say darkly.

He startles, then laughs. "Or not, Your Highness."

He's not armed, and I'm not afraid of him, so I slip the sword belt free and lose my bracers and the breastplate. My shirt is soaked from the sleet and snow, and he tosses me a dry one. I'm surprised at the hospitality, but maybe he's surprised I didn't throw him out of the army. I peel my icy shirt free and don his.

He watches me change as he stirs the *meleata*, then frowns and flexes his hand. I wonder if he hurt it when he hit me. Any dark humor has left his expression. "I heard that you were . . ." His voice trails off. "*Rahstan.*" He gestures to his back. "Whipped?"

His voice is matter-of-fact, so I make mine match. "I was."

"Some thought it was a story," he says. "A . . . a myth? To lure the queen's trust."

"She saw it happen."

"Some thought that was a story, too."

"Hmm." I'm not sure what else to say to that. This is the longest conversation I've ever had with Solt, and I'm a bit thrown. He's a seasoned soldier, well into his thirties, with the first hints of gray threading the hair at his temples. For months now, I've assumed he was speaking Syssalah in my presence as a way of mocking me, and maybe a bit of it was, but listening to him stumble over his words now makes me wonder if he was ashamed at his lack of fluency.

"My brother and I got the lash when we were young," he says. "Bryon was caught with a general's daughter when he was supposed to be on duty, and he thought he wouldn't get punished because we were . . . *kallah*. Two of the same?"

"Twins?" I guess.

"Twins! Bryon thought, surely they couldn't prove which of us it was. He was wrong." He offers me half a smile, and something about it is a little sad, a little wistful. "Nothing so bad as"—he flicks a glance at my shoulder—"that. But I never forgot."

This is the first time I've heard him mention a brother. It should make me think of any of the siblings that Lilith slaughtered when I was a guardsman, but it doesn't. It makes me think of Rhen. "They punished you both," I say.

"They did."

"Where is your brother now?"

Solt fetches two bowls from a shelf near the corner, then begins to ladle *meleata* into them. His answer is long in coming. "He fell in battle." He pauses. "When we fought the monster."

"In Emberfall."

"Yes." His back is still to me.

I knew this would be an obstacle for me with the soldiers from Syhl Shallow. I just didn't expect it to hit me in the face so acutely.

I realign all of my interactions with Solt over the past few months, putting his anger—his *hatred* of me—into perspective.

Solt turns from the fire with the bowls and sets both on the narrow table in the center of the room, then pours two cups of something dark and thick from a kettle. He gestures for me to sit, and I do, but once he's sitting in front of me, he looks at the bowl, at his spoon, at his mug. At anything but me. I wonder if he regrets telling me this.

"I'm sorry about your brother," I say. "I didn't know."

He shrugs a bit, then dips the spoon into the rice. "Why would you?"

That's probably more gracious than I deserve. I touch my spoon to the food, then hesitate. The smell is warm and inviting, almost like something I've forgotten from childhood. It's not something I expected to associate with this man.

He misreads my hesitation. "You fear *poison*?" His eyes are challenging again. He sounds amused.

"No," I say, and I take a bite. I might not know him well, but if Solt wanted to kill me, he'd do it with his bare hands.

We eat in silence for a while, and I can't tell if there's any tension to it. This reminds me of my days as a guardsman, when you could be sitting across from anyone, even someone you hated, but at the end of the day, you were part of the same team, with the same motivations—and the same enemies. I've spent weeks trying to think of how to get the soldiers to respect me, to *follow* me, but maybe I've been going about it the wrong way.

Maybe I should have been thinking of ways to join *them*.

"Are you hoping to avenge your brother?" I ask quietly.

He makes a dismissive noise. "The monster is gone. I cannot kill it."

"Emberfall isn't gone." I pause. "I'm not gone."

He shrugs a little, then scrapes his bowl with his spoon, fighting for every last bite of rice.

When he doesn't answer, I add, "You wanted to fight me. When I shoved you away from Tycho." I pause. "You didn't."

He laughs a little, but not like it's really funny. "I saw how fast you pulled those blades." He flexes his hand again, and now I can see his knuckles are swollen. "I felt you take a punch."

I take a drink from the mug he poured. It's very thick and sweet, and I can't tell if I like it. I set the mug aside and hold out a hand. "I can fix your fingers."

He loses any hint of a smile.

I affect his manner and accent from when he asked about poison. "You fear *magic*?"

He smiles as if he's genuinely amused. He extends a hand, holding my gaze as I close my fingers over his. "Fine, Your Highness. Show me such wonders that you won the heart of our queen—" He inhales sharply and swears in Syssalah, jerking his newly healed hand away from mine. He looks from me to his fingers and then back again. The swelling is gone.

I pick up the bowl and take another spoonful of rice. "Such wonders," I say flatly.

He curls and uncurls his fist, and he glances at me with a new look in his eye. Less belligerence. Greater regard.

"It's all right," I say. "You can keep hating me."

"You ask why I did not fight you," he says.

I shrug. Maybe it doesn't matter.

"I couldn't lecture the boy about respect and duty," he says, "and then attack you." He pauses. "I can't defy your orders on the field. Five hundred soldiers report to me."

I study him.

"They are good women and men," he adds. "You are sending us to war. If I risk my position, who will they trust to lead them into battle?"

Not me. He doesn't say it, but he doesn't have to. He doesn't trust me either.

Something about that is . . . almost noble. I can respect wanting to look out for his soldiers. I can respect what he's lost. I can respect his wary regard.

"Your soldiers know you hate me," I say.

"Well." He grunts. "Many of them hate *me.*"

I smile.

Solt gestures at my empty bowl. "More?"

"No." I hesitate. "Thank you."

He stacks our bowls and sets them to the side, then takes a leather cup from a shelf, shaking it before rolling a dozen wooden cubes onto the table between us. "Dice?"

I think of Lia Mara, waiting for me, but I sense we've formed a tentative truce here. I scoop half into my hand. "Sure."

He sets a coin on the table. "I've heard this is a quick way to take your money, Your Highness."

That startles a laugh out of me, and I reach into my pocket to find a coin of my own. "The dice are never my friend." I glance at him. "Grey."

His eyebrows go up slightly, and he passes the dice from hand to hand. "You should wait to see how much money I take before you offer me your given name." He pauses. "*Grey.*"

"I'll take my chances."

"*Gehr Sehts?*" he says, and I nod.

Crooked Six. It's an easy game in theory, with equal elements of luck and skill, where you keep rolling dice until you have a full set of ones, then twos, and so on. I'm fast, but as usual, fate doesn't care, and he's rolling his final six when I'm still on my fours.

He stacks the coins. "Again?"

I put two of my own on the table. He wins again. And then a third time.

"You are making me feel like a thief," he says.

"That's good, because I'm feeling a bit robbed." I put my last few coins on the table, but I don't pick up my dice. "Your soldiers can trust me too, Solt."

He says nothing to that, but he picks up his dice and rattles them between his palms. There's a new tension across his shoulders, and I regret saying anything. When his dice spill out across the table, I don't pick up my own, so he doesn't re-roll. We sit there in complete silence for a moment.

Finally, he looks up. "I did not expect you to come here tonight." He pauses. "No, that is not true. I expected you to come here and have me sent to *Lukus*."

Lukus Tempas. The Stone Prison, where Karis Luran sent the worst criminals—and the people she hated. Maybe even people she vaguely disliked. I've heard stories about the punishments that used to go on inside those walls. Some of them make the enchantress Lilith look like a doting wet nurse.

"Because of Tycho?" I say.

He nods. Hesitates. I wait.

"Many of us worry you will lead us to slaughter," he says, and his heavily accented words are slow and careful. "There are those in the city who think your magic will protect you and leave us vulnerable. That you will join with your brother and let his forces overtake ours. That you will use our queen until she has no army left to fight, and then you will destroy Syhl Shallow the way we once attacked your lands."

I've heard these thoughts before, in whispers and rumors. This is the first time someone has confronted me with them directly.

Solt looks at me, dead-on, and his voice tightens. "The day we ran drills, I thought you meant to humiliate me. *Again. Again. Again.*" He makes a disgusted noise.

"I didn't mean to humiliate you any more than you meant to humiliate Tycho."

"Exactly." He pauses, then picks up two dice to slide them between his fingers. "A man who meant to lead this army to its death would not have come here to apologize to me. A man like that would not have cared."

I go still.

He scoops the rest of the dice into his palm. "You have been running drills with Jake," he says, and he's right. I've tried running drills with the soldiers, but ever since I ran Solt into the ground, they are reluctant to fully engage. I can never tell if it's because they don't like me or if it's because they don't care, but either way, it's never been effective.

Until tonight, I didn't realize why.

"Tomorrow," says Solt, "you should run them with me."

I pick up the rest of my dice for our final game and let them spill out onto the table. Not a single "one" at *all*. Solt has three, and he chuckles.

"I'm better with a sword than I am with dice," I say ruefully.

He grins. "I am counting on it."

CHAPTER THIRTY

LIA MARA

Snow falls overnight, blanketing the training fields in a thin layer of white, turning the forest beyond into a sparkling array of ice-coated trees. The windows of my chambers are cornered with crystals and frost. These early season snows never last long once the sun rises, but when I was a young girl, I loved waking in the morning to discover my entire world had changed overnight.

Grey retired late, climbing into bed after I'd fallen asleep, but he's up before the sun anyway, fully dressed and armed before I'm even aware he's awake. I roll over in time to watch him buckle a heavy cloak into place.

He meets my eyes, and the warmth in his smile melts my heart, because I know it's a smile he only shares with me. "I meant to let you sleep," he says quietly. "I will return at midday."

"No breakfast?" I say.

He pulls on fingerless gloves and ducks to drop a kiss on my lips. "Jake and I are going to eat with the soldiers."

"Wait—you are?"

"Yes." He pauses in the doorway, looking ready to fight a war this very instant, while I'm still blinking sleep out of my eyes. "Clanna Sun and Nolla Verin will see you in the strategy room when you're ready. They intercepted two messages regarding this anti-magic faction. They would like to double the number of guards at the city gates. I agree. And many of the generals believe we should send another small company through the mountain pass."

I'm not awake enough to process this. I certainly don't feel very queenly. "I—what?"

"We've received word that Rhen has moved soldiers into position. Once you make a decision, have word sent to the fields. If you choose to send soldiers, I will speak to the captains about who is best suited."

"But—"

He's already gone. I rub at my eyes and glance at the frosty window. He's dining with the soldiers? Maybe my world really did change overnight.

Nolla Verin must grow tired of waiting, because she raps on my door before I've finished dressing, and I tell the guards to let her in. She looks irate and impatient, and she's as trussed up in leather and weapons as Grey was. I'm surprised she doesn't stamp her foot when the door falls closed behind her.

"That foolish prince has already sent a regiment to the border," she says. "And you are not even *dressed*?"

It's so silly and juvenile, but her manner is so extreme that it makes me want to slow my preparations. I dip my finger in a pot of scented cream, then dab it on my neck. "That foolish prince is likely responding to the regiment *we* stationed on the other side of the mountains. Tell me about the messages you intercepted."

"*Those* have already been dealt with. You're welcome. In regards to the army, I have spoken with Clanna Sun and the generals," she says. "We will send two companies through the pass to station them north of—"

"Wait. Stop." I turn and look at her. For as supported as Grey makes me feel, Nolla Verin always makes me second-guess myself. Even the way *he* shared this news is completely at odds with the way my sister stormed in here. *When you're ready. Once you make a decision. If you choose.* He never attempts to wrestle control from me, which is always fascinating because I'd likely yield to him without hesitation. "What did you deal with?"

"The messages," she says with feigned patience, as if I'm too slow to keep up. "This faction seems to be making an attempt to organize another attempt on your life, but Ellia Maya has replaced the messages with new ones that will lead them right to our guards."

A chill grips my spine, doubly cold due to the callous way she imparts this information. "And . . ." I have to clear my throat. "What did you do with the army?"

"I sent word that we will send two companies through the pass," she says. "One will support the soldiers already stationed there, and one will begin a clandestine assault on the smaller towns, so we can prevent word from spreading. If we can form a circle around his regiment, we can cut off their supply chain and destroy them before they can mount a defense."

"Stop." I'm staring at her. It's one thing to stop an attempt on my life, but entirely another when it comes to commanding my army. "Nolla Verin, we gave Emberfall sixty days, and their limit has not expired. I will not begin slaughtering their people just to gain an advantage."

She gapes at me like I've started speaking another language. "You do not want to gain an advantage? Sister, this is *war*."

The censure in her voice is chilling. "It's not war *yet*," I snap.

"You always naively wish for peace," she says harshly, "while war threatens to destroy everything around you. Prince Rhen has already *sent* soldiers to the border. He is already preparing to—"

"Have his soldiers engaged with ours?"

"No, but that means nothing."

I step away from my dressing table. "It means everything!"

"You wish to honor the timeline you offered, when he is clearly not?"

"He is preparing for war, just as we are." I glare at her. "I will not go back on my word."

"Your *word*." She scoffs. "You do recall that the man took you prisoner? That he killed Sorra? That he refused any attempt at alliance?"

Her words hit me like a slap. I do remember all those things.

Nolla Verin sees me flinch, and she moves closer.

"There are rumors," she says quietly. "That Grey will destroy us from within—"

I whip my head up. "He will not."

"I know he will not," she says, but there's something about the way she says it that makes me wonder if she's fallen prey to these rumors, too. I wonder just how broadly this faction against magic has begun to sink its claws into my country. "But your people will be less likely to believe these rumors if you take decisive action against Rhen's forces. If Grey is seen as following *your* order, not using his power against our soldiers."

I study her. Outside my window, the sun crawls its way up from the horizon, and the icicles that formed overnight have begun an incessant *drip-drip-drip* against the stone of my sill.

When I say nothing, Nolla Verin sighs, and some of the fierceness seeps out of her expression. She tucks a lock of hair behind my ear. "We are going to destroy his soldiers anyway," she says softly. "What is a matter of days if it prevents us from losing our own?"

I swallow. I wish Grey were here. I long for his cool, assessing judgment.

The instant I have the thought, I regret it. The decisions here are mine. I am queen. Just because I do not want to think of destroying soldiers—neither his *nor* ours—does not mean it will not happen. And perhaps she is right, and we should take decisive action to gain an advantage.

I remember riding through the hills of Emberfall, looking on the devastation we'd already brought to the country. I wanted peace then, and I want it now, but I failed. Twice. The first time because Rhen did not trust my offer, and the second time because he did not wish to come to terms when we offered him sixty days. I don't want to fail a third time. Nolla Verin is right: we should take any advantage we can.

But war doesn't bring peace to anyone. And even though Rhen did not trust me, that does not mean that my offer of an alliance wasn't sound. If I want to rule with temperance and civility, my first true action as queen should not be a betrayal of something I offered another ruler.

"We will wait out our remaining few days," I say. "We will not send another company."

Nolla Verin looks like I punched her in the stomach. "Did you not hear that Prince Rhen has sent a full regiment to the border?"

"Yes. Because *we* did."

"He sent a thousand soldiers—"

"They are within his borders, Nolla Verin! He is allowed to prepare for war!"

"Because you gave him ample warning," she says. "Because you want to be kind, and you want to be loved, and you want to be—"

"No, sister," I snap. Somehow I refrain from slapping her across the face, which would definitely make her question these accusations of kindness. "Because I want to be *fair* and I want to be *just*, and I want the best for my people *and* his."

She takes another step closer to me. "You are not fair and just. You are weak and easily led. Your people do not want you, just like Rhen's people do not want him."

"You think that the only way to achieve anything is with a blade in your hand," I say. "And it is *not*."

"It *is*," she insists. "You would not be queen if you'd not learned that very lesson yourself."

Her words shock me still. Because I killed our mother. The only reason I even have this role is because I did exactly what she said. I took this role by the edge of a blade—our very *law* requires that the role of queen be taken by violence. How could I have ever thought I could rule Syhl Shallow with anything less?

"You know," she says, and her voice is low, and not unkind. "You know what must be done."

She's so fierce and beautiful and unyielding and determined. I've never envied her any of those things, though. I once thought she would make a great queen.

But she could never stand up to our mother. She never would have made an attempt at peace.

"It is not what *must* be done," I say quietly. "It is what you *think* must be done. I will stand by my word."

Her eyes are like fire, and she glares at me steadily. "You are wrong. And you are too late anyway. I have already sent the order to the fields."

"You will rescind that order," I snap.

"I will not."

My hands form fists. "You are not queen, Nolla Verin."

"Well, at least I'm acting like one."

I suck in a breath. "No, you are not. You are acting like a girl who has forgotten who *is*. You will rescind that order, or you will have to pull your dagger and claim the throne yourself."

Her eyes flare wide. She takes a step back.

But then, for one wicked second, she thinks about it. I can see the thought flicker through her eyes. Her hand twitches toward her weapons. In that one second, my heart seems to stop. To wait.

Months ago, our mother sent her to fetch me, as part of a trial to prove her loyalty. Nolla Verin couldn't do it.

But that was different. *Then*, she was still destined to be queen, and she didn't need to kill me to prove it.

Right now, she'd have to. This tension hangs between us until I almost can't breathe around it.

Finally, an eternity later, she sighs and grits her teeth. Her hands relax at her sides. "No. I will not claim the throne." She squares her shoulders. "But I will not rescind the order, either."

My heart resumes beating, and I have to take a breath. For the first time, I realize that no matter how close we are, and how much we've endured together, there is still a part of her that sees me as weak, a queen who will need someone to handle the more . . . unsavory parts of ruling. Instead of seeing my alliance with Grey as a boon to our militaristic forces, maybe she—and everyone else—has seen that as a flinching on my part.

A *literal* flinching, as I remember the way I stood on the training fields.

Maybe it's time to change that.

"Fine." I turn away from her and head into my closet, reaching for my boots. "If you won't rescind the order, then I will."

The sky is full of clouds, leaving the air cold and damp as I stride across the fields. Since I was in a pique, I only threw on a light cloak, and I'm already regretting it. Nolla Verin is right on my heels, and she hasn't stopped trying to convince me that I'm making a mistake. In my chambers, she was so forceful and determined, but now she's speaking in a constant stream of whispers at my shoulder, her angry breath making quick clouds in the air.

"This is reckless and irresponsible," she hisses. "Rhen's army will have the advantage."

I ignore her and keep walking.

"You will look like a *fool*," she says. "Grey will agree with me. You will see."

I say nothing.

"Your officers already think you are weak," she continues, "and now you are going to change course on an order that was issued half an hour ago."

"An order *you* gave," I snap, but there's a tiny, bothersome needle of doubt that keeps poking me in the back. It *will* look weak to have such a forceful order issued—and to then walk it back. But that's her fault, not mine.

That needle of doubt tells me it won't matter, that weakness is weakness.

It's a weakness that these assassination attempts seem to emphasize as well. Too much is uncertain. Even among those who are loyal to me, magic is still distrusted. *Grey* is still distrusted. My steps almost falter.

But we draw close to the sparring soldiers, and I realize many of them have gathered to watch a match near the center of the field. It takes me a moment to recognize Grey, because it's so rare that I'm on the field to see him fight. He's so gentle and patient with *me* that I've forgotten he can be so fierce, so focused, so relentless. Their swords spin in the dim sunlight, cracking together with such force that it makes me flinch from here. The snow under their boots has turned to muddy slush, but neither of the men seems to be fighting for footing. The battle looks effortless and lethal. Downright vicious.

I don't realize I've stopped until Nolla Verin speaks at my shoulder. "You see. *He* will agree with me. This *army* will agree with me."

The needle of doubt pokes me again.

Grey's opponent is that soldier he ordered to fight over and over again, Captain Solt. Is this a *real* battle? Are they fighting in earnest?

I stride forward again. The soldiers part as we approach, bowing as I stride among them, but my eyes are on the fight. My stomach churns as I think of all the ways the army could take these small struggles.

Solt makes a move, but Grey ducks and surges forward. For the first time, Solt loses his footing and goes down, skidding through the mud and snow. At my shoulder, Nolla Verin sucks in a breath. I expect Grey to drive his blade right through the fallen man's body.

But he doesn't. He sheathes his sword. He holds out a hand. He's smiling.

Solt takes his hand and pulls himself to his feet. He's smiling, too. "You are too quick, Your Highness."

"I'm lucky." Grey shakes out his arm. "You strike like a hammer."

"You're both lucky," says Jake, standing off to the side. "I thought someone was going to lose a hand."

I lose a moment to staring. I'm not sure what just happened here.

Solt notices me first, and he straightens and sobers immediately. "Your Majesty."

Grey turns, and some of that vicious focus shifts to warmth when he meets my eyes. It's such an intent look, such a *private* look, that I feel a blush crawling up my neck already. When *he* says "Your Majesty," it makes me shiver.

I watch as his eyes take me in, then my surely fuming sister at my shoulder, then the guards that trail us. He looks to a squire standing nearby, then steps over and claims the cloak he must have abandoned before the fight. I expect him to draw it around his own shoulders, but I forgot the customs he brings from Emberfall, so I'm startled when he draws it around me. My blush fades. I see exchanged glances among the soldiers, and I wonder if this, too, will be seen as a weakness.

"Are you well?" he says, his voice very low.

"I am well." I pause. "I understand my sister issued an order to have a company sent through the mountain pass."

"We received word of Nolla Verin's intent," Grey says.

Of course he did. It hasn't been long, but Grey doesn't hesitate. He probably already sent women and men to the mountain pass.

Then he adds, "I told the captains we will have soldiers readied, but we would wait for the order to come from the queen herself."

I stare at him. I want to throw my arms around his neck. I want to burst into tears.

Neither of those options is queenly. I nod, but my voice feels breathy. "Good. I would like to wait until we have reached the end of our promised time."

"This is foolhardy!" Nolla Verin explodes. "You have an *opportunity* to take advantage, and you will *waste* it."

Grey looks at her, and his eyes are cool and hard like steel. "So you believe we need to cheat? Do you doubt the strength and ability of our army?"

That draws her up short. I watch as soldiers exchange glances again.

Our army. Such simple words, tacked into a simple sentence, but I can feel the weight of them as they reverberate through the soldiers who heard them, repeated in whispers among the others. Nolla Verin has fought among them for years. Many of them assumed she would be in my place.

But she's not. I am queen here, and she's the one who told me I had to fight for myself. Maybe she doesn't realize it, but she's the one forcing me to take a stand: not assassins, not Grey, not my people. My sister.

"Do you believe you have the right to countermand your queen?" I say, and the whispers grow in volume.

"*Nayah*," snaps Solt, and the soldiers jump to attention. Silence falls over the fields.

Nolla Verin is still staring at me. Rain, cold and heavy, begins to drop from the sky.

Suddenly, I realize she's not the one I owe words to. She's not the one I need to convince. I look at the soldiers. "I do not doubt my army," I call in Syssalah. "I do not doubt your ability. I do not doubt your loyalty. I do not doubt your strength. I ask that you do not doubt mine. We are Syhl Shallow." I take a deep breath and shout into the rain. "We have magic on our side, and we will *rise*, and we will be *victorious*."

For the briefest second, there's absolute silence, so much potential riding on the air. I'm not sure what happened between Grey and Captain Solt, but it brought us halfway to this point. I have to bring us the rest of the way, and I'm not sure if this is enough.

But then Solt drops to a knee. "Syhl Shallow will rise," he echoes fiercely. "We have magic on our side." He hits a fist to his chest. "Syhl Shallow will be victorious."

At his back, row by row, hundreds of soldiers do the same, falling to a knee in the rain on a muddy field. For the first time, all eyes are on me, not my sister.

My sister, who takes a deep breath, then drops to a knee herself. "Syhl Shallow will rise," she says, and despite everything, there's conviction in her voice. "We have magic on our side. Syhl Shallow will be victorious."

Grey steps closer to me and takes my hand. "*Our* strength," he says softly.

I nod up at him. A small flame has started to burn in my chest, and it's not love, because that's been brewing there for a while, and it's not doubt, because that's been pounded into submission. Instead, it's hope. I squeeze his hand.

Far across the field, near the road that leads away from the palace, a horn blares. The sound is loud and carries through the rain, and a hundred heads swivel to look. It's an announcement of approaching scouts, but it's uncommon for it to happen at midday. Then I hear galloping hoofbeats, and I look at Grey. It's doubly uncommon for them to return at high speed.

Something must have happened in Emberfall. Some change that requires urgent attention. Our reports said Rhen had stationed a regiment near the pass, and I assumed it was to prevent ours from moving forward.

But maybe it was intended to mount an assault against *us*.

Grey looks at Solt. "Have them get back into formation. Tell the other captains to be ready for new orders."

My heart is in my throat. I just made a vow to these soldiers, and now it's my chance to keep it. I look at Nolla Verin. "I want to meet with the generals. Find Clanna Sun and have her report to the fields at once."

She nods quickly. "Yes, Your Majesty."

The scouts cross the fields, their horses skidding to a stop in front of us, spraying slush and mud and blowing steam into the cold air. The animals are winded and slick with sweat and rain.

One of the scouts slips out of the saddle and offers me a clumsy, breathless bow. "Your Majesty," she says in Syssalah. "Captain Sen Domo is holding a prisoner at the guard station."

"A prisoner?" says Grey.

"Yes," says the scout. She's speaking rapidly, gasping between sentences. "She rode straight into the army camp. She has made many demands, including that she be allowed to see the queen. At first they believed she was addled, because she was quite injured, but she would not deviate from her story that Prince Rhen has been hurt, his guards and soldiers slaughtered."

I gasp.

"What?" says Jake. "I only caught like half of that."

Grey's brow is furrowed, too. "Prince Rhen is injured?"

"His guards and soldiers killed, too," I say. I look at the scout. "His regiment?"

"Still stands," she says. "They seem . . . unaware. Our soldiers did not engage." She pauses. "They don't know where she came from."

"Is she a soldier?" says Jake.

"Or a spy?" says Grey.

"Neither, Your Highness." The scout finally catches her breath. "She claims to be Prince Rhen's beloved, Princess Harper of Disi."

CHAPTER THIRTY-ONE

HARPER

Everything here is damp and freezing and miserable. Or maybe that's just me.

The knife wound on my thigh is swollen and hot with a bit of yellow crust around the edges, and I can't tell if I'm shivering because I'm cold or if I have a fever. Probably both, especially since I'm sitting on a stone floor, leaning against a stone wall. The pain in my thigh has long since blocked out whatever happened to my ankle when I was in Silvermoon, and now everything hurts. My wrists and ankles have been chained for two days now, the skin rubbed raw, and I can't remember the last time I ate anything. I'm only wearing calfskin pants, a blouson, and a laced vest.

My cloak and armor are long gone, but they've left me with my dagger. I've begged and pleaded for it, declaring that it was meant for Grey, babbling that it would help him. The soldiers rolled their eyes and left it strapped to my thigh—but I'm clearly not much of a threat. The soldiers haven't been *cruel*, but they haven't been accommodating either. I'm not entirely sure what I expected—I bolted away from the Crooked Boar as if I could just ride into their camp and they'd take me straight to Grey and Lia Mara.

So now it's been three days since I reached their camp, if I've been able to keep track correctly—which is rather doubtful. Seven days since I left Rhen with Lilith. For the first few days, I'd think about the moment she appeared in my chambers and tears would fill my eyes, but desperation would drive through the pain and exhaustion. I'd ride hard and fast, galloping across the terrain of Emberfall as if I could outrun my tears, as if I could just get to the border, get help, and we'd rescue Rhen from Lilith.

But a few days ago, the tears stopped coming, and now I just feel . . . resigned. Hopeless. I thought it would be so easy. *I need to find Grey,* I kept saying. Like the Syhl Shallow soldiers would gasp and say, "Well of course, my lady." Like I'm a real princess. Like we're not about to face them in a war.

There was a period of time where I thought the Syhl Shallow soldiers would just kill me. A period of time where I *wished* they would kill me, because when they first chained me up, my imagination ran wild and I thought for sure I'd be raped and left for dead. But it seems like a lot of their officers are women, and while no one is gentle, no one was forcing me up against a wall and ripping my clothes off, either.

I would kill someone for some water. Then again, it feels like a Herculean task to lift my head, so maybe that's not a good idea.

Maybe I'll be left here long enough that I'll die anyway.

I'm sorry, Rhen.

I was wrong. New tears *can* form.

Booted feet stomp somewhere on the other side of the heavy

wooden door, but I ignore it. I've stopped hoping for food. I've stopped hoping for anything.

But the lock rattles, and the door swings open. I'm staring up at a new soldier in green-and-black-trimmed armor. His expression is so severe, his eyes so fierce, that I almost cringe—until I blink and realize I'm looking at Grey.

For a moment, it almost takes my breath away. I've been so desperate to find him, and now he's here. He's *here.*

It seems so impossible that for a terrifying moment, I think I'm hallucinating. He looks the same and different all at once, like he suddenly takes up more space in the world.

"Are you real?" I whisper.

Another green-and-black-clad soldier drops to his knees by my side. I almost flinch away, but then he says, "Harp," in a familiar voice, and I discover I'm looking at my brother.

"Jake," I rasp. "Jake." My voice sounds like I haven't used it in a year. Tears spill from my eyes.

He puts a hand against my forehead, my cheeks. "She's burning up. Get these chains off her. Hey!" He turns his head, and I notice other soldiers have followed them into my cell, but they all blur into a mass of green and black. "*Bil trunda,*" Jake snaps.

I stare at him for a long moment, because I can't tell if he's speaking another language or if my brain has finally given up. Jake's dark curly hair has grown long enough to fall into his eyes, and any softness in his face has been carved away.

His eyes search mine, and he draws back a bit. "They said you were injured." His voice is gentler now. "Where are you hurt?" Another soldier approaches with keys, and Jake all but snatches them from his hand. The shackles fall away from my wrists, and he barely has time to unchain my ankles before I use all my strength to launch myself forward. The movement makes my leg ache and protest the movement, but I don't care. My arms close around his neck, and I don't ever want to let go.

"Jake," I whimper.

He catches me. Holds me. "It'll be all right," he says softly, and I'm reminded of all the times we'd hide in his room, when Dad's crimes caught up with us. Jake would whisper empty reassurances to me then, too. "It'll be all right, Harper."

But that wasn't all right. And this won't be either.

"Her leg," says Grey. "Jake, she is bleeding." He turns his head and speaks to one of the other soldiers. "Bring some water."

My brother eases me back against the wall, and I look up at Grey. My brain keeps insisting this isn't real, that I haven't succeeded, that this is a fever dream.

"Scary Grey," I whisper, and my voice breaks.

Proving worthy of his nickname, he wastes no time on emotion. He drops to a knee beside me and draws a dagger.

I suck in a breath and grab Jake's arm.

Grey's eyes meet mine, and *those* haven't changed. He's coolly intent, focused. "Do you no longer trust me?"

Maybe I shouldn't. We're on opposite sides of a war. But I stare back at him, and even through the fever and the exhaustion, I think of everything we endured together, from the moments when he first kidnapped me till the time he offered Lilith his sword on out-stretched hands in a bid to save my life. I remember when he fell through the door of my apartment, broken and bleeding, desperate for my help. I remember the passion in his voice when he stood in the shadowed hallway, when he was the Commander of Rhen's

Royal Guard, and I'd first agreed to be the Princess of Disi. When Grey challenged my trust. When he made me understand what I'd agreed to.

My *duty is to bleed so he does not,* Grey said then. *And now my duty is to bleed so* you *do not.*

Now I'm the one bleeding, and he's waiting with a dagger in his hand.

I swallow. "I trust you."

He cuts the soiled bandage free and pulls it away from my leg in one smooth movement. It must have crusted to the wound, because stars flare in my vision and I gasp. I'm choking. My back arches. I'm going to throw up. Pus and blood creep from the injury, which has turned black along the edges, with weird bruising running the length of my thigh.

My brother hisses in alarm. "Holy crap, Harp, how long has it been like that?"

"I couldn't wait," I say, and my eyes won't focus. "I think—I think it's infected."

"You *think*? Grey—"

"I can fix it." And before I have time to ask *how*, or what that fully means, he pulls off a glove and presses his fingers right to the wound.

I scream. I lied, I lied, I lied, I don't trust him at all, this is worse than any pain has ever been, ever. It's too much, too intense, like he's grabbed a fist full of my flesh and pulled it right out of my leg. This has to be a nightmare. This is torture. I'm going to pass out again.

But then—it's not. The pain eases away. For the first time in days, my head is suddenly . . . clear. I'm still weak and exhausted and starving, but the bruising and pus around the knife wound are gone, leaving only a narrow scar where the edges of the wound had turned black. I'm soaked in sweat and panting, but my body stops shivering from infection, and instead starts shivering because it's cold.

Whoa.

Jake pulls off his cloak and wraps it around me, and I'm grateful for the ready warmth, but I can't stop staring at Grey. I've heard some of the rumors of what happened between him and the people in Blind Hollow, how he saved them with magic, but until this moment, I hadn't quite understood what that meant.

Lilith tore through Dustan and the other guards with this same kind of power.

I shudder. I suddenly understand Rhen's terror. I can't tell if it's the memory of what happened or the thought of that kind of potential being at Grey's fingertips, but either way, I'm speechless. I don't know if I should be grateful or terrified.

Both. Definitely both.

Scary Grey *for sure.*

Maybe he can see it in my frozen expression, because he stands, pulling his glove back on. His eyes give away nothing.

A woman steps forward, through the soldiers, and they step back with deference. I recognize her vibrant red hair before I recognize her face. Queen Lia Mara is in dark blue belted robes, and she wears a heavy woolen cloak against the cold.

"Princess Harper," she says. I feel like I should stand, so I grab hold of Jake's arm and let him help me to my feet. Whatever Grey did didn't heal *everything*, and my one ankle nearly gives way, so I clutch to my brother to stay upright. She was able to look regal and unaffected when she was Rhen's prisoner, but I don't know if I can do the same after days of not eating, with my pants hanging in torn scraps around my knee.

I also don't know what I'm supposed to call her, and I've been in chains for days, possibly by her order. I've heard plenty of stories about the viciousness of Karis Luran—but I also know this girl once came to Rhen with hopes for peace.

Her expression isn't angry, but it's definitely not warm and inviting. "My scouts said that you told them Prince Rhen is injured," she says.

"Yes." But as soon as I say the word, my tongue stalls. I was so determined to get to Grey, to beg for his help, but now I'm here and I'm worried that I'm handing them an advantage. What did Rhen say?

This is war, Harper. Grey will use anything at his disposal.

Surely Lia Mara would do the exact same thing. I wanted to talk to Grey. I thought he would understand. I thought he would help.

Maybe. Hopefully.

Looking into Lia Mara's cool green eyes and Grey's severe ones, I don't feel very hopeful at all.

But then Lia Mara says, "This is not our doing," and her tone is grave. "My soldiers have been ordered to honor the sixty days we granted."

"Oh!" Wait. Does she think I came all this way to *blame* them? "No! I know it's not Syhl Shallow."

She frowns. "Then who attacked the prince?"

I look at Grey. "The enchantress." I take a breath. "It's Lilith. She's back."

From a distance, the Crystal Palace looks nothing like Ironrose Castle. While the latter always reminds me of something you'd see in a brochure for some kind of European fairy-tale adventure, the Crystal Palace sits well above the city, partially built into the side of the mountain. Massive sparkling windows reflect the sky, and huge snow-covered fields stretch away from the palace to end near a forest with glistening ice-coated trees. For a country that once tried to burn Emberfall to the ground, I didn't expect it to look so beautiful.

I expected Grey to react with shock when I mentioned Lilith, but he didn't. Some of the soldiers exchanged glances and murmured to each other, but Lia Mara asked for silence, and they gave it. She then said we would return to the palace to discuss the matter privately. I thought that meant me and them, but Jake loaded me into a carriage to take me away from the scout station where I was being held. So now I'm alone with my brother, rattling across rocky streets while I huddle and shiver and stare out the window at the palace that keeps growing closer.

I wish I could put a finger on what's changed about him. It's not confidence, because Jake was never lacking in that, but he's gained something. Or maybe he's lost something.

Jake speaks into the silence. "Grey would have fixed your ankle, too."

I shiver, and this time it has nothing to do with the cold. Maybe it was miraculous how Grey made the infection go away and the wound heal over, but I keep thinking of Lilith's fingers tearing out the muscle and tendons of Dustan's neck with the same kind of torturous power. I came here because he supposedly has magic, but knowing about it and experiencing it are two very different things. "Once was enough."

Jake frowns. "What does that mean?"

I say nothing. I don't even know *what* to say.

"So Rhen is terrified of magic and now you are too?" he says.

"I'm not terrified." But I am. It's obvious I am. I saw what Lilith could do. I felt her rip Zo right off the back of my horse.

"I told you to come with me, Harp. I *told you.*"

It takes me a moment to realize he means *months* ago, when Grey first fled Emberfall with Lia Mara.

I frown. "I'm so glad I showed up half-dead and you're deciding to start with 'I told you so.'"

He looks out the window, too. "From the looks of you, it's a miracle you're not all the way dead."

I'm not sure what to say to that either. "It was really hard to get here, Jake."

"I'm not talking about the *journey*, Harper." His eyes snap back to me. "I'm talking about whatever happened with Lilith. With Rhen. How many times do you need to sacrifice yourself for that guy for you to realize that you're the only one losing *everything*. Every single time."

I think of Rhen, his eyes so warm and intent on mine. *I will try for peace. I am not yielding to Grey, Harper. I am yielding to you. For you.*

My eyes fill. I'm not the only one losing everything. Rhen is too. "It wasn't like that, Jake. He's not like that."

Jake swears and looks away. "You sound like Mom."

That hits me like a bullet. My arms fold across my midsection, but my emotions can't be contained. Tears spill down my cheeks.

My brother sighs. He eases off the seat to drop to his knees in front of me, and he reaches for my hands. "I'm sorry," he says softly.

"I just—I wish you could see yourself. When I walked into that cell and saw you lying there—"

I pull a hand out of his to swipe at my eyes. "Rhen didn't do this to me."

"Yeah, well, he couldn't stop it."

"He could be dead, Jake. She might have killed him." But as I say it, I don't think it's true. She could have killed him a hundred times over. A million times over.

Once he's dead, her game is done.

"Well," says Jake. "You're not dead. You made it. You're safe."

I blink at him. "What?"

"You're here." He pauses, looking back at me. "You made it."

"You think—you think I came here because I was running away?" My tears dry up in a hurry. Is that what everyone thinks? Is that why I've been packed into a carriage instead of sitting down to strategize?

Jake looks at me like I'm insane—which confirms it. "Yes?"

"No, you idiot." I swipe at my eyes again, then shove him in the chest. "I came here for help."

CHAPTER THIRTY-TWO

RHEN

The castle is cold and silent, but I don't mind the chill. If this were midsummer, the stench of the bodies would be interminable. I'm willing to freeze to death anyway, so I haven't lit a fire in days. I still don't have the courage to look in a mirror. My left eye has been dark and blind since Lilith attacked us, and when I touch a hand to my face, all I find are raised ridges of thick scabs and swelling that aches when my fingertips drift over it.

It's only been a few months since the curse was broken, following an eternity of isolation with Grey, but somehow I quickly forgot how quiet Ironrose becomes when there are no guards and servants in the halls, no children laughing as they race up the staircases, no rattling dishes, no ruffling papers, no clanging swords in the training arena.

Lilith left the bodies in the halls, telling me to think on my crimes while they rotted around me. When the curse first held me captive, she did the same with my family, but I was a monster then.

When the season reset, everything in the palace returned to its former state from the first morning she cursed me: no dead bodies, no one at all.

This time, there's no curse—and even if the enchantress were to offer a means out of this hell, I would refuse. But maybe she knows I've learned my lesson, or maybe she thinks this is better than watching me fail for another eternity. No curse is offered. No bargain. No means of relief. Every hallway of Ironrose reeks of blood and death. I gagged on it for hours and locked myself in an empty room—but eventually, I had to eat. I might be willing to freeze to death, but starving to death felt too much like torturing myself.

Lilith probably won't let me die anyway. She won't let me run. She promised to follow if I tried, to slaughter anyone who dared to offer me shelter. So here I remain. I haven't seen her in days, though I don't dare to hope that she's done with me. Grey is gone. Harper is dead. What else can she take? Despair is all that's left.

I've spent my hours pulling bodies out of the castle, dragging them on velvet carpets one by one down the marble steps, then loading them into a wagon I've hitched myself. One horse is missing from the stable: Ironwill, my favorite steed—and Harper's, too. In a way, I'm glad he's gone, though I hope he escaped through the woods after Lilith killed Harper and Zo. Then again, the enchantress is easily vicious and vindictive enough to kill my horse, too.

For as terrible as this task is, I'm grateful for something to do. When I sit still, my thoughts churn with agony over everything I've lost. It would be worse to leave the bodies anyway. I know what happens to a corpse once it begins to decompose, and I have no interest in watching it happen by a hundredfold.

Occasionally a scout or a soldier will come to the castle, bringing messages or requests or inquiries about what actions I intend to take. The first one galloped into the courtyard, took one look at me dragging a body across the cobblestones, and screamed—then ran. I don't know what Lilith has turned loose in the forests surrounding Ironrose, but I've heard distant screams and rustlings in the leaves, and the people who make it all the way to the castle are few and far between. Maybe she's cursed another prince and turned him into a monster.

Whatever it is, it leaves me alone, and I have no desire to investigate.

Despite the cold in the air, I stop in my dragging to wipe a sleeve across my forehead, but it pulls at the wounds on my face, stealing my breath for a moment. Three dozen charred bodies already lie in a row under the trees. It feels wrong to burn them, but I can't bury them all myself, and animals have already begun to pick at the corpses.

I honestly didn't think anything could be worse than being stuck here forever, turning into a rampaging monster season after season, but clearly Lilith has no limit.

Without warning, the enchantress speaks from somewhere nearby. "What will you do with them all, Your Highness?"

Her voice sends a jolt through me, and I wish it wouldn't. I wish she couldn't still elicit fear just by her closeness.

I don't answer. I climb back on the wagon and cluck to the horse to head back to the castle.

Some people were able to escape. I know because there aren't bodies for *everyone*. At first I hoped someone would find help—but I quickly realized there is no help. No one can stop her.

Hands fall on my shoulders, and I gasp and jerk away. The horse plods on.

Lilith whispers in my ear. "I cannot believe you thought you would use that silly weapon to attack me. As if I have never encountered steel from Iishellasa."

I shiver and try to jerk free.

She leans closer, her breath hot and sickening. "As if I did not hand it to the spy myself."

I suck in a breath.

"You're so *surprised*," she chortles. "As if I have not played these games with you for an eternity, Prince Rhen." She pauses. "Who do you think has stoked the discord in Syhl Shallow? Who do you think whispers suggestions of assassination to anyone who will listen?" Her tongue touches my ear, and it's like the kiss of a forge-hot blade. "You were to use it on *Grey*, not me."

I shudder. She is diabolical. There is no stopping her.

It was useless to even try.

"I have even sent orders to your troops, Your Highness. Using your seal." Her fingernails dig into my shoulders. My back is rigid against her touch.

"Your soldiers at the border will attack this regiment from Syhl Shallow. They will bring the war into Emberfall, and we will win. I have sent for troops to surround the castle."

That's foolish. If she wants to rule Emberfall at my side, she shouldn't let Syhl Shallow's soldiers get anywhere close to the castle.

"Grey will come for you," she seethes. "The blade is gone. He will kill you, you know."

Yes. I do know. I once thought I needed to kill the heir to protect my throne—and he will have to do the same thing if he wants to claim it.

The thought brings an unexpected tightness to my throat. So many things I wish I'd done differently.

I would have yielded to him. I would have negotiated for peace. It was Harper's last request.

Almost her dying wish.

My breath shudders.

Now Lilith has ordered my soldiers to attack. No one will listen to a message about an alliance.

"Grey will come for you," she says, "and I will lie in wait." A blustering wind blasts through the trees to ruffle my hair and make me shiver, and Lilith closes her arms around my neck. "I will lie in wait so I can kill the one man who still stands in my way."

CHAPTER THIRTY-THREE

LIA MARA

My strategy room is warm from a roaring fire, and I'm surrounded by people who seem focused on a common goal for once, but my thoughts keep replaying the moment when Harper looked up at Grey with tears in her eyes and called him "Scary Grey." Or the moment when he dropped to a knee and said, "Do you no longer trust me?" in that quiet voice I thought he only reserved for me.

Jealousy is petty and useless, especially right now, and yet I cannot seem to chase it out of my thoughts. They had a history together, Harper and Grey, and even though it might not have resulted in anything more than friendship between them, it was still clearly . . . *something*. She was hurt and she ran here. For him. That is meaningful.

Nolla Verin is deep in conversation with Clanna Sun and two of the army officers, General Torra and Captain Solt, debating whether this means we should attack now, or whether this means we would be under attack from another magical creature—but

Grey's eyes are on me. He can surely tell I'm unsettled. He notices everything.

I'm not sure what to say to him.

I'm spared the need, because Jake bursts through the doors. He's never one for much pageantry, so I'm not surprised when he just starts talking. "Harper's with Noah. I brought her some food and some fresh clothes." He runs a hand across the back of his neck. "I don't know what all happened, but she's . . . she's pretty rattled."

"So she has come here seeking sanctuary?" I say.

"A bold request of an enemy," says Nolla Verin, but her voice is not as strong as it might have been yesterday. She glances at me. "Especially an enemy who once took our queen prisoner."

"She's not *my* enemy," Jake snaps, and the army officers exchange a glance.

"Perhaps we should continue this conversation privately," says General Torra with a glance at Solt.

And just like that, we're at odds again.

"Harper is Jake's sister," I say evenly. "I can understand his sympathies."

"Will she reveal information on the enchantress?" says Nolla Verin. "What is she willing to offer?"

"We should be wary of a trap," says Solt. He casts a glance at Grey, and I can tell that Harper's sudden appearance has added a flicker of doubt to whatever resolution happened between them this morning. "This could be a ploy to force our hand."

"It's not a ploy," says Jake. "And she's not offering anything." He pauses. "She wants to rescue Rhen. She's asking for help to defeat Lilith."

"Help!" My eyebrows go up. "She seeks our assistance in challenging this enchantress?"

"Not ours." Jake looks at Grey. "Yours."

Everyone else explodes with disagreement. Nolla Verin wants to interrogate Harper. Clanna Sun thinks this could be a planned distraction, especially given how few days we have left. Solt and Torra both believe this could be a trap, a way to lure our soldiers to their deaths. But Grey hasn't said much since we entered this room, and he says nothing now. His expression is impossible to read: his soldier face. I wish I knew what he was thinking.

Jake is staring at him from the other end of the table. "When *you* were hurt and desperate and nearly dead, you came looking for Harper. You literally fell through my door and bled all over my carpet. You shouldn't be shocked that she came looking for you."

I look at Grey. "Is that true?" I whisper, softer than thought.

"Yes." He looks at me. "I had no other choice."

Just as he believes that Harper had no other choice. He doesn't even need to say it. I can feel it in his words.

"She helped you," I say, and it's not even a question.

"Yes," says Grey. His gaze is steady on mine. "Harper helps anyone who needs it."

I remember the night Prince Rhen chained him to a wall, how Harper helped him escape then, too. No political gain, no posturing. At the time, I thought it was because of a spark between them, and maybe some of it was, but maybe some of it was simply . . . Harper. When Rhen took me prisoner, Harper came to my room and apologized. She didn't offer friendship, but she offered kindness. Compassion. Empathy.

The reminder makes some of my jealousy shrivel up. Not all of it, but some.

I have no idea what this means to our war, but I don't think she's lying. I don't think this is a trap. My mother would use this opportunity to attack in force, to raze Emberfall while the prince is most vulnerable. Nolla Verin is practically clutching her fingers against the table, hoping I'll do the same thing.

All along, I've wanted peace. I've wanted what was best for my people. That doesn't mean anything if I don't want it for *all* people.

"Then go speak to her," I say, and it costs me something to speak the words. "See what she needs."

Grey rises at once, and I wish he weren't so quick to action. I inhale sharply, and he hesitates, his eyes finding mine. He's waiting for me to tell him not to.

I don't. I force my lips to close.

I'm the only one remaining silent, however. "Your Majesty," says Clanna Sun. "If they are to meet in private, the rumors—"

"The hell with the rumors," Jake growls. "My sister isn't some kind of spy."

"Then perhaps an assassin?" says Solt.

"An accomplice?" says Nolla Verin.

Grey sighs. "As Jake said, the hell with rumors. If you believe Harper is here as part of a sinister plot, you are invited to come along and see for yourself."

CHAPTER THIRTY-FOUR

GREY

Jake follows me, which I expected, but so do Solt and Nolla Verin. I expected Lia Mara to join me as well, but she chose to remain behind to soothe the ruffled feathers of Clanna Sun and General Torra. She hasn't said so, but she's unsettled by Harper being here.

I am too, but likely not for the reasons she thinks.

Lilith is back. I don't know how she survived. I remember cutting her throat on the other side, in Washington, DC.

And now she is tormenting Rhen again.

I wonder how long it has gone on. I think back to the times I saw Rhen after fleeing to Rillisk. Was she there when he had me dragged back in chains? He was so frightened of magic then. And again when I arrived with Lia Mara to offer him sixty days. He flinched away when I drew near. Despite everything, worry and uncertainty tugs at me. I know what she can do. I know what she's *done*.

When we reach the hall that leads to the infirmary, I stop and turn to Jake. "You should wait here."

He glances at Solt and Nolla Verin, and while Jake has never been at odds with anyone here the way that I have, Harper's appearance has changed that. "No way," he says.

"If your sister's motives are innocent, you should have nothing to fear," says Nolla Verin.

"My sister wouldn't have come here if she wasn't *desperate*," Jake snaps.

"Enough," I say, and I keep my voice low. Jake's eyes are fierce, his jaw tight. His devotion to his sister will not help us here. "Wait," I say to him. "Please."

I watch as defiance swells in his eyes, and I expect him to try to shove past me, my request be damned. When Jake and I first met, he was belligerent and antagonistic, but he's also brave and loyal, just like his sister. In the moment I asked him to stand as my second, I said, "Taking orders requires trust, Jake. You would have to trust me."

"I can do that," he said then.

This is the first time I've ever asked him to prove it.

For an eternal moment, he says nothing, and anger clouds his expression. But he finally takes a step back to stand against the wall. "Fine," he bites out.

I clap him on the shoulder and move on. At my back, Solt murmurs something to Nolla Verin, and I inwardly sigh. All of our attempts to unite our people were beginning to have an effect, and now it's all seeming to unravel.

The infirmary is always a bit cold, because Noah often gets so distracted by his work that he forgets to add another log to the hearth, and this afternoon is no different. He's sitting on a stool beside a narrow cot where Harper is huddled under a loose knit blanket, and he appears to be wrapping her ankle in lengths of muslin. Neither of them face the doorway, and Tycho sits on the empty cot beside them, the tiny orange kitten in his lap, chewing on the corner of his bracers. He's speaking shyly. "Noah said I should name him Salam. It means 'peace' in . . . I forget."

"Arabic," says Noah.

"And then Iisak said—"

"Wait," says Harper. "Who's Iisak?"

"Tycho," I say, and he startles so badly that the kitten leaps off his lap to disappear under the work bench, where it hisses at me petulantly.

"Grey!" Tycho says, but he quickly catches himself and straightens. "Your Highness." His eyes flick to the doorway, and I don't know if he's seeing Nolla Verin or Captain Solt, but his face pales a shade. "I—I—drills were canceled—be-because—"

"I know," I say. "I'm here to speak with Harper." I glance at the door. "See if you can find Iisak. He should be made aware of what's happened." I feel pretty certain that Iisak has picked up on some of it, if not *all* of it, but Tycho needs a task.

"Yes," says Tycho. He nods. "Right away." He slips through the door.

Noah ties off the bandage. "You could've given us another fifteen minutes," he says dryly. "It's been a while since I could talk to someone who knows what a stethoscope is."

"We'll still have time." Harper looks at me and then her gaze flicks to the heavily armed people at my back. Her expression evens out. "Or hold on. Maybe I'm about to be executed."

One of the most admirable things about Harper is that she faces every challenge without fear, even when she has absolutely no reason to believe she'll come out of a confrontation alive. Lia Mara was surprised Harper was able to convince a scout to find the queen, but I wouldn't have been surprised if Harper had walked to Syhl Shallow on bare feet to knock on the front door of the palace herself.

"You are not going to be executed." I gesture to the cot Tycho just abandoned. "May I?"

"Sure." Harper glances behind me at Solt and Nolla Verin, both of whom are likely glaring at her. A light sparks in her eyes as her gaze returns to mine. "*Your Highness.*"

I can't tell if she's teasing me or mocking me, but I ignore it. I ease onto the cot, and then, just for a moment, I'm struck by a memory: sitting with Harper just like this, in the infirmary at Ironrose. Then, I was the injured one. My chest was tight with bandages, and Emberfall was under threat of invasion from Syhl Shallow.

Much like right now. Only this time, we're on opposing sides.

The spark in her eye has clouded over, and I know she is remembering the same thing.

She blinks then, glancing away, and I suspect she is chasing off tears, but her voice is even. "I can't believe you're here."

"Likewise," I say.

She gives a humorless laugh. "I'm sure that's true." She glances at Nolla Verin and Solt again. "Who are your henchmen?"

Solt takes a step forward, and his tone is vicious. "You are speaking of the sister to the *queen*—"

"Captain," I snap.

Harper's eyes narrow, and she looks at Nolla Verin. "Oh right. I remember you. You were trying to hook up with Rhen."

Nolla Verin doesn't move. "I am glad I did not," she scoffs, "if the prince and his people were so easily overcome by this *enchant-ress,* our forces will surely—"

Harper drops the shawl and surges to her feet, her hand going to the dagger on her thigh. Nolla Verin draws a blade.

"*Enough.*" I stand and put a hand up between the two of them. Harper is unsteady on her feet, but she looks ready to take on Nolla Verin barehanded if she has to.

"Please don't destroy my infirmary," calls Noah, and both girls go still. He must have gone into the hallway to stand with Jake.

I look at Harper. She's so pale, her eyes shadowed and weary. "You should sit," I say.

Her eyes flick between Solt and Nolla Verin. "I don't think so."

"Jake says you were not fleeing Emberfall," I say to her. "That you came here for my help."

"Yes," she says tightly. "I did."

"You had to know you would not find the man who was once sworn to the Royal Guard." I pause. "You had to know you would not find Commander Grey."

That gets her attention. She blinks. Falters. "I did," she whispers. "I did know." But she stares back at me as if that *is* who she sought, someone who would give her a nod, call her *my lady,* and ask to be pointed at the nearest threat.

"Sit, Harper."

She doesn't sit, and she flinches at my use of her given name.

That small flinch tugs at something inside of me.

"I came here because you were my friend," she says quietly. "Are you still?"

That tugs harder.

It must flicker in my expression, because her eyes soften and she takes a step toward me. "Grey. Please. I came here because *Rhen* was your friend, because—"

"He was *not* my friend," I snap, and she stumbles back, her eyes flaring wide. My anger surprises even me, as if it waited all this time to surface. "I understand why he did what he did, Harper. But he was not my friend."

"So—what? You're just going to leave him there with her?"

"We are at war!"

"A war *you* declared."

"I cannot save the life of a man readying forces against me," I say. "You could not possibly think that—"

"He was going to call for a truce."

I stop short. "What?"

"He was going to call for a truce." New tears gleam in her eyes. "Or peace, or an alliance, or whatever. He wasn't going to fight."

"Lies," snaps Solt.

"It's not a lie!" Harper snaps back.

He swears in Syssalah. "Your prince has sent regiments to the border."

Harper glares at me. "So has *yours*."

"I'm not their prince," I say. She inhales like she's ready to breathe fire, so I sharpen my tone. "Harper. *Sit*." I point at the cot. "Now."

She clamps her mouth shut—but she sits. Her eyes have turned cold and hard. When she first saw me in the guard station, her eyes were full of relief and desperation, but now she looks at me like an adversary.

I don't know if I can undo that. I don't know if I should *want* to undo that.

She glances behind me again. "If you're not going to help me, then just let me go, or throw me into a dungeon, or—"

"Gladly," says Nolla Verin.

I sigh and ease onto the opposite cot. "Tell me what happened."

"I'm not doing this like an interrogation. Tell them to go away."

"You do not issue orders here," says Solt. "You are a prisoner."

"Then lock me up." She holds out her arms, and in a way that only Harper can accomplish, she is both openly defiant and defeated. "I'm done."

"We will allow you the privacy you request," says Lia Mara from the doorway, and I turn, surprised.

"Nolla Verin," she continues. "Captain Solt. You will retreat to the hallway." They do, but Lia Mara stays in the doorway. "*Princess*," she says in a way that is not mocking, but implies she knows everything about Harper's farcical Disi. "I will remind you that I approached your prince with hopes of a peaceful alliance, and he took me prisoner and killed my guard."

Harper stares back at her. "*I* didn't do those things."

"I know." Lia Mara pauses. "I also know you helped Grey escape, undoubtedly at great risk to yourself." Her voice softens, just a touch. "I know he sought out your assistance once before, when he was in great peril."

Harper swallows. "I did that because he's my friend." She glances at me. "*Was* my friend."

"I do not think so," says Lia Mara, and Harper frowns, but she continues. "You may have been friends, but I believe you would have done these things for anyone who asked. I believe you are kind and merciful—and that is why you had no hesitation in riding into a country that has declared war on Emberfall, with the sole intent of finding help for a prince who has caused so much harm."

"Kind and merciful." Harper glances at me again, then frowns.

"Grey once said that kindness and mercy find a limit, and then they turn into weakness and fear."

"Truly?" Lia Mara eases into the room, capturing my gaze with her own. "Do you believe that?"

I look back at her. "Not anymore."

The smallest hint of a smile finds her lips, and her cheeks turn the faintest shade of pink. "I will leave you to have a conversation in peace. I know you have much to discuss." Her sister begins to protest, and Lia Mara adds, "If Captain Solt and Nolla Verin cannot keep their silence, I will find a task to keep them busy." She slips through the door, taking them with her, leaving us in silence.

Harper is staring at me. Her eyes are wary and uncertain. After a moment, she swallows and looks away. "I shouldn't have come here. This was a mistake." Her voice breaks, and she pauses to steady it. "I know it's war. I know you hate him. I just—I didn't know where else to go."

We sit in silence for the longest time. This moment reminds me of another, when she was weary and frightened and in a strange land—and she didn't know whether to trust me then, either. I rise from the cot to root around on Noah's workbench until I find a battered deck of cards, then return to sit opposite Harper. I drag a small table between us, then shuffle.

"Like old times," she says, and her voice breaks again.

"Like old times," I agree. The cards flip together, and I deal. Harper takes up her hand.

"King's Ransom?" she says.

"Yes." I turn a card faceup. The three of stones. I choose an eight of stones from my hand and lay it down. "I rarely play cards anymore."

"No?"

"They play dice here."

"How do you play *dice*?" Maybe the game is steadying, because the emotion has drained from her voice, and now she simply sounds tired.

"I'm not one to ask. I am terrible at it."

That startles a laugh out of her. "I doubt it. You're not terrible at anything."

"I promise I am."

She lays down a card. We play in silence for a while, the low fire crackling along the wall. I didn't forget how much I enjoyed playing cards, but I didn't realize it would summon so many memories. Not just with Harper, but with Rhen as well. In the beginning, when the curse first trapped us alone, I would let him win every game. He quickly caught on, and he was furious. He declared that he didn't need someone to cater to his pride—and when it came to cards, that was probably true. He asked if I also let him win when we sparred in the arena—and he was surprised when I conceded the truth, that no swordsman would truly risk a member of the royal family.

He drew a sword right there. "Fight me," he said. "No yielding, Commander. That is an *order*."

So I did. I disarmed him in less than a minute. I still remember him breathing heavily, staring up at me, a stripe of blood on his forearm.

I remember being startled when, instead of throwing a tantrum, he got to his feet, jerked his jacket straight, and said, "Show me how you just did that."

One of the most startling things about the curse had nothing to do with the magic, or the torments, or even Lilith herself.

It was the discovery that Rhen never realized how ignorant and sheltered he was—and how much he wanted to learn once he had the opportunity.

I lay down a card on the table. "I do not hate him," I say quietly.

Harper hesitates, then sets down her cards to press her fingers into her eyes. "He regrets so much, Grey. What he did—it's tearing him apart. I swear I'm telling the truth. He really was going to come to you with a truce."

"I believe you." My voice is grave. "I am unsure if that matters."

"Why?" she cries. "Why wouldn't that matter?"

I inhale to answer, and she says, "You once told me that if Rhen allowed it, you would take Lilith's torments a hundredfold. Now is your chance. *Now*, Grey. She is killing him. She is—" Her voice chokes on a sob. "She's so awful. He's terrified of magic. You know what she's like. You know what she'll do."

I do. I do know.

This is too much. There are too many memories. My chest is tight, my thoughts filling with ice, the way I feel when I must take action.

"She killed Dustan," Harper says. "She tore his throat out right in front of me. And Zo—somehow Lilith grew wings or created another monster, because she ripped Zo right off the back of my horse." Harper presses her arms across her abdomen. "Please, Grey. Please. Take Emberfall if you want. But please, you have to help me save him. There is no one else. No other way."

I look away. Her tears, her words, are tugging at chords inside me again. I shouldn't care. We're going to war. If Rhen dies at Lilith's hand or at my own, what is the difference?

"Please," Harper whispers. "Grey. He might not be your friend, but he's your *brother*. You spent forever together. That has to mean something. You have to *feel* something."

"I do," I say, and my voice is rough.

She stares at me. "Then you'll help?"

I inhale—but I'm not sure what my answer will be.

It doesn't matter anyway, because Harper's eyes flick beyond me, and she screams.

CHAPTER THIRTY-FIVE

HARPER

I scramble backward on the cot so quickly that I nearly fall off the other side. The cards scatter everywhere. I can all but taste my heart in my throat. A winged creature fills the doorway, black eyes gleaming in the torchlight, and I don't know if I should hide under another cot or make a grab for one of Grey's weapons.

Did Lilith find me? Did she send this monster after me? Did she do this to Rhen? Did she—

"Harper." Grey is on his feet, a placating hand held out to me. "Be at ease."

He's too calm. Too nonchalant.

Then I notice that Jake and Grey's "henchmen" have followed the creature into the room. So has Tycho. They look more alarmed at my reaction than at . . . that.

They're not freaking out.

No one is freaking out.

Jake glances from me to the creature. "Oh." He looks abashed and amused in the way only a brother can. "Hey, Harp. This is Iisak. He's a scraver. And a friend."

A *scraver*. I don't understand how this place still has the capacity to shock me. Iisak is simultaneously terrifying and beautiful, shirtless and barefoot despite the cold, his skin the color of thunderclouds. He's easily as tall as Grey, though his dark wings make him take up more space, and he's lean, with corded muscle down his arms. His fingers end in talons.

"The Princess of Disi," he says, and his voice is a dry rasp, the edges of fangs glinting in the light when he speaks. He offers me a bow, and I can't quite tell for sure, but I think there's a hint of mockery to it.

I swallow. "Hi?"

He eases farther into the room as I try to right myself. My weak leg is weaker still because of my injured ankle, and I feel clumsy and uncertain as I manage to get my feet underneath me. I'm completely off balance, which isn't exactly all that rare, and my heart is still in my throat. Am I supposed to apologize? Curtsy? Run in terror?

I glance from Jake to Grey. "Is this—did you—" My eyes narrow as I try to think of what Lilith could do, the damage she could cause. I can't shake the feeling that something like this chased me off the grounds of Ironrose. I didn't see it clearly, but I remember heavy wings that blocked the moonlight, a dark shape that seemed to absorb the shadows. I thought it was Lilith—or something she created. "Is he real?" I ask Grey. "Is this—an enchantment?"

Grey frowns. "He is real."

"An enchantment!" says Iisak, and at least he sounds amused, because I imagine if he was pissed off he could dismember me in seconds. He draws closer, and I brace myself.

He stops on the other side of the cot, and I can see that his eyes are truly black, no whites at all, and those fangs look razor-sharp. It takes my breath away, but I stand my ground.

"The young prince was right," he says. "He once said you were brave. A princess in spirit if not by birth."

The young prince. For a moment, I think he means Rhen, but I can't make that add up in my head.

But he must mean Grey . . . which means Grey once said that about me. He's been so cool and distant since I got here that I thought he'd cut off our friendship the way he once forswore his family, but maybe . . . maybe I was wrong.

I wet my lips. "I don't know about brave."

"You have come seeking assistance from a magesmith," says Iisak. "You stand and face me, even though I can smell your fear."

"Iisak," says Grey, and there's a warning note in his tone, but also a bit of long-suffering exasperation, too.

Iisak looks at him, and a cool breeze swirls through the room to make me shiver. "She has brought you a problem you cannot hack through with your sword."

"She has brought a problem we are not bound to solve," says Nolla Verin from her place by the wall.

A tiny squeaking sound near the floor draws my attention, and I glance down, ready for another nightmarish creature, but it's Tycho's tiny orange kitten. *Salam.* The kitten is winding itself through Iisak's legs. The scraver scoops it into his hands in a fluid motion, and the kitten almost immediately relaxes against the creature's chest and begins to purr. It's disconcerting to see such a frightening creature be almost . . . tender.

"I have heard enough about this enchantress to believe you *are* bound to solve it," Iisak says evenly. His pure black eyes look to my leg. "She has brought you a blade of Iishellasan steel, as well."

I take a step back automatically, my hand falling over the hilt. "You know what it is?"

"I do." He holds out a taloned hand. "May I?"

I hesitate.

"What is Iishellasan steel?" says Noah.

"It binds magic," says Lia Mara.

"Yes," says Grey. "I once had a bracelet fashioned by the enchantress that allowed me to cross over."

"This dagger likely *repels* magic." The scraver flexes his fingers, gesturing for the weapon. "May I, Princess?"

I don't want to give it to him. I thought I'd come here with a plan to rescue Rhen, but instead I've found myself among no one I can trust.

Jake's eyes find mine from across the room. "Harp," my brother says quietly. "He's okay. You can let him have it."

I wet my lips, then draw the blade.

The scraver's hands curl around the hilt. He gently sets the kitten on a cot. "Your hand?" he says to Grey.

Grey's eyes don't leave mine, but he holds out a hand fearlessly. The scraver swipes the blade across the back of his hand. One of the guards near the wall swears in their language.

Grey sucks in a breath and jerks back, slapping a hand over the wound. Blood drips behind his fingers. He looks from Iisak to me.

"As I said," says Iisak, his voice a low growl. "It repels magic."

Grey lifts his hand. The blood still flows freely. He stares at the wound with an expression of wonder mixed with frustration. "I cannot heal it."

"Indeed." The scraver looks at me. "Where did you get this?"

Noah sighs and seizes a roll of muslin from a supply table. "At least I can be useful with *this*."

Grey glares at Iisak. "Surely you could have made a smaller example."

But the scraver is still looking at me. The room temperature seems to drop by fifteen degrees, and I shiver. "Tell me, Princess." The words edge out with a low growl. "Where did you get this?"

The tension in the room has doubled.

"From Rhen," I say quietly. "He bought it."

"From whom?" says Lia Mara.

I hesitate—but Rhen has already lost. I am here. "From a spy," I whisper.

"A spy!" cries Nolla Verin. She storms across the room. "What spy? What have you—"

"Enough." Lia Mara's voice is quiet but strong. "What is the name of this spy?"

"Chesleigh Darington," I say. "She says her family was killed by Karis Luran. She was able to move among your people." I hesitate again. "She said there were people in Syhl Shallow who plotted against the throne, that there was a faction against magic that had gathered artifacts."

Grey and Lia Mara exchange a glance, and I swallow.

"She's dead," I whisper. "Lilith killed everyone in the castle—and she was there that night. She would have been among them."

The room is absolutely silent for the longest time, unbroken until Noah lifts the muslin from the back of Grey's hand and says, "You'll need stitches. I'll get a needle."

Grey sighs and gives Iisak a withering look again.

Lia Mara's gaze has turned more appraising. "Tell me more about this enchantress. Do you truly think she will stop with Emberfall?"

"She resents Rhen for his family's role in destroying her people," says Grey.

"Syhl Shallow had a role as well," says Iisak. "The magesmiths would not have been forced to find refuge in Emberfall if they had been welcome here." He pauses, peering at me, and another cold lick of wind whispers against my cheek. "Why did you think I was an enchantment?"

Literally nothing about my arrival here has gone the way I expected it to. But maybe I needed to shatter my expectations before I could start over. "Because of what she did to Rhen," I whisper. "Because of what she did to me." I glance at Grey. "Because of what she did to you."

He says nothing. His gaze is heavy.

"You know what she's doing to him," I say. "You remember. I know you do." My voice breaks. We were so close to some kind of . . . *something* before the scraver walked in here, and I wish I could reverse time to that moment. "Please, Grey. I know I have nothing to offer. No kingdom, no alliance. But please. You have to help me save him. *Please.*"

None of them look like they want to help me. None of them even look sympathetic. Scary Grey is in full effect. Jake is stoic and impassive—it's no secret how he feels about Rhen.

"I once begged him for mercy, too," says Grey.

"So did I," says Tycho, and his voice is quiet but strong.

That hits me like a dart to the chest. I know they did.

I remember. I probably have no right to ask Grey for anything on Rhen's behalf.

"What does she want?" says Lia Mara. "This enchantress."

"She wants to rule Emberfall," I say. "She wants to force Rhen to stand at her side while she does it."

"And why is she so cruel?"

The question forces me still. "Does it matter? Why is anyone cruel?"

"There is always a reason," says Lia Mara. "And if she intends to set herself as my adversary in your stead, I believe it to be relevant." She comes to stand beside Grey. When she looks up at him, he looks back at her, and his expression changes, softening.

I expect her to ask if Lilith will be a threat to her country, or whether it's worth exploiting Rhen's sudden weakness to take advantage.

Instead, Lia Mara reaches out to take his hand, and his fingers curl around hers so gently that it's almost as incongruous as the scraver picking up the kitten.

Lia Mara says, "He is your brother, Grey." Her voice is so quiet. "Do you want to save him?"

Grey hesitates, then looks at me. "Why did he buy that dagger from a spy?"

I hear what he's asking. *Did Rhen buy it to use against me? Or did he buy it to use against Lilith?*

I'm not sure what to say.

I'm not sure he needs me to say it.

"This was war," I whisper.

His jaw tightens, and Grey takes the dagger and shoves it into his belt. He looks back at Lia Mara, then to the waiting soldiers, including my brother. "Lilith will not stop with Rhen," he says. "She must know Syhl Shallow was planning to attack. She may have no interest in war, but she has plenty of interest in conflict. Rhen would have tried to spare his soldiers, to mount a defense with the least loss of human life." Another pause. "Lilith will not care. She will force him to send soldier after soldier into battle, until they're all dead. His *and* ours."

"Do you think you can stop her?" Lia Mara says.

Grey looks at Iisak. "We can try."

For the first time since arriving here, hope blooms in my chest. "Wait. Really?"

"He has a regiment already stationed at the border," Grey says. "We would need a small team of soldiers, because she is expecting a full assault, and not for another few days. Captain Solt, choose from your company. No more than ten. We will need to leave at full dark."

"Grey," I whisper, my voice full of wonder. "You'll do it? You'll save him?"

"I will stop Lilith," he says, and his voice is cold and dark. "I will protect Syhl Shallow." He pauses. "Rhen's life is not my concern."

He turns away, but he may as well have stabbed me with the dagger before leaving. I have to press a hand to my abdomen.

"Come," says Lia Mara. She takes my hand. "I will see to it that you have a room."

I don't want to like anything here, but the palace really is magnificent. I'm given a massive room with huge windows that look out over sprawling fields and the mountainside. I hoped Jake would come sit with me for a bit, but I haven't seen him. I haven't seen anyone. Food is brought, but for the most part, I'm left alone. The sun appears to be setting over the mountains, spilling pink and purple streaks across the glittering city.

I don't even know if they're taking me with them. Will they leave me here? Will I be some kind of prisoner in case things go south with Rhen? I hadn't considered that. Grey was so cold when he turned away and began issuing orders.

I once begged him for mercy.

He did beg. I remember. But is that all that matters? They spent an eternity together, enduring the most terrible things I can imagine, but their relationship will boil down to one poor choice? And even as I think that, was the poor choice Rhen's, when he ordered his guards to find some whips, or was the poor choice Grey's, when he decided to run, when he chose to keep his birthright a secret?

I don't know who I'm kidding. They were both wrong. Sometimes we make such poor choices that the good ones pale in comparison.

A hand raps at the door, and I nearly jump. "Enter," I call. I hope for my brother.

Instead, I get Grey. He's alone.

I'm so surprised that I stare at him for a long moment before scraping myself out of the chair to stand. "Grey."

"I will have armor brought," he says without preamble. "You will not be allowed to carry a weapon."

"I'm going?" I say in surprise.

"There is worry that this is a trap."

My mouth flattens into a line. "So I'm your hostage."

His expression gives nothing away. "In truth, I was hoping you would serve as an advisor. My soldiers will not know what to expect as we head into Emberfall." He pauses. "It would go a long way toward establishing goodwill."

"If I have a chance at rescuing Rhen, I'll do whatever you need."

He says nothing to that. He glances at my leg. "You are still injured. I can heal the damage."

I freeze in place. "With magic."

"It would be better if you were not a burden on the journey."

"Well." I drop into the chair. "I wouldn't want to be a *burden*."

Grey isn't one to be baited. He draws a low stool close and drops to sit in front of me, wasting no time in reaching for the laces of my boots. Noah has stitched up the back of his hand, a tiny row of black knots. Grey is so clinical, so efficient, but I shiver anyway. I have so many memories of him, all rooted in my first days in Emberfall. The way he caught my arm and showed me how to hold a dagger. The way he stood at my back and taught me how to throw a knife. How he'd catch my fist when he taught me to throw a punch, or the way he'd adjust my stance when I first began learning swordplay.

The way he was hurt and terrified in my apartment after Noah stitched him up, how his eyes kept seeking mine for reassurance.

How he unbuckled his bracers in the filthy alley in Washington, DC, buckling them onto my forearms.

I have no coins or jewels to leave you with, he said. *But I do have weapons.*

The way he saved me from the Syhl Shallow soldiers on the battlefield, how he pulled me into his arms. *I will keep her safe,* he said to Rhen.

Oh, Grey. I can understand why he's mad at Rhen, but I never truly thought about what it would mean for me and Grey to be on opposite sides of this war. Maybe I could have played fate's cards differently anywhere along the line and we could have been more than friends, but I didn't. He didn't. I think about that moment in the courtyard behind the Crooked Boar, when he went with Lia Mara and I went back to Rhen. I wonder where we'd be now if I had made a different choice. If he had. I wonder what it would be like to look on Rhen as an enemy, as someone on the other side of a battlefield, and the thought makes my heart stutter.

Whatever Grey and I are, I don't want to be enemies. I don't want him and Rhen to be enemies. My throat tightens. I can't breathe.

I must make a sound or a motion that catches his attention, because he looks up in alarm. "My lady," he says softly.

My lady. I can't take it. I throw myself forward and wrap my arms around his neck. "Please, Grey," I say, pressing my tear-streaked face into his shoulder. "You were my friend. Please don't be like this."

It's probably the most reckless move in the world, because he has about four million weapons, and there are plenty of people in this castle who think it'd be easier if I were in a grave right now.

But Grey catches me, his strong hands gentle against my waist. He drops his head, and I feel more than hear his sigh. He doesn't quite hold me, but he doesn't shove me away.

"Please," I say. "I don't want to be your enemy."

"Nor do I." His voice is very low, very quiet. "I do not want to be Rhen's either."

I draw back a bit to look at him. "But . . . you won't rescue him."

"We have been preparing for *war*, Harper. I offered him trust. I offered him friendship. I offered him *brotherhood*. He rejected them all, and I have had to make peace with that. As it is, these soldiers hardly trust me. What you heard from Solt and Nolla Verin will not be the end of it. I cannot make this a mission to rescue him. They would refuse."

"We could go alone! We could—"

"*Alone?* I have spent weeks at Lia Mara's side, convincing this army I am allied with their queen. Convincing these soldiers that I stand with *them*. How could I disappear in the middle of the night with the Princess of Disi?"

This all feels so fruitless. "But—"

"No, Harper. I will not do that to them." His eyes darken, his tone sharpening. "I *certainly* will not do it to her."

I go still. There's a protective note in his voice that I haven't heard before. A look in his eyes. I have to draw back farther, shifting into the chair to study him. I was stuck on all the loyalty and strategic talk that reminds me so much of Rhen, but now I'm focused on the last part of that sentence, on the intensity in his gaze.

Oh. *Oh.*

He's in *love* with her.

"I can take action to protect Syhl Shallow," Grey continues. "And I will." He pauses. "I cannot promise to protect Rhen," he says. "But I can make a vow to destroy Lilith, if I am able."

"And if Rhen survives, what then? What happens to this war?"

"You said he wanted peace, did you not?"

"He does," I say. "He does. I swear it."

"Good." Grey pulls the boot off my foot, all business again. "If he survives, then he can prove it."

CHAPTER THIRTY-SIX

LIA MARA

The night sky is full of clouds again, snow flurries trickling down through the wind. I can barely see the soldiers leaving, which I suppose is the point. Iisak will follow in the skies. He's already well overhead, nearly invisible in the twilit darkness.

Nolla Verin is waiting inside the palace with Clanna Sun, because we're to discuss contingency plans, but I'm standing in the iced-over gardens, watching the small group of soldiers ride toward the city gates. We've spent weeks and weeks preparing for war, but I never once thought of how it would feel to stand like this, watching the barest glints of their weapons as they ride off the training fields. I never realized that it would feel like I've given away a part of myself, a part that Grey now carries with him.

He found me before they left, stealing a few minutes of privacy during which I should have been whispering warnings and promises and telling him all the ways my heart beats for him alone. Instead, his lips were on mine, and I inhaled his breath until I was dizzy with wanting and soldiers were shouting for him.

Grey kissed me one last time, then whispered against my lips. "I will come back to you."

I hooked my fingers in his armor before he could pull away. "Your word?"

He smiled, took my hand, and kissed my fingertips. "My vow."

Then he was gone, all softness erased from his face, any vulnerability gone from his frame.

But now I'm standing, staring, watching, waiting. There's a part of me that doesn't want to leave this garden until I see him return.

I heard what Harper said about this enchantress, the things she did to Rhen and his people. I've heard Grey's stories of what she used to do.

He could die.

The thought flies into my head without warning, and once there, it takes root. I have to shake it loose.

I can't.

I might never see him again.

The thought is dizzying. I have to put a hand against my belly.

And then I throw up my dinner right there in the garden.

CHAPTER THIRTY-SEVEN

GREY

When I first journeyed to Syhl Shallow with Lia Mara, our traveling party was fractured in the beginning, with clear lines of division: me and Tycho, Jake and Noah, Lia Mara and Iisak. It made for tense conversation and uneasy nights, leaving everyone irritated and snappish.

This journey back into Emberfall is worse.

Captain Solt provided ten soldiers, as requested, and most of them are lethal and experienced, but to my surprise Solt included Tycho among them.

When I questioned him about it, he said, "The boy is from Emberfall. We may need a fluent scout."

"Wise," I said.

Solt grunted. "We'll also need someone to dig a ditch for the latrine."

To his credit, Tycho has done everything asked of him, rubbing down the horses, cleaning harness leather, fetching buckets of water—and digging ditches. He's never shied away from hard work. It's been three days, and we've only been riding at night, so I watch him pitch face-first onto his bedroll the very instant he's relieved of duty.

Harper has been clinging to her brother's side, which has generated some glances from the other soldiers, so I have tried to keep my distance from both of them, choosing instead to sit with Solt at meal times. I don't want to give anyone in our group the impression that I am separate from them. Unfortunately it leaves me with little conversation, because Solt is cool and distant, speaking only when spoken to.

My only true companion is Iisak, who takes to the skies when we ride at night, then lands at daybreak and demands that I practice my skills. Always before, magic was a struggle because I didn't understand it—and I didn't want to understand it.

Now magic is a struggle because I know where my limitations are—limitations Lilith herself does not share.

I've come to eye my bedroll with the same desperation as Tycho, but when I try to sleep, all I do is worry. I don't think Harper would lead me into a trap, which I know occupies the thoughts of the other soldiers—but I am also unsure if Rhen truly wanted peace, or if his desires were more strategic in nature. I know Harper believes the best of him, but I've seen the worst.

I know this dagger is impervious to magic—the irritating stitches across the back of my hand are proof enough of that. But I don't know if it will be enough.

I don't know if I can defeat Lilith. I don't know if I can save Rhen.

I don't know if I can help unite these countries.

And deeper, darker, a thought I almost don't want to admit to myself: I don't know if I can keep my vow to Lia Mara. I might have magic, but I don't have the skill with it that Lilith does. She trapped all of Ironrose in a curse that seemed eternal, and I now know that requires a complicated layering of magic that I am nowhere near mastering.

Sleep proves to be elusive at best, and I am no less surly and snappish than the others.

By the fourth day, we've circled around Rhen's stationed regiment, sticking close to the forest. Tonight we'll need to move out of the woods on the mountainside, which will be the riskiest travel yet, so I practice with Iisak for a shorter time, and then he goes to scout our paths from overhead to see if we'll encounter any resistance or risk of discovery.

It's barely sunrise, but most of the soldiers have already fallen asleep. It seems they've called on Tycho to guard the camp, because he's sitting against a tree not far from the fire. I slip between the trees, wondering if I'll find him dozing, but I should give Tycho more credit. I hardly make a sound, but he whirls off the ground, an arrow nocked on a string before he's fully upright.

I catch the arrow against the bow so he can't let it fly.

His eyes are wide, his breathing a little quick, but relief blooms in his gaze. "Sorry." He hesitates, easing the bow string. "Your Highness."

"Don't be," I say. "You were quick off the ground."

The praise makes him blush, just a bit. He tucks the arrow in his quiver and hangs the bow over his shoulder. "It's the first time they've asked me to sit sentry."

"Well chosen," I say.

His blush deepens. "I'm more worried I'll fall asleep."

"I'll sit with you."

He looks startled at that, and maybe a little wary, but he nods. "As you say."

I sit, putting my back to a tree a few feet away, and he sits as well, pulling the bow into his lap. The early morning forest is quiet and cold, the tethered horses just as tired as the soldiers. I've hardly spoken to Tycho since I confronted him in the sleet a few days ago. With someone else, there might be some tension between us, but with Tycho, there's none. Because the silence is so amiable, I let it hang between us while the sun fully rises, letting my thoughts drift.

If I'm not careful, *I* will doze off, so I try to fill the silence. "Do you ever think of the tourney?"

Worwick's Tourney is where I hid when I first fled Ironrose. For months, Tycho was my only companion, and my first confidant when Rhen began searching for the missing heir. It was the simplest three months of my life—until it wasn't. I used to teach him basic swordplay in the dusty arena, until Tycho learned the truth of who I was and demanded to graduate to the real thing.

Tycho looks over in surprise. "Worwick's? All the time."

"How many times do you think he spun the story of our capture?"

Tycho smiles. "At least a hundred. He's probably charging a fee just to hear him tell it."

Knowing Worwick, that's the truth.

"It's odd to be in Emberfall again," Tycho says. "Don't you think?"

"I do." I remember the first night Rhen and I discovered soldiers from Syhl Shallow were in Emberfall. I didn't expect to be wearing their colors less than a year later. I'd sworn my life to defend Rhen. I never expected I'd be standing against him.

The thought of him facing Lilith alone tugs at me more than it should.

"Do you think we'll encounter Rhen's forces?" Tycho says, and something about his voice is lower, quieter, so I look over.

"We might," I say. He's silent, so I add, "Are you afraid?"

He hesitates, and for a moment, I think he won't admit it to me, especially not now. His voice drops even lower, and he says, "I'm afraid that when the time comes, I won't be able to kill someone."

I sense there is more for him to say, so I glance at him and wait.

Maybe he's encouraged by my silence, because he continues. "The other recruits seem almost excited to do it," he says. "They have chants about the blood we'll spill in Emberfall."

I remember what Noah said, the first day I found Tycho hiding in the infirmary. I thought the others might have been hazing Tycho a bit, because of his youth, because of where we came from, because of his friendship with me. But maybe that wasn't it at all.

I don't think they're doing anything wrong, Noah said. *I think they're just being soldiers.*

I remember my days in training for the Royal Guard. "Those chants aren't uncommon here either," I say.

"I know." He hesitates.

Again, I wait. The woods around us are so silent, I can hear the wind slip between the leaves.

"When I was a boy," he says, "we had cats that would sleep in the rafters of our barn. One of them had kittens, and my sisters and I loved them. We'd play in the barn for hours after chores were done." He pauses, and sunlight breaks through the trees, painting gold in his hair. "My father lost a game of cards to a few soldiers one night, and he didn't have the coins he'd promised. They tore through our house. One of them . . . he . . . my mother . . . well." His voice tightens, and he takes a breath before changing course. "The other soldiers came into the barn. We had a cow, and one of them drew a sword and cut its throat. My sisters were screaming, we were all screaming, clutching those kittens." He hesitates, but then his voice accelerates, as if he can't get the words out fast enough. "He drew a dagger and started plucking the kittens out of my sisters' hands. Killing them one by one. He said, 'I like when they squeak.'" Tycho's eyes flash with fury. "I shoved my kitten down my shirt. It kept clawing at me, but I didn't care. And then he said, 'I bet you'll squeak, too.'" He shudders, and I can't tell which is stronger in his voice, the current anger or the remembered fear.

He stops there, and he's so still that I don't think he's breathing. There's more to this story. There *has* to be more. But this is the most he's ever told me, so I keep quiet.

"He was hurting my sisters. He was hurting me." He cringes, his eyes on the trees. "I couldn't stop him. My father was shouting for the enforcers, so he turned me loose before—before he could be caught. But I don't—I can't be like that. I can't . . . revel in it." He frowns, looking a bit abashed that he admitted all that.

I think of that kitten in Noah's infirmary. "Being a soldier does not require cruelty," I say quietly. "Nor revelry."

"Doesn't it?" he says. He lifts the bow meaningfully, then pats at the dagger strapped to his thigh. "A little?"

"When I joined the Royal Guard," I say, "I had to take a life." The moment is seared into my memory for so many reasons. I can still hear the bell of the arena ringing, can still smell my own sweat and fear. "It was a man condemned to death, but it was still a life. If I failed, I would have been dead and my family would have starved. Is that cruelty?"

He doesn't have an answer for that.

I lean back against the tree. "Those men who hurt your family—that was not because they were soldiers, Tycho. They may have had the skills and the weaponry to cause harm, but that did not make them cruel. Defending yourself—defending your *people*—that does not make a man cruel either. When the time comes for you to use deadly force, I have no doubt you'll do it well, and do it honorably."

Or he'll die.

I don't say that. I'm sure he knows it.

His eyes are on the horizon, but I can tell he's thinking.

But then his gaze sharpens, and he rolls to his feet in one fluid motion. That arrow finds his hand again, and it's nocked on the string just as my eyes see the target, a hint of motion between the trees a hundred yards away.

"Grey," he breathes.

I'm already on my feet beside him. My eyes search the trees, seeking more. This could be a lone scout, or it could be an attack.

There. A glint of red and gold, almost obscured by the trees—but far enough from the first that I doubt it's scouts working together.

"Hold," I say to Tycho, and he nods, keeping the bowstring taut.

The sun is rising beyond the forest, but it's still early, and heavy shadows still linger among the trees. As I watch, more soldiers in gold and red seem to appear among the trees, coming from all directions, easing through the foliage.

There are more than two dozen.

Tycho is frozen in place beside me, waiting for an order, that arrow nocked and ready. But everyone else is sleeping, and . . . I turn to look . . . we're surrounded. I don't know how they knew, how they tracked us, but it doesn't matter. If I shout for the others, they'll attack. If Tycho fires, they'll attack.

"Grey!" Tycho shoves me down just as I hear the *swip* of a bow-string, and I duck automatically. An arrow embeds itself in the tree where I was standing.

"Return fire," I say, but he's already doing that, snapping arrows off the string with calm focus.

I wish I had a bow. I could return fire with him. As it is, I'm thirty feet away from the sleeping camp, and now soldiers are slipping between the trees with more confidence. They're shooting at me, at Tycho, but I knock the arrows out of the air while he shoots.

"*Rukt*," I shout to my sleeping soldiers. "Solt! Jake!"

In the distance, a man cries out and falls, an arrow jutting from his neck.

"That was my last one," Tycho says breathlessly, but he draws his sword.

I grab his arm. "Come on." Arrows fill the air around us, and one pings off my armor. I'm shouting as I run back to the camp. "Solt! Jake!"

We're not going to be fast enough. There are too many of them. Rhen's soldiers seem to be appearing through the trees from every-where now. Solt is on his feet, shouting orders, but an arrow slices him right across the arm. Another soldier doesn't even make it off the ground before he takes one in the chest. My heart is pounding hard, but everything seems to be happening in slow motion, with perfect clarity. We'll be overtaken: slaughtered or taken prisoner.

Overhead, Iisak screeches in the trees, and the air thins, turning ice cold. I hear one of the Emberfall soldiers swear. Arrows point up into the sky. A soldier intercepts me, his sword meeting mine with a clash of steel. Just as quickly, I cut him down. At my side, Tycho does the same.

Iisak slashes through another soldier before he can get close to me. A blast of cold wind flares through the woods. He screeches at me, then darts higher, just missing a throwing blade. "Magic!" he snaps.

Magic. Right.

I don't know how I can focus on magic when swords are coming at me.

"I'll cover you," says Tycho.

My thoughts are flaring too quickly, impossible to settle. I once knocked out everyone in Rhen's courtyard through magic, but I've never been able to repeat it. I've been able to shove back soldiers one by one during swordplay, but that's *one*, not dozens.

But I remember the night I worked on this with Iisak, putting my power into the ground. I couldn't cover much distance, but when I thought of Lia Mara, my magic seemed to reach for her automatically. I touch a hand to the ground. Take a breath. At my back, Tycho's sword meets another, and I want to whip around, to join the fray. I send my magic into the ground, and it snaps back to me, unwilling. This isn't natural. I growl in frustration. Magic isn't automatic.

Motion flickers in my peripheral vision, and I lift my sword, but Solt is there, covering my other side.

Iisak's screech reverberates through the woods. Sunlight paints everything in stark relief, and I smell blood on the air. I take another breath and put my hand to the ground.

Another gold-and-red-armored man appears from behind a tree, his sword aiming straight for Tycho. He only has one arm, and I'm stunned to realize I recognize him. I remember how he fought, how he wouldn't yield even when he was exhausted and panting in the dust of the arena. Jamison's eyes flare wide when he recognizes me, but he doesn't hesitate.

Silver arcs in the cold air. Tycho is going to be a second too slow.

I ease my power into the ground and give it a push. Wind blazes through the trees, ice-cold in its intensity, full of snow flurries that appeared from nowhere.

Jamison is knocked back. All of the soldiers are knocked back. They're flat on the ground, not moving. At my side, Solt is breathing hard, blood seeping from that wound on his arm. Twenty feet away, most of our soldiers are doing the same, looking stunned that the battle quite literally dropped out from under us.

I'm equally stunned. My own breathing is shaking a bit.

"Kill them all," Solt calls in Syssalah.

That brings me back to myself. "No," I snap. "Leave them. Break camp. They won't stay down long."

"*Leave them?*" he echoes.

"Yes. Leave them."

Iisak settles in the leaves near us. "Your Highness. They will be able to follow."

"Then we need to ride fast. Let's go." I glance at Tycho, who's looking stunned for his own reasons. I clap him on the shoulder. "As I said. You did well. Very well."

"Thank you," he says, but his voice is hollow. He sheathes his sword.

"This was a trap," Solt snaps at me, at my back, and I look up to find Harper and Jake in the middle of the other soldiers. Her eyes are wide and frightened and angry.

"Maybe," she says. "But I didn't set it." She strides forward, toward me, stepping around the bodies of Rhen's soldiers who are lying in the underbrush. "I had nothing to do with this. Rhen had nothing to—" She stops short, looking down, and she frowns. "It's— it's Chesleigh."

Chesleigh. "The spy?" I demand. "The spy who found the dagger of Iishellasan steel?"

Solt is heading toward her, too. "Rhen's spy was among them? Wake her up. We will question her—"

"You can't," says Harper, and her voice is flat. She drops to a crouch. "She took two arrows. I'm pretty sure she's dead." She glances up at me. "I can't believe she survived Lilith to bite it here."

Solt and I reach her at the same time. Harper is right—two arrows jut from the woman's chest. She has dark hair braided tightly to her head, and a scar on her cheek that I've seen a hundred times in the Crystal Palace.

Solt swears in Syssalah, then draws his sword and plunges it into her chest.

Harper jerks back. "Holy crap. She was already dead."

"She deserves worse," he snaps.

"I agree," I say. My chest is tight with worry. I look at the other soldiers. "Break camp. We need to go."

Harper looks at me. "What's wrong? Do you know her?"

"Her name isn't Chesleigh. It's Ellia Maya." I look over at Jake. "She's not just a spy. She's an advisor to the queen."

CHAPTER THIRTY-EIGHT

LIA MARA

They've been gone for days. There's been no word, which is fine—expected, even—but I keep looking at the horizon, waiting for a scout to deliver bad news.

Noah dines with me and Nolla Verin in the evenings, and I appreciate the company of someone who's also worried about one man in particular, not just whether Grey and my soldiers—*our* soldiers—are successful. My sister rarely leaves my side, so no one has dared to attack me, but with Grey gone, my nerves are tightly wound anyway, leaving me anxious and nauseated. After growing used to sharing my bed, now it feels cold and empty at night.

"You are both so *dour*," Nolla Verin says on the fifth night. "Have you no faith in your beloveds?"

Noah and I exchange a glance.

"It has nothing to do with faith," I say.

"When I was sixteen," Noah says, "my sister was stationed in Afghanistan. It's . . . it's another place. A war zone. My parents were

fine most of the time, but the dinner table, her missing seat . . . it
was a constant reminder." He paused. "It was a depressing year."

"Your sister was a warrior," says Nolla Verin.

"Yes, she was." He pushes the food around his plate, but he
doesn't take a bite. He gives a laugh that's a little sad. "I never thought
I'd be waiting for news on a soldier *again*."

A page appears in the doorway to the dining room, and my
heart skips a beat. But the girl simply curtsies and extends a slip of
paper in my direction. "A message has been delivered for you, Your
Majesty."

I take the paper to read the message. It's from Captain Sen Domo
in the guard station at the mountain pass.

> Prince Grey has sent word that soldiers from Emberfall
> attacked their party. There were two casualties, including
> palace advisor Ellia Maya. They are proceeding toward
> Ironrose Castle. Reports indicate that another regiment
> from Emberfall has joined the first.

I have to read it three times, as if more information will suddenly appear, but of course none does.

Ellia Maya is dead? She was not with them. I don't understand.

I can't look up from this letter to look at Noah. His words just
now about waiting on news about a soldier feel prescient. Jake and
Tycho were among the soldiers. So was Iisak. Surely Grey would have
known I would receive this message. I have no doubt he would
have mentioned them specifically if he mentioned Ellia Maya.

I still don't understand why she was *there*. She has been working in the city for weeks, trying to track the source of this anti-
magic faction. She was the one who discovered the literature about

Iishellasan steel, and the one who discovered that there was a faction to begin with.

I try to consider the meaning of this letter more deeply. They were attacked? The point of the small party was to be able to travel quietly, without detection. They wouldn't have engaged in a battle.

I think of Harper, appearing to beg for help. Was this a trap? Have we been naive?

If this message came from Grey, he *had* to have a reason for mentioning her. He would know I'd be confused.

"Read it," says my sister. Her eyes are intent on my face, her voice low.

I glance at Noah, then read the letter aloud. When I get to Ellia Maya's name, my sister gasps.

Noah sets down his fork entirely. His eyes are shadowed and wary.

"Why would she be with them?" Nolla Verin cries. "Was she a hostage? Who has done this?" Her voice turns vicious. "And he has moved another regiment? They're being led to slaughter. This is a *trap*."

"I don't think Harper was leading anyone to slaughter," says Noah. He pauses. "I think Lilith is manipulating Prince Rhen."

"Regardless," says Nolla Verin. "More soldiers have moved into place. If we allow this to proceed unchecked, it won't matter what Grey does, because he'll be cut off from Syhl Shallow. He cannot stand against an army with a handful of soldiers."

"You just asked me to have faith in him," I snap. "And I do." My thoughts are spinning, refusing to settle. I feel as though an answer is there, just out of my grasp. Grey would *know* I wouldn't understand that message. Why wouldn't he give me more information about Ellia Maya? It doesn't make sense.

"Faith? Against an *army*?"

My stomach churns again. "Yes. Against an army."

But she's right. All the faith in the world isn't going to stop thousands of soldiers. Even when Grey has spoken of the enchantress, her power is limited by location, by the number of people she can affect. She's powerful, but she's not *all* powerful.

Neither is he.

Including palace advisor Ellia Maya.

I read the letter again. And a fifth time.

"What are you *doing*?" my sister demands.

"I'm thinking." I read it a sixth time. He'd expect me to be confused—and he'd also expect this message to pass through many hands before it would reach me.

Maybe I've been looking at this the wrong way. Maybe the message isn't in what he says, but in what he *doesn't*.

What did Harper say about a spy? *She says her family was killed by Karis Luran. She said there was a faction against magic that had gathered artifacts.*

Ellia Maya's family was killed. And she knew everything about the faction because she herself was researching it. She told Nolla Verin no weapons had been uncovered—because she'd sold the blade to Rhen herself.

Ellia Maya wasn't with them when she left—which must mean she was killed among the soldiers from Emberfall.

And if Ellia Maya was working against me, she might not be the only person in the palace who was involved with this faction. My blood goes cold.

This is what Grey suspected. This is why he offered no further information—not just about Ellia Maya, but about their own plans.

Oh, how I wish he were here. My people feel so uncertain about my rule, about my choices, about my alliance with a man who bears magic. I don't want to make the wrong decision.

Maybe that's been the problem all along. I've spent so much time worrying about how my actions would be perceived that I've forgotten to pay attention to what actions would be *best*.

Surely the worst decision would be to do nothing.

My army is prepared for war. Grey is in Emberfall, potentially trapped or dead—or worse, at the mercy of some enchantress.

I can't protect him, but I can protect my people.

I look at my sister. "Call for the generals. Don't send a messenger; I want you to speak with them directly. We cannot risk any further insurrection. But if Rhen has sent a force north, we will send a force through the mountain pass."

She drops her fork. "Right away."

She practically vanishes from the room, leaving me with Noah. My chest feels tight.

I look at him, my own worries mirrored in his brown eyes. "Your sister fought in a war?"

"She did."

"Was she victorious?"

"She died."

His words drop like a rock in a pond, breaking through the surface and plummeting to the bottom. "Forgive me," I say softly.

He smiles a little sadly. "She died fighting for what she believed in," he says. "I don't think she'd want you to be sorry for her loss."

"I'm sorry for yours."

He reaches out to give my hand a squeeze. "I have faith in them, too, Lia Mara." He stands. "I'll prepare supplies."

I blink at him. "Supplies?"

"You're sending an army to war." He pauses. "If I learned anything during the battle in Emberfall, they'll need a medic."

CHAPTER THIRTY-NINE

HARPER

If I wasn't popular before, I'm less so now.

The attack in the woods was terrifying, because I *know* Rhen didn't send soldiers after us, and I know he wouldn't send another regiment that far north. He was planning on yielding. I know he was.

I don't know what this means, though. Is Lilith forcing him to do this? Or is he making this choice on his own? I keep thinking about our conversation during our last night together, when I told him that I started expecting him to make bad decisions—and how he'd started expecting me to do the same.

I came for Grey in the hopes of saving Rhen, and now I'm worried I made the worst choice of all. I'm not bringing a rescue, I'm bringing an attack.

I might feel a little better if Grey weren't being so distant. It's unsettling to watch him wield magic. It's like he's Scary Grey for a whole new reason.

But it's more than just the magic. He seems to have stepped into a role, rising to a challenge he didn't want. The soldiers might not wholly trust him, but they sure listen to him. And my brother! The last time I saw Jake and Grey together, hatred flared every time they made eye contact, but now there's no tension between them. They're friends. More than friends: They *respect* each other. That might be more shocking than anything else. I've been clinging to Jake because I don't know anyone, but I can tell that his loyalty is to Grey, to these soldiers, to this army. To their cause.

I think of all the tension and uncertainty around Ironrose—throughout all of Emberfall, really—over the last few months, and it all makes me a bit sad.

Or maybe it's just the fact that I'm sitting by myself, on a log, near a dwindling fire.

It's probably an hour till full dark, and the other soldiers are beginning to pack up the horses. Motion flickers at the corner of my eye, and I think it's Jake bringing me dinner—or breakfast, or whatever we're calling it since we sleep all day and ride all night.

To my surprise, it's Grey. He's said *maybe* ten words to me since we left Syhl Shallow. Three of them were, "Were you harmed?" on the morning we were attacked, and when I said I wasn't, he gave me a nod and then moved away to look after his soldiers.

"Oh, hi," I say. "You remembered I exist." It sounds catty coming out of my mouth, but I've hardly slept in days, and I'm sort of freezing.

Grey takes a branch from the ground and uses it to stoke the fire. He ignores my tone. "We will reach Ironrose by morning."

"I know." We've been staying off the beaten path, but I've begun to recognize towns as we've passed them in the dead of night.

"Iisak is flying reconnaissance, but we were taken by surprise before. Does Rhen have soldiers surrounding the castle?"

"I don't know."

He looks down at me, and his eyes are dark and shadowed. "You agreed to act as advisor."

His tone says he's not taking my crap. Maybe that works on his soldier buddies, but I just want to give him the finger. I stare into the fire. "Well, this advisor has no idea. There wasn't an army there when Lilith or whatever it was chased me off the grounds. She killed all—all the—" I think of Zo and Freya and my chest tightens. "She killed everyone. He could be there all by himself. He could have the entire army surrounding the castle. I don't know."

He says nothing.

I say nothing.

I have to think of something other than Rhen being left alone with Lilith for days, because my imagination is conjuring so many awful things that could easily be true. But everything here is a glaring reminder of all the ways we've failed.

Eventually Grey sighs, and I expect him to turn away and storm off.

Instead, he sits down beside me.

I feign a gasp. "What will people say?"

"Quite a bit, I'm sure." He's quiet for a while, and I'm not sure how to fill the silence, so I don't. Finally, he says, "I suspect you *did* think you would find Commander Grey here. That I would rush to Rhen's aid."

"No." My voice sounds hollow. Maybe he's right. I don't know. "I thought I'd find my friend. I thought I'd find Rhen's brother." I've run out of tears, so I stare at the fire and breathe. "I had no choice."

"Choice." He scoffs. "We always have a choice."

"You're right," I say. "You had a choice all those years you were kidnapping girls for him."

"Yes. I did. I chose the path that would lead to a way out of the curse. I swore my life to him, and I meant the oath I gave."

"Until now."

That shuts him up. He sighs again.

"I know what you said about your soldiers," I say quietly. "How this can't be a mission to rescue him. How you want to see if he was serious about peace." I pause. "But what do *you* want, Grey? Do you want Rhen as your brother? Or is this just a way to take advantage again?"

"Again!" He whips his head around. "When have I taken advantage?"

"When you first went to Syhl Shallow. When you declared war. You knew he was broken and hurting. You knew he was still dealing with everything Lilith did to him."

"I did not take *advantage*." His voice is tight. "His enforcers were slaughtering his people to get to me. He tried to kill Tycho. His guards would have leveled Blind Hollow. He would have—"

"He would have listened to you, Grey." I pause. "If you'd told him the truth. From the beginning."

He looks at me. "Do you really think so?"

I want to say yes.

But I'm not sure.

I stare into the fire. "Before . . . Lilith . . . we had this big conversation about how we forgot that the other person knew how to make good decisions. For him, the big one was what he did to you and Tycho. For me, it was choosing to rescue you."

He makes an aggravated sound. "You and Rhen are drawn to

such extremes—of heroism, of generosity, of *rescue*, Harper—yet you both seem determined to accomplish these feats without assistance, without even the consideration of how your acts will be viewed by those around you."

He says this like it's nothing, like he's telling me grass is green, but I stare at him gape-mouthed. "What?"

He glances at me. "I've begun to wonder if the curse would have dragged on for so long if Rhen had just explained his predicament to each girl. If he had sought an ally instead of creating adversaries that he had to woo and charm." He pauses. "And you yourself ran from the castle—from me, from *Rhen himself*—many times. Even when you were no longer running in fear, you were taking actions without a care for how that would affect his people—for how it would affect *him*."

I can't stop staring at him. Grey was always stoic and thoughtful, but he's found a voice in Syhl Shallow, and he's clearly not afraid to use it.

"You fled to Syhl Shallow for my help," he continues, "without a moment's consideration for my position, for what your request would mean to a country that offered me sanctuary—*sanctuary*, Harper!—after Rhen had attacked their soldiers, destroyed half their army, and imprisoned their queen when she sought an alliance."

I swallow. He's right. I didn't consider any of that.

I think of my conversation with Rhen, about bad decisions that feel right in the moment you're making them. I think of how he teased me for trying to handle situations on my own, for refusing assistance. I think of how Jake said I reminded him of Mom, how I've worried all this time that I was staying with a man for the wrong reasons.

Maybe I've been like my father, too. He wasn't *trying* to make poor decisions. Neither am I. I just want to help people.

Just like Dad wanted to help our family.

The thought is jarring, and I have to put a hand to my chest—but then I straighten my shoulders.

"I came to Syhl Shallow for your help," I say, "because you're the only one who can stop her." I look him dead in the eye. "And because underneath all the talk about how much you want to be loyal to Syhl Shallow, I think you want to rescue Rhen every bit as much as I do."

He looks right back at me. For the longest time, he says nothing, but I can see the emotion churning in his eyes.

"You swore your life to him, Grey," I say. "That meant something to you, and you can't just turn that off, even if you think you can."

He sighs and runs a hand across his jaw. When he looks back at me, his eyes are cool and opaque, belying my statement. Maybe he *can* turn it off. "You don't know if he has soldiers surrounding the castle. Tell me what you do know."

Ugh. Fine. *Fine.*

"I've told you everything I know. She killed everyone." I'm reciting something I've told him a dozen times already. "The guards, the servants—Zo and I didn't find anyone alive in the castle. There were bodies everywhere." I consider the fact that I expected Chesleigh to be dead at Lilith's hand, but hope always lets me down, so I don't dare hope for anyone else's escape. "A stable boy found us in the stables, and we yelled at him to run. I don't—I don't know if he did, or if he got away. A monster chased us off the grounds. I don't know if Lilith turned Rhen into something—or if it was her. Or if . . ." I glance at the sky, and I drop my voice and shiver. "Or if it was something like Iisak."

"He and I have spoken of that," Grey says. "Magesmiths were once great allies of the scravers, but they were treaty-bound to Karis Luran to stay in the ice forests of Iishellasa. Now Karis Luran is dead, and it's possible Lilith has recruited an ally." His voice is grim.

I shiver again. "So Rhen could be stuck there with her *and* something like him?"

"Possibly."

"Could she have turned him into a monster again?"

"She did it once; I have no doubt she could do it again." He pauses. "Especially if she manipulated him into another curse. There is an element of consent in that kind of magic. Rhen agreed to the curse the first time to save his own life, and we both paid the price."

"Can you do that, Grey?" My voice is very quiet, because I'm a little scared of the answer. "Turn someone into a . . . into a monster?"

"I haven't tried." He hesitates. "Rhen lost nearly all sense of himself when he transformed. I can't do that to another."

"What if . . ." I swallow, then rush on before I chicken out. "What if you did it to me?"

He frowns. "What? No."

"You once said that when he was a monster, Rhen was a creature of magic who could harm Lilith. What if you turned me into something like . . . something like that? What if I could defeat her myself? What if I—"

"What if you tore apart my soldiers? What if you turned north and cut a swath through Rhen's ranks? What if you killed Lilith—and then Rhen himself? No, Harper. No."

"But—"

"What if you killed *me*, and no one had any hope of stopping you?" He shakes his head forcefully. "You did not see the damage he caused, season after season. You do not want that. I assure you." He shudders, just a bit, but it's not something I've ever seen him do, and it's more profound than his words. "*I assure you.*"

I set my jaw and look back at the fire. He has one dagger. Even I can see that his magic won't hold up to Lilith's. This all feels hopeless.

"As always," he says, and his voice is lower, more gentle, "your goals are noble. Heroic." A pause. "As I said once before, I could have chosen no one better, my lady."

I turn my head and look at him. He said that in the castle, when Rhen had turned into a monster. Everything seemed so very hopeless then, too.

I sniff back tears. "You do care. I know you do."

"I do." He looks back at the fire and sighs. "I'm just not sure it's enough."

CHAPTER FORTY

GREY

The night sky is ink-black and dotted with stars as our horses pick their way across the uneven terrain. We're less than an hour away from Ironrose Castle, and I could likely find my way back blindfolded. I remember riding these hills when I was a member of the Royal Guard, and then later, when I did my best to lead Rhen-the-monster away from the people.

Jake rides beside me, but we've been quiet for hours, as we've given orders to maintain silence as much as possible. There's no tension between me and him, though I worried his loyalty to his sister might cause a rift between us. But tonight, Harper is riding near the back with Tycho, and Jake is at my side, alert as ever.

Now that we're so close, my heart tightens with dread. I left Lia Mara in Syhl Shallow with a promise to return, but we've already faced one ambush—and we have no idea what Rhen could have planned, or what Lilith could have done. I have no idea who in the palace might still present a risk to Lia Mara. I have no idea whether she will have understood my message, or how she will respond. With every step I take toward Ironrose Castle, my heart beats a plea for me to return to the Crystal Palace, to protect her at all costs.

But I know what Lia Mara would want: she would want me to finish this mission, to take action to protect her people. I have no doubt Lilith will soon turn her sights on Syhl Shallow.

And as much as I don't want to admit it, I truly do care whether Rhen lives or dies.

I try to clear my thoughts, but these worries seem to press in with greater force. My horse must sense my tension, because it jerks at the reins and prances sideways until I loosen my grip and offer a soft word.

Jake glances over. "Penny for your thoughts."

"We don't have pennies here, Jake."

"Whatever."

I say nothing. I'm not sure what to say.

After a long moment, he speaks, and his voice is very low, very soft. "You're worried about Lia Mara."

"Always."

"Nolla Verin is there. Noah is there."

I glance at him. "I'm not there."

"Do you think Ellia Maya was working alone?"

I cut him a glance. "No."

"Do you want to turn back?"

Yes. My chest tightens further. I wish my magic could stretch all the way to Syhl Shallow, to verify her safety. "We cannot."

He's quiet, and bitter wind whips between us. "Are you worried you're going to have to kill Rhen?"

"I'm worried Lilith will threaten his life to manipulate me." I can feel the weight of him studying me, so I add, "I'm worried it will work."

He thinks about this for a while. "Harper once told me that when Lilith threatened to kill her and Rhen, you offered your life to spare them."

I keep my eyes on the horizon. "I did."

"I told you before," he says. "Rhen had an eternity to be your friend, and he wasn't." He pauses. "He had time to be your brother, too, but he sent soldiers after you when he learned the truth."

"I know."

But.

He glances over. "When you offered your life for them, you didn't have anything else to live for, Grey."

The words hit me like an arrow.

"Thank you," I say. I feel a bit breathless.

He shrugs like he didn't just solve the existential dilemma that's been plaguing me for days. "No problem."

The stars ahead blur and shift and darken, an indication that Iisak is descending from the sky. His black wings flare wide, and I raise a hand to call for our soldiers to halt. A cold wind rushes between the horses, and I shiver.

"Your Highness," Iisak says, his voice almost softer than breath. "I have flown to the castle. I saw no other scraver on the premises, and I tried calling in our language. No one answered."

I don't know if that's a good thing or a bad thing. "What else?"

"The castle grounds seem deserted, as the princess indicated. Prince Rhen was alone in his chambers."

I frown. "Awake?" It's the middle of the night.

"Yes. He does not seem . . . well." He pauses. "There are soldiers stationed south and east of the castle. At least two regiments."

Captain Solt has ridden close, and he swears in Syssalah when he hears Iisak's news. "Two regiments," he says, his tone hostile. "This princess *has* led us into a trap."

"Maybe not," I say.

"Just like the other attack wasn't an ambush?" he says angrily. "If we ride onto the grounds we'll be surrounded. We should return for reinforcements."

"Rhen was preparing for war, just as we were."

"We have ten soldiers. Will your magic stop two thousand?"

Well, he's got me there. I look back at Iisak. "You're certain?"

"Their camps dwarf the castle territory." He pauses. "They do not seem to be on high alert." He glances at Solt. "I do not suspect a trap."

Solt spits at the ground. "You didn't suspect one two days ago either, scraver."

Iisak growls.

"Enough," I say. "Iisak, was there any sign of the enchantress?"

"No." He pauses. "There are dozens of burned corpses along the tree line beside the castle. Many of them wear gold and red."

Silver hell.

"Let her go in and get him," says Solt. "If it's so safe."

"I will," Harper says from the darkness, her tone backed by steel. "I'm not afraid. Are you, Captain?"

He snaps back at her in Syssalah, and it's probably good that I don't know what he's saying. I glare at him. "*Enough*, Captain."

If the soldiers aren't on alert, we could possibly slip in without being detected. Then again, if Lilith is there, she rarely does anything *small*. She could cause a huge ruckus and draw the entire army down upon us.

The true irony of this situation is that I wish Rhen were here to strategize this whole thing.

I take a slow breath. "Jake."

"Ready."

At least someone is. "We'll divide into thirds. One to stand sentry on the grounds, one to guard the entrance to the castle, one to breach and find Rhen and the enchantress. I want you at the entrance."

"Got it."

"I want to breach," says Harper.

I inhale to answer, and she rushes on. "I'm going, Grey. I'm not helpless. I'm not powerless. But she took him from me twice now, and if you're not going to save him, then I'm going to—"

"Fine," I say.

She clamps her mouth shut. Then, "Oh."

I look at Solt. "Pick your soldiers to stand sentry and give the others to Jake. I only need one with me."

"Yes, Your Highness." His eyes are flinty. He turns his head. "Recruit," he barks. "You're breaching the castle."

Tycho rides forward. His eyes are wide, some combination of hopeful and worried. "Yes, sir."

I'm not sure what to say.

This feels like an insult, like a threat. But I did tell Solt to pick. And Tycho stopped the assault the other day.

I think of my conversation with Noah, when he said, *He's only fifteen.*

And my cavalier response. *When I was fifteen, I was running my family's farm.*

And how did that turn out, Grey?

My family's farm failed. *I* failed.

I don't want Tycho to fail.

I imagine him facing Lilith. I remember when I was arrested at Worwick's Tourney, how Tycho tried to save me, and Dustan caught him by the neck and choked him until I yielded. Tycho flailed like a fish on a hook.

But yesterday, he held a bow like it was an extension of his arm. He did not flinch in the face of violence. *I'll cover you*, he said, and he did, giving me time to use magic.

I put out a hand. "Well chosen."

Tycho blushes, but he reaches out and clasps my hand in his own.

I give him a nod, then look at the others. "I don't want to lose the darkness. Let's find a place to tether the horses."

CHAPTER FORTY-ONE

RHEN

I haven't slept in days.

Maybe weeks.

The night sky is full of stars outside my window, the same stars I've watched forever. I didn't realize how lucky I was that Grey remained with me for every day of the curse, because this loneliness, this *isolation*, is profound. The castle has never been so silent, so dark, so cold.

I can see a bare reflection of my face in the window, the ruination of my eye, my cheek, more clear than I'd like, but I no longer care. I wish she'd taken them both.

"You should adorn yourself in armor," says Lilith. I don't know how long she's been here, but she's grown frustrated with me. Instead of lightly cajoling or downright mocking, she now speaks to me through clenched teeth, with fire in her voice.

It likely has something to do with my steadfast refusal to cater to her whims any longer. I don't move from the window. "Wear it yourself."

"Soldiers from Syhl Shallow will invade in minutes."

"In minutes?" I say without moving. "Has war found me at last?"

"I have brought your sword, Your Highness." The reflection of the weapon glints in the window. "Do you not want to defend yourself?"

"No."

"You have two regiments stationed alongside the castle, yet you will not rise up to lead them?"

I turn and face her. "If you want them led, lead them *yourself.*"

She glares at me for a long moment. Then she huffs. "You wish for me to face Grey myself? Very well." She lifts the sword, laying the blade along her shoulder.

"Wait." The word is wrenched from me, and it causes me pain to speak it.

Grey. *Grey is here.*

I'm terrified. I'm relieved. My chest is so tight, my heart pounding so fast. Every beat seems to pulse his name. *Grey. Grey. Grey.* He is my enemy. He is my brother. He is here. *Here.* I can't breathe.

"He's here to kill you," she hisses.

Yes. Yes, of course he is.

This is war.

"He will come," she whispers, "and he will draw his sword, and he will try to take everything that is yours with the edge of his blade."

Fear spirals through my gut, until I worry I will never breathe again. "*You* have taken everything that is mine."

"Not yet." She runs a finger along the edge of the sword, and blood wells up. "Think of your people, Your Highness. I could bring you the head of every single soldier who has sworn to protect you."

I stare at that line of blood. *Not yet.* She's right. She hasn't taken everything.

Grey is here.

To kill me.

"Think of all the bodies you can drag, Your Highness."

My eyes close. I draw a shuddering breath.

"Grey is here to take your throne," Lilith says. "If he is victorious, I will simply kill each of your subjects, one by one, while you watch. While their former *prince* looks on. Each child. Each parent. Each woman. Each man. Limb from limb. Sinew by sinew."

I flinch.

Once again, she threatens the downfall of my entire kingdom, while soldiers from Syhl Shallow are banging on my door, threatening war.

Only this time, I'm alone. Harper is gone. Grey is my enemy.

I draw a long breath. My head is pounding, and my chest aches. But I reach for the sword.

My boots strike the marble floor, echoing through the empty hallways.

My hands are trembling. My armor is heavy. Or maybe I'm weak.

I promised Harper I would try for peace.

This is not peace.

As always, there is no solution here. No way out. No way to win. No matter what path I try, fate always places Lilith at the end of it. I will have to fight, and one of us will fall.

I try to find the cold edges of my thoughts. She's taken everything from me. This should not matter. Grey would not hesitate to kill me. It's proof enough that he's *here*.

This man is your brother.

The memory of Harper's words steals my breath, and I stop short in the hallway, gasping. I have to put my hand on the wall.

Lilith hasn't taken *everything.*

I hear a whisper of sound from somewhere distant in the castle. A scrape, followed by a creak of wood. I freeze. My limbs straighten, almost of their own will. My hand finds the hilt of my sword.

I nearly cannot hear over the pounding of my heart.

I count to ten, to twenty, trying to slow my breathing. In all the years we were trapped by the curse, I never feared invasion, I never feared anyone. I always had Grey by my side.

Now I'm alone.

Another scrape, maybe a footstep. Closer.

I stop breathing altogether. Every heartbeat pulses with agony. With fear. As always, there is no way out. No way to win.

A whisper carries on the air. Maybe a word. A hushed order. The sound of movement.

They're in the castle. A team of soldiers, perhaps. Dozens. Hundreds.

It doesn't matter. My heart is in my throat. I stride forward to meet them, turning the corner for the grand staircase with my hand on the hilt of my sword.

I nearly walk straight into Grey.

My thoughts stumble and panic. He's just *there*, his hand on the hilt of his own sword. His free hand is up behind him, telling soldiers to wait, possibly. He looks a bit travel-worn and road-weary, and his eyes are cool and dark, but he's here. He's *here.* Weapons at the ready, clad in the green and black of Syhl Shallow. A tiny gold crown is embedded in the armor, right over his heart.

He's here to kill you.

Just as she said.

Grey sees me and stops short. The world seems to shrink down to this moment, all the seasons of the curse narrowing down to him and me in an empty castle. Time and again, I told him to kill me. To save my people. To spare them. To end this. Time and again, he refused. My breathing is a loud rush in my ears, barely drowning the pounding of my heart.

There is no path to victory here.

Well, maybe one. I draw my sword.

Grey's gaze sharpens in alarm, but he's always been quick and deadly, and today is no different. His blade is drawn and aiming for mine before I can blink.

I step back, out of reach, and he cuts a path through the air.

He comes after me, but I drop my sword. It clatters to the marble, the steel ringing through the empty hall.

I follow it, dropping to my knees on the cold floor. Raising my hands.

"I yield." My voice breaks. "Grey, I yield. Forgive me. I beg of you. Please. Kill me. Please." I'm babbling, but his eyes are so dark, burning with emotion. He hasn't moved. "Please, Grey. You must. End it. She killed—" My voice breaks again. "Harper. She's gone. Lilith can't—she can't— Please, kill me."

He takes a step forward, and I gasp. Grey was never one to hesitate.

But his free hand reaches out and grasps mine. His grip is tight, and it's startling that I remember it, that it's *familiar*: from a thousand different sparring matches that ended with me in the dirt, from the times I would tumble from a horse, from the times Lilith would leave me in a tortured heap and Grey would drag me to my feet.

From the time, the *last* time, when I stood on the castle parapets, terrified to jump.

When Grey reached out and took my hand.

His breathing is as fast as mine.

"You're a prince of Emberfall," he says, and his voice is rough. "You kneel to no one."

I stare up at him.

And then, without preamble or explanation, Harper appears around the corner, curls tumbling loose from her plaits. She's speaking in a rushed whisper. "I told Tycho I am *not*—"

Her gaze falls on me, and her face begins to crumple. "Rhen. Oh, Rhen."

I must be dead. Or dreaming. This is a new way for Lilith to torture me. Surely.

I look between her and Grey. His hand is still tight on mine.

"You're alive," I whisper.

"I'm alive." She has to brush away a tear. "I got away. I went for help."

I look back at Grey. My thoughts cannot process all of this emotion. "You have to get her out of here. Lilith is here. She will kill us all."

"Maybe not." He gives my hand a tug. "Get off your knees, Brother. There's a battle to be won."

CHAPTER FORTY-TWO

LIA MARA

I've never led an army. The armor feels stiff and unfamiliar, but I don't mind the weight if it means I am protected. I ride with the generals at the back, and we join with my regiment on the other side of the mountain pass. Rhen has stationed his own soldiers here, as promised, but rumors fly about the confrontation with the Magesmith Prince, how he defeated an ambush but left the soldiers from Emberfall alive.

I remember the first time Grey and I rode together through these valleys, when we offered Rhen his sixty days. The people of Emberfall were eager to greet him, even with me at his side. There are many stories of the lives Grey saved in Blind Hollow, how he stood against the Royal Guard to protect the people. My generals want to attack the waiting regiment, but I wonder if there is a better way.

If Nolla Verin were here, she'd order a full-scale assault, but that's why I left her in the palace and I rode with the army.

I ask my generals to send a message to Rhen's regiment, asking for a meeting with their officers.

Clanna Sun is at my side, her tone worried. "They could attack, Your Majesty. You are alerting them to our presence."

She is the only advisor I have brought with me—and the only person in the castle who knows of Ellia Maya's treachery. She served my mother since before I was born, and she is practically more loyal to Syhl Shallow than I am myself. I may not *like* Clanna Sun, but I do trust her. "If they attack," I say, "we will retaliate. But we will try for peace first."

Their response comes in less than an hour, and their officers arrive in less than two. They're all men, which doesn't surprise me, but they're led by a lieutenant, which does. The man is missing an arm, and he eyes my soldiers warily.

Noah is in the officers' tent with us, and he looks over in surprise. "Jamison."

Jamison looks startled to see him. "Doctor Noah."

"You know this man?" I say.

"A little," says Noah. He hesitates. "He lost his arm when Syhl Shallow invaded the first time." Another pause. "And he fought in the battle when the creature drove your mother's forces out."

"Ah." I look at Jamison. "So you have brought your grievances, Lieutenant?"

"No." He glances at Noah, then back at me. "I was among the soldiers who attempted to overthrow Grey's small force a few days ago."

At that, Noah rises to stand at my side. "You saw Jake."

"I did." Jamison glances at me. "As well as Grey." He pauses. "We had them badly outnumbered, but he used magic to stop the attack."

I can't tell if he's angry about the magic or angry that they weren't successful—or if he's here for another reason entirely. "We understand the enchantress has returned to Emberfall," I say. "And she intends to take control of Prince Rhen."

"We heard the same rumor from one of our spies," says Jamison. He glances at my soldiers again, his expression uneasy. "She was in the castle when the enchantress attacked—but she died in the assault."

A spy. I bristle. "Did this *spy* tell you that Grey was leading a force into Emberfall to stop the enchantress?"

"We didn't know that's why Grey was here." His gaze returns to mine, and his voice is weighted. "She said he was here because the time has come for war."

The word *war* seems to add a layer of tension to the air, one that doesn't need to be there.

"It has," I say, "but I was hoping we could find a path to peace."

Jamison takes a breath. "I've heard rumors about that, how you tried to find peace with Rhen once before."

"Those rumors are true."

He hesitates. "I've fought at Grey's side. More than once. He is a man of honor."

"Yes," I agree. "He is."

"And he could have killed us with his magic, I'm sure of it."

"Yes. He could have."

"Our spy said your mother's army is no less vicious under your rule."

"Your spy was correct," I say. "My army is no less vicious." I pause. "That doesn't mean they need to show their teeth."

"Then you are truly here to discuss peace with Prince Rhen?"

"I am."

If I can. If Grey is successful. If he survives. If he defeats the enchantress.

My stomach begins to churn, and I fight to keep my face neutral.

Jamison glances at the officers with him. "There are regiments surrounding Ironrose Castle, preparing for an attack from Syhl Shallow. If you are truly here for peace, we can offer an escort to Ironrose for you and an entourage of twenty men." He clears his throat and looks around at my senior officers, the majority of whom are female. "Or . . . women. As you will. Our regiment will hold its position if yours will."

"Absolutely not," says Clanna Sun in Syssalah.

"Yes," I say to Jamison. "We will be ready in an hour."

"They have thousands of soldiers readied for *war*," Clanna Sun hisses when I turn away. "And you are our *queen*."

"I know." I feel a bit breathless. "Choose twenty to accompany us."

I stop by Noah before I step out of the tent. "Jake is alive," I say quietly.

He nods—then grimaces. "At least . . . he was."

I reach out and squeeze his hand. "He still is."

He squeezes back. "You're making peace happen."

I blush before I can help it. "Grey would be thanking fate. Perhaps we stumbled on some luck that Grey encountered a soldier he once knew."

"It's not luck." Noah's voice is steady, somber. "You don't luck into that kind of trust, Lia Mara. You earn it with every minute you do the right thing. So does Grey." He gives my hand another squeeze. "Go. Bring my boyfriend back to me."

"Bring him back? Noah, you must come with me."

CHAPTER FORTY-THREE

GREY

We've retreated to Rhen's chambers. The hallways are still soaked with the blood of everyone the enchantress killed, and the castle smells like death and decay. It seems Rhen is missing an eye, but it's hard to tell, because so much dirt and clotted blood cake to his face and hair. There are four long, filthy scabs that drag from his hairline across his right eye and down his cheek to curve into his jaw. The signs of Lilith's handiwork are obvious.

He is . . . not well, Iisak said.

That's very clear.

For weeks, I've been dreading the moment I would face him again. Dreading the thought of killing a man I once swore to protect, dreading the idea of falling to his blade if I couldn't go through with it.

I didn't expect to find him like this.

I should have. I remember Lilith's torments. I remember how much Rhen endured on my behalf.

I see how much he's endured this time.

Rhen hasn't let go of Harper's hand. They're sitting together on the chaise by the hearth, and he keeps looking at her as if he expects her to vanish from the room if he glances away.

"It's all right," she whispers, and her breath hitches. "I'm here."

"I would have come after you," he says. "She told me she killed you."

"She tried."

"You must go." He looks at me. "Take her out of here. Lilith will do worse. You know, Grey. You remember."

"I came here to defeat her, not to run." I've been pacing between the door, where Tycho stands guard, to the window, where I've whistled for Iisak, though he hasn't appeared. I hear him shriek in the distance. I wonder if soldiers have begun to close on the castle.

"Grey?" Harper says softly. "Can you heal him?"

I stop in my pacing and turn.

Rhen freezes. His gaze meets mine, and he seems to recoil involuntarily.

I've seen this a dozen times in the people of Syhl Shallow, but it's different to see it in Rhen. "Once healing has set in, I cannot undo that." I pause. "But I can fix the rest of it. Are you in pain?"

Rhen shakes his head quickly, but it's a lie, it *has* to be a lie. The start of infection is obvious, the places where his skin is swollen and furiously red.

Tycho looks over from the door. "It doesn't hurt," he says easily, and something about that is generous in a way only Tycho can be. Rhen hurt Tycho once, too.

But Rhen has the long, horrible history with magic. So many of the actions Rhen has taken have been in an effort to protect his people, but underneath, they've been a shield for his fear, his uncertainty, his pain.

After a long moment, Rhen unwinds his hands from Harper's and he straightens, shifting to sit on his own. A shadow of his usual defiant independence slides across his face. "Do as you say."

He might as well be saying *Do your worst*.

I cross the room and drag a low stool to sit in front of him. "I am not Lilith," I say, and my tone isn't gentle. If anything, a bit of anger slides into my words. "I won't harm you."

He says nothing, just looks straight back at me like he's bracing himself. But when I reach out to touch his face, Rhen catches my wrist. His grip is tight against my bracer, the tendons on the back of his hand standing out.

"I'm not afraid," he says, and there's a breathless quality to his voice that makes me think that's another lie. But then he adds, "I do not *deserve it*, Grey."

That pulls at a chord in my chest, and I frown. "You took her torments for me," I say quietly. "Season after season. What you did to me cannot undo that."

"You *stayed* with me," he says. "Season after season. Long after you should have fled. What I did—" His voice breaks. "What I did to you—"

"It is over," I say. "It is done." Because it is. "One poor choice shouldn't undo a thousand good ones."

He's staring at me so intently, his breathing almost shaking.

I glance at his hand, still gripped tight on my wrist. "Rhen. Let go."

He blinks, and I realize it's the first time I've ever truly told him what to do.

What's more shocking, possibly to both of us, is that he obeys.

I touch my fingers to the shredded ruin of his face, and he flinches before he catches himself. He's so tense, his hands in fists, his knuckles white. No matter what he says, he is clearly afraid of the magic. But I can sense the moment my power begins to work, because his jaw loosens. His shoulders drop. The pain eases. The swelling recedes, the infection melting away. I saved a man's eye once, but the damage to Rhen's face has gone too far, too long. His eye is sealed shut. The scarring will be profound; I can already tell.

This is not the worst state I've ever seen Rhen in, not by a long shot, so I can easily keep any pity out of my gaze.

"Had I known you were my brother," he says, his voice rough and trembling, "I would have forced you to leave on the very first day of her curse."

I shake my head. "Had I known you were my brother, I would have stayed by your side just the same." I feel the moment the healing finishes, and I withdraw my hand, giving him a narrow look. "Though admittedly, I wouldn't have put up with half your nonsense."

He startles, then almost smiles. He touches a hand to his cheek as if he's expecting the damage to be gone, but he must feel the scarring, because the smile vanishes, leaving only a bleak look in his remaining eye.

Harper takes his free hand again. "It's okay," she says softly. "Scars mean you survived something terrible."

"Ah, yes, Princess," whispers a voice from across the room. Lilith, her voice slithering into the silence. "He has indeed survived something *terrible*. But haven't we all?"

I whirl to my feet, weapons in hand, only reaching for my magic secondarily. But I'm a second too late, and her power drives me back, knocking away the furniture, sending Harper and Rhen scrambling.

"Don't you see?" she calls to me. "You are *weak*, Grey. I've had a lifetime to learn this power. You've had a few months."

"I don't just have magic," I snap, and I pull throwing blades from my bracer. They drive into her midsection, and she stumbles back. Tycho has a bow in his hands, and just as quickly, an arrow appears in her chest.

I go after her. "I'll make sure you're truly dead this time." Then I pull my dagger, the one weapon I've saved for this moment, the one weapon I know will make a difference.

I aim right for her heart.

She screams and thrusts a hand at me, driving me back. It's like a blast of cold wind, and I stagger, trying to stay on my feet. I call for my own magic, but it's like standing against a hurricane with a piece of silk. I can feel the edges of my power fraying. The bones of my fingers begin to snap, and my grip on the dagger weakens. My magic flares to heal the injury, but as soon as I heal one bone, another fractures. The wind is intense, freezing cold, and I wish for Iisak, for mastery of my power, for anything.

Another bone snaps, and I cry out. I'm going to lose the weapon.

"You are too *weak*," she says again.

"To me!" calls Tycho, and I toss the weapon in his direction, but the wind is stinging my eyes, overturning furniture, and I cannot tell if he's caught it. Harper surges forward, but the wind catches her too, sending her flying back against the stone wall.

Lilith stands in the middle of the maelstrom, her hair lifting in the wind, blood streaming from her wounds. She laughs. "You thought you could stop me?" she demands. "All I have done to you, and you thought you could *stop me*?"

Tycho gets low to the floor, crawling with the dagger in his hand, his teeth gritted, his eyes clenched against the wind.

Lilith sees him. She smiles. It's terrifying.

"Tycho!" I snap. "Tycho, hold!"

"Ah, Grey," she croons. "You've found a little lapdog."

Then she pulls the daggers out of her chest, draws back her hand, and throws.

CHAPTER FORTY-FOUR

RHEN

I don't think. I leap. The boy is wearing armor, but I know Lilith's talents, and those blades will go right into his neck. I slam into him and we roll. A knife hits my armor and bounces away, but fate never goes easy on me, so the other slices across my neck and jaw. I cry out. Tycho's dagger goes skittering across the marble floor.

But he's alive. He's panting underneath me, staring up at me in surprise.

"Are you all right?" I say.

He nods quickly. "You're bleeding."

I slap a hand to my face, and it comes away slick with blood.

Somewhere outside the window, a creature screams in the darkness. Lilith picks up the dagger. She drags the blade across her fingertip, and blood wells up. "I know what this is." She looks at Grey and some of the wind quiets, but the force still pushes against us. "Where did *you* find it?"

He seems to be having more luck than the rest of us, because he's still on his feet, facing her, bracing against her power. His eyes are dark and furious, his hands gripped tight on his weapons—but he can't move forward. "I know where I'm going to put it."

She laughs. "Look at you. You can't even *touch* me," she says. Her gaze shifts to me. "Rhen, would you like to watch me carve her heart out of her chest this time?"

"Go ahead and try," says Harper, and her voice is fierce—but weak. I saw her hit the wall. Blood glistens in her hair.

"As always, you are all too *weak*. Rhen, I have offered you many chances. Your people destroyed my people. You used me and turned me away. Your kingdom will *fall*."

"Grey brought an army," I snap. "My kingdom was going to fall anyway. And so will you, when they come for him. You can kill us, but you can't kill them *all*."

"An army?" She laughs again. "Grey brought a handful of soldiers."

My eyes snap to his, but Grey hasn't looked away from her. "You brought no army?" I say.

"I came to kill *her*," he says. "Not to take your throne."

Lilith claps her hands in delight. "You're such a fool, Rhen! This is why you are always destined to fall. You yielded to a man who didn't even arrive with a battalion of soldiers. You yielded to a man who came with a broken girl and a boy who was likely weaned from his mother's breast a week ago."

She takes a step forward, toward Grey, completely unaffected by the wind. It's beginning to flay the skin from Grey's cheeks, but it barely ruffles her skirts. "And you. Your loyalty was once a point of pride, and now you sit up and beg for scraps from your enemy. I was once friendly with Karis Luran. I imagine I can be so with her daughter."

Grey speaks through clenched teeth. His hands have turned

red and raw from the wind, his knuckles bleeding. "You will—stay away—from—Lia Mara."

"No," she says. "I won't."

The window shatters inward, exploding with glass and a large black shape that lands and rolls. Wings unfurl, and I suck in a breath, swearing, shoving myself backward, dragging Tycho with me.

But the boy doesn't seem panicked. His eyes light up. "Iisak!" he says in surprise.

The creature doesn't even acknowledge him. It launches itself at Lilith with outstretched claws, just as freezing wind blasts through the open window and ice crystals form on the walls. The room is suddenly bitter cold, and it's harder to move, as if my limbs have begun to freeze in place.

For the first time, I see Lilith falter and fall back. Her eyes no longer appear victorious, they are instead wide with shock. "Nakiis?" she says, and I don't know the word, I don't know what it means.

"Not Nakiis," the creature hisses. "His father." And then those claws slice into her, shredding the dress, shredding her flesh. Blood blooms along the satin fabric. The creature growls, and there's enough menace in the sound that I shiver. Lilith makes a choked sound. For an instant, I think this will be it, that she'll finally meet her end right here in front of me.

But Lilith still has that dagger in her hand.

I know what this is, she said.

She drives it right into the side of the creature's rib cage. Then she pulls it free and does it again.

And again.

Again.

The wind in the room dies. The ice melts from the walls.

"No!" Tycho is screaming. He's scrambling away from me, trying to get to the creature. Grey is able to stride forward, a blade in his hand, aiming for Lilith. The creature begins to fall away from the enchantress, and she makes a gurgling, choked sound, but she lifts that blade one more time.

Instead of aiming for the creature, she's aiming for Grey.

There's no wind, no resistance. I move without thought. I tackle Lilith around the midsection. There's so much blood. She was already injured, so she all but collapses under my weight.

I don't realize she still has a dagger in her hand until it stabs down into my shoulder, right where my armor ends. It's like an iron poker. Pain ricochets through my body without end. Someone is shouting. Someone is screaming. Someone is sobbing.

Lilith is panting, her face, blood-speckled, above mine.

"You're such a fool," she hisses.

I don't think anything can hurt more, but she yanks that dagger free of my shoulder, and puts the point right against my chin, pressing upward until I feel the skin split and I can barely breathe.

I can't see anything. Just Lilith's terrible face.

"Let him go," says Grey. His sword point appears at Lilith's neck.

"I can kill him before you kill me," she says. "Grey, you were once willing to swear an oath to me. Are you still?"

"No." My breath is shaking. "Let her kill me. Just let her kill me."

"No," says Harper. "No. Grey. Please. Grey."

Lilith's eyes bore into mine. "She always *begs* for you, Rhen."

"Do it!" I snap at Grey, then choke on a gasp as she presses with the dagger. "Do it, Grey. Now it's my turn to bleed so you do not."

That blade at her neck doesn't move. I can hear Grey's breathing, quick and panicked.

"Do it," I choke out. "Don't make the mistake I once made."

"Do something!" Harper cries. "Grey, use your magic!"

Lilith grins down at me, and her voice drops to a conspiratorial whisper. "Do you realize that he's just as afraid as you are?"

"Use your magic," says Tycho, and his voice is thick, and it's then that I realize he is the one who was sobbing. "You're stronger than she is."

"He's *not*," snaps Lilith. "And he'll yield right now, or I will kill Prince Rhen."

"Curse me," says Harper. Her voice is thick with tears, too. "Or change me. Make me the monster, Grey. Make me the monster."

"No," I whisper.

Something flickers in Lilith's eyes. The wind in the room picks up. "I will not wait for your oath, *Prince Grey*."

"Do it!" shouts Harper. "Grey, do it! Let me kill her!"

"No," I say again. Dread is choking me. I know what my monster did. "Grey. No."

Lilith leans down. "Remember when you tried to kill me?" she says to Grey. "Let me show you how to make a death last."

The dagger pierces my skin. "Curse me!" I cry, and my voice is nearly lost in the wind. I dig my nails into the floor, trying to lift my head. "Grey, curse me. Whatever I have, it's yours. Bind me with magic, make me something that will—"

My voice is swallowed up. The room gets smaller. The wind dies. Lilith shrieks.

And then I lose all sense of myself and become the monster once more.

CHAPTER FORTY-FIVE

HARPER

I've seen Rhen like this before, but it's still terrifying and beautiful all at once. This time, his eye is missing in this form, too, the scars mottled streaks of blue and purple that make him seem both more monstrous and more radiant.

His transformation has thrown Lilith and Grey back. Rhen roars, and my heart skips in terror.

Somewhere in the room, Tycho chokes on a breath and cries, "Silver hell."

For a heartbeat of time, I'm terrified that he'll turn on us. The monster was always indiscriminate, and I know Rhen caused a lot of damage in this form—damage he couldn't control.

Wind blasts through the room, overturning the rest of the furniture, knocking the rest of us into the walls. But Rhen-the-monster is unmoved. He growls again, ending in a shriek that makes every piece of glass in the room shatter.

Lilith screams in rage. Her fist closes on that dagger, and she struggles to her knees. Rhen's scales glitter in the light, and he rears up—leaving his chest a wide-open target.

For a stunning, terrifying fraction of a second, I feel as though we've found this moment before: Lilith with a blade in her hand, threatening to kill Rhen in his monster form.

Me, shoving my feet against the ground, running to save him.

"No!" I scream, and I leap, just like I did once before.

Rhen's growl shakes the room. I hear Grey shout, and then I feel myself slam into the marble floor, nowhere near Lilith. Rhen's monster has recoiled from the blade, and he hisses at Lilith. Grey's face is in front of me. "He'd never forgive me," he gasps.

Lilith's blade is swinging forward again, and I cry out. I'll never forgive him. I'll never forgive her. I'll never forgive anyone.

But Grey has turned away from me, and he's grabbed hold of Lilith's dress, and he pulls hard. It grants Rhen an inch of space, but it's not going to be enough.

Then her skirts erupt in flame, a sudden burst of heat from where Grey has grabbed the hem. Lilith shrieks, and the wind in the room swirls as she summons her magic to douse the flames and heal herself.

It's only a moment of distraction, but it's enough.

One moment, Lilith is there, surrounded by smoke and flames that have already begun eating away at her skin.

The next moment, the monster rips her apart.

The sound is terrifying. The sight is terrifying. I'm wheezing. Blinking. Staring. His talons are coated in gore. His beautiful glistening scales are spattered with blood.

Everything is spattered with blood.

Suddenly the room is so silent that I can't hear anything but my breathing. The fire drifts away in a cloud of smoke. Grey is on his knees. He's bleeding, his skin raw in spots. I stumble to my feet, which takes too long, and my feet don't want to work right. The monster growls, turning. Tycho is crouched over Iisak, who isn't moving, but Rhen pays them no attention. When he sees Grey, he shrieks, and the sound makes me want to cower.

"Harper," says Grey. He lifts his hands. "Harper."

"Rhen," I breathe. I stumble forward on my knees, half crawling to Grey's side. "Rhen, I'm here." I put my own hands up. "Change him back, Grey. Change him *back*."

Grey takes a breath, then carefully gets to his feet. "I can't. You remember. Only he can."

Rhen-the-monster growls again, but he presses his face to my chest and blows warm air at my knees. My gut tightens, and a tear slips from my eye. "But I already love him." My breath catches. "He already loves me."

Shouting erupts in the hallway, and the monster's head whips up. Another low growl rumbles from his chest. Voices are clamoring in Syssalah, and I can't understand a word.

But then Jake and Captain Solt appear in the doorway.

Jake swears. "Holy—"

Rhen snakes his neck and roars at him.

Captain Solt blanches, then draws a blade.

"Hold!" Grey shouts.

Rhen whips his head around to roar in Grey's face. I whimper and fall back, but Grey doesn't move.

"It cannot fly," snaps Solt. "We can kill it."

"No," says Grey, and his voice is soft. Rhen roars in his face again, and the sound makes the walls tremble.

"Easy." Grey lifts his hands. His voice is so quiet. The way he speaks to horses or children. "Rhen. Easy."

"It'll tear you in two," says Tycho. He stumbles to his feet.

"I don't think so," Grey whispers. Another growl pulls from Rhen's throat, but Grey fearlessly puts a hand against his face, below his one good eye.

"Come back to yourself," he says quietly. "Come back to yourself, Brother."

The air barely shimmers, and then Rhen stands before us. He stumbles a little, as if drunk or disoriented, but he puts out a hand and Grey catches him.

"She's dead?" Rhen says.

"She's dead."

He stumbles forward again, but this time when he reaches out, Grey catches him, and he wraps up his brother in an embrace.

CHAPTER FORTY-SIX

GREY

I don't know how long we stand there, but the time feels too short, and the danger does not feel like it has been eliminated. The enchantress is gone, but there is still an army waiting somewhere outside this castle. Tycho's breath is hitching, and Solt and the other soldiers linger in the doorway. The captain's armor is deeply scratched, and there is a claw mark across his cheek. Jake has blood in his hair.

Iisak is on the ground, unmoving.

Tycho is at his side, holding his hand.

I drop to a knee beside the scraver. His blood has formed shallow, glistening pools on the stone floor. I expect his eyes to be closed, his chest no longer rising with breath, but he blinks at me, too slowly.

"Iisak." I touch a hand to a wound without thought, reaching for my magic, but his eyes close and he shakes his head fractionally.

My magic does not heal him. The wounds continue to bleed.

The magic-resistant dagger is lying on the ground in a puddle of blood.

He's been stabbed at least a dozen times.

Iisak squeezes my hand.

"Help me," I say, and my own voice wavers. "Help me help you."

He shakes his head again, a minute movement. "Save him," he says, and his eyes flare with desperation—before they fall closed.

I squeeze his hand back, but his goes limp. His chest doesn't rise again.

"No. No!" Tycho sniffs and looks at me. "Can you . . . ," he begins, but he must see the tormented look in my eyes, because he falls silent.

I can't. All this magic, and I still can't save one of my friends. So much loss, and yet there's always room for more. My chest is tight, and I have to force myself to breathe through it.

Jake kneels beside me and puts a hand on my shoulder.

You didn't have anything else to live for, he said earlier. The words feel full of foreboding now.

But then I remember what Iisak said, and that pierces my sorrow. "Save him," I repeat. I look at Tycho and frown, then at Rhen, then at Jake and Solt. "Save who?"

Captain Solt steps forward and sheathes his sword. "The other one, I imagine. It came at us through the trees. We brought it down with an arrow through its wing, but Iisak stopped us. He spoke to the other one, but he seemed enraged. When he took off into the sky, we thought you were in danger, so I changed course and came here."

There are too many startling revelations in that statement.

The other one.

We brought it down with an arrow.

You were in danger, so I changed course.

I remember the distant screeching in the woods when we approached. Harper said she was chased by something like Iisak.

Lilith's words, when Iisak attacked her.

Nakiis?

Not Nakiis. His father.

Iisak crashed through the window to attack the enchantress. He's always patient and insightful, taking time to evaluate a threat before acting. But today, he leapt into the room and threw himself at her. He didn't care about magic, he didn't care about politics or armies or anything but unbridled rage.

I remember a conversation I once had with Iisak, when we first saw how terrible Karis Luran could be. I asked why he risked a year of service under her control, with the faint hope of ever finding his son.

I would have risked a lifetime, he said. *Would you not?*

I hesitated, and he said, *You would. Were you a father, you would.*

Tycho is a second faster than I am. He shoves himself to his feet. "You said he's in the woods? Take me to him."

The injured scraver lies in a pile at the base of a tree, his wings limp and splayed against the ground. He's almost invisible in the darkness, his eyes closed, his chest barely rising, reminding me of the day I first saw Iisak, curled up and lifeless in a cage at Worwick's Tourney. Here, though, ice coats the ground around him, glistening in the moonlight. An arrow seems to have gone through his wing and into his rib cage. As we approach, I realize there's someone with him, someone human, crouched in the darkness in a cloak.

I stop short, my hand falling on the hilt of my sword, and the others stop behind me.

The cloaked individual notices us at the same time, rising to his or her feet and drawing a blade. The scraver on the ground emits a low growl, his eyes flicking open. Clawed fingers dig into the frosted ground.

The soldiers at my back murmur in Syssalah, and they draw blades as well.

"Hold," I say.

Tycho appears at my side. "He's hurt," he says. "Grey. He's hurt."

The cloaked figure seems to straighten in surprise, then strides toward us, shaking back the hood of the cloak.

At my side, Harper gasps, then starts running forward. "Zo? Zo!"

Completely heedless of the blade, she tackles her friend in a hug. She's speaking in a wild rush. "How did you—what did you—what—how—"

Zo returns the hug, but she's looking over Harper's shoulder at me, at Rhen, at the other soldiers. She hasn't dropped her sword, and I can imagine how this looks, the crown prince surrounded by soldiers from Syhl Shallow. "What—how . . . how did *you*?"

"Stand down, Zo," says Rhen. "Much has happened."

She's staring at him, at the ruination of his face. "I see that."

The scraver behind her growls again.

At my side, Tycho's breathing has gone shallow. "Grey. Help him."

I hesitate. I know what Iisak said, but I know what Solt said, too. This scraver attacked our soldiers. He attacked Harper. He was clearly working with Lilith if those things were true.

Tycho doesn't wait for my answer. He sheathes his sword and strides forward.

The scraver's growl turns into an ear-splitting shriek, and he puts a clawed hand against the ground, his wings fluttering as he tries to get to his feet. But then he coughs, and it's a rough, terrible sound. Blood appears on his lips. His eyes are cold pools of black, very different from the warm-yet-ironic gaze that Iisak always had.

"No," says Zo. She pulls free of Harper to step in front of Tycho. "Don't hurt him."

Tycho glances at her like she's addled. "I'm not going to hurt him," he says quietly. He lifts his hands to show he's harmless, then drops to a knee in front of the scraver, who hasn't stopped growling.

Then I notice the pool of blood under his body.

Save him.

"Are you Nakiis?" says Tycho. He reaches out a hand. "Son of Iisak?"

The growling stops, but only for a moment. Then the scraver swipes with his claws. Tycho's wrist takes a hit—and he's lucky he's wearing a bracer. Those claws slice right through a leather buckle and dig a groove in the back of Tycho's hand. The boy stumbles back. Solt draws a sword and strides forward.

"No!" says Zo. "He's hurt, but he's—he's not an enemy. He didn't kill me, and he could have. He could have killed all of them. She made him do a lot of it."

"He tried to kill Harper," Rhen says viciously.

"But he *didn't*," says Zo.

Solt glances at me, waiting for an order.

I look at the scraver. "*Are* you the son of Iisak? Are you the missing king of Iishellasa?"

He growls at me. "I am Nakiis. But my father is king."

"*Was*," I say, and nothing about this moment feels gentle or soothing, but I try to make my voice convey both. "Your father *was* king. He fell facing the enchantress." I pause. "Iisak asked me to save you." Another pause. "I will, if you'll let me."

He spits blood at the ground, and I can hear his ragged breathing from here. "I will not be bound to another magesmith."

That makes me wonder what Lilith did to him, how she bound him to her will. His voice is full of rage and fury—and a bit of fear, too. Lilith left nothing but pain and suffering in her wake, and I shouldn't be surprised to find another creature whose mind was destroyed by her games.

"I won't bind you," I say carefully. "Your father once told me that the magesmiths and the scravers were great allies."

"*Were*," he emphasizes, his tone echoing the way mine did. But just the effort of speaking must exhaust him, because he puts his forehead against the ground and coughs again.

I walk up to him and drop to a knee the way Tycho did. "I couldn't help your father," I say. "But I can help you."

His voice is ragged and worn. "At what cost."

"No cost."

"You swear it?"

"I do."

After a moment, he nods.

I don't hesitate. I jerk the arrow free, and fresh blood spills. He roars with rage and tries to whirl, but he's too weak. I put my hand right against the wound. The skin closes. His breathing eases. The wing heals.

He blinks at me, then lifts his head. "You are Grey?" he says.

"I am."

"My father said you would help me. He said he was going to find you." He rolls to his knees and ruffles his wings, then seems surprised when they fold into place against his back. "His last words to me."

I hesitate. "He's spent the last few years searching for you."

"Then his time was not spent in vain." His voice is bitter.

"He was a friend, Nakiis." I put out a hand. "I would be yours as—"

"No magesmith is a friend of mine." He swipes claws against my hand, slicing open my palm, then leaps into the air.

"Wait!" cries Tycho, but the scraver is gone. We stare after him for a long moment.

Tycho's breath hitches. "Iisak died for him."

"He died for me, too," I say, and my voice is heavy.

"And his son just . . . left," says Jake.

I remember Iisak's stories about his son, how Nakiis fled Iishellasa to avoid claiming his birthright, how their relationship was complicated at best.

And then at some point Lilith got involved, and she likely made it worse. I flex my hand as the wounds close. After everything Rhen went through, I can hardly blame the scraver for wanting nothing to do with me.

I look at Rhen, Harper, and Zo, who are still standing apart from my soldiers, their expressions worn and uncertain. Captain Solt is eyeing them vengefully. The distance between them all seems to be vast. Lia Mara has so many plans for a peaceful alliance, but despite everything we accomplished here tonight, any path forward is going to be fraught with challenges.

"Wait," says Harper, turning to Zo. "Did you say the scraver could have killed *all of them*? Who?"

"Many from the castle," says Zo. "Much of the staff. Even Freya and the children were saved. The spy Chesleigh was able to sneak them through the forest, group by group. The losses would have been much greater."

Harper swears. "I guess I can't keep hating her."

"I can," I say, and at my back, I hear Solt grunt in agreement.

"When Nakiis pulled me off the horse," Zo continues, "he was going to kill me, but then he said that he'd been ordered to bring the enchantress your heart. I was able to convince him to bring the heart of an animal, and he took my armor as proof." Zo glances at Rhen. "He wasn't evil. He wasn't cruel. He was just doing the best he could to survive. In a way, he was simply . . . cursed."

"Then he has my gratitude," says Rhen. His eyes meet mine.

I'm not sure what to say. Silence swells between us for a long moment.

The space between me and him suddenly feels like a mile, too. He yielded to me in the hallway, and he saved my life as a monster— but he is still the crown prince. His army still surrounds this castle.

It's almost as if he realizes this at the same moment I do, because a new light sparks in his eye.

I'm not the only one who notices. "Emberfall's army still blocks our exit, Your Highness," says Captain Solt, and his accented voice is very low. "We should bind him. So we have leverage."

"I will face my army on my own terms," says Rhen darkly. "I will tell them to stand down."

"I do not trust this," says Solt.

Rhen glances at Harper. "Trust is built by action." He looks back at me. "I should have trusted you when it most mattered."

"So should I," I say. I look at Solt. "Rhen is not our prisoner. He is my brother."

"Indeed," says Rhen, and to my surprise, his voice isn't heavy with emotion. In fact, he sounds lighter than I ever recall. "Let us face my army. Let me introduce them to the rightful heir."

I startle, then stare at him in surprise.

Rhen smiles, then holds out a hand. "For the good of Emberfall."

I clasp it. "For the good of all."

CHAPTER FORTY-SEVEN

LIA MARA

With a small group that needs no cover, we're able to ride hard across Emberfall. I remember sneaking through the woods with Grey, how every mile seemed to take an hour, but now we seem to *fly*. My stomach churns with anxiety, and I feel as though I haven't eaten in days. I've never believed in fate for a day in my life, but Grey does, and now I find myself begging fate.

Let him survive.

Let him come back to me.

Keep him safe.

Please.

The officers from Rhen's army ride at our front and at our back, acting as escorts as promised. At first my own soldiers were wary and reluctant, but we've made good time without incident. When we stopped to water the horses, I saw one of the Emberfall soldiers lend a piece of flint to one of my officers when hers dropped into the depths of the creek. This morning, one of my own soldiers helped one of Rhen's when the girth of his saddle began to fray. Noah moves between both groups easily when we stop, treating minor wounds when necessary, but he mostly sticks to my side.

We slow the horses to a walk near daybreak, and Noah rides alongside. He offers me a heel of bread. "You should eat."

I shake my head. "I'm not hungry."

"Well, your body needs some food, even if your head doesn't think so."

I take the bread because I know he'll be relentless if I don't, but when I tear a piece with my teeth, I just want to throw up on my horse.

I shake my head and take a pull from my water skin. "I'm too nervous."

He doesn't say anything for a moment, but I can feel him studying me. "Small bites," he says.

"How far are we?" I ask. To appease him, I take a tiny tear of bread.

He looks at the horizon. "We passed the turn to Silvermoon an hour ago. If we keep up this pace, we'll make it to the castle before sunrise."

"Sunrise!" I look at my soldiers. "We rest for no longer than five minutes."

Noah chuckles. "Don't you remember Jake punching Grey when he didn't want to rest?"

I look into his eyes. "Aren't you worried, too?"

That sobers him. "Five minutes."

"We should make it three." I draw up my reins.

I love the mountains in Syhl Shallow, but there is something peaceful about the rolling hills of Emberfall, especially when sunlight first breaks along the horizon, sending early streaks of purple across the sky. The horses blow steam into the air, their hooves pounding the ground. I recognize the territory surrounding Ironrose Castle now, the wide swath of forest that surrounds the castle itself. There's one final hill to crest, and then we'll be there.

My heart beats hard against my ribs. We're here. *Grey, we're here.*

Then we sail over the hill and see the soldiers. There are hundreds of them. *Thousands* of them. All in formation.

Clanna Sun hauls on her reins. "It's a trap!" she cries. "Fall back!"

My soldiers and officers skid to a stop, too, horses rearing in protest. They quickly swarm to surround me. A shout goes up from the army at the base of the hill. The Emberfall soldiers who'd been escorting us look alarmed.

"Hold!" I say. I put up a hand and glare at Clanna Sun. "I said, *hold*!"

They hold. The horses stamp and prance, jerking at too-tight reins. I look across at Jamison, whose gaze goes from us to the soldiers waiting in formation in the valley.

Before I have a chance to say anything, he says quickly, "Your Majesty. I will ride down to them. I will explain."

A group of Rhen's soldiers have mounted horses, and they've begun to ride toward us. It's too dark to see much very clearly, but behind them, I see the shadows of archers with bows sitting ready.

"Go," I say to Jamison.

"This is foolhardy," Clanna Sun hisses at me. "Your mother would *never* have—"

"I am *not* my *mother*," I snap at her. "And you will remember your place."

She clamps her mouth shut.

Jamison gallops down the hill, and when he reaches the group that's split off, they stop. I can't hear what they're saying from here, and my heart seems to stop beating as I wait. We could never outrun this army. We could never fight. They could slaughter us all right here.

But then one soldier peels away from the small group, his horse sprinting across the turf. As he draws closer, I see the colors of his armor, the black of his hair.

I slip out of the saddle. "Move," I say to my officers. "Move."

I stride forward just as his horse crests the hill, and Grey leaps to the ground before his mount has even drawn to a stop.

My heart flutters wildly, and my knees are weak, but I force myself forward until I'm in front of him. His eyes are exhausted and full of pain, and there's blood everywhere: in his hair, on his hands, in broad streaks across his armor. I press my hands to his face as if I have to prove to myself that he's here, that he's alive, that we're together. "You're well," I breathe, willing the words to be true. "You're well."

He presses his hands over mine. "I'm well."

"Grey," says Noah, at my back. His voice is tight. "Jake?"

Grey's eyes flick past me. "Jake is fine. He's at the base of the hill. He didn't know you were here, or he would have ridden up." Grey hesitates, and his eyes return to mine. His hands tighten over my fingers. "The enchantress is dead. We lost Iisak."

My chest clenches. I knew this fight would not be without loss. I stare up into Grey's wounded eyes and think of the reason he came here. "And Rhen?"

"He survived." He pauses. "We're . . . no longer at war." There's so much weight in his voice that I know there is more to say, but Grey seems to realize we're surrounded by soldiers from both Syhl Shallow and Emberfall. His eyebrows flicker into a frown "What . . . what happened? Why are you here?"

My heart lightens, just a bit. I want to tell him that I figured out his message, that I know Ellia Maya was working against us. I want to tell him that we've brought peace, that the soldiers were willing to pause. That if Rhen is no longer ready to wage war, that we can finally put our differences aside for the good of all our people. I want to throw my arms around his neck and never let go. I want to hear his heartbeat and feel his breath and sleep for a thousand days at his side.

Instead, my stomach twists, and I jerk back, slapping a hand over my mouth.

"Lia Mara," he says, alarmed.

I inhale to answer, to tell him I'm fine.

Instead, I throw up all over his boots.

"I'm sorry," I gasp, mortified. "I'm sorry. I've—I've been sick with worry—"

And then, to my horror, I do it *again*.

"Noah!" Grey calls, and there's worry in his voice. His hands hold back my hair.

"Oh yeah," says Noah, and his voice isn't concerned at all. If anything, he sounds amused. "About that."

CHAPTER FORTY-EIGHT

RHEN

Weeks pass, and the castle again fills with people to replace those we've lost. Soldiers and guards, servants and footmen, so many new faces, new names, new voices to ring through the halls. Harper is delighted to discover that Freya and the children were among those who were ushered out of the castle by the spy Chesleigh, along with much of the staff I'd thought were killed when Lilith cut a swath through the castle.

Harper stays with me frequently, but just as often, she is with her brother, with her friends, spending her hours among the people. As always, I still feel every loss acutely, so I keep to my rooms. More so, even, because this time I do not turn my thoughts to rebuilding Emberfall, and instead I leave that to Grey. I look at the guards who survived, and I think of those who were lost. I see a servant in the halls, and I remember a body I dragged out of the castle. Instead of meeting with advisors and Grand Marshals, I cling to the shadows of my chambers.

I thought there would be an element of relief to this, but there's not.

I feel trapped just as effectively as I was by the curse.

Where can I go? What will I do? When I leave this room, people stare—or quickly look away.

Harper said that scars mean I survived something terrible. They're also a reminder that I *was* something terrible.

A knock sounds at my door one evening, long past the time most of the castle has fallen into sleep. Even with Lilith gone, my own sleep is fitful and restless, plagued with nightmares, so on the nights when I am alone, I often read in front of the fire until my eye gives me no choice.

But tonight, I straighten, and curiosity makes me call, "Enter."

The door latch clicks, and Grey comes through. He's alone.

"I knew you would be awake," he says, and I can't read anything in his voice.

"Your magic?" I say.

He almost smiles, but there's no humor to it. His eyes search mine. "No, in fact. More . . . an eternity of familiarity."

Oh. Right. I look back at the fire.

I've seen him in the castle, of course. I can't stay in my chambers *all* day. But he has been busy, always occupied, always surrounded by people, while I have slowly become invisible, as people hurry to avert their eyes. He is the heir, the crown prince, the soon-to-be-crowned king. He is the man who saved us from a terrible enchantress, using his own magic to heal the wounded and mend our fractured relationship with Syhl Shallow. I hear the adoration, the fawning, the way people have discovered that there is a new man in power, someone untested and unknowing. Someone who can potentially be tricked and swindled and cajoled.

He'll learn his way. I did. And Lia Mara seems savvy. I have no doubt.

All of these thoughts make my chest tighten, so I clear my throat. "Are you planning for your return to Syhl Shallow?"

"So eager to see me gone?" His voice is easy, almost teasing, but there's a genuine question in there, too.

"No." I hesitate, then look over at him. I don't want to admit that I don't want him to go, that I don't want this hum of tension between us to continue, but I have no idea how to voice that. Just like I can't hide in my chambers all day, Queen Lia Mara cannot stay away from Syhl Shallow forever. Snow will fall through the mountain pass soon enough, and it's a hard enough journey in the cold even when one is *not* pregnant.

Grey inhales like he is about to say something, then stops, regarding me.

I remember when he came to issue his ultimatum, how he stood in the Grand Hall and said, *Shall we draw our swords and settle this right now?* Then, the air was full of hostility, of regret, of sorrow and loss and the faintest whisper of hope.

Now it's not the same, but it's not wholly different either.

I shift forward on my chair, opening the polished wooden box on the table beside me and withdrawing a deck of cards. Without looking at him, I begin to shuffle. "Do you care to play?"

"Cards? Yes."

He sits across from me, and there's an eagerness to his voice that makes me glance up. "You've missed *cards*, Grey?"

"In Syhl Shallow, they play with dice." He pauses as I begin to deal. "I always lose."

"Truly? You should teach me a game."

"There's no strategy." He picks up his hand and looks at me over the cards. "You would hate it."

Against my will, my chest tightens again. He knows me too well. I know *him* too well.

Grey lays down a card. A nine of swords.

It spurs me into motion, and I select a card from my hand. We play in silence for a while, until the game begins to pull some of the tension out of the air.

"If you would not be opposed . . . ," he begins.

"You are the crown prince," I say as I lay down a queen to capture one of his kings. "I can be opposed to nothing."

"You are my brother," he says, with a bit of heat in his voice, "and the son of a king, and in fact second in line to the throne. You can be opposed to *plenty*."

I'm shocked by his sudden vehemence. But also . . . touched. I give him a sidelong glance. "I may be second in line to the throne, but judging by the state of your beloved, that's only for a matter of months, I would think."

He looks up, and I smile, and he looks abashed. "Well."

My smile widens. It's rare that I see Grey flustered, even for a moment. "Go ahead, Commander," I tease. "Make your request."

He blinks, and for a moment I think maybe I've pushed too far, and that wall of tension will drop between us again. But then he says, "Ah, yes, of course, my lord. I would humbly request meager lodgings for myself and Lia Mara through the winter, if it would not be *too* grand a request—"

"Wait. What?" I straighten, frowning. "Are you serious?"

"Yes." He tosses a card onto the pile. "As you know, snow will block the pass any day, so travel northward may be a bit reckless.

And Lia Mara has received word from her sister that the factions against magic have grown emboldened, and there have been attacks on the palace. We do not know who else may be working with them. The army is in place, so they are well protected, but . . ." He lifts a shoulder. "We promised a peaceful alliance with Emberfall, that Syhl Shallow would finally benefit from trade and access to the sea. We'd like to return when we can show proof that it's working."

"That's wise," I say, and mean it. "You do not need my permission to stay here, Grey. Ironrose Castle is yours. All of this is yours. I should be seeking permission from you."

"Never," he says quietly. "Ironrose is your home, as long as you want it."

My chest tightens with emotion again, and I have to look back at my cards. "I . . . will see whether Harper wants to stay."

He hesitates—then says nothing.

We play in silence again, the fire snapping. The castle is cold, the hallways quiet, but right here is a cocoon of warmth. Grey has seen me at my worst, and the scars never draw his gaze. For that, I am grateful.

"The Grand Marshal of Silvermoon," he says slowly.

I nod. "Marshal Perry."

"He has made many grand promises."

I snort. "I'm certain. He would likely promise you an evening with his wife if he thought it would buy your favor." I pause. "He often promises more than he has to give. I would be wary unless you've set eyes on what he is offering you. I don't think he's a dishonest man, just a clever one."

Grey sets a card on the pile. "And the Grand Marshal of Kennetty?"

"Violet Blackcomb. She's soft-spoken. Never too opinionated. But she's honest and believes in doing right by her people. She's a good ally. Her Seneschal, Andrew Lacky, is the one you need to watch out for." I adjust my cards in my hand and lay one on the pile.

I expect him to grill me on the others, but he doesn't. He falls silent again.

"If you leave," he says carefully. "Where will you go?"

"Ah . . . I've heard there is need for a stable hand at some tourney in Rillisk."

That startles a laugh out of him, which makes me smile, chagrined.

" 'You're a talented swordsman,' " he says, his tone low as he quotes what I said to him when we were trapped by the curse. " 'Shall I write you a letter of recommendation.' "

He's teasing, and I should smile back, but instead, I go still. I'm missing an eye. I doubt I'll have much talent as a swordsman anymore. I can already tell.

My hands are shaking. I set down my cards. Flex my fingers.

Grey sets down his own. He leans in against the table, and his voice is very low. "Rhen," he says. "What do *you* want?"

I want . . .

I look up at him. "I don't know."

"Truly?"

I shrug a little. "I was raised to be king, Grey. I don't know how to be anything else." I gesture at my face. "No one will want to look at me. Did they display passing oddities in this tourney of yours? Perhaps I could earn a few coins."

Grey blows out a breath between his teeth and runs a hand across the back of his neck. "Silver hell, Rhen. Were you quite this bleak when we were trapped together, or have I forgotten?"

I jerk back, and I'm so startled that I can't decide if I'm angry or amused.

But Grey hasn't looked away, and there's no malice in his expression. I stand and move to my side table. "I was likely always this bleak. Do you care for some sugared spirits?"

"I still have no head for liquor. I'll be on the floor."

I pour two glasses. "Good. I'll join you."

We drink. I pour two more and take up my cards. "Why did you really come here?"

He tips back this glass as quickly as the first and winces, then coughs. "I would have told you the truth without the spirits."

"I know. But it's more amusing this way." I pause. "Tell me, while you can do it without slurring."

"Harper sought me out. She is worried for you." His voice drops. "In truth, I worry for you."

Ah, Harper. I shrug and pour a third glass.

"Lia Mara had a thought," says Grey.

"Indeed?"

"She suggested that since we cannot travel north, that instead we visit your southern cities, not as allies, but—"

"Yours, Grey." I drain the glass. "They are *your* southern cities."

"—as brothers," he finishes.

I go still for a long moment, then set the glass on the table. So many emotions fill my chest that I can't make sense of them. "So a parade of their failed prince? Would you like to put me in a cage?"

A dark look flickers in his expression, and I can tell I'm trying his patience. He keeps his voice even, though. "No, I would like for you to ride at my side."

"To show me all I have lost?"

"Only half. Then you'd have to turn your head, I imagine—"

I take a swing at him, but the liquor has already hit me, and Grey dodges. I'm off balance, and I try to regroup to hit him again. Unfortunately, the liquor has hit him twice as hard, and when he tries to fend me off, we end up falling to the ground—and we take the table down with us, the wood splintering as a leg gives way under our weight. The bottle shatters on the marble floor, followed immediately by the glasses.

A guard swings open the door. "My lord! Are you—" He stops short. "My . . . lords?"

"A misunderstanding," I say. I wince and touch a hand to my head. "About which way was up."

Grey is sprawled on the marble next to me, and he looks over. He points at the ceiling. "I told you it was that way."

I knew it. He's slurring already. I look at the door. "We're fine. Get out."

The door eases closed.

Grey looks over at me. "I did not mean to offend you."

"I know." I look at the ceiling. "I think . . ." My thoughts are loosening. Drifting. "I think I sought to offend myself. You took nothing from me. I yielded."

He says nothing to that, and we lie among the broken glass and wood for the longest time.

"I would ask you to stay," he says quietly. "To join me, Rhen."

I'm not sure what to say. I don't know what I want. I don't know where to go. I don't even know if I *want* to go.

But I look over into Grey's dark eyes. "Yes, my lord. As my king commands."

CHAPTER FORTY-NINE

LIA MARA

I'm drafting a letter to my sister, my quill scratching rapidly against the parchment. For some reason, I'm exhausted all day, but by the time darkness falls, I feel as though I could lead an army. Harper's lady-in-waiting, Freya, has been a source of information for all things motherhood, and thanks to the ginger tea she brings me every morning, I've stopped emptying the contents of my stomach onto the boots of anyone who has the misfortune to speak to me at the wrong time.

Nolla Verin has written to me about how the faction against magic has grown in Syhl Shallow, about the minor attacks on the palace that have so far been thwarted. I am telling her about our plans here, how I would like to establish trade routes and promises of good relations between our countries before we return.

I have not yet told my sister about the baby. I don't want to give her hope when things feel so uncertain. Noah tells me that it's early, that many things can happen, that miscarriage is not uncommon.

Freya saw my trembling lips as he was explaining this to me, and she leaned in and said, "You've been very sick. That's a good sign."

I try to remind myself of that when my stomach feels as though I've been at sea during a storm.

But there's another reason I haven't told Nolla Verin about the baby, a reason I was relieved when Grey agreed to stay in Emberfall for the winter: this child will bear magic just like its father. It's one thing to make a target of Grey, a man who can defend himself with weapons and magic.

I will not make a target of my child.

The door creaks at my back, and I know it is Grey. "You were with Rhen very late," I say without looking up from my paper.

"I missed playing cards."

I smile, then dip my pen in the inkpot. "Well, you are—"

His hands slide down my shoulders, and he leans in to kiss my neck from behind, and I gasp, then giggle. "You've been drinking."

"Perhaps a bit." His voice is husky.

"It smells like more than a *bit*."

"It's possible we shattered a bottle."

I turn within the circle of his arms. "What?" I say, but he leans in to kiss me. For a moment it is glorious, because his hands are gentle and his mouth is sure, and he tastes like cinnamon and sugar and something sharper.

But then my stomach has other ideas, and I jerk back and slap a hand over my mouth.

Grey startles, then smiles, and there is something simultaneously soft yet protective all in that look. "Forgive me," he says.

"It'll pass," I say, my voice muffled behind my hand.

"Shall I call for some of your tea?"

I shake my head and swallow, then close my eyes.

I sense more than feel Grey drop to a knee beside me, but then his hand rests over my belly, which has not yet begun to swell and curve with motherhood. He leans in to speak right to my abdomen. "You should be kind to your mother."

I laugh softly—but the nausea suddenly passes. I snap open my eyes. "It worked."

A light sparks in his eyes. "He already knows I will not stand for disobedience."

"Perhaps *she* simply decided it was time to rest."

He takes my hand. "Ah, yes. And *she* would be quite right. It is time to rest."

I leave my letter and quill on the desk and follow him to the bed. "Nolla Verin says there have been more attacks. That the faction against magic grows stronger, not weaker."

Grey curls around me, his breath in my hair, his hand resting against my abdomen. "Have no fear, my love. No one will touch you." He pauses, and his voice gains an edge. "And rest assured that no one will dare touch our child."

CHAPTER FIFTY

HARPER

I've traveled with Rhen to dozens of cities over the last few months, and he was always at the forefront: surrounded by guards, dictating everything, smoothly shifting from cordial and gracious to haughty and aloof depending on the situation. He had a skill for reading people that was almost uncanny. Always a leader, with every action swift and decisive and absolute.

Now we ride at the back. If I weren't spurring him to keep up, I think he'd let the reins go slack so the horse could amble and graze, and we'd lose sight of the rest of the party. A leatherworker fashioned him with a patch that covers the worst of the scarring. It's dark, oiled leather, with little adornment and tiny buckles. Rhen wasn't going to wear it, but then a young child saw him and screamed for five solid minutes, so now he has it with him always. Jake told him he looked like a pirate, which I actually think he meant as a compliment, but I thought Rhen was going to put his sword right through my brother's chest.

It's colder today, and snow has begun to drift from the sky to gather in the horse's mane. Rhen looks at me. "You should ride in the carriage with Lia Mara."

"I'm worried that you'll turn back if I leave you alone."

"I won't turn back. Grey has given an order. I will obey."

"He didn't give you an *order*, Rhen."

"He's going to be crowned king. Literally everything he says is an order."

I sigh and look at the sky. The snowflakes sting my cheeks.

"Again," he says, "I insist. You should ride in the carriage."

"I don't want to ride in the carriage. I want to ride with *you*."

He glances over. "You fell in love with the crown prince, Harper. That is no longer me."

"No, you idiot. I fell in love with *you*. You, Rhen. I do not care about your crown."

"I don't either, really," he says simply. He pauses. "But . . . what else is there?"

I stare at him, somewhat shocked.

But also a little shocked at myself, that I never realized the real basis for all his brooding, his angst, the way he was moving through the castle like a ghost.

The curse is broken. Lilith is gone. Emberfall is no longer in danger.

And Rhen is no longer the crown prince.

He was a man who devoted his life to his people, and now he's . . . given all that up. A man who built his entire world around strategy and planning and thought, and now it's gone.

"You know," I say slowly, "when Grey yanked me out of Washington, DC, I lost track of any future I thought I had, too."

He looks over at me in surprise.

I shrug and keep my eyes on the back of the traveling party. "I wasn't ruling a country or anything. But still."

"And what did you do?" he says, his voice rough.

"You know what I did." I pause. "I tried everything I could to get back." My voice tightens with unexpected emotion. "And then . . . and then that didn't work. So I had to figure out a new path. A new future. A new way to move forward."

He looks at me steadily. "Are you happy with your new future, Harper?"

"Yes," I say emphatically. "You brought peace to Emberfall, Rhen. You did that. Grey was going to bring war. *You* gave him peace."

Now it's his turn to look startled.

"He missed you," I say gently. "When I got to Syhl Shallow, he talked a big game about battle and war and how he would protect Lia Mara and her people—but when it came right down to it, he marched into Ironrose Castle to save you. No matter what he said, he was going after Lilith. He was afraid she would use you against him."

Rhen flinches.

"He didn't order you to come with him," I say. "And I think you know him better than that. He *asked* you to come with him, because he wants you here." I pause. "Just like I want you here."

He says nothing.

"Remember when I first agreed to be the Princess of Disi?" I say. "We had that whole conversation where you said I couldn't help all your people, and I said that we could help *some* of them?"

"Yes." He takes a breath, and his voice turns very soft. "And you were right."

"You can do that *now*, Rhen. You don't have to be the king to make a difference for your people." I pause, as the weight of what I'm saying hits me, too. Snow flurries drift down between us. "Just like I didn't have to be a princess. I could just . . . be Harper."

At that, he looks over at me, and I can see the emotion in his eye, just for a moment, before he blinks it away. But he reaches out to take my hand, and he presses a kiss to my knuckles. "You are more than I deserve."

"Well. You did say you'd level a city for me."

I expect that to make him smile, but instead, he gives my hand a gentle squeeze . . . and lets go.

I don't know if I reminded him of what he could do as a monster—or if I reminded him of what he can't do if he's not the king, but it doesn't matter.

"Remember when you told me I didn't have to take anything?" I say. "That I could just ask for it, and you'd give it to me?"

"I do." His voice is thin and soft, and he's facing forward, so I can't see his eye now, and I have no clue to his emotion.

I plow ahead anyway. "Grey would do that for you too, Rhen. If you told him what you wanted, he would give it to you. Just—just *tell him*—"

"I don't know!" he snaps. "I don't *know*, Harper! I have never been anything else!"

My breath catches. He wasn't quiet that time, and the soldiers and guards stop short.

He's the center of attention again, but not for any reason he wants to be.

Grey was riding near the front, but his horse lopes back to us. "What's wrong?"

"Nothing," says Rhen, his tone clipped.

Grey looks at me.

I inhale to say the same, but then I stop. "Grey, we're heading into Rillisk, right? This is where they found you?"

"Yes."

"So you know your way around." I hesitate. "Maybe for the first few hours you could lose most of the guards and horses, and you could just . . . not be the future king and his brother?"

Rhen snorts and looks away dismissively. "The guards will never allow it."

Grey studies him, and then, slowly, he smiles. "Who says they need to know?"

CHAPTER FIFTY-ONE

RHEN

I have never walked through a town as a commoner. I've left anything demonstrating wealth in the carriage, as has Grey. We're in simple boots, heavy woolen cloaks, with only a sword and a simple dagger at our waist. Tycho trails us through the streets, because he knows Rillisk as well, and I told Grey it was foolhardy for us to walk the streets *completely* alone.

It's fascinating, however. The streets are crowded with people who yield nothing to me. No one moves out of my way, no one gives me a second glance. A man brushes against my blind side, and I step sideways quickly, only to nearly collide with an older woman who's missing most of her teeth.

She grabs my arm and smacks me on the back of the hand. "You keep your distance, you ruffian!"

I stare at her, shocked, and she huffs and moves away through the crowd.

At my side, Grey laughs softly. "I shall remember this moment."

"As will I."

A bit farther down, he grabs my arm and tugs me into a tavern, and the scent of baked bread and roasted meat is strong. Tycho follows us in, but he clings to the shadows and stays near the door. The place is crowded with patrons, but we find a table in the corner.

"The boy would make a good guard," I say to Grey.

"He's still young."

"So were you."

I've never been in a place like this, where the ale is flowing freely and the table seems vaguely sticky and the people speak without a moment's concern for who might overhear. At first, I'm tense, sure there could be a blade or an arrow anywhere, but as I look around, I realize there is nothing to fear.

And I no longer matter anyway.

The thought is jolting at first—but then I discover there's a bit of freedom to it, just as there was a bit of freedom to following Grey's *order*. In doing what I'm told instead of being the one in charge. I take a long breath, then exhale fully for what seems like the first time in months.

In years.

In . . . ever.

"You look better already," says Grey.

I frown. "Perhaps."

A maiden has been flitting from table to table, delivering platters of food and pitchers of ale, but when she stops by ours, she does a double take when she sees Grey.

"Hawk!" she cries with relief. "Oh, I can't believe it! You're— you're—" She breaks off. Her face pales, and she bites her lip. A line forms between her brows. "I—you—Your—Your High—"

"Shh." Grey puts a finger to his lips. "Hawk is fine."

She moves closer. "Are you in hiding? Is there a coup? I have heard that horrid Prince Rhen was going to try to kill you—"

I cough. "A truly horrid man, for sure."

"Not in hiding," says Grey. "And my brother is not so horrid."

Her wide eyes turn to me.

I shrug.

She draws herself up and takes a deep breath. "I'll bring you some ale," she says finally, decisively. Then, without warning, she gives Grey an impulsive hug, tugging his face into her impressive bosom. "I'm so glad you're alive," she says. "I was so worried."

And then she's gone.

"I'm going to tell Lia Mara," I say.

"I will personally kill you."

"Oh, Hawk," I tease in a falsetto. "I was so *worried*."

"You're worse than Jake."

I nod after the tavern girl. "What made you leave that one?" I smirk. "I'm surprised she's not trailing a little magesmith herself."

Grey smacks me on the top of the head, and I laugh.

"Jodi was a friend," he says. "Nothing more."

"Oh yes," I intone. "That seems so very likely."

"It is." He gives me a level look across the table. "When I was in Rillisk, I was too afraid of the Royal Guard showing up to drag me back in chains."

I meet his eyes. "Ah. I see."

We say nothing.

I wonder if there will always be this hum of tension between us, if all the wrongs on both sides have brought us to a point where nothing will fully dull the edges.

But then I think of what Harper said, how she kept fighting to go home, and how that eventually didn't work.

Is the tension all on my side? Is this my way of fighting to go home?

Do I simply need to . . . stop?

I look around the crowded tavern. Jodi reappears with two steins of ale. She winks at Grey and says, "Your brother looks so *dangerous*." And then she bumps my shoulder with her hip.

I choke on my drink—but I put a coin on the table. Now she winks at me.

"I'm going to tell Harper," says Grey.

I smile.

It feels good to smile.

I take a deep breath. "I'm glad you brought me here."

"As am I." He pauses. "I'm glad you stayed."

I don't tell him it was because he asked it of me. Maybe I needed him to.

"I was not raised to be a king," he says quietly. "I . . ." His voice trails off, and he hesitates. "I thought of you often, when I was in Syhl Shallow." His eyes glance away. "I longed for your counsel." He pauses. "I know . . . I know this has not been easy for you. I know you were not made to yield."

I shrug and take another sip of my drink.

"I long for your counsel now," he says softly.

I look up.

"Syhl Shallow is plagued by factions that stand against magic. Her Royal Houses do not trust me. I do not have your skill with politics or court drama. I do not know your—*my* Grand Marshals. I do not know this army, these guards." His eyes are dark, full of emotion in their depths. "I long for your counsel. If you would be willing to give it."

I stare back at him. *A new way to move forward.*

I put out a hand. "For the good of . . ." I hesitate. It's not just Emberfall any longer. "What, then?"

Grey clasps my hand, his grip tight. "You and me, Brother. For the good of all."

ACKNOWLEDGMENTS

I've been staring at the screen and crying for a good five minutes now, so that's how this is going.

I told my husband last night that this is my twelfth book, and I don't know how to write my acknowledgments without everything sounding repetitive and trite. I am truly grateful to so many people that I don't just want to write a paragraph and call it a day. (Besides which, I set a precedent for myself. I can't write long acknowledgments in eleven books and then scribble off a paragraph in number twelve.) My husband said, "Can't you write about the pandemic? That affected your writing so much!"

And yes. It did. It affected everything and everyone so very much. I'm writing this in August 2020, and who even knows how the world is going to change by the time you have this book in your hands. This has been a hard year, from the sorrow over all the people we lost to COVID-19, to the grief over the goals and dreams that seemed to turn into smoke and ash, to the daily reminder that we truly have no idea what tomorrow will bring.

That's the bottom line, friends. We have *no idea* what tomorrow will bring.

So, let me thank all the people who have been here supporting me throughout all the yesterdays that didn't seem so guaranteed this year.

I'm going to start with my husband, Michael, who's been my rock during this year and every other year. Recently he said to me that he doesn't feel like I count on him as much as he counts on me. Oh, honey. I count on you for *everything*. I basically wrote and edited this whole book while on lockdown with you and three kids. I couldn't do this without you. I can't imagine anyone being *more* supportive.

I also owe a tremendous debt of gratitude to my amazing editor, Mary Kate Castellani, who worked on this book during a pandemic, *during her maternity leave*, also while on lockdown with children much younger than mine. If anyone deserves a medal, it's Mary Kate. You always make my writing so much better, and I will be eternally grateful for all you do. Let's just hope we don't ever have to write a book this way again, 'kay?

On that same note, the entire team at Bloomsbury is always an endless source of support and encouragement, and I am so grateful for everything you do. Huge thanks to Cindy Loh, Erica Barmash, Faye Bi, Phoebe Dyer, Claire Stetzer, Beth Eller, Ksenia Winnicki, Rebecca McNally, Diane Aronson, Melissa Kavonic, Nick Sweeney, Nicholas Church, Donna Mark, Jeanette Levy, Donna Gauthier, and every single person at Bloomsbury who has a hand in making my books a success. And thank you to the Macmillan sales team for your tireless efforts on behalf of my books. Special thanks to Lily Yengle, Tobias Madden, Mattea Barnes, and Meenakshi Singh for their incredible work on managing the Cursebreakers Street Team.

Speaking of the Street Team, if you're a part of it, thank YOU. It means so much to me to know that there are *thousands* of you interested in my books, and I will never forget everything you've done to spread the word about Rhen, Harper, Grey, and Lia Mara.

My agent, Suzie Townsend, of New Leaf Literary Agency, has been an absolute rock for me since we joined forces last autumn. Suzie, thank you so much for your time and your guidance. I can't wait to see what the future holds. Additional thanks to Dani Segelbaum for handling so much behind the scenes.

Huge debts of gratitude go to my close writing friends, Gillian McDunn and Jodi Picoult, because I honestly don't know how I would have gotten through this year without you both. From reading my manuscripts to virtually holding my hand to listening to me and talking to me and supporting me, I am so grateful to have you both in my life.

Several people read and offered insights about this book while it was in progress, and I want to take a moment to specially thank Reba Gordon, Ava Tusek, and Isabel Ibanez.

HUGE thanks to all of you too. Thank you for being a part of my dream. I am honored that you took the time to invite my characters into your heart.

Finally, tremendous love and thanks to my boys. It might have taken me longer to write this book with everything we've gone through this year, but I wouldn't change one second of all the time I got to spend with all of you.